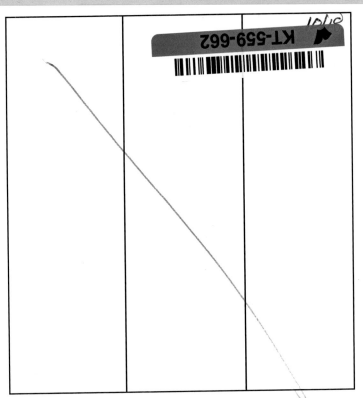

KT-559-662

This book should be returned/renewed by the latest date shown above. Overdue items incur charges which prevent self-service renewals. Please contact the library.

Wandsworth Libraries
24 hour Renewal Hotline
01159 293388
www.wandsworth.gov.uk

Everything is Lies

HELEN CALLAGHAN

PENGUIN BOOKS

PENGUIN BOOKS

UK | USA | Canada | Ireland | Australia
India | New Zealand | South Africa

Penguin Books is part of the Penguin Random House group of companies
whose addresses can be found at global.penguinrandomhouse.com

First published by Michael Joseph 2018
Published in Penguin Books 2018
001

Copyright © Helen Callaghan, 2018

The moral right of the author has been asserted

Set in Garamond MT Std
Typeset by Jouve (UK), Milton Keynes
Printed and bound in Great Britain by Clays Ltd, Elcograf S.p.A.

A CIP catalogue record for this book is available from the British Library

ISBN: 978–1–405–92343–9

www.greenpenguin.co.uk

MIX
Paper from
responsible sources
FSC
www.fsc.org
FSC® C018179

Penguin Random House is committed to a
sustainable future for our business, our readers
and our planet. This book is made from Forest
Stewardship Council® certified paper.

For JJ

Chapter One

No one is who they say they are.

I slumped into the rumbling back seat of the N159 as it roared and puttered towards Brixton and my little flat. The top two buttons were missing from my shirt, and the young guy in a Superdry jacket three seats up kept turning to stare at me, as if to say, *Go on, you can hit on me any time, it's really not a problem.*

I continued to decline this unspoken invitation, instead preferring to sink back into a fug of self-pity, all against the background of a nascent headache that had first started to pry its way into my brain somewhere around Trafalgar Square. In the window, my reflection blinked back at me, my smeared mascara making me look like a moody panda who's made poor life choices.

Around me the bus was full of the usual late-night detritus of London – drunk girls in tiny clothes; tight-trousered hipsters; weary workers on unsociable hours making their way home, nodding asleep in their seats. The unsympathetic lighting played over us all, making our skin look like meat in a butcher's shop window.

I felt sober and exhausted and oddly hollow.

* * *

Hours earlier, Tai-Pan had been heaving, the air redolent of clean sweat, perfume, yeast and aftershave – that Friday-night smell; the smell of excitement, arousal and adventure. The bar was abuzz with good-natured bellowing and delighted shrieks, and somewhere in the background music played, only the beat audible above the din.

I was out with work. James Cooper, *enfant terrible* of corporate architecture and our managing partner, had been put forward for another design award and accordingly 'impromptu drinks' had been booked for that evening.

I hadn't wanted to come.

I'd only been working at Amity for twelve weeks, but it was already clear that the company culture revolved around being 'visible' to James, a relentlessly driven New York sociopath now on his third wife – a culture of working hard and playing hard. Personally, I could have done with working hard and then playing hard somewhere else, with different people.

It had started slowly at first, an insidious creep, but gradually I was beginning to cancel my plans more and more often. First the tap class I did with Audrey, an old flatmate, faded away; then Thursday-night movies at Brixton's Ritzy with Veronika and Paul stuttered to a halt.

Tonight, I'd decided, the fightback would begin, no matter how many eyebrows were raised. I'd stay for an hour or so, then head off. It was still my weekend, after all.

But one cocktail became two, and then (with very little encouragement) three, and before I realized it, I was unexpectedly enjoying myself.

A large part of this was because I found myself pleasantly trapped against a wall, my back pressed against a giant reproduction of Hokusai's *The Great Wave*. Benjamin Velasquez, one of the senior architects at Amity, stood in front of me, his hand braced above my head as his arm created a private, intimate space, inviting me closer to where his formal business shirt hung warm and intriguingly damp next to his skin.

I'd never really spoken with him before, but I'd noticed him in his corner office with its glass walls, and every so often I'd noticed him noticing me.

He was telling me about his recent tour of the world's volcanoes, which his friends had booked for his thirtieth birthday.

'I've never seen a volcano,' I murmured, filled with low wonder. I had dreamed of seeing them, but like so many things, I'd hung on for someone, some lover to see one with, and it had never quite come off.

'There aren't many in London, thankfully.'

'Weren't you scared?' I asked, gesturing for emphasis, aware that my speech was wobbling slightly. 'They're unpredictable. They could do anything.'

'Yeah,' he replied, leaning in with a conspiratorial grin. 'But usually they don't. It's quite safe. My . . . friend, Ellie, was ter-rified at first, but she soon got over it.'

'Ellie? Who's Ellie?'

I was drunk, I realized, and my gaze danced across his chest, up to his face with its generous lips, grey eyes and per-haps, if one were to carp, his slightly weak chin.

'A friend. A load of us went together.' He glanced away, as though this line of questioning bored or pained him, and I dropped it, prepared to steer the conversation back to cooler ground.

He offered to buy me a drink, and I seized the opportunity to nip to the toilets. As I pushed open the gilded door, I saw my new friend Cleo standing before the faux-baroque mirror, the careful up-do she wore for work starting to come down around her shoulders in orange-gold ringlets. She was pin-ning it back in place, squinting at her reflection.

'Hello there, gorgeous,' I remarked.

'Ah, Sophia,' she threw me a glance over her shoulder before resuming her work. 'How is Benjamin Velasquez?' She grinned, but there was something slightly tight in it. Perhaps it was simply the hairpins she was gripping in the corner of her mouth. She took them out for a second. 'You two look like you're getting on.'

'We're just chatting,' I said, though I could feel a blush rising in my cheeks. 'He's been telling me about volcanoes . . .'

I suddenly became aware of a dull buzzing, like a fluttering heart, in my back pocket. A second later the ringtone started – a series of rising chimes – and digging the phone out I saw my mum's name and picture on the tiny screen.

I regarded it carefully for a moment, as though it might explode, before answering.

I love my mum dearly, I really do, but when she phones at this time of night it usually means only one thing.

'Hi, Mum,' I said. The clock on the phone read 9:50.

'Sophia, where are you?'

There was always this tiny shiver of alarm in her voice as she asked this, like I was still a little girl and she had just looked up from one of her tasks in the garden and noticed I was missing. 'I tried your flat.'

'I'm in a bar,' I supplied, though surely she must have been able to hear the background music thumping. 'I'm out with work.'

'Again?'

'Yeah,' I scratched my temple. 'I know. They do this a lot.'

'Oh, right. I see.'

A long pause followed. Every time she called me like this a kind of bewildered impatience wafted down the line, as though I'd called her instead of the other way around, and was dancing around some deep and dangerous issue, refusing to share it with her.

When I was a spiky, cruel teenager I used to bark, 'Mum, what do you actually *want*?' at this juncture, but it was completely pointless and always made me feel terrible. She'd tell me all in good time, whenever that was, but I didn't have time to spare. I had Benjamin waiting and I could hear the first few chords of the throbbing drum-and-bass hit that had been the sound-track to the summer so far.

Having slid the last pin into her hair, Cleo turned and raised an eyebrow, flashing a cheeky grin at me in farewell.

I waved her off as she left.

'How are you, Mum? Is everything OK?'

More silence. I tried not to sigh, to be patient. I worried about my fragile, gossamer mother a lot, and lived in terror whenever she called that this would be the one night she gen-uinely needed me.

'I want you to come home. We have to talk.' Her voice, as always, sounded thin and small, like something heard from the other side of an expanse of clear, still water.

'Mum, this isn't a good time.' I sighed, tried to calm my voice. What was the point of getting upset? My mum's my mum and it's just the way things are.

But disappointment cut me.

I'd been sure she was getting better, and these calls, always late at night, had started to tail off over the last few months. I'd begun to let myself believe that she was finally coming to terms with the fact that I wouldn't be moving back home to Suffolk; that this constant anxiety about my whereabouts was slackening its hold on her.

'This is different, Sophia. This is important.'

'You always say that. *Always*. And then I get there and it isn't.'

'Jared and I need to talk to you.'

That was strange. Why was she calling my dad Jared? It was

an off note, a troubling ripple. 'Mum, is something wrong? Are you two OK?'

'Yes, we're both fine.'

'Then why can't it wait until morning? We can talk then.' I glanced at my watch. 'There's no way I can get out to Pulverton tonight anyway. I'm over the limit, and even if I left now, I'd never make the last train.'

Silence, then: 'Sophia, sweetheart . . .'

She was always doing this. Always, always. The devil by my left ear whispered, *Hang up.*

I glanced over my shoulder, as though someone was watching me.

'I'm sorry, Mum, I just can't get there tonight. I'll call you tomorrow and we'll have a good long chat.'

Silence, then: 'If you feel that way, Sophia.'

'It's not about what I feel.' I am trapped again, racked with guilt for something I just can't fix for her: her luminous, melting unhappiness, always understated and yet somehow always there, and seemingly without cure. I pushed the feeling down, bolted it tight. 'I'm sorry. I'll be in touch first thing, I promise. Goodnight.'

I tapped the screen and, just like that, she was gone.

* * *

By the time the taxi rounded Millennium Way his hands were already in my bra and I was plastered to the door while he kissed me as though it was the end of the world. Both of us had neglected to put on our seatbelts and the driver was probably too mortified to remind us.

It was a terrible way to behave really, but I expect that's why I found it so erotic.

'Carnarvon Mill, mate,' said the cab driver, a balding middle-aged man, who carefully kept staring straight ahead.

Benjamin released me and I gasped in some air, straightened my shirt while he cheerfully extracted a couple of tenners from his wallet. 'Thanks, mate, keep the change,' he said, before drawing me out after him into the sultry night.

We were outside one of those po-faced riverside developments that line the banks of the Isle of Dogs. Behind us the Thames lapped against the pebbles, in the wake of a party barge full of fairy lights and dancing people, speeding towards Woolwich. The thin sound of Michael Jackson's 'Wanna Be Startin' Somethin'' wavered in its wake. The air smelled of rotting wood and the brackish blood of the river.

'Come on,' he said, pulling me towards the lobby with its muted walls and spartan expensive-looking pewter fittings.

There had been a lift without music – or there might have been music, it was just that I was too caught up in his searching kisses to notice it – then pale corridors and dark wood doors. I was thrust through the one at the end into an impossibly compact open-plan penthouse flat, one large wall entirely constructed of plate glass. About two hundred feet below, the river glittered in the streetlights.

He pushed and manoeuvred me up the hardwood steps to the mezzanine.

'Nice flat,' I remarked, falling backwards on to the massive oak sleigh bed, pulling him down with me. 'Lovely view.'

'Yeah,' he gasped, yanking my stripy work shirt over my head with a breathless inefficiency that made us both giggle. 'I bought it through Amity.'

'Very nice,' I repeated, while he unbuttoned my printed trousers, tugging them down with a single swift stroke. My shoes were already gone. I had no idea when that had happened.

We were kissing again, my hands were in his shirt, scrabbling against his chest as I tried to unfasten the buttons, and then I realized:

'Sorry, I need the loo,' I said. 'Where is it?'

'What, now?'

'You don't want me to ask later, believe me.'

He laughed then and pointed to the only other closed door in the flat, slapping my buttocks as I hurried over to it. 'Don't be long!'

* * *

I stood barefoot on the cream rug, the mirror reflecting me in my pink knickers and bra. I grinned as I sat down on the toilet, my eyes sparkling, my chest and face flushed – I had chosen one of my only two matching sets for tonight. Usually when I got lucky I was wearing embarrassing mongrel underwear. Fate was smiling on me.

As I sat down, I noticed that one of the cupboard doors under the sink was hanging slightly open. As an architect, I'm well aware of how these new-build riverside developments are made – location is everything, but the apartments themselves are frequently poorly designed and badly fitted.

I shook my head, smiling to myself. I was not at work now.

Nevertheless, I couldn't help noticing that within the cupboard glinted glass and gold. My bathroom cupboard had very similar contents.

Don't look, Sophia.

But it was too late. I had seen.

I sorted myself out and flushed the toilet. Then I bent down, carefully opening the door. A crowd of colourful bottles, a make-up bag bursting with jars and lipsticks – all higgledy-piggledy, as though they'd been scooped off the counter and hidden. Next to all this was a plain white paper box.

I turned the tap above, quickly rinsing my hands; then left it running, hoping its rushing sound would cover any others. Aware that this was very, very naughty of me, I picked up the box.

8

I already knew what it was.

The white pharmacy label read 'Mrs ELIZABETH VE-LASQUEZ, 127 Carnavon Mill, Millennium Way'. I wondered if this was Ellie, the 'friend' he'd climbed the volcano with. The date was two weeks ago. 'Microgynon 30 – to be taken once daily with water'.

It was the same contraceptive pill that I took.

I peeped inside the box. The blister pack for the first month was missing. She must have gone away for a few days, taken it with her.

I closed the cupboard doors and turned off the tap. In the mirror, my sparkly flush was gone, replaced by a cold, humiliated pallor.

She could have just left him.

No, I thought to myself with a dull disappointment, *she'd have taken all her pills. And her make-up.* She'd gone somewhere on business, most likely – wherever it is these high-flying Canary Wharf types go – and couldn't get the bigger bottles through hand luggage so left them here.

And while the cat's away . . .

You're not the one married to her. Just pretend you didn't see. You shouldn't have seen. You wouldn't have seen if you hadn't been prying where you didn't belong. Oh come on, it's just a bit of fun.

If it wasn't you it would be somebody else . . .

I gazed down at the marble counter. I could see the shadows left by her things now that I looked for them, in little water-stained circles.

It was hopeless, I realized. Another fucking married man, another liar by omission, his ring probably jammed somewhere in his trouser pocket. I'd turn up to work on Monday and everyone would be darting looks at me, quietly sniggering amongst themselves.

They'd seen me leave with him, after all.

Why hadn't Cleo said something? Did she not know?

At any rate, the evening was over.

'Hey, hurry up in there!' he shouted. 'Do you want a drink?'

'No,' I replied, coming out, my mind made up.

He peered at me, catching on quickly. He was practically sober, or at least a good deal more sober than me.

'Something up?'

'Sorry, I have to go.' I snatched my trousers up from the floor and pulled them on while he stared. Outside, the faint sound of buoy bells interlaced with the splash of the river.

'What's wrong?' he asked, but that slightly weak chin looked a little weaker right now, and his eyes were small and hard.

'Had a change of heart.' I plucked up my shirt, jerking it over my head.

'What? You can't . . . you can't just wind me up like that and then walk out.' His voice was rising.

'Oh, I *so* can.' My shoes were lying by the dresser, and I wormed my feet into them, gathering up my jacket and my bag from where they lay on the floor.

He was out of the bed, impressively naked. I felt a fleeting sense of regret for what might have been. 'What do you think you're playing at, you fucking mental cocktease?'

Instantly he was in front of me, too close, towering over me. His shoulders were hunched, the muscles tense, fists balled at his sides, and I understood in a whiplash moment that what he really wanted to do was hit me.

I'd realized he was no Prince Charming while I was in the bathroom, but his sudden viciousness, his sense of entitlement, still managed to be an unpleasant surprise.

Shit, I thought, *this guy is practically my boss. What have I done?*

Still, he didn't get to speak to me like that.

'How sweet. Do you kiss your wife with that mouth?'

'What are you talking about, you crazy bitch?' But his

anger was now laced with panic, and he sat back down on the bed.

I'd made an enemy tonight, that much was clear. And I had no idea what the fallout from that would be.

I should have been more careful.

'Night, Benjamin,' I said, blowing him a kiss. 'Don't wait up.'

* * *

As the bus roared and jolted along, I let my head rest against the dirty window and closed my eyes.

Another married man. Bloody hell.

As I looked down at my phone, my mother's call stood proud in the log. I had brushed her off for some chancer, a married chancer no less. I felt a clammy sense of shame.

We were approaching my stop, and I pressed the button and swung to my feet, feeling unpleasantly sober and clear-headed. She might have been summoning me home for no good reason, but she was still my mum. I didn't need to hang up on her like that.

That, at least, was something I could fix.

I trudged down the steps, pushing myself out past the steamy, booze-smelling crush at the doors and into the night.

Chapter Two

It was morning, and I was speeding towards the coast in my little purple Ford KA. I'd been driving it for over ten years now and it was held together almost entirely by rust and willpower.

If I'd been less hungover and cranky, I would have enjoyed the rolling Suffolk landscape, the winding tree-shadowed roads, the orange burst of the nascent sun streaming through the thin barred sea clouds. It was going to be a beautiful day.

I had barely slept, tossing and turning until I could stand it no more. In the end I'd given up and staggered upright. The pale haze of dawn was just beginning to cast a weird pall through the bedroom curtains. In the kitchen, I tinkered with the expensive coffee machine the salesman had talked me into buying instead of the one I'd wanted, and after ten minutes I finally managed to extract three syrupy thimblefuls of espresso.

I sipped this mournfully at my kitchen table. In front of me, the plans from my latest project – a new visitors' centre for Scottish Heritage, which was going to be built on a tiny, rocky islet in Orkney and would need to be a) eco-friendly, and b) impressively storm-proof – were up on the laptop.

For a while, I sat there, pretending I was achieving something and likely to do some work, before coming to my senses and grabbing the car keys.

It was roughly a three-hour drive, and I tried to support my caffeine hit by switching on the radio, but within ten minutes my pounding temples had vetoed the idea. Instead I drove along to the soundtrack of an irritating tapping that had started somewhere in the back of the car about a month earlier, and which a friend had assured me was probably due to shot wheel bearings.

I was nearly twenty-seven years old. It was high time I stopped wasting money on expensive coffee machines and upgraded the car.

High time I stopped living like a student.

Stopped living like my parents.

I crushed this thought down with a hot flash of guilt.

You shouldn't have hung up on her.

I didn't know why this was bothering me so much. Mum used to call me two or three times a month, usually between seven and ten at night, overcoming her horror of the telephone to breathlessly urge me to return to the fold, to leave London in general and Brixton in particular and come home to her.

'And do what?' I would ask, exasperated.

Her eyes would roll doubtfully sideways – I couldn't see this, of course, but I knew she was doing it. 'You could help me and your dad in the gardens. You're always saying you want to update the café.'

'I know I am. And you're always saying it would cost too much. Look, why don't you come down to Brixton and visit for a weekend? We could go do clichéd London things together, like afternoon tea and the London Eye and a show . . .'

'Oh no. No, I don't think so. No thank you.'

I turned off the A12 on to Moncton Lane, noting that the weathered sign stuck into the grass reading EDEN GARDENS AND CAFÉ 300 YARDS was now broken and skew-whiff – someone must have clipped it with their wing-mirror when they'd turned the corner.

I pulled up just past the sign, switched off the ignition and let myself out into the cool morning.

Birds sang all around me, as though they had been waiting for my arrival. The sea, though still a few miles away, was a salty tang mixed in with the grassy scent of hay. Breathing it in, I could feel something within me relax and settle.

I walked over to the broken sign, my blue pumps sinking into the soft, dewy mulch. It lay in two pieces, one sporting a wide tyre track, dissecting GARDENS AND from CAFÉ. It had happened recently; with a sigh I uprooted the post from the ground and carried both pieces to the boot of my car.

I was vaguely surprised that my dad, a perennial early riser, hadn't been out this way on his daily visit to the north field and done it already. I shaded my eyes and peered towards the gates of the gardens, just a few hundred yards down the road.

They appeared to be still locked.

* * *

At the gates, painted a cheerful apple green but now starting to show rusty patches, I drew out the keys and undid both locks, the metal still chill despite the warming morning sun. They swung open with a creak.

I glanced at my watch – it was 8:27. I felt as though I'd been awake for ever. The gates were normally open earlier, in order, as my dad would say, to capture any passing custom. Though, of course, any passing custom that did actually stop and approach, looking for herbs or plants or even a cure for chronic insomnia, would then be treated with the utmost surly suspicion, since my dad would have to interrupt his early-morning routine of maintenance and watering to serve them. It was Mum that supplied Eden Gardens' human touch, and she never got out of bed before nine.

Yet somehow the place remained in business, despite my plaintive urgings to add a new tea room instead of the corrugated, spider-haunted shed that currently served this purpose, with its mismatched chairs and draughty windows; or to consider stocking more mainstream gifts and houseplants as opposed to their weird collection of dusty bric-a-brac and yellowing greetings cards.

I let the gates clang shut behind me and moved off along the gravelled path, with its pots of marigolds and ceramic fairies, to the shop itself, rimmed with a little circle of white stones like tiny megaliths. Two mouldering picnic tables sheltered under the cheap awning at the front, as though cold or embarrassed.

'Dad?' I shouted out, though he was clearly not around — the stable door to the shop was bolted shut, the padlocks in place. I frowned at the blue painted wood, turned up the path, my footsteps crunching beneath me, and headed for the house beyond.

* * *

The house was accessible through another blue painted door set in a wooden fence that had long since been given over to trellising. Heavy apricot roses, just past their best, nodded their scented heads above my own as I let myself into my parents' private garden.

The house was suddenly visible, like a magician's trick — the perspective from the gardens and the frowsy thatch of thorns and blown roses shielding it from public view until you opened that final blue door with its rotting wooden sign marked PRIVATE.

This was not only a description but a personal injunction. When I was a little girl, it seemed to me that the world of the house and my parents was a kind of fantasy kingdom, separating us from the milling visitors in the nursery outside. It was an enchanted place, small enough to be hidden in a glass bottle, a realm accessible only to those who knew the right words or where the secret key was kept. Visitors who accidentally wandered out of the grounds and ended up here were given very short shrift by my dad.

I was under strict instructions at all times to keep the garden door locked, the key tied around my neck so I wouldn't lose it or give it away. Even as I grew older, this feeling that we lived in our own tiny private universe never left me, though by the time I was a surly teenager with a brow full of storm clouds, the downsides of inhabiting a magical pocket island were already starting to become clear.

'Hello!' I sang out across the small square of lawn, the one patch that my mother had saved from my father's all-consuming lust to plant more practical species, either for eating or selling.

No one answered.

The house had been beautiful once, a handsome Georgian building constructed for a prosperous miller – the millstream still wound through the public part of the gardens, bridged by chicken wire and wooden paths my dad built over the top of it. But perhaps that beauty was simply a projection of my memory. All I knew was that in my visits as an adult it seemed ever more ramshackle – the white portico of my childhood was now damp-stained and rotting, and as I climbed the steps I could smell its decay.

As I drew near, I saw that one of the little stained-glass panels in the door had been smashed and boarded over with plywood, which was neatly nailed into the window frame. I ran my hand along it – the wood was still pale and new. This could only have happened since my last visit a fortnight ago.

How strange that Dad hadn't fixed it already. Mum wouldn't be pleased.

They were an odd couple, my parents, both unlikely and yet somehow well matched, and they had muddled along together all my life. They had met, my dad told me, in a café in Cambridge. My mum had been heading east; my dad was heading north. He'd liked the look of her and asked her to come with him. She'd said yes. She must have been a bolder creature in those days.

I had followed them, nine months later.

They'd never married – the pair of them had a horror of paperwork and viewed all government services with suspicion and dread. I bore my mum's last name, as my dad wouldn't set foot in the registry office. At one point Mum seriously considered home-schooling me, but in the end common sense prevailed. I've lost count of the times this intractable paranoia has made me want to tear my hair out by the roots.

The key was no longer around my neck – I had slipped that shackle long ago – instead it was attached to my keyring with the lucky rabbit's foot, a gift from my dad. I let this assemblage rattle in the lock, hoping to give my perpetually late-sleeping, perpetually nervous mother sufficient warning that someone was entering, especially since my dad would be out in the grounds and fields for hours and wouldn't return to the house until lunchtime. I also knew that when I got in and shouted up to her, she'd reply in a startled gasp, as though I was the last person in the world she expected to appear.

'Mum, it's me,' I called out into the pale hallway.

Silence greeted me. Now I was inside, I noted with disapproval that the patches of damp above the dark wooden stairs had grown exponentially; indeed they now met, like two little branches reaching out, as if holding hands. The house smelled of dust and curry powder and the ghost of sandalwood incense. An untidy row of shoes littered the foot of the staircase, and I spotted my mum's work boots, caked in mud, one lying on its side, like it had given up.

I clumped up the stairs, the carpet dusty and littered with mud, shaken loose from the cuffs of jeans and hand-knitted socks. On the way up, I stopped and wrestled a window open to let the fresh air in.

'Mum? Are you up there?' I glanced at my watch. At this time of the morning, it would be hard to imagine her being anywhere else.

Still no answer. I sighed and mounted the remaining stairs, heading for the master bedroom at the end of the corridor.

But as I drew near I saw that the door to her room was open. Sunlight streamed through it, illuminating piles of books and curios and ugly sideboards in gold.

'Mum?'

The bed was made – well, pulled together – and as I poked my head in, I saw that this room, which like the rest of the house was usually in a state of dishevelled shiftlessness, had been tidied. No, not only tidied but *cleaned*, and thoroughly, since my last visit. The dresser had been dusted, the bottles of perfume and make-up, some so old they probably pre-dated my birth, had acquired a shiny order I had never seen before. The wardrobe was shut, the stacks of books and papers beneath the big bay window were now in neat piles.

I gazed about myself in confusion. The rest of the house was as scruffy as ever – why was this room so tidy? The unkempt disorder of this strictly maternal space was something I always associated with my mum, its condition mirroring that of her mind. To see it neat and clean, while the rest of the house continued to moulder, was like happening upon her dressed in a safari suit, as though she had become a different person, or rather, that a different person had been lurking beneath, ready to spring out.

The tiny hairs on my arms stood up. Where was she?

'Mum?' I called out with more urgency.

The soft creaks of the boards beneath my feet as I moved to the big bay window were the only reply.

I looked out over the lawn, past the rows of bean poles and netting tents and sprouting green shrubs that grew the food I'd been raised on. My gaze tracked down to the shed at the bottom, where my father spent 90 per cent of his spare time, then to the weather-stained trestle table where we ate family meals, all overshadowed by thick-trunked trees of all kinds, as though we dined in a sacred grove.

The branches of these trees were festooned with small fairy lights all year round, and I noticed uneasily that they were still lit.

'Mum?' I shouted again, though I knew the house was empty, and once more I heard that note of alarm in my voice.

Something was wrong in the grove at the back. Something was there that shouldn't be there.

I leaned against the window, peering hard through the grass. There was a shape amongst the trees – a human shape, barely visible through the leafy branches.

A shape with extended, dangling feet.

It becomes harder to remember now, because everything in the world was suddenly replaced by this sick, sinking panic. I breathed it in as I ran along the corridor, stepped on it as I tumbled down the stairs; it buoyed me up as I fell through the door and raced down the garden, crushing sprouting carrots and squash and turned earth beneath my stumbling feet.

And as I drew nearer, my mouth dry, my heart hammering, there was no mistaking it; that hideous, obscene bundle I had seen from the window, in my mother's floral yellow blouse and grey-blue jeans.

My mum hung suspended from the branches of the big sweet chestnut, the stepladder sprawled on its side, discarded.

I let out a noise – a kind of elongated animal wail.

I snatched up the stepladder, righted it and clambered to the top.

I couldn't see her face and she made no sound, there was nothing but the rustling leaves and the faraway rattle of a magpie. From the branch above, the thin electrical wire we used to hang the lights on was wrapped twice, three times, around the tree limb, biting into the bark, and she swayed slightly from it, the cord descending and hidden at her neck by her long dark hair.

I dragged her into my arms, trying to take her weight off the spiteful cord, and that was when my heart knew what my mind had instantly understood. She was cool and stiff and incontrovertibly dead. As her hair fell away the sight of her wine-dark face was like a punch in the gut.

I toppled from the stepladder, landing hard on my back on the mulch below, incapable of feeling anything. Above me, my mother's purpling feet dangled, swinging now that I had disturbed her, accompanied by an eerie, horror-movie creaking as the branch took her weight again. I lay below her, transfixed with disbelieving terror. I think I was waiting for this to be revealed as a nightmare, something I had dreamed, the price of being a terrible daughter who would awake, like Scrooge, with a chance to make amends.

But waking didn't come, just one leaden, sickening second after another. My mouth was open and nothing was coming out, not even breath.

Then a noise – a kind of choking. I grasped, helplessly, at the idea that it might be her, that in spite of all I had seen and felt and experienced, she might yet live, because she could not be dead. That was unthinkable, impossible. But instead it had come from the mulch, somewhere to my side.

I turned my head, wondering what new nightmare this could be.

My father was lying in a small huddle behind another of the

trees, curled up into a ball, and his arms and chest were stained crimson.

'Dad?'

He was absolutely white, as though he'd been carved from marble. But he made the noise again, and his bloodstained shirt moved, just a fraction, and I realized that he was still alive.

Chapter Three

I barely remember what followed next. Maybe I just prefer not to.

I do know that I spent most of my time in the hospital. I sat next to my dad on a little white plastic chair while he breathed into a tube, lost in the depths of a chemically induced coma, oblivious to the world and its woes.

I stared at his white, lined forehead, where it emerged from the mask, waiting for it to wrinkle with a sign of consciousness, but there was nothing – no feeling, no emotion.

Some desperate, gnawing part of me envied him.

People in white coats explained things to me with gentle tact, as though I was a bomb that might go off.

My father was very badly hurt, they said. He'd been stabbed twice, once in the lungs and once in the stomach, and this last wound had ruptured his bowel. Sepsis had followed. No one said as much, but it was not clear that he would live. The secret of those last hours of my mum's life might go with him to the grave, following her as he had followed her in life, a morose presence drifting behind her as she moved through the house, his mouth in a permanent frown under his dark beard.

I would reach out and take one of his cool, limp hands in my own, and weep, but quietly, because I knew he didn't like drama.

Nothing made sense.

Whenever I called to check in with the police, they kept telling me that 'the investigation into the course of events was ongoing', but it was very obvious what they all believed. I'd had the chance to read all about it in the paper a few days ago, when it was shoved into the groaningly full mailbox bolted to the gate:

WOMAN DEAD, MAN CRITICAL IN PULVERTON MURDER – SUICIDE

The body of a woman and a critically injured man were found at a house in Pulverton on Saturday morning after what appears to be an attempted murder – suicide.

Police and ambulance were called at 9:05 to The Old Mill, Pulverton, after the couple were discovered in the garden of the property.

The dead woman was confirmed as Nina Mackenzie, 46, and the injured man her partner, Jared Boothroyd, 51. The couple ran Eden Gardens and Café together, a garden centre attached to the property in which they were found. Mr Boothroyd is currently in a coma in the Royal Suffolk Hospital in a 'critical condition'.

The woman is understood to have died by hanging and the man sustained serious knife wounds during the evening of Friday, 28 July. Both were discovered in the garden by their daughter, Sophia, 26, who lives in London.

Local woman Babs Moran, of Brightley Cottages, Pulverton, described Nina Mackenzie as 'a nervous little mouse of a woman' and 'rather strange, though she seemed very nice. You'd never imagine she was capable of such a thing.'

Detective Inspector Rob Howarth told the *Mercury*, 'This is a tragic and baffling event, and it's far too early to discuss the motives involved. Indeed, we are very keen to hear from anyone that can shed some light on the mindset of Nina and Jared in the weeks leading up to the incident.'

He confirmed that the police were not currently looking for anyone else in connection with the matter.

The conclusion would seem to be obvious to everyone but me. My mum had planned to kill herself, and tried to stab my dad when he attempted to stop her. The DI, Rob Howarth, had shown me her pair of green kitchen scissors, bloodstained and with bits of grass still stuck to them, the blades gaping apart – these scissors had stabbed my dad so hard that the little rivet holding the pieces together was broken, and now both halves rattled about in the clear plastic evidence bag.

'Do you recognize these scissors, Sophia?' he asked.

'Yes,' I whispered, because I did. Mum had had them for years, and my dad would sharpen them for her in his shed.

Fingerprints were dried into a maroon crust on the silver steel.

It made no sense at all.

I had never known my mum to commit a violent act. Ever. She was the kind of woman who would spend the best part of half an hour wafting a trapped fly towards the open windows of the house.

I told all this to Cleo down the phone, as I took a short break in the hospital coffee shop to wolf down a bland cheese sandwich and some vending-machine coffee. I'd looked for a vegan sandwich but couldn't find one. Despite the fact that I'd rejected their vegetarianism years ago, for some reason it felt important to stick to it now – perhaps, if I did, the unseen forces of the universe would relent and let my dad get better.

'But there's no change? I mean, in his condition . . . ?'

'No,' I said, setting the paper cup down. Then, as kept happening, I burst into tears.

'Oh, Soph, Soph, don't cry . . . I'm sorry. No news is good news, isn't it? He's not getting worse, right?' She paused, as though reluctant. 'Do you want me to come down?'

I did. I'd become increasingly cut off from my old friends

by my new job at Amity, to the point where calling them felt more awkward than I could cope with in my fragile state. 'I could do with—'

'I mean,' she interjected quickly, 'I've got some reports due in for James on Monday morning, so I have to work this weekend, but maybe next . . .'

I understood instantly and with a flash of annoyance replied, 'It's all right, Cleo, thanks, I'll be fine. Rowan is here.'

'Who?'

'Rowan, a friend from when I was a kid. He works for my dad.' I tried to rein in my impatience. I'd told her this already. I seemed, on top of everything else, to have developed a savage, hair-trigger temper. It's very hard to explain. It was as though I was constantly spoiling for a fight, for someone to beat up.

Perhaps the person I wanted to smack was myself. I'd hung up on Mum that night, after all. My own mother. Even though I knew something had been slightly off about her call.

It was the last time I would ever speak to her.

'Look, Cleo, I'd better get back up there.' My horrid sandwich and bitter coffee were finished. I'd promised the nurses I would eat something today and I had.

Mission accomplished.

'Sure, sure. When are you back in work?' asked Cleo.

'I don't know.' I couldn't think about that now. Amity, Benjamin and my little flat in Brixton seemed like something that had happened in another life, to another Sophia. 'I'm not sure it will be any time soon.'

There was a significant pause. 'Oh.' She swallowed. 'If you're sure. Well, I'm positive they'll understand . . . under the circumstances.'

'I'll ring you over the weekend, OK?'

'OK. Take care, Sophia.'

'Will do. You too.'

I stumped back up the stairs towards the ward, and when I got there, a visitor was waiting – lurking near the entrance by the hand disinfector, his shirt limp with the heat, his chin and cheeks red with razor burn. His blonde buzzcut glistened faintly.

'Hello again, Sophia.'

It was Detective Inspector Rob Howarth, the man telling me and the papers he wasn't looking for anyone else in connection to my mum's death and my dad's hideous injuries.

Our relationship had quickly become tense and confrontational – in the main, because he believed my mum had hung herself, after attacking my dad when he tried to prevent her, and I knew that every single element of that scenario was impossible.

There was no way my mum would kill herself. It was inconceivable that she would do such a violent thing, and leave her body to be found like that by anyone, especially me. The mere idea would have horrified her, struck her as selfish and . . . and *rude*, strange as that may sound.

Even if I was wrong and she *was* capable of this, there was no way she would hurt my dad that way, stabbing him so hard the scissors snapped apart. That kind of passionate violence and rage – it just wasn't who she was.

Someone else had done this to them. Someone – and my heart clenched to think of it – who might have been stood behind Mum while she was on the phone to me that night, perhaps holding a knife to my dad's throat, while I drank in that stupid bar and tried to get rid of her so I could get off with some worthless married man.

The thought of it was too horrible to contemplate.

The police didn't see it this way because of course they didn't know my mum and dad, and that was hardly their fault.

It was my job, I reminded myself, to set them straight and make sure they kept looking for whoever had done this.

I might have failed to help my parents that night, but it wasn't a mistake I would make again.

I fought to still my shaking hands and decided to cut to the chase. 'Well?' I asked.

DI Howard seemed to bear my abruptness no ill will. A kind of pity lurked in the creases of his dark blue eyes and the tight lines surrounding his mouth. I understood instantly that whatever he had come to say, I would not want to hear it.

'So, we've had most of the results back from the crime scene,' he said. 'Including the DNA samples from the scissors and the fairy lights.'

'What . . . already?' I felt breathless. 'What does it say?'

'We've found no evidence that anyone else was involved in the incident at Eden Gardens.'

I blinked at him. 'Well . . . well, that can't be right.'

His face did not move, and his seriousness made a chilling impression on me.

'I know it's not what you were hoping to hear, Sophia—'

'It's not about what I'm *hoping* to hear,' I said, my anger rising. 'Whoever it was could have been wearing gloves or something. I mean . . . the fact that you can't find any evidence just means that whoever this was . . . whoever did this was clever about leaving no trace.'

He looked down at his shoes for a second, as though trying to muster his patience. 'Sophia, I know this is hard to accept . . .'

I raised my hands, as though warding him off. 'No. *No.* Everyone keeps saying, "I know this is very hard to accept" in that tone of voice, and the fact is, *yeah*, it *is* hard to accept, because it's impossible—'

'Sophia—'

'My mum would not kill herself!' The tears were coming back, and I wiped them away impatiently. 'She was down sometimes, but so is everyone. And she wouldn't hurt my dad. I know this, do you understand? I know *them* . . .'

My voice was growing louder, and nurses and visitors were turning towards me to see what the commotion was. I tried to collect myself. This wasn't his fault.

This was *my* fault.

'So here's what we have, Sophia,' he said carefully, with a thin veneer of brisk compassion as his Adam's apple reddened above his loosened shirt collar. 'There are no fingerprints or any other evidence that anyone else was there, except for you.'

'But—'

'There are no defensive wounds on either of them, no signs of any forced entry to the garden. Your mother's ligature wounds are consistent with how she was found . . .' He swallowed and I almost pitied him. 'Sophia,' he laid a hand on my shoulder, very carefully, as though I might bite it. 'I know this is, uh, a lot to take in. But it's the only explanation that fits all the facts, when you consider the problems your parents were having.'

'What problems?' I asked sharply.

Surprised, he blinked at me. 'The burglaries? The vandalism?'

'*What?*'

'You don't know?'

'I . . . no . . .'

'They reported incidents four times in the last six months. They promised the officer who came out last time that they were going to buy CCTV cameras,' he said, tapping his notebook with his pen. 'It doesn't look like they ever installed any.'

I was too stunned to reply. Burgled?

And four times in six months?

Eden Gardens is out in the middle of nowhere, and not an

obviously prosperous place. Who would bother breaking in even once?

And why had my parents never mentioned it? A burglary is a traumatic event – I'd been burgled once in Brixton and had spent the next three weeks sleeping with the lights on.

My confusion must have been obvious to DI Howarth.

'You really didn't know?' he asked.

I stared at him bleakly and shook my head.

'Sophia, I think that number of break-ins would upset anybody. You're sure she wasn't depressed?'

'*Yes*. Well, she was always a little . . . needy. But not depressed. If anything, she'd seemed – I dunno . . .' I fought to capture the feeling I'd had, the thing that had been in the back of my mind for months. 'She seemed a little more together – she'd . . .' My cheeks were burning with shame. 'When I first moved out, I had constant phone calls begging me to come home, to find a job nearer them, but in the last few months it had started to calm down.'

I was paralysed by all these new, impossible doubts. 'She tries to manage her moods, though. She meditates . . . sorry, meditated. You know, the standard hippy thing.' I rubbed my sore eyes. 'She was just, I dunno, everything was always a bit chaotic with her. She was always going to learn to paint, or write a book about her "spiritual journey".' I dropped my hands. 'But she'd been saying that for years. She never got around to it.'

'One thing you learn, being a police officer, is that people are always surprising you.'

I folded my arms around myself miserably, and considered this bizarre, strange, but yet plausible scenario for a second. When said out loud, it could have played out that way. They were frantic with anxiety; they were both insular, self-contained people, and they were under attack in their little garden world.

But here's the thing. I knew them.

Or at least I thought I did. Then.

* * *

Rowan and his wife, Kayleigh, had urged me to stay at their cottage two miles down the road from Eden Gardens, and at night they fed and housed me alongside their charming, chaotic children. I would sit at their table at mealtimes and watch them, feeling like Banquo's ghost, aware that I was intruding but unable to face staying at my parents' house alone.

I had grown to rely on Rowan, who worked for my dad at the gardens. The sound of his heavy boots clumping down the hospital corridors soon became recognizable from dozens of yards away. The untidy mass of his pale brown dreadlocks tied loosely away from his face was a challenge to the sterile decor and starched uniforms around me.

'Hiya, Soph.'

I raised my eyebrows at him as he sat down next to me. I didn't have the energy for much more.

'How is he?' he asked.

'The same.'

He nodded, as though this was progress, and leaned back against the wall, letting his head fall against it. He closed his eyes.

There was blessed silence.

I have known Rowan for ever – since we were children. His father, Cliff, had a tiny farm on the edge of Pulverton Down and worked with my dad sporadically, each helping the other out with the bigger gardening and farming chores. For years Rowan was my only playmate and we did everything together.

I'm not sure when that changed. Maybe when I hit my teens and became a dark Goth rebel with *ennui*, poetry and boys on my mind, while he stayed with the things he loved – hiking, fishing and working the earth.

And I think, if I'm being honest, that I was more than a little jealous of him.

Rowan's dad died a drunk, but Rowan stuck around, working at Eden Gardens full time. He married a local girl, rented a cottage just down the road from us, sired two children and effectively became the son my dad had always wanted.

As I sat indoors, studying for my A Levels, I would often look up from my books and out of my bedroom window, where I'd see them lounging comfortably together at the trestle table under the trees, mugs in hand, smoking tiny roll-ups with glowing orange tips in the dusk as my dad gestured expansively, doubtless telling him some story that made them both laugh.

My dad wasn't like that with me any more, and it made something in my heart curl up and ache.

I'd been gone for years now, and I thought Rowan and I had grown apart. But distance is quantum, and frequently imaginary, or so it proves. He was acting as though I'd never been away.

'Rowan, did you know my parents had been burgled?'

His eyes flicked sideways at me. 'What? Again?' His tanned brow wrinkled.

'The police said four times in the last six months.'

'Oh, yeah, I knew about that.' He seemed to relax, as though worried I'd been talking about some other, additional crime. He caught my expression. 'Jared and Nina never told you?'

I shook my head.

'They probably didn't want you to worry,' he said, but his tone was clipped, his gaze evasive. We both knew that my mum always wanted me to worry about her. It was one of her tools for getting me to come home. 'It wasn't like any big deal – nothing important got stolen.'

'But doesn't four times in six months strike you as excessive?' I asked.

He shrugged. 'You know, it did at first. But the police reckoned it's quite common. If a criminal gets in successfully once, you know, he'll try again. It's not like there's an alarm. Your dad never got around to installing any CCTV. What's to stop them?'

I sighed in exasperation. I knew all about my dad's views on the surveillance culture. 'Never be photographed,' was his maxim, as though he subscribed to the old belief that cameras could steal your soul. 'But what is there to rob from my parents? They don't even have a TV.'

Rowan shook his head. 'Who knows? Money, jewellery, and we have loads of tools in the sheds – though they didn't take any.' He shrugged again. 'If it's druggies, they don't have to steal a lot, just anything they can pawn. Jared reckoned it might just be kids, you know, after the thrill of the thing.'

He looked uncomfortable, realizing he'd been in on a secret from which I'd been deliberately excluded. That ancient childhood jealousy and paranoia was stirring within me again – I pushed it down, locked it back in its box.

There was a horrible irony to all this – while I had railed to the detective that he didn't know my parents, *I* hadn't known this was happening to them, and Rowan had. Why hadn't they told me?

Probably, I realized with a flash of insight, because I would have gone crazy at them both. 'You need a burglar alarm. You need cameras. You need locks on the windows and doors . . .'

I would have got *involved*.

'I've got a list of people your parents knew locally – you know, like . . . for the funeral,' said Rowan after a few moments.

'Thanks,' I replied listlessly.

'Did the coroner get back to you?' he murmured, glancing over at my dad, as though anxious not to be overheard.

I nodded. 'The funeral directors are picking her up tomorrow.' I swallowed hard; my eyes were growing hot and it was becoming harder to think. 'They've done the autopsy, so we can bury her. The next thing we're waiting for is the inquest . . . whenever that will be . . .'

I could say no more. Everything was falling apart again.

'Come here,' he said, and before I knew it I was sobbing into Rowan's arms, my dad's dislike of drama notwithstanding. 'Soph, I'm so sorry about this. So sorry.'

'I don't believe my mum killed herself. I just don't believe it.'

'I know, Soph.'

'I just don't . . . I mean, why did this happen to them? I don't know *why*.'

'No,' he said, stroking my hair. 'Neither do I.'

* * *

'It was a beautiful service.'

We were in Eden Gardens, drinking from rented glasses in the public garden. I was facing an earnest young couple in black. The girl, Sonia, had worked for a while in the café before leaving for uni. I'd never met her before.

'Thank you,' I said. It was easy to do – I was numb and cold and utterly alone, even in this throng of kindly people, in a chemical cloud of alcohol and Valium and wretchedness. I was a waxwork Sophia, poised with my glass. My reply sounded thin and reedy, as though someone else were reading my responses out through a cheap loudspeaker. 'And thank you for coming.'

'Sophia,' Kayleigh, Rowan's other half, appeared at my elbow, gently clasping it in one hand. 'Someone's asking to see you.'

I nodded and smiled at Sonia – it must have been a rictus,

but she took it in good part – then Kayleigh was leading me back to the house. Her round cheerful face was pinched with discomfort. 'They just arrived . . .'

'Who?' I asked, though I didn't really care.

We were already up the steps to the house, moving into the hallway. Two elderly people I didn't recognize were standing there, dressed in muted black. The woman hunched around the jacket bundled in her arms, as though the very walls could reach out and touch her somehow. Her cheeks were scored with deep downward lines, as though she had been carved from some pale warped wood, and her escort was a tall thin old man with a round beer belly and a tiny, bitter slit of a mouth.

I paused on the doorstep.

'Sophia?' asked the woman. Her teeth were yellowing, her grey hair tinted the colour of steel.

There was something here, some barely suppressed intensity that I didn't understand. They both made me feel distinctly uneasy.

'Yes?' I asked.

'I'm Estella – Nina's mother. Your grandmother.'

This I had not expected.

Several conflicting emotions overtook me. I had never met these people before in my life. They'd fallen out with my parents, or more correctly my dad, at some point shortly after my birth, and that was that.

'Your grandmother,' she repeated.

At her shoulder the man blinked at me. 'We're Nina's parents,' he said, with a brusqueness borne of embarrassment, I sensed. It appeared to be an emotion he had trouble processing as little red spots appeared on his cheeks. 'What part don't you understand?'

I just stared at him.

'*Thomas.*' The word was a short, staccato bark. Estella's black gaze flashed at him.

He subsided, though his eyes darted about. I think he was someone not used to being at a loss.

I considered them for a long moment. As self-absorbed as I was in my misery, it struck me suddenly that they had lost their daughter, and most horribly, before they'd had a chance to make up after that long-ago quarrel.

I had no idea what their quarrel was about – my mum would only tell me that they didn't like Daddy. But there was always a kind of strained, stretched tone in her voice when she talked about them, and from this and various half-remembered stories she told about her youth, I got the impression that they were not very kind people.

'I see.' Kayleigh let go of my elbow as I tried to compose myself. I couldn't just stand there staring at them; I had to say something. 'I'm afraid you missed the service.'

'Yes, we know,' muttered Thomas, looking about in disapproval.

My grandmother's hand came up, the knuckles grazing his chest, as though warding him back, very gently, but it was enough. His bitter little mouth shut and his gaze dropped.

'We just came to let you know how terribly sorry we are that you've lost your mother.' Something trembled then, at the very corner of her eyes, but she mastered it. 'Thomas and I think you . . . you perhaps have questions, about us and the rest of the family. With Nina gone . . .' She paused for a second, as if it had only just occurred to her that it might be true. 'With Nina gone, perhaps we have questions, too.'

I didn't know what to say, but I nodded through my sedated fug.

She nodded back, as though relieved, as though we had

come to some agreement. 'I'd like us to meet. Not here, not now – I know you have things to organize – but soon.'

I nodded again.

'Take this, and when you're ready, call us.' She reached into her black patent leather handbag and removed a card from a silver case. 'We need to talk about the house in any event.'

'The house?' I blinked at her.

Thomas looked about to speak then, but once more the hand came up.

'It's not important now,' she said. 'But we do need to talk at some point, Sophia.'

She came forward, and as I realized what she was about to do, I nearly flinched, but managed to master myself while she kissed me decorously on the cheek, smelling of face powder and some heavy perfume that hung around her like a wreath of lilies.

She pressed the card into my hand firmly, then slipped her arm through Thomas's.

'Till then, dear,' she said.

Just like that they left, and I was too surprised and dazed to even say goodbye, leaving all that to Kayleigh, who seemed to understand.

I glanced down at the neat, mint-green card. 'Mrs Estella Mackenzie, The Gables, Pinsworth, Oxfordshire' was printed in a faux-cursive script across it.

I dropped it on the windowsill near the front door, on top of a pile of unopened post.

* * *

'Amity Studio.' She sounds as she always does – endlessly poised and utterly disengaged.

'Hello, Olympia,' I said.

It was August, and the heat had moved from pleasant to

stifling. The plants in Eden Gardens wilted around me despite Rowan's best efforts. He told me there was talk of a hosepipe ban.

'Oh, hello – who is this?'

'It's Sophia Mackenzie.' I dug at a stain on the kitchen table with my thumbnail, feeling it scrape across the distressed wood.

'Oh . . . Sophia, sorry, of course.' She didn't sound sorry. I had a bad, uneasy feeling. I hadn't been back to Amity for nine days. 'We were so sorry to hear . . .' She lowered her voice to an almost pantomime whisper. 'How are you?'

I had no answer, because I had no idea how I was. In front of me, the faintly rusting wind chimes hanging over the kitchen window twirled infinitesimally slowly, though I'd no idea what could be moving them as there hadn't been a breeze in days. A single drop of sweat was crawling down over my collarbone, and I crushed my shirt to my skin to catch it.

'Thanks – I'm getting by,' I replied.

'Oh it must be *awful*,' she said.

'Well . . .' I said. 'Yes.' I paused, derailed. 'Look, Olympia, sorry, but I have to get back to the hospital soon and see my dad. I need to speak to James. Is he in?'

This request elicited a long moment of silence.

'Oh,' she said. 'Sure. Just let me see if he's available.'

With a click I was on hold, and my uneasy feeling intensified. A few seconds passed, punctuated by gentle double beeps, and I glanced down to see I'd gouged the varnish from the table with my nail.

I stopped, balling the offending hand into a fist.

Another click.

'Sorry, Sophia, he's busy with a client at the moment. Can I get him to ring you back?'

This was the third such message I had left in four days.

'Thanks,' I said, ceding defeat. 'But it's OK. I'll email him.'

'If you're sure,' she said, and there was a tension underlying her bright tones. 'We're all thinking of you.'

'Thanks,' I said. I was sure that was true. 'Speak to you soon.'

She hung up with a quick clatter, and in it I sensed her relief.

I wrote an email to James, the managing partner, updating him on the situation.

I had been given seven days off work when I phoned in with the news of my mum's death and the harrowing circumstances surrounding it. They had delayed my presentation of the plans for the visitors' centre to Scottish Heritage, which should have taken place last week, but this had been granted with poor grace.

I had wanted to reschedule for later in August to give me more preparation time, but nothing came back from the office except hazy mutterings about the client having problems setting a date.

I had a bad feeling about the vague yet intransigent tone of these emails – nobody actually phoned me, and when I phoned them nobody was in or they were too busy to talk to me.

One word kept running through my head while I considered all this – Benjamin.

Looking through the email correspondence with the client, his name had suddenly cropped up in a truncated part of an email I hadn't been cc'd into, but which the project manager had unwittingly forwarded to me earlier when I'd asked for clarification of who would be at the presentation. In it, Benjamin described himself as 'caretaker for the project while Sophia is "indisposed"'.

He hadn't shown the slightest interest in the project while

I'd been working on it, and anyway his area was corporate architecture, not leisure and heritage like mine.

Normally I would be challenging all of this, but I was exhausted, heartsick and too overwhelmed to indulge in the luxury of anger or self-defence. Besides, he was one of James's favourites, and much more senior than me at Amity.

The only way to resist successfully was for the presentation to blow them all out of the water. Somehow, I had to find the strength to do just that.

* * *

Dad was not getting any better. In fact, every day he looked more sallow, more drawn, as if the infection was devouring him from the inside out.

I left him at eight o'clock. It was still daylight as I reached the front door of the house and pulled out the keys. I was so dispirited I had to try three times to open the door.

I shuffled into the damp landing with its sour, mouldy smell, which the hot weather didn't seem to be helping. I moved off towards the kitchen, switching on the light, and put my hand-bag down on the table.

Lying in the middle in a rusting wire basket was some new post. Rowan must have brought it in for me – he'd always had a key to our house.

There were two letters. One was from the water company, with some terrifying figure on the bottom in red and a threat to cut us off in capital letters. I threw it back in the basket.

The second was in a white envelope. I turned it over and saw an embossed address – Paracelsus Press, with an office somewhere in Clerkenwell.

I tore it open. Inside, there was a single sheet of high-quality paper.

Dear Nina,

Thanks so much for your note, which I was very excited to receive.

Do let me know when is a good time for me to come up to Suffolk and read the completed *Morningstar* manuscript. I can't tell you how much we are looking forward to seeing it!

Any questions, just ring me.

Best wishes,
Max Clarke
Senior Editor

So my mum had finally written a book, the one thing my dad and I had been convinced would never happen.

It had even found a publisher.

I read the letter – once, twice – then burst into tears.

Chapter Four

'Hello, I was hoping to speak to Max Clarke.'

It was the following morning, Tuesday, and the torpid heat continued unabated. I was sitting inside Eden Gardens' café and my head ached.

I'd spent hours going through the old, rumbling freezers and cupboards, throwing bags of frozen food, stale flour and rotting root vegetables into the bins outside – I hadn't been able to decipher my mum's system of stock rotation and nothing she'd prepared herself was marked with dates. The last thing we needed, with the business so parlous and short-staffed, was to poison someone.

Serving in the café had been one of my chores since my earliest memories, my mum hovering over the pots in the background, filling the tea urns, sometimes humming the latest pop tunes to herself while I ferried plates back and forth to the dishwasher. If I'd been very good, she would give me a sliver of cake, which I would wolf down at one of the tables while she cleared away the Tupperware boxes of salads and garnishes lying out on the work table.

My own, very average aubergine and coconut curry bubbled away in the background on the wonky stove with the same broken hob that had given up the ghost in 2008 and never been fixed. The plan was to sell this concoction to visitors as the Special of the Day, but a cursory tasting a few minutes ago had thrown doubts on this scheme.

The minute the clock struck nine I picked up the phone.

'Who's calling, please?' replied a female voice, cultured yet brusque. Paracelsus Press had clearly sourced their receptionist from the same factory where Amity got Olympia.

'Hi,' I said, scratching anxiously at the back of my neck. 'My name is Sophia Mackenzie. I'm calling on behalf of my mother.'

'I see, and what's it in connection with?'

'A book my mother submitted to your company.'

'I see.' There was a wary note in her voice, as though this was a ruse I'd constructed to get round her vigilance. 'And what was the name of the book?'

I groped through my mind for a minute, the name forgotten. But then, in a flash, it came to me. '*Morningstar.*'

There was a profound silence for one, then two beats.

'Oh, of course. I'll put you through now, Ms Mackenzie.'

A click, and then:

'Hello? Nina?'

He was young – I could tell that immediately – and he had a slight accent I couldn't identify beneath his smooth London media patina.

'No, I'm sorry, I'm not Nina,' I said. 'I'm her daughter, Sophia.'

'Sophia? This is *Sophia* I'm talking to?'

'Um, yes,' I said, disconcerted. Why was he asking after me as though he knew of me? 'Listen, I got your letter.'

'My letter . . . *you* did?'

'Um, yes. Are you sitting down . . . ? I mean, I'm afraid I have some bad news. About my mother.'

'What do you mean?'

'I . . .' I didn't even know how to begin. Before I'd picked up the phone, I'd decided I would cut to the chase, but it wasn't working out that way. 'You see . . .' *Just come out and say it.* 'My mother's dead.'

42

Silence. No, not complete silence. I could hear him breathing. Just about.

'I'm sorry,' I said after a few moments. 'I know it's a shock.'

'Uh . . . no, I'm sorry. Forgive me. I had no idea. Um, how did . . .'

'She . . . well, she . . .' *No. I will not weep. Or at least I'll get this over with first.* 'I'm afraid the police think she killed herself.'

I'd thought the silence before had been profound.

'*Killed herself?*'

I didn't reply. Sometimes you just have to let people absorb things. I was discovering this for myself.

'B-but that's . . . I'm sorry, I don't understand.'

'No. Neither do I.'

'I mean . . . She'd just . . . she was so excited about the book. About *Morningstar*. We'd been talking about the manuscript for the last six months . . .'

Six months? Where had I heard that recently?

'I . . . I have to confess, I had no idea she would ever get around to writing a book.' I felt light-headed. 'So you've read it? What's it like? What's it about?'

'Well,' he said, and I sensed a pulling back, an equivocation, in him. 'I've got to be honest – I haven't seen the completed manuscript yet.'

'No?' A little shiver of disappointment, of sadness, went through me. Perhaps there was no book. Perhaps my dad was right; she could only talk about it, not actually do it. Perhaps . . .

'. . . But I've certainly seen the notebooks.'

'Notebooks?'

'Yes. The manuscript existed in the form of handwritten notebooks. Nina wouldn't let me make copies, but once we'd talked on the phone a few times I came up to Suffolk in

43

person and met her in a café in Southwold. I read the first two while she waited, and I was *very* excited by them. I immediately made an offer for the whole thing once it was complete. She wrote to me a fortnight ago to let me know she'd finished the final third. She said she'd start putting them all together into a single manuscript.'

'I still don't understand,' I said, my head spinning. 'My mum always said that she wanted to write a memoir.'

'That's right. *Morningstar* is a memoir.'

'Don't get me wrong,' I pictured Mum in this very room, placing the menus on the table, wiping the counter with a ragged cloth, that tiny half-smile on her face. In my memories she was always here, always in Eden Gardens. 'I loved my mother dearly but . . .' It felt like treachery to say it, but still. 'Why would you be excited by a book about her life?'

Silence fell, and within it I sensed an enormous surprise.

'You don't know . . . you don't know about her time at Morningstar?'

I shook my head. 'I don't even know what Morningstar means. What is it?'

'Sophia — may I call you Sophia?'

I shrugged. 'Sure.'

'Do you have any idea where the notebooks are now?'

'No,' I said. 'I mean, they're not in the house, as far as I know. The police—'

'Have you looked?' Those chummy tones had grown sharp — I'd alarmed him.

'I've spent the past two weeks going through their things. I haven't seen anything that looks like handwritten notebooks.'

'I mean,' and he sounded faintly desperate, 'you might not have recognized them for what they were. Would your father know, perhaps?'

I swallowed hard. 'Maybe, but, um, I'm afraid he was very

44

badly injured during the, er, incident, and . . . well, he's in a coma now. It's not clear if he'll wake up.'

I shut my mouth with a click, trying to squelch my oncoming tears. I can't start crying every time I discuss this with strangers. They can't help and it doesn't help me – all it does is make them feel wretched and uncomfortable, which only compounds my own misery.

Silence again.

'Good God,' he said eventually. 'You poor, poor thing. I can't tell you how sorry we are . . . how sorry *I* am. Listen, this can all wait. It's a lot for *me* to take in, for you it must be absolutely . . . well, I can't imagine what you're going through.'

'No,' I said, with a firmness in my voice that took me aback, as though there was another person inside me that had very distinct views on the subject. I wiped my face with barely concealed impatience. 'It's all right. If there's really a book I want to find it. It's the least I can do for her.'

'If you're sure.'

'Yes.' And as I said it, I knew it was true. 'Quite sure. I'll have a look for these notebooks tonight, once the café closes.'

'I wouldn't like to—'

'No. I want to read them. There might be . . . it could . . . you know, there might be some clue in there about what happened.' I screwed my eyes shut, forcing my breathing to calm.

'There might be,' he said, but he had an aura of reserve now, of caution. 'Sophia, I should probably tell you that there are certain disturbing elements in your mother's past and these are . . . well, possibly a little explicit, especially for her daughter to read.'

Explicit? My mother? I'd loved her desperately, but she'd spent her whole life avoiding being explicit or clear or straightforward about anything. All had been a ragtag bag of distraction strategies, designed to head off the real questions. 'I don't—'

'If you find them, you can just send them straight on to us, or decide what to do later.'

'All right,' I said. I thought for a moment. 'God. She's written a book.'

'Yes,' he said, with a gentle tolerance, as though realizing that the majority of this conversation had been a body blow. 'Yes, she most certainly has.'

* * *

It was true. I'd never thought she'd do it. When I was a teenager, she'd already been talking about it for years. Initially, I'd felt the thing to do was encourage her in this, a respectable hobby, something to distract her from my forthcoming escape into the real world. I knew that in her youth she'd been thought clever and been interested in literature and poetry. Nowadays this manifested solely in her compulsive habit of buying books at charity shops. Perhaps this buried interest could be awakened as a bulwark against her loneliness.

So I bought her manuals on writing and leather-lined notebooks, silver engraved pens and brightly coloured pencils. I brought them for birthdays and on visits to the house and I sent them as offerings when I felt particularly guilty for ignoring her pleas to return home for good.

Sometimes I would invite my dad to pitch in with the more expensive gifts, but all he would do was raise a single cynical eyebrow and offer me a half-smile. He knew there would never be a book, that all this talk about writing and the absolute lack of action was a screen for my mother's insecurities; busywork to disguise her feelings of restlessness and thwarted potential, and in time I began to believe that, too.

But we'd been wrong. She'd not only been writing, she had gone out and got herself a publisher.

Did my dad even know about this?

And if he did, I wondered with a bitter little sting, would he even have told me? Maybe this was another thing that Rowan knew about and I didn't.

I shook my head to clear it of self-pity.

I needed to find those notebooks.

Together with this, and getting the visitors' centre project together for tomorrow (Amity had never called me back about rescheduling), I had a full agenda, but I couldn't get to any of it straight away. The gardens were open for business again and I was taking over the role of hostess for the day, until we could find someone to run the café.

So far only two people had responded to the advertisement. One was Laura, a shifty forty-something. I'd interviewed her a couple of days ago and her vague CV ('Why did you leave Annie's Seaside Café then?' 'Ooh, me and Annie, like, we didn't get on.') and elusive eye contact had already convinced me she wasn't right for this, or possibly any, role. But the truth was we were desperate; we needed someone to start immediately.

Nevertheless, I'd held off calling her back. I hadn't been able to get Annie from Annie's Seaside Café on the phone to check her references, and I was starting to wonder if she even existed.

The other candidate, Tina, had told me that her daily attendance was entirely dependent on her being able to get her sister to look after her kids. Her sister, however, sometimes got agency work, so she wouldn't be able to work on those days.

'Any idea when those days would be?'

'No.'

'Ah. Right. Thanks. I'll be in touch.'

If Laura's references continued to be elusive, I probably would be.

When a couple of old ladies came in ten minutes before

four, it was all I could do not to tell them we were closed. I was due at the hospital in an hour. But this was my parents' business, and my dad would need it if he recovered. I had to keep it afloat.

When he recovered, I told myself firmly, as I cleared away their empty cups after they left. It's been a fortnight and he's survived this long. I know my dad. He is strong and dark and tenacious, like tree roots. He's had a terrible shock and is badly hurt, but he'll be fine. I know he will. He's going to wake up, and then he will tell me what the hell happened. Somebody did this to us all, and whoever they are, we are going to catch them.

We *are*.

'Oh, hello there. Are you Sophia?'

I blinked away these dark considerations and looked up.

A woman stood in front of me. She was pretty in an unremarkable way, blandly dressed in a white shirt, brown skirt and belted jacket, her highlighted hair tied neatly at the base of her neck in a ponytail.

I'd been so distracted I hadn't even heard the bell on the door jangle.

'Yeah, I'm Sophia,' I said. My heart sank. Was this another journalist? 'Can I help you?'

'I'm Monica. The guy outside – Rowan – sent me to talk to you.'

I blinked at her.

'About the job?' she ventured. She had a slight accent. 'In the café? You put a card up.'

'Oh! Oh, I'm so sorry, yes I did!' I carried the cups away to the counter. 'Sorry, there's been . . . things are kind of disorganised around here. Can I get you a cup of tea? Coffee?'

She looked at me and her head tipped sideways, like a clever little bird. 'If anyone looks like they need some tea, it's you.'

48

I opened my mouth to refute this, but in those days any small act of kindness was enough to set me off.

In the end she fetched the tea and talked.

When she walked out thirty-five minutes later, she was hired and set to start the following morning. Her name was Monica, she'd worked in a tea shop in Aldeburgh, and now that she'd had her daughter she was looking for something nearer home.

She was the first person I'd interviewed who didn't seem to have some incipient personality disorder or be on the lam from the law.

When I locked up, I was smiling for the first time in over a fortnight.

A little stroke of luck, at last.

* * *

That evening, after my visit to the hospital, I searched for the *Morningstar* notebooks.

A quick look around the house revealed nothing beyond what I'd already found since I'd first discovered my mother dead. Searching the same places again failed to make the notebooks magically appear.

I sighed, already hot and pink in the louring summer heat, my mother's dusty-rose room lit by her favourite mock-Tiffany light, which gave everything a hectic, multi-coloured cast. The curtains for the bay window looking out into the garden, with its view of the tree she'd been hanging from, remained resolutely closed. I wasn't sure I would ever open them again.

I needed to get back to work – day-job work. The Scottish Heritage presentation was happening tomorrow and I needed to make the final adjustments to my files. Already, Benjamin's email was playing in my dreams.

'. . . while Sophia is "indisposed"'.

Those insolent quotation marks haunted me. As if my mum's death and dad's injuries were on a par with a hangover.

The project or the notebooks?

Choose, Sophia.

I started from the ground floor up, turning out the wardrobes, the drawers, the hundreds of random chests and dressers, revealing moth-eaten clothes, dusty papers, broken tools, lost pieces of plastic; unintelligible and gnomic now they were separated from whatever had spawned them.

There were things I didn't recognize – the most notable being a tall silver cabinet bolted to the wall of the office. It looked sturdy and expensive, but had been empty except for a pair of brackets at the top and bottom. Perhaps Rowan knew its purpose.

Wearily ascending the stairs, I went to my mum's room next.

Her old jewellery box sat on a faded, yellowing doily on the dresser. My dad had made it for her years ago, and I had varnished it, badly. It had been a joint birthday present from us to her.

I'd checked through this already – the jewellery was long lost, and only a few odd pieces remained: a cloisonné brooch with chunks of missing enamel, a tiny finger ring, a strange pendant – a thin gold cross within a circle with barely legible characters etched into it. You'd be hard-pressed to fit any notebooks underneath the box, but I moved it back to look anyway.

There were indeed no notebooks, but there *was* something thin and white hidden beneath the doily.

It was two folded pieces of paper.

Surprised, I opened them out.

The first was a receipt, from somewhere called Trevor and Hartley Country Supplies in Woodbridge; it was for a Baikal SPR 310 (second hand) and two boxes of smokeless 3-inch cartridges. It had been bought on June 21st of this year, about seven weeks ago.

I opened up the other piece of paper – stiff and glazed with plastic, and with something glued to it – and was stunned to see a small photo of my mum. She gazed out unsmilingly at me, her hair piled up on top of her head.

Above her, on the paper, was the title 'Shot Gun Certificate', and an expiration date for four years from now.

Several things hit me like a blow to the gut.

Firstly, my mum had a shotgun licence.

Secondly, according to the receipt, she'd bought a gun. Presumably in response to the burglaries.

And finally, I thought, as I turned around the room, scanning the surrounding junk, if that was so, and we'd already searched the house, then where the hell was it?

* * *

It was after nine when the sun finally set. I was covered in dust, tired and hungry but not ready to stop looking.

I shut my eyes against the bright light of the single suspended lightbulb and sighed, the phone clutched to my ear, a weak cup of coffee at my elbow.

'A *gun*, you say?' Rowan sounded as alarmed as I felt. 'You're sure?'

'Yep. I looked Baikal SPR 310 up on the internet. It's a twenty-bore shotgun made in Russia – cheap and, er, cheerful. And there were two boxes of cartridges as well.'

Rowan sighed. 'Sorry, Soph, can't help you there. I don't know anything about guns, and I never saw one in the house. Jared never mentioned it either.'

We were both silent for a while.

'So, here's the thing,' I said, reluctant to form the words. 'If it's not in the house, might it have been stolen during one of the break-ins?' I rubbed my dusty forehead. 'We need to tell the police it's missing, and sooner rather than later, before someone uses it.'

Rowan was silent.

'Are you absolutely sure it's not still in the house?' he said eventually. 'If they were being burgled like that, Jared and Nina would have been cunning about where they put it. I'll bet you any money they were going to try and scare intruders off with it. You know, fire a few warning shots.'

My heart sank. 'That sounds like such a terrible idea, it could only have come from my parents.'

'Hmm,' said Rowan with deliberately vague diplomacy. He never liked to hear me criticize my dad. 'I don't know much about guns,' he went on, 'but I *do* know that if you apply for a gun licence, you need to tell the coppers where you'll be keeping the gun. You can't just prop it up next to your door with the umbrellas, like.'

'I found a metal cabinet in the office,' I said. 'But it was empty.'

'Oh, oh yeah, that. I put that up. Was it for guns? Neither of them said.' I could hear him yawning.

'Did you not ask them what it was for?'

The question seemed to make him uncomfortable. 'I dunno . . . I might have done. They didn't mention guns anyway.'

If they had, would you have told me? I thought. *After all, you didn't tell me about the burglaries.*

'We can talk about this when you get in anyway,' he said. 'Shall we see you back at the cottage in a bit?'

'Look, Rowan, I've been thinking. I'm going to keep on looking for this gun. I'll sleep here tonight.'

The idea seemed to shock him into a moment's silence.

'Oh, Soph, you can't do that. Come back to the cottage.'

'I'll be fine,' I said, with far more conviction than I felt, and my voice tightened. 'If I hear so much as a creak I'll call you straight away.'

'Sophia . . . if you're sure.'

'Yeah, I'm fine, Ro. Honestly. And I'll see you tomorrow night at the hospital.'

* * *

I wasn't looking forward to spending the night in the house alone, but this business with the gun had rattled me. They'd bought it in June, less than two months ago, while the break-ins were in full swing.

Clearly something about these crimes had frightened them on some deep level as, even by my parents' standards, fire-arms were not a rational decision.

Had something else been going on? Something else that Rowan wasn't telling me? I needed to corner him, question him more closely. I picked up the phone, but realized it was now late – his kids would be in bed. It would have to wait.

I cast my mind over the last few months and all my inter-actions with both of my parents. Other than my mum seeming a bit more independent, nothing unusual sprang to mind.

As far as I could tell, the only thing that had changed about my parents' lives before these troubles began – before all this death and horror – was that my mum had written a book.

I didn't even know what it was that I suspected, but I realized I'd have no peace until I found her notebooks.

* * *

By midnight I'd searched everywhere. There was nothing but moth-eaten boxes of old clothes in the attic. And nothing in the damp basement, with its glinting rows of jars of preserved fruit, its cans of supplies, its empty crates.

Eventually I had to admit that the gun and the notebooks simply weren't in the house.

But maybe, I thought, they were outside it.

Maybe they were in my dad's shed.

I stirred uneasily at this thought.

My dad's shed is, to all intents and purposes, his home. It's a small blue-painted shack he built himself at the bottom of our garden, where he plays with his woodworking tools. It's shaded by the same trees I found my mother hanging from.

I didn't want to go into the garden at all, particularly now that it was dark. I didn't want to see them both there again, even in memory.

For a while I sat there, letting my coffee go cold, before I finally forced myself to my feet and pulled the Maglite out of the kitchen cupboard.

* * *

The garden was so much darker than I remembered. I paused at the door, staring out into the night, putting off the moment before I stepped forward and triggered the sensor on the security light, illuminating the darkened lawn and revealing whatever gloomy spirit was out there waiting for me.

Out I went, and there was that audible click as the flood-light came on.

There was nothing out there. The very bottom of the garden was still black because the fairy lights were gone, of course, and the floodlight only covered the first half of the lawn. Beyond it there was just the lush darkness of leaves and thick springy grass.

I switched on the Maglite as I drew nearer the shed.

An eerie feeling descended on me as I tripped quickly along the garden. I kept imagining that the beam would jiggle away from the shed door where I focused it, and there would be my mother, not a figure of terror but of dread, dread and soul-crushing guilt, her heartbroken disappointment in me made manifest on her dead white face, a dire visitant from beyond the grave that I would never be able to unsee or undream.

The key to my dad's shed came up out of my pocket and scratched at the lock while the flashlight shook and I breathed in short sharp little gasps.

If my dad dies – oh God don't let him die – but if he dies I am selling this place, I thought. *And I will never come back here again. Never never never . . .*

The door opened, squealing against the floor as I shoved it and nearly fell in, my hand feeling desperately against the rough walls for a light switch.

Nothing.

Stop panicking, Sophia. You know there is one. You watched him switch it on a thousand times . . .

There.

The strip light above juddered into bald, clinical life, and I let myself draw breath again.

My dad's tiny lair had an unkempt, dishevelled appearance even when inhabited; now it was like the *Marie Celeste*, complete with a coffee cup sporting a film of scum, which I'd made for the policeman but he'd never drunk.

I had only been in here once, to let the police in a couple of days after my mum died, and they'd searched the drawers and abandoned dresser in a desultory way for clues. I had stood in a corner, looking away, towards the house.

Before then I'd never come in here alone. It wasn't allowed. The few times I'd attempted it, as a small child, had led to a smacked bottom and a week of growling disapproval.

I honestly, at the time, never thought it strange that my dad lived in a small separate building, and came into our large house to eat meals before retiring to his den in the garden for a few more hours.

I looked through the drawers and dresser, each moment expecting my dad to appear, offering a furious scowl at my trespass. There was nothing resembling notebooks or a gun – only tools, some paperwork and, in the bottom of a dresser drawer, a small stack of soft pornography, dated no later than the early Nineties. I dropped it quickly.

I wanted to go back into the house, in the worst way, but I had made it this far, and I wanted to be absolutely sure there was nothing I had missed. I had no interest in coming back again.

I slumped into my dad's overstuffed and frayed leather swivel chair, and let myself feel a little charge of daring at taking over his space.

The chair faced the window, and beyond it the house proper, with its fusty yellow lights, appeared welcoming and safe.

I let my head fall backwards against the headrest, my gaze wandering the walls.

That's when I saw them.

Above the window was a wooden pelmet, shielding the rod that held the dark curtains up. On top of it, almost hidden but visible in the strip light, was a thin stripe of red-gold, and one of red.

I recognized them. The red-gold line was the spine of the first notebook I'd bought her, years ago, when she'd declared she was going to write a book. She must have liked it, because the other one was similar – A5, the size that could fit in a handbag, with ruled pages.

I couldn't reach them, so I climbed up carefully on to the rickety dresser, aware that I wouldn't like to break a leg and have to spend the night out here with only the poor signal on my mobile for company.

At the top I grabbed them – two notebooks. Max had mentioned three, so one must be missing.

I opened the one I had given her.

I recognized my name on the very first line – 'For my Sophia' – and her handwriting made my heart clench with love and loss.

'Everything is lies,' she'd written, 'and nobody is who they seem.'

The First Notebook

For my Sophia

Everything is lies, and nobody is who they seem.

That always seems to be the lesson. It was the lesson for me, and now, if you're reading this, it will be the lesson for you, too. I apologize, dear heart, if the lesson is a hard one, but I hope and pray it will not be as hard as my own was.

I must have started writing this story a thousand times, only to throw it away after a few pages, burning the papers in the Aga before Jared ever saw them. In all that time I never thought to use this, the beautiful notebook you gave me, and now that I have begun here, I have a feeling I will finish – one way or another.

I should have finished this a long, long time ago.

I hope you will not be too angry at me, Sophia, for the choices I made. After all, you were always the bold and brave one, the adventuress, whereas my whole life has been an example of cowardice in action. Or inaction.

But never mind, my darling girl, all of that's about to change. I will plant my flag and issue my call to battle, and this little world will burn down around me. And as much as I long for it, and I am ready for it – dying for it, in fact – I am frightened for you. I think we will all be bruised and battered at the end, and you most of all.

After you've read this, I'll answer any questions you have, as best as I am able, but not before.

I'm so sorry. I didn't mean for it to go this far.

All of my love, for ever,
Mum xxxxx

Chapter Five

Once upon a time, Sophia, long before you were born, I arrived at St Edith's College in Cambridge, on a blustery Saturday morning in 1989. I was eighteen years old and conscious then of only two immutable truths – the first being that I would never amount to anything, and the second that the plunge-necked, shoulder-padded purple velvet dress I'd bought with Uncle Malcolm's Christmas money made me look like a 'common streetwalker'.

I'd packed it anyway, and it was folded carefully in the bottom of the scratched red canvas suitcase I'd brought up with me. I remember the car journey on the way up, and the dread that my father would ask to take the suitcase back home to Oxfordshire with him once I'd unpacked it. When I emptied it, the lurid presence of this dress would be discovered. Terror, and something else, a little like excitement, threatened to smother me at the mere thought.

We'd arrived in Cambridge and been greeted at the tottering stone gatehouse by a brace of porters who'd directed us to join the other new arrivals. Ahead of us were more students, by the look of them, some accompanied by parents, some on their own, forming a loose queue. They were freshers, like me, and they were being processed by a trio of self-confident young people seated at a trestle table with a sign saying WELCOME COMMITTEE taped to it. The wind worried at the sign with ragged teeth, and the papers on the table were all firmly pinned down with rocks, mugs and, in one instance, what looked like a pint glass half full of beer.

Of course, I realized, I would be allowed to drink here – be expected to, in fact.

Here, all things would be permitted.

The thought made me giddy.

I stole a nervous glance sideways at my father. Already he was bristling at this trivial delay, displaying his signature tic for displeasure where his upper lip compressed almost white, as the boy fronting the table chattered idly to one of the newcomers. He had asked the girl for her name, and she tossed her lush curly perm and blushed.

Daddy did not like to queue – for anything, ever.

My mother slipped a hand through his arm, a gesture that appeared companionable, but which I knew was secretly checking, restraining. *Don't make a scene, Thomas.*

It occurred to me in a breathtaking flash of blasphemous insight that I couldn't wait to get rid of them both.

Nevertheless, I made nervous conversation to skate over the building tension – 'How old do you think these buildings are?' 'Do you think I'll meet anyone famous here?' – which my mother answered with cordial boredom, offering me no assistance, and my father ignored.

Finally it was our turn at the desk.

'Oh, hello there. Sorry to keep you waiting,' said the boy. He had a shock of blonde gelled hair and wore a grey blazer. He was almost indecently handsome and self-assured. 'I'm Adam, welcome to St Edith's!'

He offered me his hand and a gleaming white grin.

In that instant I glimpsed the potential for a new world and all of its dazzling potential. It made me dizzy, like a sudden rush of blood to the head.

I went to switch my bulky handbag from one shoulder to the other, in order to take his proffered hand and offer up the gift of my own name, when Daddy growled, 'About bloody time. Would it be too much trouble to tell her where her room is? We've been up since dawn with all this carry-on, without having to wait for you to stop flirting with all and sundry.'

The golden smile faltered, the hand dropped and the moment was gone. The blood burned in my cheeks, swelled my throat.

'So sorry,' said the boy, with clipped politeness but clearly angry. Unlike me, he was doubtless unused to being spoken to that way. 'What's the name?'

I groped for my voice . . .

'Nina Mackenzie,' snapped Daddy.

The boy's head dipped to the list, and without another word he fished out a pale envelope that rattled metallically. The girls bookending him at the table gazed pointedly away from me as he rose. 'Follow me please.'

The walk through the quad and up the wooden stairs to the rooms happened in agonizing, icy silence, though it seemed to me that Daddy's gait now had a rolling, satisfied air, as though the day was finally going his way.

'This is the room,' said the boy, as we reached a door marked thirteen. 'If you need any help with anything, just come to the orientation desk or ask at the Porter's Lodge.' He held out the envelope, waited for me to take it. 'Enjoy your time at St Edith's.'

'Oh.' I wanted to say something to make up for the humiliation in the courtyard, some friendly rejoinder, but nothing came to mind, and from the set, cold expression on his face it wasn't clear how it would have been received anyway. 'Thank you.'

He turned on his heel and walked away quickly down the stairs. The envelope was plucked out of my hand in an instant and torn open. 'Ah.'

My father was opening the door, struggling with the unfamiliar mechanism, and he was smiling – that thin, satisfied smile he wore when he had, in his own words, 'cut one of the uppity buggers down to size' at his factory.

'Why did you do that?' I asked before I could stop myself.

'Do what?' asked Daddy, and that hard, vicious look was back in his eyes. It would be the work of seconds to cut me down to size, too, small as I was, and I knew it.

My courage was deserting me, draining away like water down a plughole. 'I mean,' I back-pedalled, despising myself, 'he didn't do anything *that* bad . . .'

It was not quite enough. That hectic colour was back in his face, spreading up his neck from the opening of his green Ralph Lauren shirt. 'You might be happy to stand around being kept waiting by spoiled little trust-fund brats, but I have better things to do, my dear.'

'He was just being nice,' I mumbled, aware that the wisest course of action was to drop this, but unable to help myself. 'Welcoming. Like he was supposed to be. We were only waiting a few minutes. I don't understand . . .'

My mother's warning flex of eyebrows came too late.

'Is that so? Well, maybe your new friends can hump your bloody cases about.' With a theatrical gesture he dropped the little red suitcase and the grey holdall, and inside something clattered as it broke – the new mug they had bought for me.

'Daddy . . .'

He threw up his arms in a theatrical shrug – *see what you've driven me to!* – and stomped off down the staircase.

My mother stepped over the bags and kissed my cheek with hard, disapproving lips. 'Honestly, Nina. You should know better. You can call and apologize tomorrow. Try to have fun in the meantime. And behave yourself.'

With a brisk wave, she was gone too.

I stood alone on the landing, surrounded by my bags. From above and below came the sound of laughing voices, opening and closing doors. I could smell cooking and polished wood and dust, dust that danced in the shafts of sunlight coming in through the high thin windows.

I should run after Daddy, I knew, and verbally prostrate myself. If I headed off the storm early, he might yet be palliated, and we could go for a pub lunch as we had planned, shop and sightsee like a normal family might.

A normal family.

But I would have had to pass the desk in the courtyard again, and as I peeped out of the window, I could see the boy, Adam, laughing with the two girls, their chatter vaguely audible through the glass.

'What do you suppose his problem was? What a nutter.'

The girls laughed; tinkly, cruel, ingratiating laughter.

I stepped away from the window, picked up the red suitcase and holdall, and let myself into unlucky room thirteen.

* * *

'Where are you from?' bayed the boy from room twenty over the electronic stutter of 'Pump Up the Volume'.

'Shelford,' I squeaked. My mouth and glass was redolent with the sharp spice-and-vanilla taste of Southern Comfort, which was almost but not quite masking the thrilling, unfamiliar tang of alcohol. I clutched the glass tightly, revelling in it.

I'd decided to be the sort of girl who drank Southern Comfort. A wild yet cosmopolitan creature, not afraid of hard spirits. Hard spirits that had, admittedly, been diluted liberally with lemonade. But I had to start somewhere.

The boy frowned at me, his forehead creasing like an old man's. 'What?'

'Shelford,' I said, raising my voice, and it cracked against the unfamiliar exercise. At home I rarely spoke in more than a whisper. 'It's in Oxfordshire. In the Cotswolds.'

The boy already looked bored, painfully so, and I was sure he was about to walk away when he suddenly shouted, 'Are you going to the Freshers' Fair tomorrow?'

I had heard of the Freshers' Fair. It was where you went to join university societies. At that point I had barely been part of society, never mind *a* society, and I was very excited by the prospect. I imagined a group of cool, clever people – funny girls with spiky wits but hearts of gold, intense young men with frosted hair and expensive shirts who might ask me out for coffee and a cigarette

(I didn't smoke, I would need to start) and passionately discuss books with me in their rooms until I fell into their arms.

My life would finally *begin*.

Though it didn't seem to have *begun* quite yet.

Perhaps it was because I wasn't dancing.

'I'm going to dance,' I said.

'Really?' The boy screwed up his narrow little face again, and even the coloured lights of the disco couldn't hide his acne. He glanced into the plastic cup of beer in his hand. 'Oh, right.' He shrugged. 'It was nice to meet you.'

I smiled thinly and walked off towards the dance floor, his perceived lack of enthusiasm scalding me.

Perhaps I shouldn't have walked away. Perhaps I should have lingered, flirted, done whatever Bright Young Things were supposed to do. This was the problem. I had no idea of what I was supposed to *do*.

What I didn't understand then was that nobody else knew what to do at that age. We were the generation before smart phones, the internet and reality TV. Our hearts were hidden from each other.

We were innocent in ways that no one would ever be again.

I drifted into the centre of the dance floor as the track changed to 'Never Gonna Give You Up' by Rick Astley – I didn't like the song that much, but everyone around me burst into enthusiastic dancing. I tried not to notice their electric-coloured clothes and deep necklines, already inwardly contrasting these with my own minimal make-up and lavender pastel dress, and thinking how anaemic, unworldly and desperately uncool I must look compared to everyone else's burgeoning, energetic confidence.

Nearby, I spotted one of the girls from the matriculation dinner on the dance floor. Her name was Saffron, and she'd sat nearly opposite me at the long table in the Great Hall where we'd made passing small talk. She was bobbing away with another couple of girls I'd seen in passing. I think they'd all come up from the same school. I offered them a tentative smile as I started dancing a few feet away, but received a sharp grimace in return, and then Saffron quickly looked away. That boiling sense of humiliation moved through me again.

I shuffled along to the music, thinking all the while that I should just go back to my room. My sense of disenchantment was growing and swelling, making my belly feel queasy, making me feel . . .

Sick.

Within moments I was running for the door, my hand to my mouth.

* * *

'Are you all right?'

The voice was soft, tentative, and with my hair streaked with vomit and my cheek pressed to the cold tile of the toilet floor, it took me a minute or two to work out that the question was addressed to me.

'Unh?'

'Are you all right?'

A shadow moved over the tiles outside, at the level of my eyeline.

'I . . . uh, I don't know. Feel sick.'

'Oh.' A pause. 'Do you want a hand up?'

I blinked. 'No. Um, maybe. Actually . . . yes.'

There was the gentle creak of someone opening the cubicle door wider, and then soft hands carefully sliding under my armpits, gathering my back against a pillowy, ample bosom that heaved with my weight. I scrabbled to help this unknown person, my sticky hands bracing myself as I was hauled up to my feet and released.

I was a disgusting object. My hair straggled over my face and I smelled the re-emergent stink of Southern Comfort, making my gag reflex hitch once, twice, before it reluctantly settled.

I would never touch that stuff again.

'Thanks,' I mumbled, letting myself totter and collapse against the cubicle wall. 'Sorry. I'm in such an awful state, I know . . .'

'It's all right. Where are you from?'

I nearly raised my hand to wipe against my mouth, but grabbed instead for the toilet roll on its holder, pulling a swatch of white tissue away. 'Sorry . . . I . . . I'm from Shelford . . .'

'No, I mean *here*. Are you a fresher?'

'Yeah.' I let my face sink into the tissue, raised a cautious eye to my good Samaritan. In the spinning, giddy-sick centre of my vision was a sallow, plump girl with thin fawn-coloured hair, clad in a tight blue top and long silky black skirt, her skin make-up remarkably pale, but giving contrast to small, light blue eyes overwhelmed with sparkly eyeshadow and thick, cloggy mascara. She was peering at me through this clumped net of make-up, and her expression was both kind and doubtful.

I immediately recognized someone like myself, someone who found the rough and tumble of teenage sociality exceptionally hard work and who wasn't very good at it.

'Yeah,' I repeated, attempting to gather myself. 'I'm a fresher.' Everything was moving, and I felt hollowed out, but at least I no longer wanted to throw up.

'Well, come on. I'll walk you back to your room. Do you want a glass of water first?'

'You don't have to walk me back. Don't you want to stay for the disco?'

'No.' The girl replied crisply, then let out a little good-natured laugh at my surprised expression. 'None of this is really my sort of thing. I came down with a friend and he's already gone. I was just on my way back to my quad when I popped into the loos and . . .'

'Found me.'

The girl smiled then stopped, a tiny, tentative expression, as though she was perfectly happy to help out but not really interested in pursuing a friendship, and as I approached the sinks I saw why – a Hieronymus Bosch illustration of debauchery stared back at me. I was sheet-white, my mascara smeared down to my cheekbone, my fussily applied lipstick smudged to my chin. I looked as though I'd been drinking diluted blood.

'Oh God,' I said. 'I'm a mess. I—'

'Forget about it,' said the girl quickly. 'It happens to us all at one time or another. Come on back to your room and get to bed.'

* * *

The girl led me through low stone corridors and across flagged paths spanning geometrically perfect lawns, while all around us the tall buildings of the quads loomed overhead, crowding out the night sky, giving me a queer kind of vertigo.

My self-consciousness flooded back as my nausea retreated, and I was now far too embarrassed to speak. How many people had seen me lying there like that, puking my guts up? What would Mummy and Daddy have said?

And then we were back at the staircase, and I was stood in front of the door marked thirteen, murmuring my thanks while my guide urged me to drink lots of fluids and wished me goodnight, before vanishing up the stairs to the floor above. She hadn't mentioned that she lived here, too.

I staggered into my room, exhausted and sick of myself. I grabbed my towel and soap and made my way to the little communal shower on my floor. I stood under the water for what seemed like hours, my forehead pressed to the wall tiles while various people came looking to use the bathroom, knocked on the locked door and left disappointed. I scrubbed myself raw, and only switched the limescale-encrusted knob off once my skin began to prune.

I padded out, scalded by hot water, my teeth brushed to bleeding point, and feeling a little faint, and was startled to see the girl who had walked me back standing in front of my door. Her back was to me, and she was carefully setting down a can of Coca-Cola and a folded piece of paper on the brown carpet.

'Oh, there you are!' said the girl, embarrassed. Her own make-up was gone, and she looked a different person, somehow – her natural pinkish colouring made her small blue eyes and thin red lips more vivid and generous, more balanced. She shrugged. 'I got you a Coke from the vending machine. I swear by Coke when I'm worse for wear. Caffeine, sugar and water, you know?'

I gazed down at it, astounded. I wasn't used to random acts of kindness, and didn't know how to respond.

'Thank you.'

'It's nothing.' The girl flicked a hand, dismissing the gesture. Her eyes were red and a little wet. She had been crying, or was about to start. 'Well, sleep well . . .'

'Wait,' I said, aware that something was wrong. 'Do you want a cup of tea?'

'No, you don't have to . . .'

'Look, I'm fine.' I grimaced. 'But won't you have a cup of tea?'

The girl's mouth opened, as though considering what to say, and I added, 'Because you look like you could use one.'

The other girl blinked and the deal was sealed.

* * *

Her name was Rosamund, but most people called her Rosie. I never understood why – Rosamund, the 'Rose of the World', was a much better name, and I rather boldly said as much, and was rewarded with a wan smile.

Rosie took her tea strong with a lot of milk and two sugars, as though fortifying herself to tell her story. She was a third-year student, reading astrophysics, and had gone to the freshers' disco with her 'friend' Piers. The evening had proved to her that her definition of 'friend' and his were elastic and ultimately incompatible, especially after he dissolved almost immediately into the arms of a starry-eyed blonde fresher, while she retreated to the ladies' toilets to regroup before he saw her crying – this would have proved the nail in the coffin of this 'friendship', for reasons that I couldn't

71

quite understand. It was then that she'd spotted my pale blue high-heel poking out from under the toilet cubicle door, and the rest, as they say, is history.

I'd drunk a cup of strong tea with a Coke chaser and was now feeling much restored. In a selfish way, hearing about Rosie's woes distracted me from my own.

'It's not his fault,' continued Rosie as she restlessly twisted her star-shaped pendant between her fingers. 'I mean, I've never said anything to him.' She sniffed. 'He has no idea I feel this way.'

This seemed unlikely to me.

I tightened the belt of my flannel dressing gown, keeping my eyes carefully averted while Rosie sighed. My own romantic history comprised entirely of a mini-flirtation with Niall, the son of one of my father's friends, who had once kissed me after a boozy wedding in the village church.

Between that and my crush on Simon Le Bon, I was certainly no expert in matters of the heart. However, my feeling was that if Piers was ever going to get together with Rosie, he would probably have done so before today.

'Maybe,' I ventured, 'if you saw him a bit less, he'd have a chance to miss you more.'

Rosie raised an eyebrow. 'I dunno,' she said. 'We hang around with the same people. We're into the same things.' Her hand drifted up to her throat and played with her pendant again.

'What is that?' I asked.

'What?' A guarded look came into Rosie's eyes. Her hand covered it, as though shielding it.

'That, around your neck.'

'It's a pentagram.'

I peered at the necklace Rosie reluctantly revealed. It was a five-pointed star contained in a circle, wrought in slightly tarnished silver. 'I'm a pagan.'

'*Really?* A pagan?'

'Yes,' replied Rosie with a testy air, but there was something a tiny bit smug about her now, as though we'd stumbled on to a topic close to her heart. She had enjoyed my reaction, even if she couldn't admit it.

'I . . . wow. What does that involve?'

'It's about being in tune with the Earth and nature,' supplied Rosie. 'Good things.'

This was 1989, and there was nothing mainstream about Paganism then. I was astounded, and, as Rosie had doubtless wanted me to be, scandalized and impressed. In my family, even listening to the vicar in church was considered an unhinged ideological position. Spiritual belief existed solely as a means of cementing networking opportunities. Mummy's sister, Aunty Yvonne, had become a Buddhist after a year of yoga classes, and was spoken about within the house in hushed tones, as though she were a lunatic.

Mummy delighted in sneaking secret meat into the meals she served her whenever she visited, though visits had been thin on the ground since Yvonne fled to an ashram in Norfolk. My parents had been contemptuous, but I had admired her daring.

It must be wonderful to believe in something, I'd thought at the time.

Rosie believed in something, even though it seemed very strange to me. But you are what you do. She'd taken me under her wing and brought me gifts and asked for nothing in return.

I could use a friend in this place.

And, I had to admit, I was desperately curious about her beliefs, full of forbidden glamour as they seemed. Perhaps I sensed within them the tiny sparking potential for rebellion.

Chapter Six

So that, Sophia, is how I ended up hanging around with Rosie and her group of third-year students instead of the other freshers.

Perhaps another part of the reason was that I was so used to being the most junior person in the room at home that taking up the same role at university seemed like a logical next step. At the time, I think I craved leadership. Somebody had to be in the driving seat and it needed to not be me. That's the way I've always been.

Well, until now, that is.

Sometimes, when I watch you, with your seemingly boundless confidence, I wonder where you get it from. It must have turned up in some weird genetic lottery, a winning ticket in the form of a character tic. It's not a trait you learned from watching me scurry about like a frightened mouse in the foliage at Eden Gardens, desperate to avoid exposure.

But somehow I gravitated towards the company of Rosie and her friends, and before long it felt as though it had always been that way. We fell quickly into well-defined orbits and regular habits.

On weekdays, for instance, we were usually to be found in the Eagle, on Bene't Street. Lunch was largely liquid, interspersed with packets of crisps, which we tore open and shared amongst ourselves.

Piers, who had been quickly, almost carelessly, introduced to me by Rosie a few weeks ago, returned to the table in the outside courtyard with a tray full of drinks. The two boys – Piers and Tam – drank real ale, and Rosie and Meggie, our friend from Trinity who sported jangly bracelets and an elaborate blue streak in her hair, had ordered cider with a splash of blackcurrant cordial. I followed suit, too shy to request my usual of vodka and orange squash.

Piers was a lean, spare boy with huge brown eyes and long hair that had grown into a single messy dreadlock which the college dons were always tutting over. He smelled of the spicy oil he dressed his striking coiffure with.

He tore open a packet of smoky bacon flavour crisps and placed them in the centre of the table.

'Didn't you buy any veggie crisps?' asked Rosie, frowning.

'These are veggie crisps.'

'They're bacon.'

'They're bacon-flavoured.' He lifted one, raised it to his mouth and crunched ostentatiously.

'I'm vegetarian, Piers.' Rosie raised an eyebrow. 'I can't eat bacon, as you well know.'

'They're not bacon. They contain no bacon. Nil bacon. *Nada*.' He lifted the packet, careful not to drop any crisps out of the foil packaging and peered at the tiny writing on the back. 'They're E-number, E-number, E-number, monosodium glutamate, dried lactose powder, salt, E-number, paprika seasoning, preservatives.' He dropped the packet again. 'Also oil and potatoes. Probably. Hopefully.'

I wasn't sure if I'd imagined it, but I thought he winked at me.

'Well, I'm not eating them,' said Rosie.

'Oh, I give up.' He reached into his pocket and drew out a packet of salt and vinegar crisps. 'Here you go.'

He tossed it to Rosie, who caught it gracefully.

'Thank you, Piers,' she said.

'You're most welcome, fair Rosamund.' He offered her a courtly nod as he drew out a small tin of tobacco from his slightly tattered leather jacket. His eyes alighted on me, narrowing. 'What about you? Do you have any crazy food fads?'

'Me?' I gulped, startled by this sudden attention. 'Uh, no, no . . .'

'Good.' Piers was rolling a thin cigarette, and the smell of fresh-cut tobacco was masculine, grassy. 'Is she bullying you to become a lettuce-lover, too?' He laughed and shot a look at Tam; a gargantuan, stooped and largely silent figure who usually, like me, sat on the outside edges of our conversations.

Tam worked in applied mathematics and was always complaining that his supervisor, who had just published a bestselling book, was too busy for him. The suggestion was that we should be asking more about this, but when we did, he grew red about the ears and became maddeningly vague. In fact, it wasn't until years later, when I was stood in the kitchen and you came in with a battered copy of *A Brief History of Time* that I put two and two together.

'Any other vices, Nina?' Piers squinted at me.

I froze. 'Um . . .'

'Tell him to piss off and mind his own business if you want,' supplied Meggie kindly to me. 'That's what I do.'

'Your charm is the stuff of legend, Megs.'

'Just like the bollocks you talk all day, then,' she shot back.

Piers merely laughed. 'What is it you're studying again, Nina?'

'English,' I said, suddenly on safer ground. This was a subject I had strong opinions on.

'I remember now. How's it going?'

'Good. I'm going to specialize in mid-twentieth-century literature, I think.'

' "War is peace, freedom is slavery, ignorance is strength." ' Piers grinned. '*1984*. It was the only A Level book I had any time for.' He stuck his completed roll-up between his lips and lit it.

'I love Orwell,' I said, for once forgetting my shyness as I was borne away by enthusiasm. 'Not just the big ideas, you know, but the tiny details, the sheer *panache* of it all. I—'

'Does this cider taste all right to you?' cut in Rosie loudly. She was peering into the depths of her glass.

'What?' asked Meggie. She sipped. 'Mine's fine.'

'What about you, Nina?' she asked. 'Is yours all right?'

'My drink?' I sipped, though I suspected, from Rosie's slightly raised voice, that this question was merely a way to derail my outburst, and the way it had obviously captured Piers's attention.

A fleeting annoyance moved through me then, followed by a wan pity. I knew the score with Rosie and her feelings. I should be more sensitive to them.

But looking back, I felt other things too. Rosie wasn't a bad person, but she was controlling on occasion, and like many manipulative people (and I know of what I speak, Sophia) she thought she was far cleverer than she was. Though I was almost morbidly naive, I still knew I was being undermined.

'Mine's fine,' I said of my drink. 'But take yours back if you think it tastes off. No point getting sick.'

'No indeed,' murmured Meggie, giving Rosie a sharp look.

'Nina, you're coming out to the Meadows tonight, right?' Tam asked earnestly.

'Of course she is,' said Piers, with a dismissive wave of his hand. 'Aren't you, Nina? It's going to be a beautiful night.'

I nodded happily. 'Wouldn't miss it.'

It was Friday, a couple of nights before Bonfire Night. There was a plan to go out to Grantchester Meadows and join some other people with similar beliefs that Piers knew – drinking and laughing and just talking quietly amongst ourselves as we sat beneath the velvet night.

I loved it. I made me feel alive. And though I wasn't sure whether I believed in it, it made me feel like I belonged.

Halloween, which I had now learned was really called Samhain, had been something of a failure for us. Tam had driven us all over Wiltshire in his creaking Mini Metro before finding Avebury. Though I was officially little more than an interested observer, my heart had been pounding with excitement, an electric frisson I'd picked up off the others.

It had thus been all the more disappointing when, ten miles from

Marlborough, the heavens opened, drenching the darkened night in unstoppable, unceasing rain. We had shivered and sneezed all the way home, our soaked clothes and close breath steaming up the windows so much Tam could barely see through them, the inadequate little heater in the car no match for the crushing, damp cold.

The others had moaned endlessly, but to me the whole affair had been enchanting, something to which the rain had only added a patina of magic. We had stood amongst the vast grey stones in the downpour, while others who appeared to have gathered from far and wide had played drums and sang while friends held umbrellas to protect their instruments, colourful hair and bright clothes. I had peered up into the louring dark sky, and for a fleeting moment, with my newfound friends at my elbow, I'd felt that sense of *connection* we all talked about and pursued; connection to nature, and the world, and all the things you could see and all the things that you couldn't.

When Rosie had gently nudged my elbow with her own and smiled at me, offering me a smouldering joint with a tenderly conspiratorial air, I felt as though I had finally come home.

I was looking forward to the meeting that night.

'So,' said Rosie. 'Grantchester Meadows, near the start of the Grind, at half seven, yeah?'

We all nodded.

'Don't be late.'

I got up. I had to rush, I had a supervision. As I left, I could hear Piers saying, 'Rosie, Tam was saying he was going to bring some friends . . .'

'What friends?' she asked.

'New friends . . .'

* * *

Night fell mere hours later – the early darkness raised strange mists from the river. I cycled after Rosie, the pair of us little more than shadows as we sped over the bike path through Lammas Land in the darkness.

Around us, the twisted shapes of ancient trees held aloft spiky branches, and through the dying leaves early fireworks lit and fell with faraway bangs, spreading the scent of gunpowder and the colours of the rainbow, and leaving a sheath of smoke over the still air.

I sped up, drawing abreast of Rosie, who was muffled in something she called a 'snood' which covered her head and neck in swathes of dark green wool. Rosie occasionally made these self-conscious fashion statements, quickly seizing upon them, then just as quickly abandoning them.

'I wonder who these friends of Tam's are?' I said aloud. 'The ones that are coming tonight. Did he tell you about them after I left?'

'Hmm,' she said. 'It's his mate Gary,' she sniffed. 'And some people he's met.'

'You don't know them?'

'No.' Rosie's shadowed face flashed sideways at me. 'Or at least I've never met them myself.' She looked troubled. 'But I hear things.'

'What things?'

'Oh, nothing. Just gossip.' She sighed. 'I wish it was just us tonight.'

We were drawing up to the corner of Barton Road and Grantchester Street with its packed terraced houses.

'So what *do* you know about them?' I asked. 'You must know something, to have heard gossip.'

She looked quickly around, as though searching for spies. 'Nothing much.' She paused, sniffed again. 'One of them used to be the singer in the Boarhounds.'

'What?' I asked sharply, dumbfounded. 'Really? The old or the new singer?'

'Oh, I dunno which one he is. I was never into the Boarhounds. He's called Adam or Arran or some such thing . . .'

'Aaron,' I corrected her, astonished. 'You mean Aaron Kessler? How does Tam know Aaron Kessler?'

Rosie shrugged. 'I don't think he does. But Gary, his mate, does, and for some reason him and some of his . . . *group* are coming along tonight.'

I laughed. 'Wow. That's so weird. The girls at school fancied him like mad.'

'Hmm,' said Rosie, and her *hmm* let me know we had alighted on the nub of the problem. 'Plenty do, to hear it told.'

'How d'you mean?'

'Oh, nothing. C'mon, we're going to be late.'

We pedalled silently through the tiny streets while my head whirled – *I'm going to meet Aaron Kessler!* – until we reached the small car park at the foot of Grantchester. There we dismounted as the overgrown passage ahead was too dangerous to cycle along in the dark.

Far above us, a stray rocket exploded into green and pink falling sparks. Rosie glanced up at it, vaguely distracted. She was anxious, I could tell.

'Rosie?'

'Yeah?'

'You're sure there's nothing wrong? You don't look very happy.'

She shrugged again, a tiny, quick little movement. 'I'm fine. I just . . . look, Piers and I had a bit of a row after you left at lunchtime.'

This was not that uncommon. 'You did? What about?'

'Nothing, really. I just didn't like the sound of these people and Piers totally went off on one, saying how I'm "judgmental" all the time about anyone who's the "wrong sort of pagans", and I told him he was a desperate starfucker and we . . . we kind of left it there.'

Bloody hell, I thought. I considered asking her why she'd come at all, then thought better of it. I didn't want her to change her mind.

Also, I knew why she'd come. She would never have let Piers go alone – he might meet a girl.

'But . . . what don't you like about them? How are they the wrong sort of pagans?'

'I didn't say that. He did,' she snapped in annoyance. I knew that the accusation of being judgmental must have stung her. 'I *might* have said that they were creepy.'

'But—'

Rosie silenced me, raising her hand. 'Not now. I'll tell you later, when we can't be overheard. Look,' she whispered.

Through the darkened thickets I could make out a tiny orange glow, lying close to the river in the distance – a fire. And now that we'd stopped, straining to see the source of the flame, we heard voices, male and female, murmuring, and the flicker of laughter. Though the moon was bright, the smoke from other people's bon-fires had formed a deep mist that swirled above us, obscuring our vision. There was only the tiny point of the fire to draw us forward.

And voices – many more voices than I was expecting, perhaps as many as a dozen – and music too, small and tinny at this distance, doubtless being played on someone's ghetto blaster.

Then Piers clearly said, 'Yeah, I'll have another, thanks,' and there was something about his tone that sounded unlike him, almost ingratiating. The difference between this and his normal self was so marked that Rosie stole a glance backwards at me.

Then a deeper male voice I didn't recognize said something in reply. We couldn't hear, but it made Piers laugh, almost spasmodically.

The sound of Piers seemed to galvanize Rosie. 'Come on, then,' she said, her shoulders squaring, leaning low as she pushed her bike forward, 'let's get on with it.'

* * *

'Well, well, what have we here?' asked a low, amused female voice.

We had left our bikes chained to one another near the cattle

81

grid, and stomped down the uneven grass to the river's bank, which in the cold and smoke felt like traversing the surface of the moon. Everything smelled of burning: wood, tobacco, gunpowder, marijuana. Ahead of us there was low laughter and the crackling noise of the ghetto blaster, playing some track I recognized from one of Rosie's mix tapes – was it The Cure? Rosie had loved The Cure back then.

We approached the outermost ring of people around the fire, which encircled a smaller gathering in the centre, the tiny lights of their cigarettes and joints animated like fireflies as they were passed around.

'Rosie! And little Nina!' said Piers, rising to his feet, somewhat unsteadily. He had been sitting in the centre on a large tartan blanket, next to Tam and a quartet of people I didn't know, but one of whom I was sure would prove to be Aaron Kessler, should I dare to raise my head and look. In fact, as I scanned the various faces in the firelight, there were a lot of people here I didn't know, and Rosie neither, judging from her expression. 'Where've you two been?'

I frowned – we were actually early.

'Nowhere much,' said Rosie. 'Hallo, Tam,' she said, deliberately ignoring the girl who had spoken first in greeting, a slender brunette spilled decorously over the blanket, her lips slicked with some dark colour, her small breasts cinched in a tight bra and threatening to burst out of her jersey dress. Her long hair fell over her back and arms in a startling pre-Raphaelite effect that she was using to maximum potential, judging from the wolfish grin Piers offered her.

'Heya, Rosie.' Tam raised vague eyes towards her and reached down very slowly for his can of Pilsner. 'Want a spliff?'

'Aren't you going to introduce us?' asked the strange girl on the blanket, rolling upright. Her voice was low, her mouth wide and wicked, her eyes shadowy. I envied her obvious showy confidence. She was mistress in her own world, and she knew it.

'Oh, yeah, sorry,' said Tam, rubbing a muddy hand on his Killing Joke T-shirt. 'This is Rosie and Nina, from my college.' His voice was soft, the words slurred. 'Guys, this is Lucy. She's here with Aaron.'

There was something in his tone that implied no further introductions were necessary.

'Hello,' said Lucy's companion. There was nothing slurred about *his* voice.

I stole a tiny, surreptitious glance at him.

The main thing that struck me at the time was how little he looked like he belonged there. Everyone else was exactly what they were – self-conscious students smoking drugs and pretending not to feel too cold as they huddled on the damp trampled grass of the water meadow.

But Aaron, whose high-boned good looks I instantly recognized, appeared to feel utterly comfortable here, in his finely cut leather jacket and designer jeans, his long boots crossed over one another. His shoulder-length dark hair was tied behind him; his eyes narrow, his brow smooth, his lips full and sensuous in the dim, flickering light. I was drawn to the way his tight stomach disappeared under his shirt into the waistband of his jeans.

Transfixed, my eyes lingered on him, just a fraction too long.

He noticed me looking, and I instantly dropped my gaze to the ground, my face heating with embarrassment.

I didn't raise my head as Rosie took the joint from Tam, and I waited uncomfortably for it to be passed to me, so I would have something to do, anxious as I was.

I risked another glance in his direction; his face was turned to me, studying me with an absolute lack of self-consciousness, as though showing me how it was done.

He offered me a single smile.

I looked away again.

Finally the joint was in my trembling fingers, and I sucked in hard, harder than I ever had before, eager to be diverted from my self-conscious embarrassment, to blend back into the crowd. It was too much, I realized, as the smoke rushed in, burning my throat and lungs all the way down, and I was coughing, no, whooping like a distressed seabird, and people were looking at me and laughing at my gaucheness, and I just wanted to die.

All the while Aaron just kept *staring* at me.

'You all right there, Nina?' asked Piers, patting my leg with a friendly hand.

'She's fine,' said Rosie coolly, though she touched my back to take the sting out of the words. She pulled forward her backpack, set it on the toes of her boots to keep it dry. 'Here, I've got some cider. Have a drink.'

'No,' said Aaron, from the blanket. 'Have some of this.' His voice was deep, slightly hoarse.

He held forward a thin crystal glass with such authority that I took it and sipped. The contents were dry and sour and fizzed against my burned throat all the way down – it was champagne.

'Better?' he asked with a smile.

The relief was so sweet I almost groaned, and a bubble of self-indulgent laughter erupted from Lucy, the girl with the long dark hair. I handed the glass back down to him. 'Thank you,' I stammered.

'You're welcome. Keep it. Sit down.'

The habit of obedience had long been instilled in me, and before I knew what I was doing I lowered myself down on to a corner of the tartan blanket. The fire was a warm presence at my back.

Rosie did not join me, staying resolutely on her toes, and I could feel her absence, her disapproval of these strange new people and their laughter and commands. But it was too late to get up again now. It would just make everything worse.

I cast around, looking for Meggie, or anyone else I might know, lost as I was in this strange field with an angry Rosie, stupefied Tam and servile Piers, who had settled with puppyish abandon next to the newcomers.

Even Aaron had now turned away from me. He was watching Piers flirt with Lucy, his sharply chiselled face wearing an indulgent expression, as though he were watching toddlers play.

'Are you all right?' I murmured.

'I'm fine, why wouldn't I be?' replied Rosie crisply.

Lucy was showing Piers her necklace, which appeared to be a kind of stylized cross in a circle, studded with gems that winked in the firelight. This involved Piers leaning over Lucy's chest and picking up the amulet with his fingers while she laughed coquettishly. I threw a sideways look at Rosie, who was drinking cider straight from the plastic bottle with stony determination.

'Do you recognize that symbol?' I whispered to Rosie.

'No.' Her expression told me that nothing could have interested her less.

'It's the symbol of our group,' Aaron said, looking at me again, and there was something unhurried and utterly unabashed about it, as though he had every right to do it. Then he reached into his low-buttoned shirt, and drew out the amulet's twin, except that his was plain, made out of some unpolished metal.

I peered politely at it, aware of my spreading blush. 'Oh, I see.'

'Do you?' he sounded amused. After a long moment he unhooked it, the chain catching briefly in his hair, and handed it to me.

I let him drop it into my hand, since there seemed no alternative, and the metal was warm from his skin and smelled faintly of cinnamon. I turned it over, and on the back, only dimly visible in the firelight, there were little letters engraved on the circle. I ran my finger over them.

'What does it say?' I asked.

'Oh,' he said, smiling. 'I can't tell you. It's a secret.'

'Sorry.' I flushed, as though I'd been slapped, and quickly handed the amulet back towards him.

He laughed and shook his head. 'Don't apologize. It wasn't a criticism. Some things you can only know once you're ready for them.' He ignored my outstretched hand, and I let it retreat back into my lap.

'You said you were . . . you mentioned your group?'

'Yes. We're all about fostering artistic inspiration – exploring ways to be more creative, more switched on. You know what I mean?'

I nodded, though I didn't.

Years later, I would understand that he didn't just pitch up in a field in Cambridge because he fancied a night out in the Fens with a bunch of students. He was on the hunt, with Lucy, his glamour-ous little hawk, and that night he had correctly identified prey.

'Are you a creative person . . . it's Nina, right?'

I squirmed. He'd been paying attention, had caught my name. Everyone around me had grown silent, was following my conversa-tion with the Great Man. The night seemed full of eyes. 'I've always wanted to be a writer.'

'Yes, I can see that about you.' He smiled. 'There's a light in you.' He picked up the nearby bottle and refilled my glass, as though we were the only people there. 'But I think you've never had much encouragement at home.'

'Oh, I don't know,' I said, troubled, embarrassed, and yet struck by his unerring perception. 'I think they try . . .'

He raised a dark eyebrow, as though he knew I was lying. Beside him, Lucy smiled and settled down, curling up next to him. I had the fleeting image of a man and a sleek dark dog – if Aaron had scowled, Lucy would snarl.

As it was, it seemed more likely that Rosie would be the one snarl-ing. She stiffened next to me as Aaron filled my glass, and a tightening wire of irritation pulled at me – what was Rosie's problem?

Was it that another man was paying attention to me?

'What do you write, Nina?' asked Lucy.

'Oh, nothing really.' I said quickly, growing alarmed. 'A bit of poetry, sometimes.'

'Recite some for us!' demanded Lucy. 'I am in the mood for poetry.' She fell backwards on the blanket, her head in Aaron's lap, her hair tangling in his hands. She flung her arms wide and closed her eyes. 'The Full Moon demands it.'

'Yeah, go on, Nina.' Piers grinned at me.

The thought of repeating my few fragments of scribbling in front of this crowd filled me with a terror that bordered on nausea. 'Oh no, no, I couldn't possibly.' I stammered. 'It's t-terrible and I can't even remember any. Please don't ask me.'

'Oh, go on!' said Lucy playfully.

'Come on now, Lucy, you're embarrassing her,' said Aaron, stroking Lucy's hair back into straight locks. 'Nina, perhaps you can recite for us once you get to know us better.'

'Hear hear!' said Lucy with a full-throated laugh, and not knowing how to respond, I tipped my glass anxiously at him in return and drank again.

Rosie did not move.

At the time, I don't know what I thought. No, wait, that's a lie, and I'm trying not to lie to you – even when it doesn't cast me in the best light. The truth is, I thought Rosie was jealous that this beautiful, famous man was paying me attention. She was tormented by unrequited love and it frequently made her difficult. I understood that it was a disease of the heart, not something she could master or shake off like a cold.

It didn't occur to me at the time that Rosie's jealousy usually only focused around Piers.

Something else was bothering her.

The conversation shifted to Tam and a friend of his called David and the band they were in – I can remember nothing about it. I realized I was still gripping Aaron's amulet. I should offer it back, but I was too nervous to interrupt the men while they were talking.

'We should go,' Rosie whispered to me.

'What?'

'I'm freezing out here. And I think I'm getting a migraine. Drink up and come on.'

There was something so peremptory about this command that I was tempted to rebel. I didn't want to leave – I wanted to stay here, and bask some more in Aaron's enigmatic attention, to be told by this gorgeous, high-status man that he could see the light in me, but then I sensed that she was shivering.

I quickly tossed down the rest of the champagne, and as I did so Aaron Kessler gazed at me again, and I had the sense that he had been half-observing me throughout.

A shiver of melting pleasure went through me at the idea.

'Thank you very much,' I said, handing the amulet back to him. 'But Rosie's not well. We need to go back. It was lovely to meet you.'

Aaron regarded me with quizzical amusement, as though in my tentative manners I was a time-traveller from Victorian times. He reached out, taking the amulet but also gently seizing my hand.

I was so surprised when he raised it to his lips and kissed it that I gasped and nearly dropped the glass.

'It was a pleasure, Nina,' he said. 'And I hope to see you again very soon.'

'Nina,' said Rosie, her voice having the character of an order.

Aaron ignored her, releasing my hand as Rosie rose to her feet, tersely answering Piers's and Tam's questions – yes, she was ill, it was a migraine, she had to go.

And then I was abandoning my glass, being pulled by my arm across the pitted marshy surface of the field, too surprised and self-conscious to object.

I turned over my shoulder, for a last final look at the small gathering, and saw Aaron Kessler raise his glass in a parting gesture.

I didn't know it yet, but I was already lost.

Chapter Seven

So, Sophia, it will come as no surprise to you that after that Friday night I quietly obsessed about Aaron Kessler and our meeting on the meadows. I recalled the warmth of Aaron's hand, the sun of his personal interest blazing on my face, and Rosie's obvious envy, which she had not yet bothered to excuse or explain.

'Why were you so rude to them?' I asked Rosie once we arrived back at college.

'I've heard things about them. You should stay away from them, apparently.'

'What? Really? Why?'

'It's just something I heard. They're dodgy people. Like a cult. Fakes doing it for attention, dropping hints and coming over all mysterious, and everybody runs around after that man because he's famous.'

It was as if she'd slapped me.

'Heard? Heard from who?' I said, and the ratcheting hurt in my voice was obvious even to me.

Her face was flat, impassive and pale. I do believe, now, that her head was hurting. Watching the sexy Lucy flirting with Piers had doubtless shredded her fragile nerves. That night, I was merely collateral damage from her ongoing obsession with Piers.

And I resented it.

'It sounds like rubbish to me. Like jealousy.' My teeth were gritted. 'Like these people have nothing better to talk about.'

'I need to lie down, Nina. Goodnight.'

* * *

It was nearly two o'clock on Monday and I had to meet my supervisor in King's College in five minutes. I'd said farewell to Rosie and Meggie in the refectory and was wrapping my woolly scarf around my neck. Through the gatehouse windows there was a swatch of blue sky, but I already knew it was deceptive – the wind was freezing outside, and by the time I got to King's my cheeks and ears would be pink, as though I'd been slapped.

Passing by the Porter's Lodge, I stepped into the mail room to check my pigeonhole. There had been no communications from Daddy since the row when he had dropped me off, though I still spoke to Mummy weekly on the phone.

I felt torn and guilty about this. I should call him, I knew, and offer him the grovelling apologies he wanted. On the other hand, my tiny inward rebel thought there was something about not hearing from either of them that I could grow to love.

Looking back now, I can see that I was ripe for a change in regime.

There was nobody in the mail room, and I scooped up the small pile of correspondence in my pigeonhole – mostly flyers for college events, a message from my Modern Poetry supervisor asking to move our meeting on Monday, and then a folded piece of expensive blue paper:

Nina,

It's me, Lucy. We met in Grantchester last week. Aaron wants to see you again. We're having a party at a friend's house tonight – we'll send a car to college for you at nine.

Bring your friends. If you want.

Lucy XXX

I read this extraordinary note three times, attempting to make sense of it. Each time raised more questions than answers. No, there was no doubt about it – I was being summoned, not invited. They'd send a car? What did that mean?

I lingered in the mail room, conscious that I was running late. I crushed the letter into my bag, wondering what Rosie would say about it when I saw her tonight, and hurried on to the bike sheds.

There was no question of going, of course. The icy handlebars nipped my fingers as I gripped them, straddled the bike. I didn't know these people, or the house, or indeed anything else. Rosie obviously thought they were dodgy. Even if they weren't actively dangerous, they were abominably rude – after all, I could have plans for tonight. In fact I *did* have plans. My essay on political language in the works of Anthony Trollope was due tomorrow.

They were *presumptuous*, as Mummy would say.

Absolutely no question of going. Of course not.

But it was desperately intriguing – and, of course, extremely flattering.

In this brave new world of St Edith's, I knew I was a follower, someone who tagged along with others. This consideration did not trouble me, as following was easier, and more social, than swimming against the tide. It also made my introverted nerves jangle less in public. The circle of people I had joined was gentle and undemanding, and it made me feel safe. It sheltered me while I found my feet in this milieu that was so decidedly different from the ordered autocracy at home.

And I was grateful.

But still, there was something intoxicating in being singled out, in being the main event rather than the warm-up act. A little part of myself kneeled and warmed its frozen hands on the individual interest the letter conveyed.

And the crushed velvet purple dress I had sneaked into my suitcase from home was hanging in my wardrobe, after all. Just in case I changed my mind.

* * *

'Hello, Mummy.'

I sat on the staircase in St Edith's, my fingers curling compulsively around the cord on the public telephone. All about me was genial busyness, as the other girls on the staircase stepped around me on their way up to dump their books in their rooms, or tripped back down on their way to dinner or meetings.

'Ah, hello, stranger! The prodigal returns. I thought you might have become too grand for us now.'

My mother sounded amused and faintly drunk, as she often was at this time of night, particularly if she was going to be entertaining guests.

'No, Mummy, sorry, I've just been very busy.' I swallowed, wound the curling line of the phone tighter around my fingers. 'With work.'

'Oh, if you say so. I can't speak for long, darling, the Sallisses are coming round for dinner. I told you last week. I haven't time to chat.'

'Sorry, Mummy, I forgot.' This was a lie. 'How is everyone?'

'They're fine, they're fine. Teddy's taking Martina to Bali for Christmas.'

'Oh, how lovely,' I said automatically. I had long ago learned that this was the only response to give to news about my cousin and her husband. These stories about Martina's glamorous life were intended as a rebuke. If I had been a proper girl, they seemed to say, and valued my looks and charm over the inexplicable draw of academia, I, too, could be on my way to Bali.

'He's about to get a big bonus, he thinks, from the bank, and they're talking about buying a summer house in Wales.'

'That sounds nice.'

'Yes, he works very hard. And even though you didn't ask, Daddy and I are fine. I saw you hadn't sent Daddy an apology present yet for your behaviour when he drove you up there, so I've bought him some glasses and added it to what you owe me.'

'Thanks, Mummy. I meant to, I just haven't had time. I'll pay you back when my grant finally comes in.'

'So, are you all right, then? Not calling to ask for money, I hope.'

'No, Mummy, I'm fine. Actually, I . . . I was invited out tonight . . .'

'Oh, of course you were, drinking and dancing all hours, I'm sure. Listen, darling, I can't stand here all night listening to you talk about yourself, the Sallisses will be here in half an hour and Daddy still hasn't changed. Ring me next week – but not Saturday. You know Mummy and Daddy are busy on Saturdays.'

'Yes, Mummy. I love you.'

'I love you too, darling. Goodnight.'

There was a brisk click before the dial tone purred in my ear.

* * *

'You're not going to go, are you?' asked Rosie over our sausage and mash (or, in Rosie's case, just mash), raising her voice over the chatter and clatter of the hall. Around us, the college founders gazed down from the portraits on the walls, with serious eyes, elaborate hats and dark, voluminous clothing. They disapproved of me, I'm sure. I don't entirely blame them.

'What? Go? On my own?' Even the thought of this horrified me. This was the Eighties, after all. Back then, the prevailing public opinion was that girls who went out alone were 'asking for it'. These opinions were practically legal canon at the time. 'No. Absolutely not.'

Piers sniggered. 'I'll go with you if you want, Nina. I'll *chaperone*.'

'I don't think you should,' said Rosie. Her tone was sharp. 'Either of you.'

'Why not?' asked Piers.

'Well,' said Rosie, as though explaining something to an idiot, 'firstly, because it's mad. And secondly, it's mad.'

'I don't think it's ridiculous that this guy would invite Nina to a party,' said Piers.

'I didn't mean it that way. You know I didn't mean it that way. Stop trying to twist my words . . .'

'So,' said Piers, ignoring her and turning to me, 'do you want to go to the ball, Cinderella?'

'I . . . well, I mean, I hadn't . . .' I began.

'Brilliant! I'll see the pair of you in the bar at ten to nine.'

Rosie regarded Piers and bit her lip as he sprang to his feet and span away with his tray.

I cast my eyes down at my plate. Already this unorthodox invitation was playing havoc with my relationships.

'You know, Rosie . . .'

'No, it's fine. He's right. I'm being paranoid. We should go. It'll be fun.' I could hear the way Rosie was trying to inject some enthusiasm into her voice, like someone squeezing the very ends out of an empty toothpaste tube. Piers was going, so she was going. That was the end of the matter. 'It'll be an *adventure*.'

In spite of everything, I was getting my way.

So why did I feel so frightened all of a sudden?

* * *

'Ah!' said Lucy. 'You came!'

The promised car had appeared at precisely five to nine, a gleaming black Bentley, driven by a chauffeur with a suit and cap, who had got out to open the doors for us. The trip had been short – a mere ten minutes – before we were rambling slowly past the elaborate houses of Newton Road out near the Botanical Gardens.

Lucy greeted us at the door before we even had a chance to knock. She wore a floor-length black dress, gathered at the hips, and her dark red hair was loose again.

She seemed delighted but not surprised to see us, and came forward to kiss me lingeringly, her breath sweet and hot, kissing Piers and Rosie with brisk efficiency. Her scarlet lipstick left a red mark on Rosie's cheek, but I was too paralysed by self-consciousness to tell Rosie to rub it off.

Lucy took my hand, as though we had been friends for years, and led me through the hall, past a variety of stylishly dressed people chatting in a vast open-plan kitchen, surrounded by glasses and bottles and smouldering ashtrays.

'This is a lovely house,' I said, for want of anything else to contribute.

'Yes,' said Lucy, but it was as though I was boring her. 'It's Penelope's aunt's house. We're just borrowing it.'

'Who's Penelope?'

A catch, a beat of hesitation, as though she'd been about to say something offhand and dismissive, before she remembered herself.

'One of us. You'll meet her yourself.'

I had nothing to add to that.

Lucy drew me after her, past the staircase and into a conservatory paved in beautiful painted tiles. A long leather couch was at the far end of the room, a man and a woman seated on it; both turned to look at her.

I could feel it, a kind of electric excitement, transmitting from Lucy to me as I was drawn out of her wake by hand and deftly presented, like a gift or a rabbit out of a hat.

I blinked, overwhelmed, unbearably nervous and excited. Sat on the low couch in white shirt and black jeans was Aaron Kessler, his arms spread wide along the armrests, looking every inch the jaded artist, with high cheekbones and unreadable eyes. His skin was perfect and smooth, unlike that of most of the other men in my life, who were either spotty, elderly or razor-burned, and I was filled with a forbidden, unaccountable desire to touch it, to see if it was real.

He nodded at me, took my hand and kissed it. His lips were warm. 'Hello again, Nina.' He had a slight brogue, Irish, but it must have been a childhood thing, so long ago it had nearly vanished, only its ghost remaining. 'I'm delighted you could make it.'

'Oh,' I said, trying not to stammer. 'Thanks for inviting me. I mean, us,' I supplied, remembering myself. I glanced over my shoulder,

95

looking for Piers and Rosie, but they seemed to have vanished on the short journey from the front door.

Panic gripped me. 'Oh . . .'

Aaron politely followed my gaze, as though humouring a child talking about her imaginary friends.

'Would you like a drink?' On his left was a willowy girl holding a tall glass full of ice. Her voice was cool, cultured. She was almost shockingly beautiful, her blonde hair piled upon her head in an artful mess of crystal-headed pins, her lips painted the purest pale rose. She rested a hand on Aaron's arm.

Looking at her, I felt a disappointment I hardly dared articulate to myself. Of course he had beautiful girls surrounding him. That's what rock stars did. There was no way he was interested in *me*. What did I think was going on here?

'She would love a drink, I'm sure,' said Lucy. 'What will it be, Nina? Champagne?'

'I . . . oh, yes, thanks . . .'

'Excellent choice,' said Aaron, making a careless gesture at the blonde girl, who immediately rose to fetch a glass while I wondered what on earth to talk about.

And where were Piers and Rosie?

'It's a beautiful house,' I said again, for lack of anything else to offer.

'Thank you,' said the blonde girl, returning with two glasses, one for Aaron and one for me. 'It's my aunt's. She's based in South Africa.'

'Oh,' I said, like an idiot. 'I see.'

'This is Penelope,' said Aaron, waving at her. 'But don't just stand there. Sit down.' He patted the seat right next to him, practically in the shade of his arm as it stretched out across the back of the sofa.

Tentatively, I took my place, aware that this was closer than I usually got to any man, including Daddy. I was immediately conscious of the masculine smell of him (even now I cannot smell sandalwood or cinnamon without being transported back to that moment, in a kind of fever dream). Moreover, I felt the *heat* of him, burning through the side of my purple velvet dress, my exposed right arm with its cheap plastic bangles, my powdered cheek. He blazed like the sun, and strands of my fringe glued themselves to my forehead with nervous sweat.

But slowly, as he turned and spoke to the others about various matters of no apparent importance, such as a forthcoming trip to London, or the shooting they would do when they got home to Kent, I began to relax. In fact, with the champagne everything took on a lovely golden glow; the candlelight, the elaborate make-up and dresses of the girls, Aaron's profile, like that of a sculptured Greek hero. I ceased to miss the others or wonder where they were.

Lucy smiled broadly at me and passed me a spliff, carefully placing it between my fingers. Though my own glass kept being refilled, I had noticed, almost in passing, that Aaron's stayed at the same level throughout.

'I was watching you, Nina,' he said suddenly, his eyes lighting upon me. 'That night on the meadows. Or maybe' – he seemed lost in thought for a moment – 'I was looking for you.'

'Me?' I squeaked. I was conscious of Lucy and Penelope turning towards me, as though on some signal.

He laughed then. 'Yes, *you*. You listen, you don't speak; not unless you have something to say. Everyone else is talking, talking all the time. They've got something to prove. But you – you're a thinker, a dreamer. You're a seeker – not one of these dilettantes and fakes,' he gestured expansively all around him, taking in the other guests, 'but a *real* seeker, someone not satisfied with surfaces. That's why I wanted you to come here, Nina. I think we have something in common.'

I didn't know what to reply, astonished by this assessment, unable to frame how I should respond. I was also, and I was not so

97

drunk or naive that I was incapable of realizing this, very flattered to be told how discerning and authentic and admirable I was by a famous and handsome man.

There had been very little of this in my life.

So I was stunned as Aaron reached out and gently took my chin in his warm fingers. 'You're so beautiful, aren't you? Inside and out.'

And though I wouldn't realize it until much later – indeed too late – such attention is deeply addictive, more so than the weed, or the champagne.

'I . . . thank you . . . but I don't think . . .'

'You are,' he said flatly, in a tone that brooked no contradiction. 'It was fated that you came here to us. You're a gift, Nina. Together we'll do great things.'

He released me then, and Penelope and Lucy shared a glance, smiled, as though a much-loved project was coming to fruition.

'Tell me about yourself,' he said quietly, holding me with his eyes. 'Tell me about your family.'

It was the sort of question that most people would have asked at the beginning of a conversation, and in reply, when sober, I might have said that my parents lived in a village in the Cotswolds, and that my father owned a successful double-glazing company. We would have left it at that. It was, after all, much too dull to discuss any further.

But I felt golden and emboldened, light-headed and suffused with a vague euphoria. The heat from Aaron's fingers still lingered on my chin.

I am beautiful and a gift.

'My family?' I shrugged, still self-conscious, but it was a medicated twinge that felt very far away, a mere tic. 'Daddy makes money. Well, really he makes double-glazing, but hates to look outside his own little world. All windows, no vision. At the factory, everyone has to jump to his every twitch. At home, too.' I took another sip of champagne. 'And my mother is about peace at any price. She's the female equivalent of Neville Chamberlain.'

98

I was rewarded with their laughter, even Aaron's deep chuckle, and then his arm slid downwards, circling my shoulders with a gentle squeeze. A hot blush of pleasure and excitement stole over me.

'I probably shouldn't talk about them that way . . .'

'Oh, I'm sure they deserve all of that, and worse. I doubt they appreciate the tiniest part of your worth,' Aaron said. He gestured at Penelope with his champagne glass, and this appeared to be another signal, as she took it from him. 'But you seem distracted, dear Nina. Is something the matter?'

'Oh no, not at all, I just . . . I wonder where my friends have gone.'

He nodded. 'They won't be far away. You two, go find Nina's friends,' he said to the girls. 'I'll show her the house.'

The other two smiled swiftly and, rising to their feet, kissed me, their soft hands alighting on my arms with an almost caress, their lips lingering against my cheek, and then Aaron's. And as they did so, I saw that his hands moved over their waists with an easy familiarity as he embraced them.

They tripped lightly out into the hall, and I was alone with him. The couch suddenly seemed very small.

'Is something wrong?'

'I . . . I dunno.' I giggled, blushed again. My heart was fluttering against the too-tight bodice of the purple dress. 'I just can't tell which one's your girlfriend.'

He cocked his head at me, offering me a crooked smile. 'Maybe both. Maybe neither.' He took my hand and drew me to my feet. 'Come.'

* * *

Aaron didn't speak as he led me past rooms of antique furniture, past a knot of men and women gossiping within their own self-generated cloud of cigarette smoke and tea lights. They fell silent as we passed by.

My hand was hot and damp in his. I was trembling, and he must have felt it. He was leading me up the stairs – of course he was; this was what happened now, what the plan had always been from the moment that blue invitation had been written and posted into my college pigeonhole, and it occurred to me that I needed to say something, to stick a wrench in this slowly ascending rollercoaster of expectation and desire before we reached the top; before the fall began and my momentum became unstoppable.

'I . . . I wonder where the others . . .' I couldn't bring myself to say any more. The words sounded absurd even as I said them, and he was paying them no attention anyway.

He pushed open a door on the hallway and pulled me in after him, and I had the sense of a larger room, mirrors glinting in the semi-darkness, the white expanse of a bed. The moon shone in through a veiled window.

He kissed me then, and he tasted of champagne. His hands were everywhere, stripping the purple dress from me, his lips on mine, on my throat, on my suddenly, shockingly, naked breasts, which he clasped in his hands, and I attempted, half-heartedly, to resist these caresses, more out of a thwarted desire not to appear slutty than any genuine wish that he should stop.

I definitely didn't want him to stop. This was the most exciting thing that had ever happened to me. He wanted me, and he was beautiful and famous and older and so knowledgeable, and I was desperate, absolutely desperate, to be wanted by someone. Anyone.

Don't misunderstand me. I wasn't stupid enough to think this was true love, or at least I didn't then. I grew stupider over time. Mostly I was just enthralled, enchanted, and thrilled. My life was actually beginning, at last.

And in a big, *big* way.

He told me not to be scared, and I wasn't, not really, at least until he took the condom out of the drawer in the bedside table. He bore me down on to the bed and I realized that this was *It*, as the girls said in school in hushed voices. I squeezed my thighs together anxiously until he teased them apart with deft fingers and soft words. My hands were pressed against that perfect skin and it was smooth and warm; his mouth was on mine and he was crushing me, pushing into me, and it hurt in a vague way, like an afterthought. But more than anything it was unbearably exciting, just to be wanted, just to be desired, and I yielded completely to him, because in those days, yielding was the one thing I knew how to do.

* * *

'I feel rough,' said Piers. He looked pale and smelled vaguely of spirits.

'Good,' said Rosie, her lipstick gone, her lips visibly cracked, even in the low light of the Bentley. 'You deserve to.'

I was sitting between them in the back seat. Something had gone on between them, some boundary had been breached. I should be paying attention, but it was impossible to gather my wandering thoughts.

Every time I shut my eyes I saw things – myself shamelessly splayed on the bed under Aaron's gaze, or the thick purplish rod of his erection as he urged me to take it into my mouth – flashes of my evening, as sharp and clear as photographs, filling me with an odd mixture of tearful mortification and yearning.

'Where did you vanish off to?' asked Rosie, and it took me a second to work out that this question was for me.

'Nowhere much,' I said. 'Lucy took me into the conservatory. Aaron was there with this other girl, Penelope.'

'Another one of his harem, then?' sneered Rosie. 'What did you get up to?'

I blushed hard, though it was hidden in the dark womb of the car. 'We just chatted, really.'

'Oh yeah? And what's the great Aaron got to say for himself?'

'I dunno . . . just chit-chat. He keeps lots of guns. They were going to shoot clay pigeons at his house.'

And he told me I was beautiful and a gift. That I was a seeker after truth. That together we would do great things . . .

'I don't approve of people who are into guns,' said Rosie.

'You don't approve of anyone,' snapped Piers with unexpected bitterness.

I threw him a sharp glance, but he was already rolling down the car window and shouting to the driver, 'Mate, mate, stop the car, stop the car, I think I'm going to be sick.'

* * *

I woke up the next morning sore all over, my head pounding, and hurried down to the mail room to see if Aaron had left a message.

There was nothing.

There was nothing at lunch either.

The purgatorial silence went on and on. I told no one what had happened. Piers asked me if something was wrong, Rosie did not.

And then, four days later, long after I had given up hope and almost come to terms with the way I had been picked up and dropped, another note appeared in my pigeonhole.

Nina,

Aaron wants to see you again – this time you're going to stay for the weekend with us at the house. The car will come by to pick you up at seven tomorrow morning.

Sorry, but there's only room for you – your friends will have to do without you this time.

Love and blessings,
Lucy XXX

Chapter Eight

Let me tell you, Sophia – it's a long way to Kent from Cambridge, especially when you're in a frenzy of nerves and erotic anticipation. I sat in the back of the Bentley, staring out of the windows, trying to look like the sort of girl that was regularly chauffeured from place to place.

I had packed two bags – one of clothes, my small collection of Body Shop toiletries, a brand-new underwear set consisting of bra, French knickers, suspenders and stockings in electric blue (dear God, what was it about the Eighties and stockings and suspenders?), at least three pairs of shoes – and the other containing my textbooks, notepads and a novel. I was reading two or three books a week at the time. This one might have been *Beloved* by Toni Morrison.

When I'd been collected at the college gates at seven in the morning, these bags had been swiftly put in the boot of the car. The impeccably suited chauffeur had slammed it shut with such decisive force that I hadn't dared ask for the novel, or the pink bubblegum lipgloss I'd packed for the occasion.

Instead I'd clambered into the back seat and regarded the closely cropped rear of his head beneath his peaked cap as he started up the car.

'Excuse me?' I worked up the courage to ask eventually.

'Yes?'

'How long will it take to get there?'

'Two and a half hours.'

'Oh, that's quite far, isn't it?' I chirped, more for the sake of conversation than any other reason.

He didn't reply, not even giving me a backward glance in the mirror as he'd pulled out on to Trinity Street, the car purring over the cobbles.

I decided to try again.

'So, do you know Aaron Kessler well, then?'

'Who?'

A little dart of alarm shot through me.

'Aaron Kessler.'

'No. I don't.'

There was something in the way this was delivered; perfectly polite, but with a final, almost hostile edge, that put paid to the conversation.

Through the window, the ornate college buildings gave way to the villages on the outskirts of Cambridge, then there was nothing but flat plains filled with crops and the occasional lone garage on the winding country roads.

Now I had nothing to distract my attention away from the forthcoming enigma that was Aaron Kessler.

I crossed my legs, wondering if my flimsy hippy skirt with tiny bells sewed to the ends of the belt-string had been the right choice. Maybe it was all too flower child. Perhaps I should have worn jeans and the bright geometric jumper I'd bought for the trip, or perhaps even the purple dress I'd worn to the party, though now, of course, he'd seen me in it. And out of it.

Perhaps I should have told the others where I was going.

This last was troubling me most of all. I'd thought about it for days, but ultimately, I hadn't wanted to tell them to their faces that they weren't invited.

And I'd been frightened that they might talk me out of it.

I sighed and tried to relax, enjoy the admiring glances the car engendered in motorists passing in the other direction. None of this was a big deal. I'd just ask Aaron if I could give them a quick call when I arrived, and then I'd ask Rosie to keep an eye on my pigeonhole.

They couldn't persuade me not to come if I was already here.

* * *

There was nearly two hours of motorway, during which I sat, silent, in the back of the car. Then forty-five minutes of twisting, plunging roads lined with thickets of yellow-gold and copper trees standing knee-deep in fallen leaves. The sky was a perfect cotton blue.

We passed what seemed like miles of impossibly high yew hedge, and then a red brick wall at least ten feet tall with triangular coping stones. This ended in a tiny entrance with a high gate made of wood and cast iron. On the wall next to it was fixed a slate plaque, and carved on it was a single word: MORNINGSTAR.

The driver reached out, pressed buttons on a metal box mounted on a pole near the drive, and the wood and iron gate swung wide to admit us.

On the other side was Morningstar, appearing like a mirage, its crenelated roof poking up over the sweep of poplar trees. It was not so much a house as a castle, or rather a fortified manor – small, but perfectly formed, with high walls and leaded windows and, at the top, a square turreted tower with a flag flying from it.

I gasped and raised my hands to my mouth.

'Oh, it's gorgeous! Like a fairy tale!'

The driver didn't reply, but did a peculiar thing with his shoulders, a sort of not-shrug, as the gate slowly closed behind us.

That little pang of confusion, not quite discomfort, again rose within me, like a jarring note in some music. At the time, his responses on the journey mystified me, but looking back, I can see that he was operating under the twin engines of pity and contempt for me. This was a little more advanced than my emotional register was capable of understanding at the time.

Had I but known it, I would soon be expanding this register in a variety of new ways.

As the car crunched down a winding gravelled path, I caught details – an orchard full of drooping trees, the fruit long gone, interspersed with the white rectangles of beehives; a perfectly flat, still stream with gliding ducks upon it, and, as we grew near, the front door was under an archway with a real portcullis and narrow moat.

Whatever I had imagined, it was not this.

And soon, soon, I would be in Aaron's arms again. The thought paralysed me with nervousness and desire. My heart fluttered under my silky blouse, another new purchase.

'Nina!' Lucy emerged on to the drawbridge, barefoot and seemingly oblivious of the autumn chill. Her toenails were painted scarlet, like her lips, and she was in a long black shift, her only other clothing a heavy gold chain with the amulet on the end.

I waved through the car window as it pulled to a stop, and she was running up to the door, pulling it open to let me out, throwing her arms around me. 'You came! Oh, it's going to be great!'

I returned the embrace, overwhelmed and touched by this enthusiasm – Lucy barely knew me. I was confused, but then I thought, *Yes, some people are more demonstrative than others, more impulsively friendly than I am. You could stand to be more like her, in fact.* A thousand small fears that had grown with me in the back of the car as I sat with the silent driver were dismissed and dissipated into the cool mid-morning.

'Come on, come in, we're waiting. Well,' chattered Lucy, 'I say *we*. We won't see Aaron for a couple of hours yet. But that will give you time to meet everyone else. Have you got bags . . . Oh, he's got your bags. He'll put them in the Blue Room. Do you need to change?'

'I . . .'

'Oh, you don't need to change, you look so great, but you can if you want to.' Lucy threw her arms around me again and kissed my cheek; and once more I subdued the voice that suggested this was strange. 'Oh, it's so good to see you! We're going to have so much fun! It's going to be *amazing*.'

I was drawn after Lucy into a small cobbled courtyard, enclosed on all sides by the house. In the centre an astrolabe glinted in brass. I was being led through a big wooden door. I had a sense of dark carved panels, tables covered in antiques, an old-fashioned cream telephone with a brass rod for a receiver and Bakelite mouth- and ear-piece to speak and listen into.

We emerged into a hall with a spiral staircase leading upwards in one corner. Lucy went left but I dawdled behind, my breath taken away by the sheer scale of the building, with its wooden and plaster ceilings, dusty portraits and wide windows admitting pale autumn light. It was a vision of unparalleled luxury and privilege, of baronial splendour.

Lucy tugged me forward out of my reverie, into a high room papered in green flowers and containing a long billiard table.

Two men – boys, really – were playing at the table, and both stopped what they were doing to raise their heads and peer at me.

Lucy took both of my hands, and then, to my surprise, twirled me around, as though displaying me, as if I were a prize. There was something troubling about this, something . . . objectifying about it, and within me, something bridled.

'Nina, this is Tristan, and this other one is our Wolf.' She came forward, running an almost possessive hand over the back of the smaller, swarthier of the two men. 'He may look scary but his bark is worse than his bite . . .'

'Speak for yourself.' Wolf had blue eyes that gleamed quickly at me before looking away. He was dressed in jeans and a checked shirt and nodded brusquely.

'Tristan, Wolf, this is *Nina*,' she said.

Tristan was taller and heroically blonde, like a Nordic prince, with wavy hair and high cheekbones naturally tinted pink, as though he spent a lot of time outdoors indulging in wholesome sports.

'Nina,' he said, and took my hand while I blushed. 'Lovely to meet you. We've heard a lot about you.'

'Oh!' I said, unable to reply, because I'd had no idea that either of them existed until this moment. 'Are you here for the weekend too, then?'

'We live here.' It was Wolf that spoke. He had a flat, northern accent, and his hand curled around a bottle of lager.

'We all live here,' said Lucy, taking Tristan's hand.

Tristan grinned. 'It's so great that you'll be joining us, it really is . . .'

I blinked, confused by the strange turn of phrase. I was already here, wasn't I?

'C'mon Nina, you still have to meet Peter and Tess,' said Lucy loudly, cutting him off and dropping his hand. 'So much to see and do! Come on!'

'Peter's gone,' remarked Wolf, as though to himself, bending low over the billiard table again. 'Left this morning.'

'Will he be back tonight?' asked Lucy, raising an eyebrow. 'Did he say?'

Wolf shrugged. 'Doubt it. Think he went back to London.'

'Never mind,' said Lucy, sharing a look with Tristan. 'Perhaps that's for the best.'

I allowed myself to be led away, my confusion smothering me. 'You know, Lucy,' I said as we passed the great staircase once more, 'I thought it was only for the weekend . . . I've only brought a few clothes and I have college—'

'Oh, don't be silly! He didn't mean *you* were moving in. Silly Tristan, got his wires crossed – he does that.' She waggled her eyebrows at me. 'No, you've got college on Monday, we know, we'll get you back. Though you will be busy this weekend – never a dull moment here!'

'Don't *you* have to get back to Cambridge on Monday?' I asked, once again surprised. 'I thought you were—'

'Penelope!' shouted Lucy up the stairs suddenly, 'Nina's here! Come on down and say hello!'

There was silence.

'Ah, let's go look for her.' Lucy bounded up the steps, and once again I sensed that an awkward line of inquiry had been blocked.

* * *

We emerged on to a landing underneath a large porthole window, and I blinked happily in the sunlight and warmth that slanted through it while Lucy shouted up to Penelope a few more times.

'I was sure she was up here . . . Ah, there's Tess!'

I turned. Emerging on to the stairs was a girl, sleepy-eyed and clad in a pink silk dressing gown, her small feet bare. She seemed very young to me, little more than a child, especially as she rubbed her huge blue eyes with her hand, and her thick honey-coloured hair was messy and disordered.

'Tess! This is Nina.'

Tess smiled, holding a hand over her mouth to stifle a yawn. 'Hello, Nina. We've heard all about you. We're all very excited . . .'

'Now now! No giving away any surprises!' Lucy reached out and gently slapped at Tess's hand. I eyed them both, unsettled. 'So, if you're up,' Lucy continued to Tess, 'I guess Aaron soon will be?'

'I think so, he's in the shower.' Tess yawned again.

As she said this, I had a sudden, horrid suspicion that this girl had come from his bed.

And once this suspicion entered my head, it latched on to my thoughts like a leech. What was going on here?

You're being paranoid, that's what's going on here, I told myself.

Lucy slipped her arm through mine. 'All right,' she said to Tess, 'We'll leave you to it and see you downstairs. Wolf said Peter left this morning?'

'I don't know, I haven't spoken to him since last night.' Tess looked over her shoulder down the corridor, and though I had no real evidence for this, I sensed that the question made her uneasy.

They were hiding it as well as they could, but nobody seemed very fond of this Peter.

'Never mind. He'll be back soon enough, I'm sure.' I was tugged again, this time down the stairs once more. 'Come on!'

* * *

Aaron appeared at some point after noon, clad in a loose pair of trousers and a white linen shirt.

I was sitting in the billiard room with the others, engaged in idle chat around cups of herbal tea and cigarettes, though Wolf smoked spliffs, one after the other, so that his small eyes were permanently pink.

Though I asked them questions – where had they come from? What did they do for a living? – and they gave friendly enough answers, I couldn't shake the feeling that they were being vague and evasive. The most I could find out was that Wolf had first met Aaron somewhere in South East Asia, though I couldn't pin down where.

Their elusiveness troubled me.

But Aaron's arrival changed everything. First, there was the sound of a door opening upstairs, and the energy in the room transformed. I realized that I wasn't the only one who had been desperate to see him. The others were the same, their upturned faces moving towards him like sunflowers in a field, following the sun's light in unison as the stairs creaked beneath his footsteps. Tess fiddled with her thick dark gold hair, Lucy sucked in her already flat stomach, and cool, willowy Penelope, who had just joined us, bit her pale lips to redden them. Even Tristan seemed to bridle with excitement.

When the door swung wide and he came in, there was almost a little cheer as he greeted their enthusiasm with a smile.

I had literally no idea what to do or how to react. His beauty mesmerized me once again. I froze, panicking, completely at a loss, and it was only when he approached me first, leaning over to kiss me warmly, that I started to relax.

He tasted of toothpaste and smelled of some astringent, woody aftershave. It was going to be all right, I realized, as the others beamed at me without apparent jealousy. It was going to be all right.

Lucy and Penelope had already risen, fussing to make coffee, while Aaron settled into the comfortably stuffed leather chair which I noticed had been left empty throughout the afternoon.

'So you're here,' he said, as though we were the only two people in the room. He lit a cigarette, something with dark brown paper and a strong scent, his broad hand cupping around the tiny flame as he sucked in hard, his dark hair stroking his cheek as he leaned forward. 'Good. Good. Excellent, in fact.'

I managed a weak smile.

'But you're wondering what you're doing here.' He leaned back in the chair, meeting my gaze, while the others were silent, contemplating us both.

'Well,' I said anxiously, wrapping one of the skirt-belt ties tight around one finger and letting the tiny bell ring gently. 'I had wondered. A little.'

To be truthful, I'd come in hopes of becoming his girlfriend, but in this room full of intent, evasive strangers watching me, this was more frank than I was capable of being.

'But you came anyway,' he said, as smoke curled out of his mouth. He offered me a faint knowing smile. 'You are an *adventuress*.'

I just stared at him. Nobody in my wildest dreams had ever described me as an adventuress. I saw myself suddenly in a pith helmet, compass in hand, deliberately lost in uncharted, unknown territory.

I shook my head, to clear the illusion. 'I don't know about that . . .'

'Nonsense,' he drawled. 'Of course you are. You are many things, Nina, and I don't think you realize half of them yet. But you will. All of you will.' He tapped the table, as though bringing us to order. 'So, are we all ready for the next phase?'

Everyone around me nodded in unison.

'What is the next phase?' I asked.

Aaron regarded me for a long moment, his dark eyes considering me. 'Hmm. Well. The next phase of what I and the other Ascendants do here.'

The what?

Everyone nodded again, looking at me.

I didn't know what to do with this circular conversation, Sophia. I find straightforward conversations difficult enough, as you probably know. I'd already asked a direct question and been rebuffed, and I wasn't sure what my next move should be.

'What do you know about the Creative Spark, Nina?' he asked.

The others waited in expectant silence.

'The Creative Spark?' Was this a test? 'I . . . not much.'

'Divine creativity, the kind that swoops down and possesses you.' He inhaled smoke and watched me. 'That's the kind we're interested in here at Morningstar. Maybe it's the kind that interests you, too. And if that's the case,' he said, leaning forward, 'then maybe we can do something about that.'

I didn't understand what he meant.

But also, and this was the nub of the matter – I was incapable of telling love from desire. Aaron was, at the time, all I knew of desire in the world, and after those hours in his arms, and being charmed by his expensive car, his beautiful house and the kindling flame of his admiration, I would have persuaded myself to accept almost anything he suggested.

I was aware of them all awaiting my reaction, and it was making my cheeks heat with a blush.

He leaned back in the chair, those deep-set eyes fastened on me. Nobody, I realized, looked at me like that, with such fearless interest. And now I could feel myself growing wet and flustered.

'So what do you say, Nina?' he asked. 'Do you want to take a risk? To learn a little more?'

I sat, paralysed. I had no idea what they were talking about, but if it kept me near Aaron – *he called me an adventuress!* – then what was the harm in it?

I tried to imagine the mortification of saying no, I couldn't possibly stay, of getting back in that car with the driver and being borne away, followed by the waves of their disappointment, like a cold, lapping tide.

It would be the end of me and Aaron – so much I understood.

There was no way I could allow it to end. Not yet.

'I . . . I don't know anything about this kind of thing, but . . . yeah, sure. It sounds like it will be a fun weekend.'

The others broke into wild cheering, hugging me, kissing me, and I let them, inwardly stunned and confused (and a little bit suspicious, if we're going for full disclosure) as to how I had caused this reaction, but also happy.

They were nice to me. They seemed to *like* me. I wasn't tiptoeing around them like I did with Rosie and Piers. They all seemed free and easy and . . .

And this could be *fun*. All I'd agreed to do was find out a little more. To hang out with them.

What could go wrong?

* * *

There was no more talk of the Creative Spark that day. Instead, Aaron declared that since the weather was good we would go clay pigeon shooting.

'I don't know anything about guns or how to shoot,' I confessed to him.

'You'll learn.'

113

Men in overalls drove us out across the green fields in two jeeps. I sat next to Aaron, between him and Lucy, Wolf riding shotgun. I kept catching Wolf's eyes in the rear-view mirror, narrowing at me.

My first taste of shooting suited me down to the ground. I loved everything about it – far more than I thought I would. The smell of the gunpowder and oil and the crushed green bracken, the fulsome bang as I tracked the luminous discs of clay, even the subdued violence of the recoil into my chest, bruising me again and again, was exciting and dangerous.

'To learn to shoot is to learn to surrender,' that brogue of his murmured into my ear, raising the tiny hairs on my cheek as his warm breath brushed them.

'I don't understand.'

'You have to fire once the clay falls into your sights. You can't wait, you can't hesitate, you must pull the trigger right at that moment and let the gun slam back into you, let the shot fly, whether you're ready or not.' He chuckled, and his hands fell about my waist, caressed my hips, and just for a second one brushed over my crotch, with a deliberate, featherlight pressure. 'It's all about surrender. It's a metaphor for sex. For life.'

* * *

That evening, after a good dinner that his cook prepared, we stayed up late into the night in front of a roaring fire in the library, smoking spliffs and making inroads into a bottle of cognac that Aaron had told us was worth a thousand pounds.

He sat in his armchair by the fire, his hair like a dark lion's mane, his gaze lingering on each of us, one by one.

'You first,' purred Tristan, settling in next to me on the couch, combing back his rumpled blonde locks with long fingers that had clearly never done any kind of manual labour. 'You're the guest, after all.'

There was something very gentle yet clumsy about Tristan's gestures, like a lot of very tall men. I intuited that he was someone

114

like me, someone who had never been sure about himself or his place in the world.

He poured me a glass of the brandy while I giggled. This is what I remember about him – that there was an uncomplicated kindness to him, a trustworthiness, that didn't make me think twice. The others were friendly and kind too, but not in quite the same way.

I tried to justify this to myself, because I wanted to like them, and Aaron clearly liked them, which was why we were all there. It wasn't that they were false, I rationalized to myself, it was just that if I'd met any of them as a stranger, Tristan would be the only one to treat me exactly the same way.

Poor, poor Tristan.

'This is wasted on me,' I protested. 'I'm not an expert.'

'You don't have to be an expert,' said Penelope coolly. 'Just enjoy it.'

Next to her Lucy offered me a lazy smile, her head lolling against Aaron's knee by the fire. 'Just taste it, Nina.'

'Why's this cognac worth a thousand pounds?' I asked, watching Tristan fill six tumblers with a fingersworth of the amber liquid. The bottle had a decaying and dusty label: *Bisquit Dubouché Grande Fine Champagne Cognac Année 1856.*

'It's a pre-*phylloxera* bottle,' said Tristan, carefully pouring until all were level.

'Preffilloxery?' Tess asked, confused. I was struck again by how young she looked – barely old enough to drink. 'What's that?'

'Pre-*phylloxera*,' he repeated. 'In the eighteen fifties in Europe, nearly all the old vineyards were destroyed by a parasite, the larvae of a fly called *phylloxera*.' He held up a glass and offered it to me, which I cautiously accepted. 'They were never the same afterwards. This bottle is one of the last survivors of a vanished age.'

'It's a waste of fucking money, that's what it is,' muttered Wolf.

'Quiet, you,' said Aaron. He reached forward, ruffled Tristan's golden hair affectionately. 'My sweet boy Tristan is also one of the last survivors of a vanished age.' He gave his shoulder a light squeeze, almost a caress.

This gesture threw me: men didn't act like this around one another in public then, and I was very innocent. I was still recovering from my surprise when the others took up their own glasses, Lucy sniffing hers greedily.

'To the Creative Spark!' said Aaron, raising the glass.

'To the Creative Spark!' rejoined the others, clinking their tumblers together.

'Drink,' Aaron commanded me, seeing me hesitate at this strange toast, and I instantly obeyed, as I was wont to do. The brandy was warm on my tongue, but burned all the way down, while I tried not to wince or hiss.

'What does a thousand pounds taste like, Nina?' asked Tristan, grinning. His cheeks were pink, his eyes shining. Aaron's hand was back on his shoulder.

'A thousand pounds tastes like caramel,' I replied boldly, and filled with a kind of drunken bravado, I drained the glass in one, though it excoriated my throat all the way down. 'And also alcohol.'

'You little savage!' said Aaron. 'That's an atrocious way to treat good cognac!' He stood, and I found myself swept up and swung over his shoulder. He was unexpectedly strong. 'You shall go to bed with no supper.'

'Goodnight, Aaron! Goodnight Nina!' came the cries from the room. I couldn't see the others, as I hung upside down along Aaron's back, the room spinning, my long hair shading my eyes as I tried to raise my head.

'Oh, put me down!' I cried weakly, giggling with nerves and desire. 'You're making me dizzy!'

'Yes, yes.' We were mounting the stairs and my heart was pounding. My hands moved against his back, his skin warm through his shirt. I knew what was coming next, and it made me breathless to think of it. 'I'll put you down. All in good time.'

* * *

'Nina! Where have you been?'

It was five days later and I'd finally called, sitting on the Queen Anne chair next to the old-fashioned Bakelite telephone in the morning room.

It was hard to concentrate on what Rosie was saying. It was as though my attention and focus had somehow been moved out of my body, so that it hovered perpetually somewhere around Aaron.

Even now, I knew he was in the main drawing room playing pool with the boys while the girls sat in the bay windows, watching and calling out advice, and the feeling of wrongness in being separated from him for even the time it took to check in with Rosie was overwhelming.

I was in love. But it was more than that. I was understood here. I was accepted.

I was *home*.

'Nowhere. Away. I'm with friends. In Kent.'

It was Thursday, and I'd made no plans yet to go back to college. The thought of it hung over me like a black cloud. I was missing lectures, supervisions, writing no essays. It had been quietly suggested to me by Aaron that I didn't have to go back if I didn't want to, not immediately, anyway – his driver could take my key and collect any things I needed from my college room.

'But . . . I can't just give up!' I'd said, as we'd lain in his huge bed, tangled together in his glossy silk sheets.

'It was only a suggestion,' he murmured into my ear, then nipped the lobe.

Aaron was contemptuous of how much you could learn in a university. He didn't see the point. He'd never needed to go. As much as it embarrasses me to admit it now, I had started to wonder whether he was right. Late at night, while I lay there with him, he told me the world was just a dream, the froth on the real existence that lay just underneath, beneath the surface. How was university supposed to help me access that?

Since my capacity for rational thought was draining away on a diet of sex, drugs, luxury and love, I didn't resist much.

Of course I would go back to university, I told myself. *At some point. Very soon.*

In any case, Aaron was too clever to obviously disapprove of my plans, or forbid me. The few times I'd seriously mentioned returning, or at least checking in, getting my assignments and contacting my friends, had resulted in indifferent non-committal grunts and a vague feeling that I was disappointing him. He'd speak to the driver, he'd say dismissively, but then somehow that never seemed to happen.

Besides, the others told me, my focus should be here. I had been chosen, and handed a great opportunity. Everyone depended on one another here.

What was involved was still a mystery, but doubtless all would be revealed in good time.

'What are you talking about, Nina? What friends? What about uni?' Rosie sounded utterly perplexed, as well she might. 'When are you coming back?'

'Oh, I'll be back. Soon.'

There was a long pause.

'Nina, are you at Morningstar? With Aaron Kessler and his lot?'

I was aware, though there had been no prohibition – nothing was forbidden here, after all – that Aaron and the others didn't like to talk about their group with 'outsiders'.

'Look, Rosie, I . . .'

'You *are*, aren't you?'

'No . . . I'm just with friends . . .'

'Nina, listen to me. Just please listen. You have to get out of there. They're not good people.'

This was, on the face of it, such an absurd statement that I had trouble comprehending it.

'What?'

'No, listen. They were *so* weird with us when we came to that house party last week. They wouldn't let me look for you, wouldn't tell me anything, kept trying to get us drunker and drunker . . . they're shifty. They're into . . . some strange things. People say it's a cult.'

I couldn't help it. I snorted out a laugh. 'A cult?'

Of course they were into strange things. But a cult? That was ridiculous. Rosie was just too provincial to get it.

Aaron had already said as much about her. He'd seen it the minute he'd laid eyes on her, he told me.

'That's absurd,' I said. 'They just have, you know, their own beliefs. You wouldn't understand and I'm not supposed to talk about them—'

'So you *are* there! Why did you lie to me?'

'Rosie, I need to go,' I said, deciding to lie again. 'Dinner's ready, and I have to set the table.'

'Nina . . .'

'Rosie, I'll ring you back tomorrow, yeah? And please don't worry about me. I'm absolutely fine.' I smiled, happy now the call was ending and I could get back to the others, to Aaron's side. 'Never been better.'

Chapter Nine

It was nearly three in the morning. It was cool now in my dad's shed, and my legs were stiff and my nails bitten.

I hadn't been able to read past the first notebook. I didn't have the stamina. I needed to think about what I'd already learned. I gathered both notebooks up in my shaking hands, determined not to spend another second in the shed, with my mum's ghost so vibrant and visible I could have reached out and touched her. She was the shade of a pale ingénue from a life she'd had before I was born, so young and innocent and so, God forgive me for saying it, so bloody, bloody *stupid*.

I took my feet off my dad's desk and stood up, realizing with a shock that this had always been his gesture – when I glimpsed him through the window and he hadn't been working, he had always been half-perched on this, his favourite chair (which had proved to be exceptionally uncomfortable, with its bunched cushions and slightly wonky leg), his shabby socked feet crossed over one another and parked on top of the scarred surface of the desk.

It was almost as if, by mimicking their gestures and reading their experiences, I could conjure my parents back to life again.

But the tragedy was that the people I conjured were still my parents, and as huge as my grief was, they both still drove me mad. I had recognized my mum in her writing, her hesitant patterns of speech, her desire to make everybody happy at her own expense, her almost pathological self-effacement . . .

I was just thinking about them both as I stood beneath the

striplight over the desk, my irrational fear of the shed and the garden and the late hour gone, and without my noticing, for a nanosecond my grief was gone, too.

Yes, my mum had done a foolish, reckless thing, and Aaron Kessler had used his age and status to take advantage of her, of that there could be no doubt.

My mum and Aaron Kessler.

Wow! I bit my lip.

I'd heard of him, of course.

The Boarhounds were from well before my time, and I'd never been that interested in them personally. All I knew of them was that famous first album; the one that was always featured on lists of all-time greats in the music press, alongside Pink Floyd's *Dark Side of the Moon* and Led Zeppelin's *Houses of the Holy*.

An ex of mine had been a bit of a rocker on the quiet, and his copy of *Green Eyed Monster* had always fascinated me with its iconic cover, depicting a stylistic hand-drawn swamp in brilliant viridian. In the centre, the knotty forehead and cat's-slit eye of an alligator lurked, barely hidden beneath the surface of the still water.

I rubbed my eyes. This was all just too much. I needed to get to bed; I had work in the morning. I could think about all this tomorrow night once I got the Scottish Heritage presentation out of the way. That had to be my focus, at least for now.

I had picked up the Maglite, the notebooks still crushed to my chest, when suddenly there was a faraway but very familiar click, loud in the pre-dawn silence.

I turned and froze.

Through the window I could see that the front of the house was lit up in stark white. Something had tripped the security sensor and the floodlight had come on.

It's just a fox, I told myself, *or an owl, setting it off. This happens all the time.*

But almost without thinking about it, I had withdrawn to the wall of the shed and snapped off the striplight.

All was darkness as I tiptoed to the window, peering out from behind the sill.

There was nothing there. No sign of anyone, no noise, just the bald fact of the floodlight illuminating my parents' front door, shining on to the path leading up to it. Around the shed the trees were black, the air too still to even stir the leaves.

Five seconds became ten, and then fifteen, as I crouched there, with my father's signature scent of creosote and old tobacco emanating from the curtains, my knees brushing the wooden wall as I struggled to control my breathing and urge myself to stay calm.

Nothing moved outside, and there was no noise.

After twenty seconds, the security light snapped off again with another click.

The inside of the shed was completely dark, except for the long shadows cast from the house. The lamp on the kitchen table glowed cosily at me from the window as I cowered by the shed's windowsill, as though beckoning me back indoors.

I waited, my heart pounding.

Stop this, said a firm inner voice. The security light was frequently set off at strange hours by random wildlife; it had happened for as long as I could remember. It didn't require an intruder to behave this way. *Get a grip, get up and go back inside.*

But I couldn't move, not to save my life. My mother had died a little over a fortnight earlier not twenty feet away from where I was huddled, and as far as I was concerned, her killer could still be out there.

After all, someone had been troubling my parents with break-ins in the months before . . .

I would ring the police, that's what I'd do, and report a prowler. I didn't care that I might be wasting their time, that it might just be a stray cat. Under the circumstances, a little caution was only to be expected. I would ring them now and not move from here until they . . .

Except, I realized, patting my jeans, I'd left my phone in the kitchen.

'Fuck,' I whispered. 'Oh, *fuck.*'

Now what?

I couldn't stay out here all night.

And besides, I told myself firmly, I had the Maglite, which could double as a wickedly heavy cosh if required, which it wouldn't be. I just had to run up the garden, through the unlocked door, and this would all be over, this non-event I was making a fool of myself over.

I rose silently to my feet, took a deep breath, and crashed out of the shed door, running.

Ahead of me the house loomed across the long strip of lawn, the lamp in the kitchen window shone in encouragement as my legs pounded, and then, with that self-same click, the security light came back on.

The front of the house was immediately drowned in white light.

Nothing was there.

I threw open the door, stumbling over the step, then turned and locked it, my hands shaking with adrenaline, the notebooks and Maglite at my feet, my blood singing in relief.

I checked every room in the house before retreating back to the comforting haven of the kitchen, unable to shake the idea that someone could easily have slipped inside while I was reading out in the shed.

There was nobody there.

* * *

I left the notebooks lying on the bedside table in my room and crawled into the narrow little bed of my girlhood. My posters of pop stars and actors were gone, only the smudged traces of Blu-tack where they'd been hung remained.

And I started to think.

Who were these people my mum had known? I wondered. I had never heard any of their names mentioned, not even in whispers. I had gone through years and years of correspondence after my mother's death, and hadn't found a single reference to any of them.

If you'd asked me before she died, I would have told you that my mum didn't have a degree and had never gone to college.

Why would she conceal such a thing from me? No matter how I tried to pitch this to myself, there was something sinister about it, something that spoke of guilt and flight.

Once I got this bloody presentation out of the way, I would get on with tracking down these people. Max Clarke would be able to help with that. And one of them at least should be easy to find. The famous one.

I sat up, pulling my laptop towards me, aware that I should be trying to sleep ahead of my career-deciding meeting tomorrow morning. Instead I opened Google and typed in 'Aaron Kessler'.

There was a sudden, astounding plethora of entries and images. Pictures of a youngish, square-faced man with impossibly high cheekbones and brown flowing hair. He was frequently shirtless or wearing buttoned garments that had come undone, revealing a superbly muscled, hairless chest.

I grunted a little at this. I suspect if you worked out that much, you probably wanted people to see the results. I wasn't much disposed to like him, considering what I'd read about him, but there was no doubt that he'd been very good-looking back in the Eighties, and this didn't appear to have changed much.

I tabbed through to the articles, which were all roughly similar, at least in the beginning. The initial results tended not to be about Aaron Kessler himself, but about the band, only mentioning in passing his stint as their lead singer from 1984 to 1986, though the dates themselves only added up to a little over thirteen months. The split was apparently due to irreconcilable differences, which struck me as the sort of wording you would use in a divorce.

I let myself fall back against the pillows, astounded. I couldn't get over it – my mother had been sleeping with the guy that sang 'Mean River', which had been covered multiple times since I'd been born and became a hit again a few years ago when it was used as the music for a smartphone ad.

If I closed my eyes I could hear 'Mean River' playing in my head, with those dark, portentous chords and that baritone boom – 'And now in my arms I can feel you shiver/Oh baby time is a mean mean river . . .'

I shook myself awake. I wasn't interested in his musical career right now.

After a while, the pages of Boarhounds results started to give way to something less generic and a little more interesting – IS THE ORDER OF ASCENDANTS A MIND CONTROL CULT?! screamed one tatty website that didn't look like it had been updated since the Nineties. The answer, a brief glance through the glowing fonts assured me, was definitely yes.

There was an article in the *Guardian* from 2008 – WE LOST EVERYTHING TO A GURU – 'How Martin and Sam bounced back after losing their house, jobs and almost their children to an ex-rock star's Society for Spiritual

Enrichment' – where an unhappy bohemian couple, a slouching man in a loose shirt and glasses; a woman in jeans and a pink tunic, shared how their relationship had broken down and they had signed over everything they owned during a brief flirtation with 'a secretive organization run by Aaron Kessler, ex-musician', who had declined to comment on the article, according to the reporter.

Looking through the links I'd turned up, he must have rebranded at some point in the Noughties. Judging from his own website, what they seemed to do now was host very expensive seminars – £2,000 for a week, including food and accommodation – called Creative Spark Workshops.

The Society for Spiritual Enrichment exists to promote a healthy work–life balance and to provide our clients with the tools to enable them to get in touch with their creative self. We believe that this creative identity is the inner wellspring that fully ignites all human beings to live more passionate and authentic lives.

A full engagement with one's creative self encourages stress reduction, increased focus and concentration, and a growth in mental and physical energy. All of these things lead to more successful and fulfilling business and personal relationships.

Get in touch today to find out more about how the Society for Spiritual Enrichment can help you unlock your inner creative nature.

There was a picture of Kessler in the 'About the Society' section. He looked older, but still handsome in that deep-set, dark-eyed way that my mother had correctly described as 'intense', standing near an antique wooden desk with his arms folded, well-defined muscles barely hidden by a white shirt.

But I couldn't think of this now – I was insanely busy and had to prioritize. Once I got back from London I would be able to look again and read the second notebook.

It would soon be morning. It was nearly time to shower and get on a train.

Chapter Ten

'Oh, you're back.'

My timing was terrible or wonderful, depending on your point of view. I was in my smart blue office dress and jacket, laptop slung over my back, and mounting the steps to Amity Studios when I heard the brisk clatter of male feet behind me.

I tossed a look over my shoulder, startled. It was James, the managing partner, who'd been studiously ignoring my emails and calls.

I made myself smile and appear relaxed. 'Yes, today's the day.'

'Are you sitting in on the Scottish Heritage presentation then?' he asked. There was nothing remotely remarkable in the way that he didn't offer me any condolences. I had expected none.

'No,' I said coolly. 'I'm not sitting in on the Scottish Heritage presentation. I'm giving the presentation.'

'Is that still your project? I thought Benjamin took it over.'

'No, it's still mine.' I'd chased up the client yesterday and straightened this out with them, remembering to copy Benjamin into the confirmation email, letting them know I was back at work and thanking Benjamin for his 'caretaker' duties during my compassionate leave.

He had not replied.

'You're sure you're up to that?' James asked.

'Quite.'

He said nothing further, pushing open the steel and untreated larch-clad door, and I passed in behind him.

* * *

I was early; it was only half seven in the morning. I had wanted a little peace and quiet before the project manager, Trish, and the other guys from Scottish Heritage got here, so that I could update the model with the work I'd done at home. I was looking forward to this time, this return to normality – tinkering with the model is my favourite part of the process. I get lost in the software, designing fly-throughs and filling in the virtual background. I like to make the biggest mug of coffee I can manage, and vanish into the machine.

'Oh, Sophia!'

Cleo was in the kitchen, her small hands clasped around a mug of tea. She looked bleary and tired, her top crumpled, her hair pinned back unevenly.

'Hello, stranger!' I grinned. 'I see you got lucky last night.'

She looked at me like I'd slapped her, and her cheeks went a fierce pink. 'What do you mean?' There was something hard in her face.

'You're in early,' I said, taken aback. 'Relax, I was only kidding.'

She seemed to calm down. 'Sorry. I hate this time of day.' She yawned, or rather, I thought, she pretended to. 'It's good to see you, Soph,' and I was pulled into a little embrace. 'Are you sure you're . . . I mean, you're good to come back?'

'Yes.' I reached around and selected a clean mug from the cupboard. 'I was going mad at home. Look, my morning's rammed, but do you want to grab a coffee later this afternoon at Café Louis?'

I turned back to her and was surprised: there was something

both shocked, eager and pitying in her expression. I couldn't understand or interpret it at all.

'Cleo?'

She shook her head. 'Sorry, Soph. I just . . . I can't believe your parents are . . .'

'Well, my mum is,' I interjected crisply.

She blushed again. 'Sorry, sorry, I know, I didn't mean . . . sorry, I know about your dad. How's he doing?'

'They say he's comfortable and stable.'

'Oh, well that's good news. When did he wake up?'

'He hasn't.'

She bit her lip. 'Sorry,' she said again. 'You would have said. I just don't do mornings. But yeah, of course I'm up for coffee. What are you doing till then? Catching up?'

'I'm doing the SH presentation, remember?'

'What, still?'

'Today's the day. And it's my project.' I tried to smile. 'My Amity debut.'

'Oh. Yeah. Anyway, I've got some stuff I need to crack on with before ten. So yeah, see you after lunch.'

I nodded. 'OK.'

After she'd gone I made the coffee on the company machine, hitting the button for one, then two extra espresso shots, all the while feeling troubled.

* * *

It took me a little while to work out that something was wrong – I scanned through my emails for anything urgent, then loaded up the modelling software.

I tried to open the last project I'd been working on, the Orkney visitors' centre.

'The system cannot find this file: please browse to new location or attach missing external drive.'

Shit, I thought. I'd updated the file from home. I must have saved it locally on the laptop. But a search on my laptop showed nothing.

It was gone. In fact, not only was it gone, but the folder with the other drafts and their backups was gone. It was empty.

No, I thought, feeling the blood drain from my face. *It had been emptied.*

I leaned back in my chair, staring at the impossible blankness of my screen. A seismic tremor of sobs was building somewhere around my diaphragm and moving upwards.

Had I done this, in my desperate grief, my confusion, my conflicting duties? Had I hit the wrong button and lost all of that work?

And then the door to Benjamin's office opened.

He emerged into the main office floor, heading for the kitchen. He was constantly drinking filtered water from the dispenser there. As he came back, glass in hand, I made sure that my face was turned to my iMac, but still, in my peripheral vision, he paused, just a fraction, slowing down in the same way that cars slow down as they pass a wreck in the opposite lane, just so they can check the mangled metal for bloodstains.

I didn't stir, not even as he moved off again, and there was something almost like a satisfied sway in his hips as he glided back into his office, throwing the door shut behind him.

I did not move.

Oh, you fucker, I thought. *You absolute bastard.*

Shit. Shit.

What am I going to do?

I was shaking with rage. I was going to cry. I was going to pick up the po-faced iMac from my desk and fling it through the steel-silled glass wall of Benjamin's office . . .

And then I had a sudden memory of my mother.

She was standing in the garden, not far from the tree I'd found her hanging from. She was leaning forward and drawing in a deep breath, inhaling the scent of our lavender bush.

I didn't remember when I'd seen this, only that I had.

My breathing started to slow down.

From when I was a little girl, to when I was a teenager and moving out to university, my mother had said the same thing – no matter what my moods or rages: 'Do whatever you want, my darling heart. You get to choose. But before you do, first of all, you need to take a deep breath and *think*.'

This moment felt like a gift and a lesson for me.

Now was the time to breathe slowly, to be calm. And to think. *Think*.

* * *

It took three hours.

It was desperately ramshackle and if anyone asked too many questions I would be in trouble, but I built that bastard again from the ground up, based on my locally saved notes and preliminary drawings. All the whizz-bang plans I'd had for the presentation would have to be shelved, so it would be very low-key. Noticeably low-key.

I'd have to wing it on charisma and sheer nerve.

And the design, of course.

When Olympia rang through, her voice was so tentative, I wondered if she was in on it. 'Sophia, Scottish Heritage has arrived. Do you want me to . . . ?'

'That's fine, Olympia, I'll come and collect them now.'

* * *

I was on the 16:00 to Ipswich, then another train change. Once I arrived, I had a long drive ahead of me to the hospital.

The presentation had been awful. I'd been tired and

muddled – I hadn't slept a wink the night before – some things all the espresso in the world can't fix. There had been a couple of times when I'd had to ask the Scottish Heritage contact – a big guy in a grey suit and bottle-bottom spectacles – to repeat himself, which had been mortifying.

The only bright spark had been the design itself. As I talked them through it, with its slate and seawater inspiration, I felt a tiny rush of the excitement I'd had when I first conceived the idea.

It *was* a great design; my best yet, and I'd salvaged it at the eleventh hour, rather than falling to pieces.

My mum and dad would have been proud of me today.

The train was noisy and hotter than hell. Through the window, the urban sprawl of Ipswich had given way to the secretive greenness of Suffolk proper. I tried to let it soothe me.

The man next to me was reading a free paper which he kept rattling, as though trying to shake crumbs out of it; and in my exhausted state it was driving me ever so slightly mad. I wanted to get back to my dad and then go home and curl up in my little bed at Rowan's cottage with the second notebook.

I'd be up at dawn to do all of this again.

God knew when, if ever, I'd return to my cosy little flat in Brixton with its scrap of garden and single scrubby deckchair, where mere weeks earlier I would sit and enjoy the sunset with friends and a glass of cold white wine. It seemed a lifetime away now – a golden age where I'd been blessed and happy and dearly loved, yet never once realized it.

I was on the brink of tears again.

Hoping to distract myself, my gaze drifted to the other passengers. A woman sitting opposite me was reading a copy of some dog-eared historical romance with a lady in Tudor dress on the cover. There was something odd about her, with her sharp chin and messy, pale brown pixie haircut.

I tried to let the rhythmic rattle of the train soothe me. Sometimes I think it's like music, a backbeat to my journey home for when I'm too tired to engage with my headphones. Stupidly I'd forgotten to pack a book when I'd left this morning. I had no interest in reading the second notebook in public, crowded as I was on all sides by strangers. It was hard enough to cope with seeing my mum that way on my own. Maybe I had something to look at on my phone . . .

I glanced at the woman opposite and realized what I found odd about her.

She wasn't turning the pages.

Perhaps I just hadn't noticed her do it. I fell back against the seat and let my lids close, leaving just a slit of vision, and in this facsimile of dozing I watched her.

A minute or two passed by, possibly less. The pages continued not to turn.

Then her triangular face turned upwards towards me, giving a glimpse of freckles and a little snub nose. But the remarkable thing, the scary thing, was her eyes – pale blue and utterly focused, her expression cold but intense, filled with some overwhelming but unidentifiable emotion.

She was rapt, yes, but not in her book; in *me*.

The strangeness of it made my mouth go dry.

Then she stole a glance towards my side, and I felt the man next to me stiffen, stir.

I understood instantly. They weren't strangers on a train; they knew one another, but were pretending not to. And for some reason they were bracketing me in the seats.

But why? Could they be reporters? Police? Was I suspected of something now? I couldn't quite believe it, but there was just something about the way the woman had fixed me with that strange, ardent, yet cold look.

Somehow, I was a big, big deal to her.

I had to get away from these people.

I made a big show of jerking awake, as if I'd been dozing, and her face dropped to the book. His paper shook annoyingly again, but this time I recognized it for what it was – nerves.

Do whatever you want, my darling heart. You get to choose. But before you do, first of all, you need to take a deep breath and think.

We were five minutes from Wickham Market. I needed a plan. I had to get off the train before Darsham, lead them off. In the crush of commuters I could catch a cab, perhaps, and shake them. Call Rowan – hell, call the police – but no, that was ridiculous, I realized, what would I say? That some strange woman on the train gave me a funny look?

Explaining it all was a problem for another time. I had to get off the train *now*.

I began to slowly, almost theatrically, pack my headphones away, carefully winding them into a little coil, then tucking my phone in and removing my sunglasses, as the announcer told us all that the next station was Wickham Market and this was the train to Lowestoft.

With a sinking heart I felt rather than saw the free paper being folded away, the woman closing her book. I had been hoping, I realized, that I was imagining all this.

I stood up and joined the small knot gathering at the doors, clinging on to the sweaty handles of a nearby seat as the train slowed, its rattling rhythm changing tempo.

Within moments I felt him behind me, close enough to hear him breathing. I hadn't had a chance to get a good look at him – just a sense of a pink nose and cheeks, and a receding hairline. I stole a quick glance in the windows, hoping to catch their reflection and find out where she'd gone, but the sunlight was too high and bright for that.

'This station is Wickham Market.'

The doors seemed to take for ever to open, but after the

beeps, the expectant movement in the waiting crush, and the first cool draught of air, I was alighting on to the platform, walking quickly, almost running, alongside the train towards the exit. I had no idea where my followers were, as I didn't dare look around. I passed the first carriage while commuters were disgorged on to the hot tarmac, nearly pushing and elbowing several in my haste.

The exit was ahead of me. The handful of people waiting to get on the train were ascending into the second carriage, and through the gate the station's tiny car park was busy with waiting cars. I glanced at my watch and made a show of moving my head, as though searching for one in particular; for someone waiting for me.

The doors started to beep in warning.

I turned on my heel and barrelled along the last few feet before launching myself back up into the train as the doors slid shut behind me, cutting me off from my pursuers.

I retreated to the other side, scanning the windows. I couldn't see them. *Oh God, had they followed me back on?* I peered along the carriage on either side. No sign. No . . .

No. Wait. *There.*

It was the woman, standing against the painted white fence enclosing the platform. Her face was frantic, her head whipping from side to side, her mouth moving though I could not make out the words.

Then, as though she had felt my attention on her, she glimpsed me just as the train lurched forwards, nearly knocking me off my feet. Her blue eyes were wide, her mouth thinned.

Take a picture of her. Take a picture of her with your phone.

I tore through my bag looking for my iPhone, but by the time I laid hands on it she was long gone and the train was chugging on to Saxmundham. Soon I was babbling to Rowan as the signal wavered in and out, trying to control my tears while the other passengers nudged one another and stared.

'Rowan, listen – some people were following me on the train . . . No, I don't know them. But they were definitely following me, the pair of them. I pretended to get off the train and they got off, then I rushed back on as the doors were closing, and I could see them hunting for me on the platform. That's the . . . Look, I'll tell you more when I get to the hospital – you're there now, right? Can you just hang on until I arrive? No . . . No . . . I'm fine. But something is wrong. Something is very wrong. I'll explain more when I get there. Sorry, Rowan, you're breaking up, it's Saxmundham. I gotta go.'

I dropped my phone into my pocket and sank into one of the few empty seats, ignoring the looks I got.

Because there was absolutely no shadow of a doubt in my mind.

Someone was after me, and they meant me harm.

Chapter Eleven

'Sophia!'

Rowan was waiting in the hospital corridor, calling out to me, animated and urgent.

'What? What is it?' I yelped at him, terrified it would be more bad tidings, and then I noticed he was smiling.

'Soph, Soph, calm down.' He took my arms in his hands. He wasn't just smiling, he was beaming. 'It's all right. You're safe now. Listen. They're saying Jared's showing signs of waking up.'

* * *

It's not what I would have called 'waking up', but he definitely looked different when I entered the little side-room they'd put him in, with its aggressively cheerful checked green curtains alongside the spiky chrome and plastic medical equipment.

Strangely enough, he also smelled different – often when I'd sat with him with my laptop, I used to catch a hint of a death-like, sickly scent, which would appear and then vanish the minute I tried to properly register it. It lurked over his bed like a ghost, content to make itself known in tiny but terrifying ways, in the yellowish cast of his skin, in the utterly slack yawing muscles of his face.

And yet . . . there was no doubt, tonight he was different. His colour was slightly better, still ghastly, but this time faintly tinged with pink rather than green and, perhaps it was desperate wishful thinking, but his breathing sounded easier, so that you could almost believe he was simply asleep.

I took his pale cold hand with its cannula needle in the vein on top and gently stroked it.

'Dad?' I asked. 'Dad, are you there?'

There was no response.

'Dad?'

Nothing.

I turned to Rowan.

'What do you mean, "waking up"?'

'Well,' he said, scratching at his dreadlocks. 'Maybe waking up is overstating the case, but the nurse said that you had to talk to the doctor.' He shrugged. 'I got the impression the news was good, but they wouldn't say anything to me, as I'm not family.'

I nodded. 'Stay with him for a few more minutes while I try to find them, will you?'

He sighed. 'I can't stay long. Kayleigh needs me at home tonight. Her sister's coming for dinner.'

'Just a few minutes, honest, Ro.'

He shrugged, as though defeated. 'Fine.' I felt a rush of irrational anger – I had sobbed out my fears to him over the phone on the train, and yet I had the impression he didn't quite believe me.

'Just a few minutes,' I said. 'I promise.'

He replied with a tired nod. 'Yeah sure.'

* * *

Tracy the staff nurse was a middle-aged woman with a blonde menopause bob and a deeply lined forehead, as though it had been built out of flesh-coloured bricks and the mortar had worn away over time. I found her in front of her computer screen in the nurses' station in the centre of the ward.

'Hello, lovey. Did Rowan send you in?'

'He said my dad had woken up . . .'

'Not quite, he's a little overexcited. He's a lovely lad, isn't he? He dotes on your dad.'

'Yes,' I said, my cheeks heating, assuming the seat in front of her desk. Rightly or wrongly, I felt the implied contrast between him and me, the neglectful daughter, who'd left my dad to scurry off to London for the day. 'So, what *did* happen?'

She sighed. 'Well, you know how we test your father to see how he responds throughout the day?'

'Yes?'

'So, at lunchtime there was a tiny bit of a response when I asked him to squeeze my finger. The doctor ordered some bloods taken, and soon we'll know if the antibiotics are starting to kick in.'

'Oh . . . that's good news, isn't it?' I replied. I was slightly shocked and felt lost. There hadn't been much good news recently.

'Well, yes, but you need to speak to the doctor, lamb. She can tell you more.' She sighed, thinking. 'Can you be here tomorrow morning? Around ten?'

I found myself nodding; of course I could. I would think of something to tell Amity.

'Don't look so worried, love,' she said kindly. 'He's not out of the woods, but things are moving in the right direction.' She patted my hand, and I let her. 'If I were you, I'd get off early tonight and get some sleep. You look all done in.'

Rowan was stretched out in one of the chairs, his head lolling back. There were dark shadows under his eyes.

'I'm to talk to the doctor tomorrow morning, about ten.' I pulled up one of the chairs next to my dad's bed and took his hand. I wanted to ask him to squeeze my fingers, too, but worried about overtiring him. I kissed his forehead instead and sighed.

'Did Monica start OK today at the café?' I asked.

'She did,' Rowan snorted out a grunt of approval. 'She was really good. After the first hour or so she hardly needed me.' He gave me a sidelong look. 'How did your presentation go today?'

'It nearly didn't, but all was well in the end.'

He raised an eyebrow while he shook out his arms. He must have been here for an hour already and he was also single-handedly running Eden Gardens and supervising Monica. He must be exhausted.

'That sounds good. I think.'

I shrugged. 'They deleted my work.'

'What d'you mean, "deleted your work"?'

'Deleted my work for Scottish Heritage. All the files. I had to redo the whole thing.'

He seemed to think about that for a moment. 'Why would they do that?'

'Trying to get rid of me.' I plopped down on the seat next to him.

'But they hired you.'

'Well, um, something nearly happened with one of the partners the night . . .' I swallowed. 'But it turned out he was married.' I shrugged. 'He got quite nasty when I called him on it.'

'Right . . . but still, to delete your work . . .'

He looked doubtful.

'You wouldn't give me that look if you'd met him.'

'What?' he bridled. 'What look?'

'That look. Like I'm mental.'

Something stiffened in his expression then. 'I never said you're mental.'

I should have stopped myself, but I couldn't. It was eating me up inside. 'But you think it. I can tell that you think it.'

I felt a fleeting moment of respect for him, in that he didn't attempt to deny it.

The silence glowered between us. My eyes felt hot and stabbed with little pinprick tears.

He sighed.

'Soph, I don't think you're mental, not in the way you mean anyway. I really don't. But I might as well be honest. I think, like, that you're under phenomenal strain. Something has happened here that nobody could have expected in a million years, and it is . . . there is no doubt, it's something none of us knows how to cope with.'

I didn't reply.

'It's huge. You need to, like, *process* it. It takes time, and space. But, you know, you aren't giving yourself any time or space. I'm sure the world seems very scary and hostile right now.'

'Rowan . . .'

'You need to talk to somebody about this.' The words came out in a rush, as though this were a prepared speech, and he had gone bright pink. 'I mean, properly talk to someone. Not just your friends. A grief counsellor.'

It was as if he'd slapped me.

'So I'm paranoid, then? My mum supposedly killed herself and stabbed my dad, and now I've lost my mind?' I snapped.

'Soph . . .' His brow was damp. He was not enjoying this conversation. 'I don't know what happened to your parents. Neither do you.'

'You said you believed me!' I shouted, not caring that the nurses were exchanging glances and hurrying over, or that the visitors on the main ward had stilled, craned their heads to watch. That even my dad might be able to hear this. My sense of betrayal was racing away; it felt like I was falling through space. 'You said you believed me when I told you my mum didn't kill herself!'

'I believe that you believe it!' he snapped back, and then

mastered himself. 'You are *so* upset, Soph. And it's . . . it's hard to see things clearly.'

'Excuse me,' said one of the staff nurses, a woman I didn't know with a neat black ponytail who appeared at the door, 'This is a hospital. There are sick people in here. If you can't keep your voices down you'll be asked to leave.'

She turned on her flat brown heels and was gone.

I was about to blurt out some rejoinder when there was a noise, a kind of choking cough from the bed, more of a sub-audible rumble, then stillness. Both of our heads whipped round.

'Dad?' I bent by his head. 'Dad? Are you all right?'

But it was gone, and though we cajoled him and stroked his arms, there was nothing more but slow breathing.

We regarded each other across the bed, the heat gone out of our argument, but the atmosphere tense with all the words that neither of us could take back.

'So,' I said, 'you'd better be getting back to Kayleigh. It's getting late. I'll stay at the house tonight.'

'Sophia, don't be like this.'

'Be like what?'

He opened his mouth, about to speak, but something about my expression changed his mind. His jaw shut tight, and then he was out the door and tramping from the ward, his shoulders sagging.

I should have run after him, but I didn't. Instead I let myself slump down in the chair next to my dad. My eyes were prickling again.

No. I'm not going to cry. I'm going to carry on.

I picked up my bag and set it on my lap. The notebooks were within, and with a mixed sense of sinking dread and determination, I pulled the next one out and started to read.

The Second Notebook

Chapter Twelve

I know it must sound ridiculous to you, Sophia, but I had more or less forgotten that the order had a religious nature, and that what they were doing was 'spiritual practice', even if they were very scanty when it came to details. Meditation would be involved, and chanting, they said, but I never saw much of this.

At any rate, there was no spiritual practice at Morningstar in those first ten days, or not that I saw. In retrospect, of course, they were softening me up, and they were very good at it.

They'd done it before.

While the sun shone, we all amused ourselves on the estate during that Indian summer – driving the jeeps through narrow farm lanes while rabbits and tiny muntjac deer scampered out of our way, their tails flashing white in their panic; losing ourselves in the Yew Maze in a haze of giggles; or shooting pigeons, clay or real, in the grounds with Aaron's handsome shotguns, and coming home redolent of gunpowder and bruised grass.

At night, we drank and smoked weed, talked philosophy and read poetry out loud by the fireside to one another (or rather, most of us did, as Wolf had no truck with poetry). Even now, in my memory, if I hear that line from Byron: 'She walks in beauty, like the night . . .' nearly thirty years and hundreds of miles fall away from me. I am back at Morningstar, and my anger and hatred and the doughy burden of my middle age have vanished. I am that Nina again.

That poor deluded fool.

I remember the sex even now. I was Aaron's creature, as he posed me on his giant bed with its antique carved headboard. He commanded me to open for him and I did. There was nothing

I would not do for him as I panted, moaned and yelped out my prayers to him.

Afterwards he would stroke me like a pet, between lines of cocaine, and murmur into my ear, 'You're so beautiful. You're so unique, so innocent, so *hot*. You're not like the others.'

Despite my flattered vanity, I wondered why he would compare me to the others. I didn't dare ask him – anything like sexual jealousy would arouse his forbidding displeasure, and I was not about to displease Aaron. Instead I chose to hear: *He loves me best!*

He never once said he loved me, though he was always talking about love, or rather 'Love' as a general concept. Rather, he told me he loved things about me; such as my hair, or my laugh, or the way I gripped his cock.

Sometimes I would stop for a second in the middle of all this bacchanal and think, *This is not real life. Nothing about it makes sense.*

Sometimes I would think *he* didn't make any sense. He was engaged with me; passionate, intense and vigorous. He didn't like me to close my eyes during sex, or look away from him, while I swirled my tongue around him or he pounded into me, my feet trembling by his ears. He was always *present*. I had no prior experience to fall back on, but I could never quite shake the feeling that I could have been anybody, and I would have elicited exactly the same responses from him, just with the names changed. It was a mere ghost of a feeling, but at stray moments in the wee hours of the morning it haunted the foot of his bed, regarding me with mournful eyes.

But I'm describing mere bubbles of uncommon wakefulness in an ongoing sea of euphoria, perhaps a little more detail than you would like, dearest one. I'm sorry for it, but I need to explain myself. I was in love, I was out of my mind. I was living the dream, as they say nowadays. I had no idea it would ever become a nightmare.

* * *

I had been at Morningstar for ten days before I finally spent the night in the room they had given me, a pretty bedroom facing out over the moat, decorated in what I suspected was original William Morris blue wallpaper.

I lay in my quaintly ruffled bed, surrounded by dusty china ornaments, weeping. Like them, I had been put on a shelf.

That evening, we'd had yet another splendid dinner. This time it was duck a l'orange, which I'm not sure people still cook. It was served to us by Michelle, a silent woman with thin tawny hair. Like the driver, she gave the impression that while she worked for us, we were not people she wished to know any better.

'You know, Nina,' Aaron murmured into my ear as Lucy chattered to the table at large, 'I'm tired. I think I need to just sleep tonight.'

'Oh, yeah, whatever you want. I could do with an early night too, I mean,' I breathed, my mouth tasting of good Malbec. 'It's enough to be together . . .'

'No.' There was a hidden ring of steel in his whisper. 'I mean *alone*. You go to your own bed tonight.'

'Oh,' I said back, the blood draining from my face. 'Of course, if that's what you—'

'Thank you, Nina.' He moved his head away from me and rejoined the conversation at the table.

It was the end of the discussion.

The evening had gone by in a kind of dark dream. Was I being rejected? Had I done or said something to offend him?

I was gloomy and silent and on the verge of tears all evening as the others drank and smoked and laughed, while I pondered what this announcement could mean. No one remarked on my obvious pale misery.

Finally, I fell asleep in my single bed, and woke early. I lay awake there in a fug of dread, my hair stuck to my face by dried tears. I stayed there during the bustle and gentle clanging from

Michelle in the kitchen below, presaging the rising smell of bacon and eggs.

I didn't want to get up. I was terrified of what I might find.

Then came the footsteps in the gallery, amplified by creaking – Morningstar was a *grande dame*, beautiful and luxurious but with arthritic bones that snapped and popped as we crossed her floorboards or clung to her bannisters. At night, her plumbing gurgled and murmured.

'Where's Nina got to?' asked Wolf. His voice shocked me with its suddenness, its loudness. He must have been mere feet from my closed door.

He'd been looking for me, I realized. I froze, not ready, in my unhappiness and dread, to be discovered.

'She's in the blue bedroom.' I recognized Tristan's voice. 'You know. Sarah's old room.'

Who is Sarah? I wondered.

I rose, silent, and stole towards the door, my curiosity piqued.

'Oh right. Are you going into town today, mate?'

'Yeah, yeah, I need to get to the bank with Lucy.' Tristan sounded anxious.

'Great. Can you pick me up some rolling tobacco from the offy? I'm nearly out.'

'Yeah, sure thing, of course.' There was a doubtful edge to this reply.

'I'll pay you back, you know.' Wolf's tone rose in confrontation, as though Tristan had accused him of something. 'And the rest.'

'It's no trouble, Wolf.' Tristan's voice had moved off, his tread heavy on the ancient stairs now. 'Really it isn't.'

There was a beat of silence after Tristan had gone.

'Fucking pillock,' I heard Wolf mutter under his breath.

He must have been standing right next to my closed door now. If he knew this was my bedroom, he must have meant for me to hear him.

Seconds passed as I stood, perfectly immobile, waiting for him to move on. It seemed to take for ever, but eventually the creaking recommenced and he thundered down the worn stairs and away.

* * *

'Ah, there you are!' Lucy bounced up to me and threw her arms around me, kissing my cheek. 'How did you sleep?'

She seemed very happy and animated, her big eyes made up, her long hair a dark red shawl around her.

'Very well, thank you,' I lied. My head felt thick and my heart felt hollow.

'Oh, good, good! Big day today!' She was grinning broadly, and swooped back into her chair at the breakfast table, her white teeth quickly tearing into a slice of buttered toast.

'Is it?'

'Oh, yeah.' She swallowed quickly, brushing at the crumbs on her mouth. 'Don't worry, all will be revealed when Aaron comes down. But first I have to just dart into town with Tristan.' She glanced over at him, caught his eye, and his already ruddy cheeks blushed.

'That's all right, isn't it, Tristan? Today's still good, yeah?'

'Oh, yeah, yeah, it's fine. We'll go after this.' He gestured at his plate with his knife, noticed me and offered me a grin in welcome. 'Morning, Nina.'

At the table, Penelope, still in her dressing gown but with her white-blonde hair pulled up into another flawless chignon, offered me one of her small, cool smiles. 'Good morning, Nina.'

There was, naturally, no sign of Aaron yet, but everyone else was there. Tess chirped out a happy hello from underneath her messy dark-blonde hair and dimples. 'Are you coming into Tonbridge with us, Nina?'

A little flutter of interest moved me. I could call Rosie maybe, try to apologize for my previous behaviour, and then run this recent development past her and see what she thought. I hadn't realized it, but growing within me was a restlessness to talk to somebody from outside, to get some perspective.

Before I could answer, however, Penelope did.

'Lucy and Tristan are going to the bank, Tess.' She did not raise her eyes from her muesli. 'Nobody else.'

'Oh,' Tess's face fell in childlike disappointment. 'I wanted some chocolate. Some Dairy Milk.'

'Ask Lucy and Tristan nicely to pick some up, providing they have time.' Penelope's voice was cold. 'Though it might be an idea to stop gorging on chocolate for a while. You're getting rather plump.'

Tess crimsoned, as did I, in empathetic embarrassment.

Lucy scowled behind Penelope's back.

'You're gorgeous, baby.' Lucy kissed Tess's pink forehead. 'Never change. I'll get you a bar on the way back.'

Penelope ignored this, resuming her breakfast.

I pulled up a chair, hiding my confusion by helping myself to toast and bacon. I felt I wanted to confront Penelope on Tess's behalf, but the moment had passed, and Tess in any case now seemed content, slurping away at her tea.

Mostly, if I'm being honest, I very selfishly didn't want to fight with the others now that my relationship with Aaron felt so suddenly, inexplicably tenuous. But the whole incident troubled me. Having been raised by bullies, I knew what one looked like.

In my self-conscious unhappiness, I forgot to ask the others about Sarah.

* * *

We were to meet in the dining room at noon, Penelope told us archly, as Michelle took our plates away and got on with cleaning the kitchen. We were not to be late.

This was very unusual. We never went in there during the day. We didn't even dine in there.

I was there first, by some accident – the others were downstairs, greeting Tristan and Lucy, who had just returned from town – and I was peering out of one of the three big sash windows, at the grounds beyond.

Normally the room stood empty, cleared of all furniture, completely bare and wooden-floored, with only what looked like a mobile television camera mounted on a tripod in one corner. A case of tapes lay next to it, and nearby, a microphone stood in its stand. I had always assumed it was something to do with Aaron's music career.

I didn't like the camera. There was something plasticky and alien about it. Its single blind eye, facing the empty centre of the room with nothing but the stirred dust to film, gave me the creeps.

'There you are! Little Nina!'

From behind I was swept up into strong male arms, and I shrieked in alarm until I caught the smell of his sandalwood aftershave, that low laughter.

'Aaron!'

'Hey, baby, it's me.' He crushed me to him and kissed me. 'Did you miss me?'

My agony had lasted all night and morning, and it was all I could do not to burst into tears.

'Oh you did! My little Nina, you did. I'm sorry. I just . . . I sometimes need to be alone. It's been so *intense* with you. But we're good, right?'

He had my shoulders and was gazing deep into my eyes.

I nodded, blushing. I had been so stupid. So clingy and desolate, and here, look, nothing was wrong. I felt such a fool. I let him squeeze me in his embrace.

As the others filed up the stairs, he let me go with a final kiss on my chin. 'Time to get to work, right?'

I had no idea what he was talking about, but I nodded enthusiastically anyway.

* * *

'So, the time has come,' said Aaron, addressing the room, 'to get on with the main business of our lives, which is preparing for the ritual.'

Lucy and Tristan let out little cheers, and everybody clapped. The sound reverberated through the high ceiling of the dining room, its emptiness giving everything a strange echo. In a flash of insight I realized that it had been chosen for this; these peculiar acoustics.

What ritual? I wondered.

'Lucy,' he gestured to her and she performed a brief, self-mocking curtsy, 'is going to read the cards tonight and find the best time to perform it. In the meantime, we need to get this place ready. We've got rid of the most obvious negative influences . . .' Here the others' grins faltered as Aaron's expression grew stern. 'This time it has to work.'

Everyone nodded.

I still had no idea what was going on.

'Um, Aaron?'

'Yes?'

'Sorry, I still don't . . . get what we are doing.'

'We're going to perform a ritual, a symbolic marriage that will enable us to get in touch with our deepest subconscious urges.'

I blinked at him. 'I don't understand,' I said. Everyone stared at me. 'What do you mean, a "symbolic marriage"? And isn't the point about subconscious urges that they're subconscious, that you can't control them? I mean . . .' I tailed off, too overwhelmed by their collective conviction to continue.

'We can access our subconscious by using drugs and herbs, which we source naturally,' said Lucy, glancing towards Aaron, who ignored her, keeping his gaze on me. 'We call it the Sacred Draught. It puts us in touch with our untrammelled inner selves, allows us to abandon our consciousness and ego and explore the inner course of our instincts within the context of the ritual.'

Nothing about this explanation reassured me. I, for one, did not want to abandon my consciousness and pursue my untrammelled inner self through the medium of pharmaceuticals. The weed we all smoked was one thing; even Aaron's coke was merely a different mood applied to his normal state of mind.

This sounded like something else. Something unknown.

'You don't want to be involved, Nina?' asked Aaron patiently, but that hidden ring of steel was back again, lurking beneath his calm demeanour.

'I . . . I didn't say that,' I stammered. 'It's just that . . . it sounds very . . . strange. And maybe even dangerous.'

It sounded crazy, to be honest, but I thought it best not to point this out.

'I suppose you could call it strange, but it's not dangerous – or at least not physically dangerous. Everything worth having comes with an element of risk. We're getting in touch with our divine, creative heritage. We are working to manifest the World Soul.' He leaned back and sighed. 'It's worked for me so far. It's worked for all of us.' He fixed me with a look. 'It could work for you, too, Nina. If you let it.'

I didn't know what to reply.

But he was Aaron Kessler, and he was regarding me with those dark, assessing eyes, his lips pursed as though he was concentrating on me, nailing me to the ground with sheer force of will. My heart was pounding, my thighs shaking.

I didn't believe in what he was saying, but I absolutely, positively, believed in *him*. He was the most overwhelming physical and emotional experience I had ever had, an experience that would not be supplanted until the squalling, bloody bundle of you, Sophia, was pressed into my trembling arms by the midwife.

'We would never let you do anything you were uncomfortable with, or that put you in danger. You can observe, if you like, until you're ready to commit.' Lucy smiled and reached across to gently move a stray strand of my hair out of my face.

I swallowed . . .

'No,' he said. 'I can see you retreating. This is a lot to take in, Nina, I know. This is a whole new thing. You don't have to say yes or no right this instant. Think about it for a little while.' His face darkened. 'But by the time Lucy chooses the hour tonight, you're either in or you're out. OK?'

Where else could I have gone, what could I have done? I couldn't let it end yet. Which is what refusal would have meant, I knew.

'You don't have to worry about me. I'm in.'

Aaron came over and wrapped me in his arms, while the others cheered and clapped and embraced us both. 'This is great, baby, just great,' he murmured. 'We couldn't do it without you. You're the missing piece of the puzzle.'

'Uh . . . thanks . . .'

'Go with Penelope and she can tell you what needs to be done.'

'Sure . . .'

I followed Wolf out of the door, Tristan and Tess ahead, Penelope leading the way. Tristan was pressing a bar of Dairy Milk into Tess's hands behind Penelope's back, and they both giggled quietly.

But as I was leaving I heard Lucy murmuring to Aaron. 'The bank went OK. He signed the forms and they accepted them. The cash will take a little while to come through, though. Maybe as long as ten days. I'll drive him down and we'll pick it up then.'

'Great,' said Aaron, as though the subject bored him.

'Shall I call Peter? Tell him we've got the money?' Lucy had lowered her voice and, intrigued, I paused just outside the door, pretending to adjust my skirt, while listening in.

'Sure,' said Aaron. 'Do it.'

The mention of Peter stirred my curiosity. Lucy had spoken of Peter when I first arrived.

Nobody had seemed that fond of him at the time. I wondered why.

I was soon to find out.

Chapter Thirteen

After a late dinner we sprawled, as usual, in front of the fire. We did this every night, Sophia. Tonight, however, something was different. The lamps were off and the room was lit by white church candles in a variety of purloined and mismatched candelabras. Lucy, with a newfound primness, carefully carried in a carved wooden box and seated herself in front of the fire.

'This is it!' she said.

She told us to sit around her, close our eyes, join hands and focus on her. This we did. Penelope's hand in mine was hard and chilly, like a doll's hand. Wolf's, however, was large and sweaty, and he gripped mine tightly. A little too tightly.

I tried to dismiss him from my thoughts and concentrate.

When we were told we could open our eyes, Lucy had opened the box and three tarot cards lay on a swatch of black silk before her.

Lucy spread her hands above the cards, as though they were coals warming her.

'The message is clear. The ritual must take place in twenty-one days . . .'

I was not entirely ignorant of the Tarot. Rosie had tried to teach me a little. That said, I couldn't make out how the cards had said what Lucy thought they meant. 'What does the fact that it's upside down mean? That card, the Knight of Swords?' I asked.

Aaron's brows flexed at me in displeasure.

'What?' Lucy snapped, surprised at the question. The disapproval of the others was palpable. I had a sudden sense of myself as the neophyte trying to undermine her, undermine them.

'Oh, nothing,' I said, falling silent.

Tristan reached over and discreetly patted my arm to re-assure me.

'So who's the focus?' asked Penelope, sitting upright and wind-ing her arms around her knees. 'The Receiver?'

There was a brief pause while Lucy pulled out another card – this one a Princess of Wands.

'It's Wands,' said Lucy. 'So it's me.'

There was a tiny burst of clinked glasses at this.

'Hooray for Lucy!' said Tess, and the others cheered and drank. In the scattered conversation that erupted afterwards, I turned to Tristan and gently tugged on his sleeve.

'I don't understand,' I said quietly. After my humiliation before, I was reluctant to approach any of the others with my questions, even Aaron. 'What's going to happen at this ritual?'

He ran his fingers through his golden hair. 'Well . . .' He glanced uneasily over his shoulder. Penelope's attention was focused on us, her pale brows lowering. The change in Tristan was sudden, startling. 'Oh, I don't know . . . really Aaron or Lucy should be explaining this to you.'

'Nina's instruction will begin tomorrow,' said Aaron. I nearly jumped. I hadn't the slightest idea he'd been listening to us. 'So there's no need for more questions now.'

'Right,' said Tristan nervously. 'I wouldn't want to do anything out of place.'

'No, you wouldn't.' Aaron rose from his chair and beckoned to me. 'Come on. Sleep well, everybody.'

* * *

That night I lay next to Aaron in his giant bed, the sweat drying on my skin. The night was low, cloudy and close, the moon a smudge of distant light through the window. In the background, 'Child-hood's End' from *Green Eyed Monster* started playing on the tiny, hugely expensive CD player he kept in his bedroom.

It was the one song on the debut Boarhounds album that Aaron hadn't sung on.

He lay on his back, cupping the end of his cigarette with one large brown hand, which he lit with a golden Zippo. Burning tobacco joined the scents of sex and joss sticks in the room.

Noticing which song was on, he reached towards the bedside table, grabbed the remote and quickly skipped it forwards so that 'Mean River' started playing.

'You always do that,' I murmured from my pillow.

'What?'

'You fast-forward through "Childhood's End". You never—'

'Why would I want that arsehole Geoff Carter singing in here?' His bitterness was raw, acidic enough to etch glass. He dropped the lighter back on to the bedside table. 'He can't even hold a tune.'

It was the first time I had ever heard Aaron directly criticize anyone. Normally, he just talked vaguely of 'negative influences'.

I knew who Geoff Carter was. He was one of the Boarhounds' founding members. I had seen his picture all over the house, in any group photo of the band. He was a smallish, slender man with a sandy ponytail, invariably dressed in tidy new blue jeans and a checked shirt.

'Geoff Carter. What a cunt,' muttered Aaron. That cold, steely tone was back. 'He's desperate to destroy me.'

'Oh,' I said. I had no idea how to reply. No one had ever said that word to me out loud in conversation before. It's practically mainstream now, but back in the Eighties it existed in some Neverland beyond the F word.

The world was still young then. When I was sixteen, Daddy had nearly slapped me for saying 'bloody hell' to him.

Aaron lay back and let smoke plume out of his nose. I had wanted to start smoking – the others did, except for Penelope – but Aaron had remarked, in a seemingly offhand way when I mentioned it, that he loved the fact that I didn't taste of smoke when he kissed me, so that was that.

'It doesn't matter,' I said, shifting towards him. 'The solo album will be huge. He'll be so jealous. I'm sure he's already sorry you left.'

'Hmm . . .' said Aaron. He sucked in smoke again.

The solo album, provisionally titled *The Magus*, played constantly in the background during our days and nights. Lucy danced before the fire to the slow ballads, and the others nodded along to its beats in the car or kitchen.

I nodded and danced too, praising it effusively along with everyone else. But in my private, secret self, I dreaded the moment it was put on, usually on Lucy's suggestion. The fact was, I didn't like it. It was ponderous, thudding, but also thin-sounding; Aaron's voice was a low groaning in it, the high notes escaping him with embarrassing ease, leaving him squeaking in pursuit, and the lyrics were facile, boring – nothing like the sexy, slow-burning innuendo of *Green Eyed Monster*.

There wasn't a single discernible tune on the whole thing. And I had heard it over and over and over. If there were one, I would know about it by now.

You might be wondering right now, my dearest heart, how I handled learning my idol had feet of clay, or at least a tin ear. The short answer is, I didn't learn. Or rather, I rationalized it away, as I did much else – after all, I told myself, I understood nothing about rock music.

Yes, it was true, there were tracks from the Boarhounds which I enjoyed, but the Boarhounds were so much more commercial and sold-out than Aaron – mere pap for the masses, as Penelope drawlingly described it. Aaron was operating on a much higher plane.

'You think the solo album will be a hit?' he asked, tapping his cigarette into his glass paisley-printed ashtray. His tone was flat and bored, but not enough to hide his need.

His vulnerability stirred a deep tenderness within me.

'I know it,' I said.

I simply couldn't understand his genius properly, I decided, and the fault was mine, not his. Plenty would understand it, in time. Perhaps, with practice, so would I.

'I have so many enemies, Nina.' He sighed and exhaled more smoke. 'You wouldn't understand, in your sweet, simple little world, but I do. So much envy, so much doubt . . .' He closed his eyes, and for a long moment I enjoyed the unguarded spectacle of him.

The silence deepened, lengthened.

'We all have to band together, Nina,' he breathed, reaching out to ruffle my hair. 'I told you, when you first came here, that we have to *deserve* revelation. To do that, we have to live communally. Love communally.'

'Yes,' I said.

'And that demands big, big sacrifices, sometimes. Things that might hurt us. But it's for the greater good.'

His eyes were still closed.

'Yes,' I said, but a little prickle of anxiousness was stirring at the nape of my neck. The close air was chilly now on my bare skin.

'The bonds between us – they need to be strong. Reinforced.' He opened his eyes and looked at me. 'Can you do that?'

'Of course.' I had no idea what he meant.

'You're sure?' he asked.

'Of course I'm sure. I love you. I'd do anything for you.'

His eyebrows raised and he let out a bitter snort. 'People have said that before, Nina. Actions speak louder than words. We have to give all we can to the work.'

'Just tell me what to do.' I reached out and stroked the perfect muscles of his arm. 'I'll do it.'

There was a long pause. 'OK,' he said. 'We need to pool our love, our resources, our energy.' He sucked in more smoke. 'Primarily sexual energy,' he said.

He kept looking at me.

'I d-don't understand,' I said, but horribly, I thought I was beginning to.

'It's important,' he said, slowly and clearly, so there was no mistake, 'that we don't get hung up on exclusive attachments. As one of the focuses of the ritual, I need to share that energy with the others.'

'I see,' I breathed. My chest felt crushed.

'We need to share. To become more than the mundane. To become more than we are.' His voice was rising again in that declamatory way.

'I . . .'

'Oh, little Nina. I know this is hard for you. But it will make you grow so much as a person.'

'I . . . I see.' I didn't know what else to say. 'But I don't know if I could . . . you know, sleep with the others . . .'

'Baby, you don't have to do anything you're uncomfortable with. It's enough that you understand it. That you understand my role.'

I didn't answer, but I didn't have to. He had stubbed out the cigarette and was leaning over, taking me in his arms, and his mouth was on my own, swallowing up any further questions I might have. He tasted of smoke. 'You'll see,' he said, raising his head for a second to pierce me once more with those dark eyes. 'And it will be beautiful, Nina. Trust me.'

Chapter Fourteen

This is so much harder than I imagined it would be, Sophia. It's almost impossible to describe to someone who wasn't involved what the experience of being in that house, in the Order of Ascendants, was like.

It was an all-involving lifestyle – Aaron provided everything for us, and very quickly we became infantilized; rarely sober and dependent upon him for so many things; for his approval, his conviction that we were all special, gifted, meant to be together. I'd noticed that the sunlight of his love was every day becoming just a tiny smidgeon harder to obtain – vanishing like the end of a rainbow into a hazy distance; retreating as you walked towards it.

He was sure of me now. He no longer had to work at seducing me. It was up to me to do the running.

We were standing in the dining room, my back to the camera on its tripod. Together we would perform the ritual in this very room. We would rehearse in the mornings, so I could learn the proper words. A large part of this rehearsal would involve meditation to 'open me up' to the 'creative energies' that the chants would raise.

'We have our own special chants that Aaron has devised,' said Lucy. She was looking rather self-satisfied in her floaty black skirt, her eyes huge with kohl. She was wearing her talisman and tiny silver ankh earrings. I think she was enjoying being in a position to school me.

Nobody had offered me one of the order's talismans yet – the circle with a cross in it. Tristan's was visible whenever he leaned over, and Penelope's gold talisman usually nestled somewhere under her high-necked frilly Princess Di blouses.

I was too shy to ask when I would get my own. Presumably once I mastered whatever Lucy was going to teach me, and I became a fully functional member of the order.

Wolf didn't seem to have one either, or if he did he didn't wear it.

'What does Wolf do?' I asked, curious.

'Wolf chronicles our spiritual journey,' said Aaron, with a drawl that was becoming more and more common, the one that signalled the conversation was boring him. As if I was boring him.

'Like a reporter?'

'No,' said Aaron, while Lucy's expression underwent a strange change, her bright coral-painted lips thinning. 'Wolf films the ritual.' He waved towards the camera on its tripod.

'*Films* it?'

'Yes,' said Lucy. 'All iterations of the ritual are taped for posterity.' She didn't meet my eyes when she said this. 'It's so that we can capture any spoken revelations during the ritual that we can't remember later.'

'Oh,' I said. 'Cool.' I felt uneasy. Lucy was, if nothing else, enthusiastic about everything at Morningstar, Aaron's cheerleader-in-chief. She was the good cop to Penelope's genteelly sneering bad cop. That said, she did not seem particularly happy about Wolf and his role, and furthermore, I could tell Aaron sensed this about her and that it was making him angry again. That icy disapproval radiated out of him, and I knew that whatever happened we needed to stop making him feel that way.

'So are there a lot of tapes?' I asked brightly. I could hear the rising lilt in my voice – this ebullient chatter was exactly how I used to deflect Daddy's bad moods at home.

'A few,' growled Aaron.

Lucy remained silent.

'The taping isn't always successful. We've suffered from the negative forces that some members bring. It's vital,' he continued, eyeing Lucy as he spoke, 'that we work hard on the meditations so that these negative, wheedling forces of doubt and negativity are crushed. We can't expect revelation while we're whining and second-guessing the process.'

'Absolutely,' agreed Lucy. 'If Nina has problems with the ritual being filmed, that creates problems for everyone, not just herself.'

'You don't have to take part if you don't want to,' said Aaron to me, as though I was too painfully stupid to be bothered with. 'I have important things to do. Lucy, you carry on.'

'Of course.'

And out he went, leaving me alone with her.

'Now, first of all . . .'

I blinked, wondering whether I had missed something. Some-how, right before my eyes, Lucy's reluctance about the camera had been transmuted into mine, and I was in trouble with Aaron over it.

You'd think I'd have said something, but I was too powerfully confused and taken aback. I wasn't sure what had just happened.

It was a feeling I would grow more and more used to.

* * *

Ten days after Lucy and Tristan's trip to the bank, we were sitting together in the kitchen around the oak table when the news about the money came through. It was about four o'clock. Aaron had been in London to talk to his agent about his solo album. He'd returned and gone upstairs, and we were waiting for him to come back down and join us.

We were always a little lost, aware of ourselves as lacking, when he wasn't with us.

Over time, it was becoming clearer to me what everyone's role was. Penelope managed Aaron's business affairs. It was she who answered the phone, her impeccably spoken 'Hello?' soft and yet capable of being heard in nearly any room of the house. It was she who booked the car, organized his diary, read his post – either at the breakfast table or in his private study, a place on the upper floor near his room which I had never been admitted to.

Lucy recruited newcomers and trained them.

Wolf was allegedly the photographer, though I never saw him with the camera. As a rule, he sat about and smoked endlessly with the other men, sometimes jamming with Aaron on his instruments, can of beer in hand.

Tess's role was still hidden, unless it was simply that of mascot, but this evening I was about to find out what purpose Tristan served.

Michelle had cooked us a lasagne for later, and we had cooed over the crates of champagne and other treats that had been pre-emptively ordered in anticipation of Aaron's return.

Tristan had been telling a story about how he'd first met Lucy.

'It was Glastonbury, I think,' he said.

'Who knows?' said Lucy, sitting cross-legged on the stool near the door, enjoying the attention.

'Somehow I'd lost Xanthe . . .'

'That was your girlfriend's name?' asked Wolf, disbelievingly. '*Xanthe?* Who gets called Xanthe?'

'I think it's a pretty name,' I said.

'You would,' replied Wolf, with a contemptuous snort.

'You're one to talk about names, Mr Wolf,' said Penelope, regarding him through lowered lashes and offering him a small smile. 'What's *your* real name?'

'Mind your own business,' he said curtly.

'So, while I was there,' continued Tristan, 'I got talking to some other guys at the chillout tent, and one of them was Lucy—'

'FUCK!'

It was Aaron, upstairs in the master bedroom, which was on the other side of the house. His roar thundered through the long gallery and barrelled down the stairs alongside the crashing sound of some object being hurled with immense force against the wall.

'FUCKING FUCK!'

We all froze. In the resulting silence I could hear the kitchen clock timer ticking, the tiny burning hiss of Wolf's perpetual spliff as it flaked into ash.

We all looked at Lucy, who appeared lost. The colour had drained from her face, and her red lipstick looked like dead blood. She in turn cut her eyes at Penelope, and without another word the two of them vanished into the hall, where we heard the stealthy creak of them mounting the stairs.

We waited a few seconds, straining to listen.

'What is it, do you think?' asked Tess, wide-eyed.

'Bad news,' said Wolf. 'That's what I think.' He looked at Tristan, who had gone sheet-white. 'You sure there wasn't a problem at the bank when you went, mate?'

Tristan stood up and rushed out as well.

Wolf watched him go, and Tess followed Tristan to the door, peering up after him before disappearing herself.

'What's going on?' I asked.

Wolf grinned nastily. 'I think Tristan's family have turned the tap off, love, that's what I think.'

'What do you mean?'

He raised a dark eyebrow and waggled it. 'Who do you think pays for all this?' He gestured around theatrically, bottle of Pils in hand.

'Aaron does, right?'

He smiled thinly, shaking his head. He leaned forward, stealing a glance towards the door the others had melted through. 'You reckon, eh?'

I was completely confused, as though I was being told a joke and didn't understand the punchline. 'Of course he does. Aaron's rich. He's got this house, he's a star . . .'

'A star?' Wolf drummed his heels against the legs of his chair in mock excitement. My naivety obviously delighted him. 'Yeah, a *star*! With one album behind him, just before he got his spoiled, prima donna arse fired from the band?' Wolf laughed. He reached into the pocket of his denim jacket and pulled his tobacco tin out. 'He lives *waaaaaay* beyond his means, petal. He's spent every penny he owns and he's not getting another cheque till February. And the taxman will be having all of that.'

'What do you mean?'

'He's broke, that's what I mean.' He was putting together yet another roll-up. 'Not a pot to piss in.'

'No.'

He nodded. 'Yes.'

'But how . . . that doesn't make any sense.'

'Tristan's paying, the daft fucking twat. The thousand-pound brandy, the food, the lights, the firewood, even the rubber johnnies. This used to be Tristan's house. Aaron's his *guru*.' His head leaned in to mine, and I smelled the mixture of cannabis and sweat on him as he whispered, 'Tristan's parents were killed a couple of years ago in a car crash. He's from this crazy-wealthy family, just in case you couldn't tell. They'd set up a trust fund in case they died, like rich people do, so Tristan couldn't touch it till he was twenty-one. He was wandering around the festival scene, like a little lost puppy, when he met Lucy, who then put him on to Aaron. What can I tell you?' He shrugged, as though enjoying himself. 'Tristan got the first part of his payout sometime in June this year. Thirty thousand pounds and the deeds to this house. Signed it straight over to Aaron.' Wolf opened his hands and made a little *poof* sound. 'Five months later. All gone.'

I was speechless.

'Of course, there was always a risk,' said Wolf, 'that the people running Tristan's trust would do their fucking nut if they found out what had happened. But what can you do?' Wolf shrugged again. 'No fucker's got a gun to his head.'

This conversation was like a punch in the gut, and I hated him, perhaps more than I have ever hated anyone in my life. How dare he tell me these things about Aaron?

'I'm sure Aaron has every intention of paying Tristan back,' I said stiffly.

Wolf snorted out a little laugh. 'Yeah, love,' he said. 'You keep believing that. The real question, of course, is how Aaron is going to pay Peter.' He blew out a long stream of smoke, as though very pleased with himself. 'Because Aaron also owes Petey, and Peter Clay does not offer credit.'

'Peter?'

'Oh yeah.' He screwed his face up, as though tasting something bitter. 'Peter. You've got that special pleasure still to come.'

* * *

At breakfast, Tristan had been like a ghost, and Penelope silent and chilly, as though we had all collectively offended her in some deep and unforgivable way.

I reported to Lucy in the dining room.

Through the week, I was being taught to chant and meditate. This had been going on since Lucy had set the date for the ritual, and attendance was compulsory, at least for Tess, Penelope, Lucy, Tristan and me. There was never any sign of Aaron or Wolf.

It had been drilled into me by Lucy and the others that for the 'ritual energy' to work we all had to 'open ourselves up' psychically, which involved sitting in the lotus position and chanting lengthy prayers I barely remember now, containing phrases such as 'To you I pray most earnestly/That I be filled with creativity', often for hours at a time.

The others seemed to find this experience euphoric, even sublime, reporting that they'd had small epiphanies or felt lifted out of their bodies. This never happened to me, not once – all I felt was bored and sore from sitting in the same position all the time, though I was careful to never let this show, to keep the same elated smile on my face as the others. Lucy, however, was not fooled, and I was constantly being singled out for extra 'training'.

I would never have admitted it to myself at the time, even under torture, but looking back I could see that there was, in these chants and songs, the same leaden phrasing and puerile rhyming as in Aaron's solo album.

'The others have already mastered this, Nina. Now come on. Try again,' said Lucy.

Lucy didn't seem impressed with my progress, and increasingly when I entered a room where she already was, the conversation would either stop or turn low. I couldn't even solicit Aaron for reassurance – Lucy, Penelope and Tess were sharing his bed now on different nights, and I rarely saw him, except in the evenings, alongside the others.

My misery bloomed, sprawling out of me. I had only myself to blame, this was becoming clear from everyone's reactions.

What if I was becoming the thing the others most feared – a negative influence?

My loyalty to Aaron remained absolute, perhaps even growing stronger in his absence, and when I did see him it was as though my tedious lessons with Lucy, and Penelope's constant supercilious snipes, were the dream, and my nights with him, the reality.

Then morning would come, and things would crash back down to earth.

That day I was particularly distracted, as I knew the others were going into town and I had been desperate to join them. A longing had risen in me lately to call Rosie, to talk to another human, to run my situation past her. It wasn't something I could do at Morningstar as we were always together, always watched.

I would even have spoken to my parents. Lucy had urged me to write a postcard a week or so ago, to tell them I was staying with friends and not to worry. It was important they didn't show up and start interfering with my 'spiritual training', and no amount of explaining that this was the very last thing they would do would satisfy her. Cowed, I'd written the card, and it had been plucked out of my hand and surrendered to Penelope.

As far as I know, they never responded.

At breakfast, Penelope had quickly squashed the idea of me joining the trip to town, with one of her cruel little smiles. 'Don't you have practising to get on with, Nina? I hear you still need work.'

That was that.

'Try the chant one more time . . .' Lucy said, with a disgusted sigh. She never gave advice, merely scowled when I got it wrong. 'It's going to be even harder to get right once you're doing it for real . . .'

'You know, Lucy, maybe it would be easier if I could watch one of Wolf's tapes.'

'What?' She seemed stunned by this suggestion, verging on sudden fury. 'Why?'

'Well,' I said anxiously, 'if I could watch what other people do during the ritual, it might help.'

'What do you want to watch the tapes for?' she asked, her voice loud and strident. A spreading red rash appeared above her low-cut top. 'You'd be far better off paying attention in here. I have better things to do than this, you know, Nina. I have *lots* of other demands on my time. I'm doing you a favour and if you're going to be ungrateful—'

'No, not at all! I just thought it might . . . you know, help.'

'Has Wolf put you up to this?' The redness was moving up her throat.

'No.'

'What's going on in here, then?'

Without us noticing, the dining-room door had opened and a strange man stood on the threshold. He was heroin-thin, with a round pot belly and lined skin. Though he had greying hair, cut in a mullet, he was dressed much younger, in a bright geometrically patterned jacket with huge asymmetric lapels and white Converse high-tops.

He didn't look to me like someone who shot a lot of hoops.

'Hello, Peter!' sang out Lucy, lifting up that come-hither smile. She might have seemed pleased, but I could tell she wasn't happy.

I offered him a cheerful 'Hello.'

He looked me up and down with saggy yellowing eyes of indeterminate colour, then turned to Lucy. 'So this is Sarah's replacement, then?'

'Who?' asked Lucy, without skipping a beat. Her expression didn't change.

'Like that, is it?' He grinned at me. 'How d'you fall in with these mad bastards?'

I didn't know how to reply. I literally didn't know the answer to that question.

In any case, he was talking to Lucy again. 'Is he in?'

'Aaron? No, no,' she said. 'He went out shooting. We weren't expecting you until this evening . . .'

'Out shooting. Yeah, right, Luce. Lazy twat is probably still in bed. Has he got my money?'

I felt like I'd been slapped. Nobody spoke about Aaron like that. Wolf had wounded my sense of Aaron, and for some reason, instead of inspiring me to see reason, it merely ignited my furious loyalty. Aaron needed me. He was beset on all sides. Negative influences did indeed surround him.

An invisible fist of rage bloomed inside me. If he said anything else . . .

'I thought you were still in Germany,' said Lucy.

'Nah. I got back from Stuttgart early, drove over from Heathrow.' He looked at me again. 'So, what's your name, New Girl?'

'Um, Nina.'

'Nina, is it?' He grinned, his gaze travelling up and down me again. 'Very nice to meet you, *Nina*.' His attention settled on my chest. 'Yes, very nice.'

Chapter Fifteen

The odious Peter stayed for the next four days, which soon adopted a similar pattern. We'd decamp upstairs and he'd get high with Aaron and the boys. Sometimes they'd jam together on Aaron's instruments. We girls would sit on the floor around them, fetching drinks and pretending to laugh at his jokes.

Then, at about one in the morning, he'd choose a girl, usually Tess, and retire for the night.

But on the second night Peter had shown a lot of interest in me. After that first evening, when he'd called me Knockout Tits all night, Aaron had explained to me in his most earnest, intense way that Peter had always been, despite his rough but honest manner, a father figure to him. He loved him with all his heart.

'He's his drug dealer,' Wolf had said when we'd discussed it later alone. 'That's all you need to know.' He'd gestured with his ever-present spliff and grinned. 'You girls – you're a fringe benefit for the pusher man.'

* * *

In fact, on that second night, Peter had remarked that I was the only one he hadn't had sex with.

Aaron hand-waved this away. 'Nina's new, man. She doesn't know you.'

'This is a good chance for her to get to know me! Biblically!' Peter had grinned, revealing his blackened cracked teeth.

I had offered a slightly bemused smile, as though this were all a joke, while inside I felt a kind of sick, falling sensation.

But on the third night, when Peter had mentioned it again, Aaron had seemed to pause and glance over at me, almost assessingly.

Something about my horrified face must have made him change tack.

The next morning, I found myself alone with Lucy as we tidied up the empty glasses and bottles in the long gallery. The others were mysteriously absent.

'You know, Nina,' said Lucy, with that careful, prim enunciation of hers that presaged a lecture, 'it's rather selfish to keep expecting the rest of us to entertain Peter.'

'Aaron told me, when I first came here, that I didn't have to do anything I didn't want to.' I had been up preparing this defence since five o'clock that morning. 'Anyway, Peter isn't even a member of the order.'

'I know, I know,' said Lucy, taking my hand as if in sympathy. 'But Aaron is still very fond of him, and it makes Peter happy when we . . . take care of him. Which makes Aaron happy. You know that Aaron is under huge, huge stress at the moment.'

I didn't reply.

'Don't you want to help Aaron out? I mean, we both know he's been very good to you.'

I felt heartsick, hollow. Appearing selfish to Aaron was a horrifying prospect.

'Anyway, you have to do what you think is right,' said Lucy, letting me go, reaching down to pick up an overflowing ashtray. Her face changed into something harder. 'But there are no free rides here. We're all expected to contribute to the work.'

'How is sleeping with Peter part of the work?'

'Aaron needs to be supported. He needs to be free to concentrate on all of this important stuff.' Lucy turned on her heel, ashtray in hand. 'So think on.'

I looked at the ashtray. 'What are you doing with that? Won't the cleaners take care of the ashtrays?'

Lucy seemed to expand, suddenly furious. 'What, are you too lazy to clean up after yourself too?'

'Sorry?'

'Aaron sent the cleaners away. Yesterday was their last day. *We'll* be doing the cleaning from now on.'

'What? Why?'

Lucy snarled. 'Because they were whispering about him. Because they were spreading all this negative energy. The next time we do the ritual, it has to work, and everything that doesn't contribute will have to go, do you understand? There can't be dead weight.'

I could come up with no reply.

'Do you understand, Nina?' Lucy's face was red, her eyes bright.

I swallowed hard. I might have been naive, but even I knew that this whispering and negative energy had not come from the cleaners, but from the coke that Peter constantly offered Aaron. And, as I'm sure you, darling girl, have already guessed, since you were always much cleverer than me, the cleaners had been dismissed because the income from Tristan's trust fund had dried up and we couldn't afford to pay them any more.

Nevertheless, a little shiver went through me.

'Yes, I understand.'

* * *

After my miserable day of solitary meditations and chanting (Lucy had professed to be 'too busy' to manage me) I had finally been released. Avoiding her, I'd gone upstairs to sit cross-legged on the floor in the long gallery, which was one of the few rooms where we still kept the fire going all day. Wolf lounged opposite me, rolling up a very small spliff. Supplies were evidently running low.

Outside the leaded windows, swirling snow brushed the glass, and the roaring fire felt good, almost a little too hot, at my back. The sky was dimming – it was four o'clock in the afternoon, and the cards were becoming harder for me to see on their pool of black silk.

'Right,' said Wolf, peering down at the three tarot cards I'd pulled from the deck and spread out on the little swatch of silk. 'What have you got?'

'It's the Star, the Emperor, and the Three of Swords.'

'Anything else you want to tell me?' asked Wolf, sticking the spliff between his lips and quickly lighting it. His familiarity with tarot cards was one of many quixotic things about him, since he professed to believe in nothing.

I stroked my chin and thought. 'The Emperor's reversed.'

'Which means?'

'Um . . .'

'An insecure and controlling man.' He put his hands behind his head and scrubbed at his scalp. 'So, the question was, will Aaron's ritual be successful this time? And the answer is . . . ?'

'I don't know.'

'It means it won't work. It's never going to work.' He shrugged. 'But I could have told you that anyway.'

Wolf did not have anything like the sense of investment that the rest of us did. He just filmed everything. The others seemed ambivalent about this. Whether they were conflicted about the idea of filming the ceremony, or they just didn't like Wolf, wasn't clear.

As to whether *I* liked Wolf, I was never quite sure I knew the answer to that either. We had Morningstar in common. Beyond that, in our Garden of Eden, with Aaron as God, Wolf always struck me as a little too happy to play the role of serpent.

I didn't trust Wolf, not really.

But if I'm being honest, by then I didn't trust anyone – I just refused to admit this to myself. I mean, did I believe in the ritual, or the order, or in whether my days chanting and meditating in the dining room in a kind of endless esoteric punishment would do any good? I don't know. The question was irrelevant.

I believed in Aaron, and in throwing everything I could into making him happy.

And yet I couldn't stop these tête-à-têtes with Wolf. There was something grounding in them, something I needed, even if I dismissed the lion's share of what he said as envy.

'If you think that,' I asked, 'why are you even here?'

'Where else would I be?' He shrugged and grinned.

'Oi!' came a hoarse male voice from downstairs. 'Anybody in?'

It was Peter.

'We're up here!' Wolf shouted, then he offered me a little apologetic shrug.

There were heavy footfalls on the stairs then, and I picked up the cards, quickly shuffling them back into the pack.

It was indeed Peter, his grizzled head the first thing we saw. He paused on the stairs, blinking at us. He'd been gone for a day and a night, 'taking care of things in town', he'd explained. 'What are you two doing up here alone?'

Wolf shrugged. 'I'm teaching Nina Tarot.'

'I'll bet that's not all you're teaching her,' said Peter, with one of his trademark guffaws. He was walking down the gallery towards us, wet snow falling off his boots. Over his back was slung a cracked leather satchel.

I was careful not to look up as he came over, bringing the cold in with him like a cloud. Wolf, however, got to his feet and they clapped each other's shoulders.

'How's things?' asked Wolf.

'Good, good. London is a fucking madhouse. Everything's frozen solid. Took me two hours to get out of Mile End.' He toed my thigh with the tip of his wet boot. 'Hey, love, run down and get us a cup of tea, eh? I'm parched.'

'Sure,' I said, standing up, careful not to make eye contact. 'Do you want one, Wolf?'

'Yeah, ta.'

'I'll bet he fucking wants one, eh? Eh?' He reached out and smacked my bottom as I passed him, and I offered him a blank, submissive smile; my usual disguise.

Downstairs, I watched the kettle moodily as it began to steam. *A watched pot never boils.* I could hear the men upstairs, talking, not the words but a kind of enthusiastic rising and falling in their tone.

I thought about the ritual, and my greatest fear, the one that my reading with Wolf had stoked rather than calmed: that it wouldn't work. Aaron would not be divinely inspired. He wouldn't get his solo deal.

The demo of *The Magus* was being shopped all over town and Aaron's manager kept sharing exciting snippets of gossip that Penelope would repeat over the dinner table while Aaron nodded amiably next to her ('Louis told me today that Beggar's Banquet loved the second side of the demo!' and 'EMI are going mad over it – they just have to run it past some people Stateside'). It all sounded incredibly hopeful and positive, which always made us cheer.

But none of this ever seemed to materialize into anything as tangible as a contract, or even a meeting.

And the other troubling part was, where was Penelope getting this information from? These were reported conversations, but apparently there were now no telephones in the house – Aaron had ripped them out in a rage over a week ago, roaring that they were nothing but sewer pipes pouring negative influences into the house. I was in the dining room all day with Lucy and would have heard the car going out, so Penelope can't have been using the payphone in the village.

The obvious answer was that there was still a phone in the house, it was just that I wasn't allowed to use it.

I understood that if *The Magus* didn't work it was going to be someone's fault, and with the cleaning staff gone the next logical step, I considered with something like terror, was that he would start weeding out and replacing *us*.

When he was low, or drunk, or both, he had started to refer to this obliquely, watching us with his dark eyes, searching for a reaction.

Now the threat of eviction was being raised, I found it impossible to imagine a life outside of these walls, a life away from Aaron and the others. The university, I presumed, had already kicked me out as I hadn't returned. The postcard I'd written to my parents a fortnight ago had garnered no reply.

The men sat on the seats near the fire, and I handed their tea to them. Outside the snow had worsened.

'Might get snowed in, eh?' Peter was expansive. I waited and waited, as though expecting a beat in music. 'Just us and the candy bag, Knockout Tits.' He shook the satchel.

And there it was. I offered him a wan smile which I carefully judged. I didn't want to look amused and encourage his sallies.

Though, really, I thought with a dull pang, you'd think he'd have got the idea by now. The fact that he still keeps it up is a sign that he knows you're not interested – it's just that it doesn't *matter* that you're not interested.

A spark of flickering anger lit within my breast, and I tried to smother it before I said or did something rash.

'So where's Aaron?' asked Peter.

'I don't know. Upstairs, I think.'

He leaned back in the chair, scratched his thigh through his jeans. 'Go on and fetch him, darling. That's a good girl.'

* * *

Aaron was in bed. I knocked on the door and was greeted with a hoarse 'Enter!'

He was alone for once, scribbling frantically into his black note-book, the sheets around his waist and his fine torso rosy with sleep and warmth.

'Hello, Aaron,' I said, my heart in my mouth as I surveyed him, as it was a thousand times a day. 'Peter's here.'

179

'Is he? Good, good.' Aaron didn't look up or stop writing. His voice was fast, almost high. On the nightstand next to him, a pair of rolled-up five-pound notes lay in a residue of white dust. 'Can't stop this now. Can you pay him?'

I was astounded. 'Aaron, I don't have any money . . .'

'No, you pay him with *my* money, you dozy cow. The key's in my trousers.' He glanced up at me. 'Sorry, Nina, very important I carry on with this.' He gestured carelessly at his jeans where they hung from the back of a rococo chair. 'The little gold key on the ring. Take two grand out of the safe and give it to him. And make sure you lock it afterwards.'

'OK. Sure, Aaron.'

'And if he asks for more tell him to go fuck himself, right? Use those exact words.'

'OK.' I nodded, but Aaron had turned back to his notebook.

* * *

All in all, I could not have been more thrilled by this trust, but I was also apprehensive. Only Lucy and Penelope were ever allowed in Aaron's study – this was the first time I had even seen inside it.

Feeling like Bluebeard's wife, after a moment of nerves I unlatched the door and walked in. It was a big room under the eaves and frigidly chill as there was no fire burning yet. The irregular oak ceiling beams sloped down to three low leaded windows. Peering out of one, I could see the blizzard had calmed, but snow was still falling, and below the hedges were heavily frosted with white, the grass a featureless pale plain. I could see my silhouette on it, as I stood against the window, as though I was a shadow puppet in a play.

But I had a purpose, and it wouldn't do to look as if I was dawdling in Aaron's private place, as much as I wanted to leaf through the untidy piles of papers stacked on his desk – many of them bills with bright red numbers printed at the bottom, together with the words 'FINAL NOTICE' – or linger over the collection of framed photos of the band and gold discs on the walls.

I knelt on the deep rug by his little grey antique safe and turned the key in the lock.

Within were bundles of banknotes, roughly fastened with rubber bands, though not very many. As I started to count the money out, losing track every so often and, with a few soft expletives, starting again, putting the notes in piles, I saw that I was making serious inroads into the money that was left.

By the time I had £1,765 in front of me on the carpet, I had cleared a space in the safe, making a small stack of letters visible at the bottom.

I would have reluctantly ignored them, like the papers on his desk, except that as I picked up another of the bundles of cash, underneath it, in a large neat hand, was written 'Ms Nina Mackenzie, Morningstar, Hetherton, KENT'.

I froze, astounded.

I carefully lifted out the letter, forgetting the money. Examining the stamp, I saw it had been posted two weeks ago. On the back, near the top, was written, 'Ms R. Balcombe, Flat 2, 137 Mill Road, Cambridge'.

This letter was from Rosie.

Why was it here? Why hadn't it been given to me?

It was unopened, and squeezing it between finger and thumb, I sensed a fattish wodge of paper – Rosie had written at length.

My first impulse was to tear it open. In fact, my finger was already sliding towards the gap at the corner of the seal . . .

But what if this was a test?

I held it, trembling, at arm's length. I'd been trusted with access to Aaron's office. I'd been trusted with the safe keys. I knew that whatever was written within this letter, it was going to be critical of Aaron and the others.

He must have known that I would see the letter. It was unthinkable that he could have just forgotten and sent me in to find my purloined post. Even now, he could be in his room, waiting to see what I would do. He'd looked very preoccupied, but . . .

It must be a test.

Suddenly there was a burst of muffled shouting, a furious female storm. It seemed to be coming from the direction of Aaron's room, though I could make out no words, nor understand the hoarse burr of his reply.

Penelope. And she was raising her voice, which she never did – screaming, in fact.

My heart clenched. This could mean nothing good.

Abruptly it stopped. There was a whirlwind of flying footsteps heading towards the office door. Reluctantly, I slid the letter back, just as the door flew open and she burst in.

She stood in the doorway, glaring, and her long white-blonde hair seemed to snake about her in rage. Her face was pale and pinched.

'What are *you* doing in here?'

Alarmed by her obvious passion, I shrugged helplessly. 'Aaron asked me to—'

'What are you doing in the *safe*?'

'Aaron asked me to pay Peter. He gave me the keys—'

'Get out! Get out, do you hear me? Never go in there!'

Penelope flew forward, grabbed my wrist and hauled me up. As her hand connected I felt not just Penelope's anger, but also, in a kind of trembling undercurrent, her fear.

'Let go of me right now!' I snapped, yanking my arm out of Penelope's grasp. 'Aaron told me—'

Penelope slapped me across the face.

The shock was worse than the pain. I raised my hand to my cheek, stunned. Nobody had hit me since I was a little girl. Nobody. Even in his very worst excesses, Daddy had smashed my possessions in front of me, but he had never laid a finger on me.

'Get out!' shrieked Penelope, spittle landing on her lips. '*Out!*'

* * *

I stumbled out, running for Aaron in the master bedroom, sobbing. I ran past Wolf and Peter, who called for me to slow down, stop. I banged furiously on the studded wood and iron door, calling his name, to no response.

I tripped down the spiral staircase, nearly falling. I could hear the voices of the others in the converted dining room, raised in some kind of excited debate, but when I walked in, everyone fell silent.

They were standing in a semi-circle, ranged against me. Penelope stood on the end, still shaking with adrenaline, her arms crossed over her chest.

'Money is missing from the safe.' Aaron's face was a closed book.

'What?'

'You stole the keys.'

'*What?*'

'Where is it?'

'I don't . . . You *gave* me the keys, Aaron, you said to pay Peter . . .'

Nothing changed in his expression as I said this. The others crowded more closely together, their disgust with me palpable.

Everything was becoming unreal.

'Where is it?' barked Penelope. 'Where did you hide it?'

'Hide what . . . ?'

'Search her,' said Aaron, almost wearily.

'*What?*'

Penelope lunged at me, tearing at my clothes, while Peter sniggered in the background. My dress was ripped at the shoulder as Lucy came forward, too, and grabbed me.

'Where's the money, Nina?' asked Lucy, sorrowful rather than angry.

'I . . . This is crazy! I haven't taken any money . . . Aaron, you *gave* me the keys!'

His face didn't change; if anything, it hardened.

'Nina, you're going to admit to this one way or another. Where's the money?'

I could no longer even plead my case; I was too confused to

answer. He knew I had stolen nothing. Penelope – all of them – knew I had stolen nothing. They would never even have had time to count the money, never mind notice any was missing. What was—

'Put her in the barn.' Aaron made a dismissive gesture.

Hands were upon me – Lucy, Penelope, Tess and Tristan, yes Tristan, had grabbed me, and Wolf was opening the front door. The first blast of the cold night hit me, the darkness and its banks of snow, and I burst into tears as they dragged me to the barn, threw me in and locked the door.

'Let me out of here!' I screamed. 'Let me out!'

Barefoot, in my ripped dress, I lay on the cold concrete, weeping.

Now that I was alone, I couldn't shake the sense that if they all thought I'd stolen money, then that *must* have been what happened.

Why else would I be here? Nothing about this made any sense, and by default, when things didn't make sense I assumed the problem was me.

I rolled into a sitting position and got up. I was in complete darkness and freezing cold, but I knew there was a light switch somewhere.

I stumbled carefully towards the walls, feeling them with my hands, every so often my palm slapping against dusty cobwebs or sharp steel edges.

I found the door. There was a tiny gap between it and the jamb, and by pressing my eye to it I could make out a sliver of the house and the golden light coming from the windows.

My fingers suddenly discovered the old-fashioned plastic switch. I clicked it on and the shed was flooded with light, revealing the stacked tools lying against the wooden walls all around me.

The floor was chilly beneath my feet, sending shooting pains through them, up my legs. I wiped at my eyes, tried to calm down. Eventually the others would relent, I told myself, and work out they had made an error somehow.

Meanwhile I had to put something between my feet and the freezing floor.

I scanned the walls. There were rakes, machetes and shears hanging from them, and big pieces of equipment covered in tarpaulin – ah, the lawnmower. It was a four-wheeled one, the kind you drove rather than pushed. I grabbed the tarp, wrapping it around myself, and sat on the seat.

The tarpaulin was chilly and thin – meant to repel water and dust, not keep abandoned girls from the cold – and the seat was uncomfortable. But my feet didn't hurt so much any more. In fact, they felt, like my fingers, increasingly numb. I welcomed my shivers. They were all that was keeping me warm.

My breath emerged as little white puffs into the still air.

Not long now. They were bound to come soon.

'Oi! You in there?'

I started and nearly fell off the seat. I recognized that voice. It was Peter.

'You going to let me in so you can work off your debt?'

An icy panic filled me, worse by far than the cold. I got up quickly and crept over to the door. There was a latch on the inside, and as quietly as I could I fastened it.

There was the sound of the padlock outside being undone, rattling in the hasp.

Where had he got the key?

The door was tried; once, twice, and then Peter shoved it with all his strength.

Within, the latch jangled hard in its hook. I looked around. Saws, axes and hammers littered the walls. I picked up a sickle and held it before me, watching the wood of the door shake and shudder, like my shivers earlier.

Then it stopped.

'Come on, Nina, open the door. It's time to talk this through.'

Naive I may have been, but I was not fooled. I knew what he was here for, and if I opened the latch I understood that he would rape me.

For a fleeting moment, it all flashed through my head. It was as

185

though I was standing outside of myself and another Nina was speaking in my ear, very slowly and clearly. She told me that the others wanted me to have sex with Peter. They didn't have the money to pay him for everything – Aaron's coke and Wolf's endless weed – and giving him the money out of the safe would have left us destitute. Tristan's money had dried up. Aaron may not have realized this when he gave me the key, but Penelope certainly would have. I'm sure she'd had no trouble explaining to Aaron exactly what she was afraid of as she screamed at him in the master bedroom – the conversation I hadn't been able to hear.

And Aaron needed to keep Peter sweet, by any means necessary.

I stood there, absolutely paralysed, then shook my head. No, it couldn't be true. It was too monstrous. Aaron would never do such a thing.

Would he?

'Fuck it,' I heard Peter mutter after endless seconds of silence. 'Fucking freeze to death, then, you silly bitch.'

I retreated back to the lawnmower.

Time passed.

I grew more and more tired, but I'd stopped shivering, passing instead into a series of strange falling dreams that I kept waking from with a start. At one point, I was sure I'd found Aaron's money, a strange purple bag full of gold doubloons, and when I kicked it over as I fell off the seat of the lawnmower, they spilled out over the concrete. It was good that I'd found them. But when I tried to blink awake to gather them up, I realized that I'd dreamed them, and there was only the sickle, still clasped loosely in my numb hand.

I felt warm now, almost hot. Perhaps it was a fever. I kicked the tarp away and lay down.

The floor wasn't cold any more. This struck me, distantly, as being quite strange, and something within me kept saying: *You're freezing to death*. But I was too tired to move.

Soon I was fast asleep.

Chapter Sixteen

I was back in Morningstar and people were shouting.

I was lying on my back still, but this time it was on a blanket, and I was in front of the fire in the long gallery. Somebody was stroking my forehead, with an almost gloating pressure. I wished they would stop, but I felt too numb to move. And the fire was too hot, though I felt very cold.

'She's waking up.' It was Wolf. It was him touching me, his hand stank of tobacco.

'See? I told you she'd be fine.' Lucy's voice sounded a little trembly but sharp.

I spent the night wrapped up in a goose-down duvet, shivering in front of the fire, my thoughts foggy and wandering – I was so, so cold. Various smiling people brought me hot drinks and brandy (not the *Bisquit Dubouché* – that had long ago been finished off), plumped my pillows where I curled on the chaise-longue they had carried into the gallery for this purpose.

The fire roared, the flames flickering constantly wherever I turned, visible even in the periphery of my vision. Visible even as I dozed.

There was no further mention of the money I was supposed to have stolen.

There was no sign of Aaron.

* * *

Even now, years after the fact, I'm not sure what was going on in Aaron's head. I'm so angry at him still. It would be easy to say that it was all his plan from the minute I knocked on the bedroom door – a set-up – but to be honest, I don't believe that. Not out of any misplaced loyalty, dear heart – I am long beyond that – but Aaron's genius was never in plans, but opportunism. He knew how to *carpe diem*. Out of the materials to hand, he reconstructed the world in his image and according to his desires, and we were all plastic, pliable, more than ready to jump to his command.

He may have been an appalling musician, lyricist and human being, but by God, he had that Creative Spark.

Later Wolf would tell me the real story of that evening, or real as he saw it – Penelope had crashed into Aaron's room that night, perhaps after glimpsing me vanishing into the study, heartbroken and furious that yet again another woman was being handed her privileges. He'd promised her – *promised* her – that Lucy would be the last time.

Most likely the germ of the idea had taken root in Aaron's mind while she was shrieking at him and he hadn't wanted to admit to Penelope that he'd given the keys to me.

He must have realized, on the spur of the moment, that this was a great way not to give Peter two grand. It could always be explained away afterwards as a misunderstanding, a mistake.

I'd play ball, he was probably sure of that. I always had before.

They'd had to break down the barn door with one of the jeeps to get me out.

I had a sense from all the others that this episode had brought them closer to me, had sealed up some hitherto unknown breach.

Whereas to me, the dangerous fracture the cold had made in my devotion now yawned wide and split me in two. On one side there was the Nina who adored Aaron, who yearned for revelation, who wanted to be lifted out of her ordinary life by love and spiritual adventure. And on the other there was the Nina from before, Nina who had studied hard and wanted to read English, perhaps be a poet. A lost, buried me, who came suddenly to the surface, gasping for air and stunned at her newfound liberty.

For the first time in a long while, this Nina was in control.

What are you going to do? asked the other Nina, the docile, quiet one, Aaron's creature.

'I don't know,' I whispered aloud to myself when the others had gone. 'But I'm *not* staying here.'

Chapter Seventeen

They caught me by the gates of Morningstar at dawn. I had waited for the sun before opening the big sash window and crawling out, slipping and sliding on the tiny lip of icy sloped grass at the edge of the moat. I judged the grand creaking of the front door to be too dangerous to risk at that quiet, still hour. The swans on the bank had hissed at me as I pattered round to the drawbridge, both of my bags with my meagre possessions banging against my back, my breath misting in the cold air.

Wolf had been sat on the front step, smoking – his perpetual, omnipresent habit. I had not been expecting him. Why was he awake now?

Had he been keeping watch for me?

Shit.

'Nina . . . what are you doing?'

'What does it look like? I'm leaving,' I said, with a defiance I didn't feel. I shrugged myself into one of the big waxed jackets, which was cold and smelled a little mouldy, and slipped my feet into a pair of wellington boots I'd purloined from the porch while he stared at me.

'What? Where will you go?'

I buttoned up the coat, shoved my shoes into my already over-stuffed bag. 'Dunno.' It was a question that I dared not contemplate the answer to. 'But anywhere's better than here.'

'Wait . . .'

'No, sorry.' I had no interest in speaking to him. I remembered how he'd held the door open while the others carried me out to the barn. 'Have a nice life.'

I strode off quickly, and his calls soon faded, though when I looked over my shoulder, he was gone and the front door was lying open.

I started to run. The wellingtons were too big for me and made me ungainly, the path was slippery with slush.

I took another look over my shoulder, my breath steaming in the air. The sun was getting higher and, despite the cold, it was a beautiful morning.

Then, coming from the direction of the house, I heard the tiny mechanical roar of an engine turning over.

Wolf's told them I'm running, I thought with a tiny flare of rage at such betrayal, but also, oddly, a twinge of gratitude.

Out on the drive, the trees lining the gravel were bare and the fields covered in snow. There was nowhere to hide, and besides, they could probably just about see me from here.

I realized I had no choice but to confront my pursuers.

Within two minutes I could hear the hot growling of a jeep drawing up alongside me as I stomped through the slush.

'Nina!' shouted Lucy. 'Nina!'

It was very hard to look at Lucy. Lucy, I knew, could be persuasive.

'What?' I shouted eventually.

'Where are you going?' Her head stuck out of the jeep window. She had a haunted look, as though she'd seen a ghost, but she could have just been hungover.

'Home. I'm going home.'

'You can't go home,' said Lucy. Her dark brows knitted together. 'Are you mad?'

'I'd be mad to stay,' I snapped back.

The jeep came to a halt, and Lucy jumped out and ran in front of me, holding out her hands as though to slow my progress. 'Nina, please. Please don't leave like this. I know last night was bad.'

'*Bad* is one word. I can think of others,' I said, trying to hold on to my fury at the expense of my fear. '*Criminal* is another.'

'It was horrible, I know. We all know it was. But if you want to go, let's talk about it and do it properly – at the very least we can give you a little cash and a lift to the station. If you're still sure.'

I regarded her silently, my chest heaving. Despite all that had happened, this offer was unbearably tempting – maybe I would see Aaron one last time.

You don't want to see him again, remember? That's why you're leaving. And if he is that keen, why hasn't he come out here himself?

I shook my head a little to clear it.

'At least you can say goodbye to the others. And I know Aaron is desperate to speak to you, to sort things out.' Lucy's eyes were huge, sorrowful, and she took my hand, as she had in the beginning, and tugged me. 'Come on.'

* * *

When I opened the door to his study, I felt it, that old Bluebeard's wife feeling, as if I was in the wrong room and if I were caught there I'd be in trouble. I had to stop my gaze from darting to the safe.

Aaron was sat on the chair in the corner, and from it somehow he seemed to occupy the whole room. I swallowed, tried to meet his gaze, but found I couldn't. He had an instant, almost terrifying effect on me, always – a mixture of fear, faith and a boundless desire.

He was everything I thought I knew about love. It was that simple.

That said, today he was subdued, his shirt buttoned high, as though he was working hard to appear harmless, contrite.

It's a performance, said that newly re-emerged inner voice of mine. *When are you going to get it through your thick head? That's what he does. He performs.*

'You were going to leave,' he said. He looked inexpressibly sad, almost betrayed.

'Yes,' I tried to keep my voice firm. 'I thought that was what you wanted.'

'I never wanted that, Nina,' he said softly.

'Well,' I said, shivering, because in the cold light of day, the habit of contradicting him was a difficult thing to navigate. 'You must have wanted it last night, when you accused me of breaking into your safe and stealing your money.'

'Everyone said a lot of things last night that they regret.' His face had gone very still, and I sensed this was difficult for him. I realized, with a little flash of insight, that this was the nearest I'd ever seen him come to an apology. 'Things everyone said and did to hurt, not things they truly meant. I know I keep telling you how much stress I'm under, Nina. Stress you could barely imagine. Things have to work here, I have to get that deal, and it takes great energy. Sometimes that energy breaks free, you know what I mean? Dark things as well as light are attracted to what we do here.'

'And I have seen these dark things,' I said, with real bitterness.

'Don't be that way,' he said, with a commanding gesture, and I felt again that thrill of terror at contradicting him. 'You know you need me. And now I know I need you. You, more than any of them.'

'You don't need me. I'm here to make up the numbers. I'm here to replace Sarah, whoever she was. Someone smarter than me, I'm guessing.'

He was, just for a moment, absolutely still, as though I'd surprised him. 'Who told you that?' he drawled as though this was a risible notion.

I offered him a tiny, nervous shrug. I had no interest in getting Tristan into trouble. He was probably in enough trouble already now his cash had dried up.

'Can you really understand so little about me? So little about yourself and what you mean to me?' he said, and I could see he was growing impassioned, rising from his chair and coming towards me.

And of course, the sad thing is that he was right, I didn't understand him then. I didn't understand that if anyone was doing the rejecting in our relationship, it had to be him. I didn't understand then that my value to him was conditional – while he was sure of me I meant less than nothing, and when I was walking out the door I was worth my weight in diamonds.

Seconds ticked by, measured by the sonorous clock on the mantelpiece, the flickering of the flames in the fireplace.

'Nina, you must not go. I *need* you. You're a gift I've been taking for granted for far too long. Last night, I realized this. It's so very clear now. It's *you* that needs to be at the centre, not Lucy. You're the strong one. You alone know the way.'

My mouth was dry, my head felt light.

'Me? I don't . . .'

He nodded ferociously. 'It's got to be you and me in the ritual.'

What?

'I don't . . . I don't know what you—'

'I know, I know,' he said, stealing over, soothing me with his hands, caressing my shoulders. 'But you *must* be my Receiver. You're the vessel that will be filled with revelation, don't you see? Already last night was full of revelations – about you, about me . . . there's a light in you that shows me the way.'

'I . . .' I didn't know what to say. 'I don't . . .'

'Don't be afraid. It will be so, so beautiful. The best yet. Come here.'

'But what will happen? What am I supposed to do?'

'I'll show you what to do. You will do what the Creative Spark moves you to do. It will be glorious. Transcendent.'

I was overwhelmed. I was going to be the centre of the ritual. My terror, imprisonment, flight – they had all been worth it. It had all been worth it. I could have wept.

You don't think this is all a little convenient?

'Ah, Nina.' He kissed me, his hands warm beneath my dusty, mouldy coat. 'Everything is going to be perfect.'

It sounded perfect. I had no idea what it actually meant, but it looked like I was staying to find out.

Chapter Eighteen

Wolf was not happy with the new announcement for some reason.

It made him even more foul-tempered than usual, and I felt that he blamed me more than Aaron for the change. There was almost a rage in him when he discovered that the ritual would centre around me now.

But Lucy appeared to bear me no ill will, embracing me as Aaron announced the alteration to the room. Penelope, on the other hand, seemed to be working hard to mask her obvious cold displeasure, but then again, Penelope never recovered from finding me in the safe that day – possibly she never recovered from my coming here in the first place. I noticed that her smirking bullying of Tess seemed to ramp up, as though, since I was now off-limits, she had an excess of stored-up bile that needed to be vented.

And me? I had no idea what was now expected of me. 'The spirit will move you in divine ways,' was all Lucy would say, 'and you will respond to Aaron as the Creative Spark.'

Aaron would only tell me that he and I would be enacting a symbolic marriage. 'You don't need to worry, little Nina,' he said, drawing me into his arms and kissing the top of my head. 'You just follow my lead; you only have to do what you feel comfortable with.'

That was all I was getting.

Everything about it was a source of anxiety. If the ritual failed this time and Aaron didn't get his deal, it would all be down to me. And I was too caught up in it, in them, to realize how monstrously unfair this was, a poisoned chalice I'd be drinking from at the same time as the Sacred Draught, whatever that was.

Perhaps this was why Lucy was so sanguine about giving up her place.

You can leave anytime you want, I told myself, but in truth, I was not so sure. The feeling that I was being watched, and constantly gently probed about my loyalty, was becoming stronger and stronger. At this point I don't think I could have chatted with Wolf the way I had in the past, even if he'd managed to put his inexplicable anger aside.

For now, we were all concentrating on the preparations for the ritual – the morning prayers, the led meditations, Aaron cross-legged in the centre while we sat circled around him, at the compass points. The days filled up with spiritual busywork.

The gender division of labour at Morningstar continued as always. We women cooked and cleaned, fetched mugs of tea and instant coffee for the men upstairs. The men played with the recording equipment, jammed together on Aaron's collection of instruments, or smoked and waited for dinner in the kitchen below.

One good thing came of it though – there was no sign of Peter. I seemed to have scared him off.

* * *

'So, you know what this all entails, do you?' Wolf asked, leaning against the back door. In the moonlight his face was hidden, saturnine. 'You know what it means?'

He'd said he'd help me carry the rubbish from the kitchen out to the compost heap – Michelle the cook had left the week before, after a quietly hissed conversation with Penelope about her continually delayed pay.

His offer had surprised me – we hadn't really spoken since he'd betrayed me on the front steps of Morningstar, and I hadn't shaken the feeling that he was furious with me for some reason I couldn't fathom.

I was still pretty angry at him, too, truth be told.

'Do I know what's entailed in chucking out the peelings?' I asked.

'No, you silly mare. Entailed in the ritual.' Even in the darkness his cynicism was crystal clear.

'I hope so.'

'And you're happy with that, yeah?'

'Happy with what?' I asked.

'Being filmed in your own personal porno with your Magus?'

'What are you on about, Wolf?' I asked irritably.

'What I say. You're going to be engaging in this bloody stupid "divine marriage" with him. Sharing the "Sacred Draught".' He rolled his eyes theatrically. 'Where does he come up with this shit, I wonder?'

'Look, Wolf, I've had this out with Aaron already. I don't have to do anything I'm not comfortable with. We can have a symbolic union. It's not like we're going to be getting it on in public.'

He didn't reply.

'What?'

'That's exactly what you're going to be doing,' he said. 'And furthermore, Aaron is counting on it.'

'That's not what he says,' I said, getting angry.

'I would have thought, Nina, that by now you would have worked out that there's a big difference between what Aaron says and what Aaron means. You don't know what you'll be doing. You'll be off your face.'

'So?'

'All the others have gone on to have sex with him. I have the tapes. You'll do it. You won't dare say no.'

I blushed hotly.

'I know what's involved,' I snapped. 'And anyway, I hate to break this to you, but I have slept with Aaron before. We've seen each other with no clothes on and everything.'

Wolf's face darkened and he looked about to speak.

'What? What are you trying to say?' I asked peevishly.

He shook his head. 'Have you ever wondered why it has to be on camera? Why I'm here?'

'I know why. We've all been told why. It's to capture evidence of revelation.'

'I don't mean what you've been told about capturing spiritual evidence and all that bullshit. I mean the *real* why.'

'No,' I said, flustered, trying to lift the bin up so I could drop the rubbish into the heap by the field without getting any on my clothes.

Suddenly the bin was out of my hands and he was emptying it. Its organic stench accompanied us back to the house. He wouldn't give it back to me, insisted on carrying it to the door. Our feet crunched in the snow. His voice grew low, quiet.

'See,' said Wolf, 'we think different things about all this, you and me. You think that this is all some big experiment. I'll bet you think, *Well, even if I do have to admit he's a gigantic fucking fraud in the end as well as a bully* – as I know you already know in your heart of hearts – *I'll have taken the risk. I'll have nothing to regret.*'

'I'll admit nothing of the sort. And I *do* have nothing to regret.'

'Well, nothing *yet*.' His pale eyes glittered. 'But see, I think, if you go ahead and do it with that man in there?' He leaned forward, pointed at me. 'He will *own* you, Nina. And for all time. The same way he owns all of those other silly bastards, did they but know it.'

'That's a little melodramatic . . .'

'For. All. Time.'

His gaze did not waver as he lit a cigarette with a little flick of his Zippo, sucking it into burning life. 'And he'll make you know it.' Wolf offered me a tiny, bitter smile. 'One day, when you really leave here, leave for good,' he dropped the lighter back into his jacket pocket, 'and sooner rather than later.'

'What do you mean?' I asked sharply.

'What I mean is that five, ten years down the line, you'll be holed up with some fat bastard who does accounting or risk management or whatever the fuck else in some nice village in the Cotswolds with the two-point-four children you've managed to squeeze out, and you won't have a care in the world.

'And then not him – he's too clever for that – but some other twat he'll send, will come knocking on the door. Reminding you of that film, at just the moment you don't want to be reminded of it. Wanting something off you. And whatever you give them, and however much you give them, they'll never be satisfied.'

'That's a horrible thing to say!'

Wolf shook his head at me, one eye always on the door.

'You might have no time for that dickhead Peter Clay, but let me tell you, when us lads are upstairs drinking and snorting the end of Tristan's fucking trust fund away, that man can tell a story or two about your Magus. If you'd gone with Uncle Petey to see some puppies like you were supposed to, you'd have heard them, too.'

I was trembling. Every one of these words cut me like a knife.

Wolf appeared not to notice, or if he noticed, not to care. If anything, he had a little grin on his face.

'If ever there lived a man who was destined to die with his throat cut in a dark alley, it would be Aaron fucking Kessler. Or Tim Littleton, to use his real name.' He shrugged. 'Do you still want me to film you naked with him?'

* * *

By four o'clock the next day, we were deep in preparations for the ritual. Aaron was barely present, unable to concentrate; he kept vanishing from the dining room, lingering in the hallway by the front door, as though waiting.

It gave me a sinking feeling, almost of déjà vu.

If you just walked out now, they're so distracted you could be halfway to Tonbridge before they noticed you were missing.

For a long second I thought hard about it, before realizing I would never dare. It was too late in the day.

And Aaron had promised I wouldn't have to do anything I didn't want, I reminded myself firmly. It was just Wolf stirring, because it was all he knew how to do.

I loped down the stairs, pausing in the hallway, and that's when the front door swung open. Aaron was there, with someone else.

'Hello, Knockout Tits. Long time no see. Got a kiss for your Uncle Peter?'

* * *

'What's he doing here?'

I could barely speak for my rage, my shaking.

We were stood in the dining room.

'Why are you freaking out?' Aaron laced his fingers against his scalp. Behind him, I glimpsed Wolf rolling cable into a coil. 'Obviously we need him. What do you think goes into the Sacred Draught? You're like a nagging wife, Nina. It's not hot.'

Aaron was twitchy, and though I might be imagining it in my nervousness and paranoia, his scaling anger and anxious rubbing at his nose made me think he was high again.

'I thought the Sacred Draught was made of natural ingredients – herbs and stuff . . .'

'Don't be stupid.' Aaron shrugged, and it was a jerky, hitched movement, and something in my heart sank. 'Where would we get that in winter?' He snarled at me. 'You know what? Do this or don't, but if you let me down now after all this preparation, you and I are through. Do you understand?'

I swallowed and met his eyes. Even after everything that had happened, the prospect seemed unimaginable. 'I never said that.'

'Good.'

'But I can't be out of control if I know Peter's in the room. I don't trust him.'

'He's not going to be in the room – don't be ridiculous,' said Aaron. 'Do you think I'd let anything happen to you?'

I didn't know the answer to this. The only thing I knew was that if I'd kissed him, he would taste of coke.

So I didn't kiss him.

'You promise?'

'Yes. I promise.'

I was torn then. Even at that moment, things could have gone either way. There was still a chance, vanishingly small, yes, but still a chance I could have walked out.

They wouldn't have been happy, true.

But not as unhappy as they were going to be.

'OK?' he asked. 'So, are you ready?'

Choose, Nina.

So I chose. I managed a wan smile for him. 'OK. I'm ready.'

Behind him, Wolf's knuckles tightened on the coils of cable so much I could see it.

'Great,' said Aaron, clapping his hands. He reached into his pocket and pulled something out.

I realized, with a little shock, that he was holding one of the order's amulets, only this one was silver.

He looped it over my head, and it lay, heavy and chill, upon my breast, as he kissed me. 'Let's get this show on the road.'

* * *

After that it becomes difficult to remember clearly. It happens in flashes.

I remember that we held hands, surrounding Aaron. We started the first chant. The words felt sticky, too big for my dry mouth. Behind me was the incongruous sound of metal and plastic as the camera clicked and whirred. Wolf was there, but I couldn't see him.

Nervous sweat soaked me, despite the coldness of the room. I wore a corona of flowers on my head, and it was slipping down over my left ear, the sharp ends of the pins scraping across my damp scalp. With my hands tightly held – Tristan on one side, Lucy on the other – I couldn't find a way to right it.

Lucy's nails cut into my hand, little sharp half-moons, as though she sensed my reluctance, my sudden fear.

I didn't want to do this, I realized. And now it was too late, far too late to stop. I'd chosen wrongly.

Chapter Nineteen

The next thing I knew, Sophia, I was running for my life.

Above me the stars and the thin moon wavered and blurred, the stars breathing in and out, the moon swinging back and forth, lolling like a drunk. The trees on the horizon with their stark bare branches loomed ominously on all sides, like an angry mob.

My thin gown stank of burning wood and incense. Beneath my bare feet, dried twigs and stones embedded in the ice cut me, but I felt these wounds at a strange, dreamy remove, and they had no power to stop my flight.

I had no idea what I was running from, no memory of it, but I knew it was vital that I escape. There had been a terrible noise – male voices screaming, shouting, fighting, and then a rolling boom, like thunder . . .

But however much fear could give me wings, it could not prevent my silky gown from catching in my flying steps, tripping me, and I was thrown forward, rolling on the cold wet slush, winded and gasping for air.

Above me, the stars were falling, falling down on top of me. The wind howled, and faraway, voices were raised, men and women, but they were not near enough to hurt me.

I raised my hands to my eyes and rubbed.

My hands were sticky, hot, and they smelled of iron and tasted of salt.

In the moonlight, as I held them up to inspect them, they looked blacker than the inky sky.

Far away, possibly from the direction of the house, or from the other side of the universe, there came a wailing, rising and falling. Someone was screaming and it sounded like Tess, and as I drifted, it threaded in and out of my nightmare.

'He's dead, he's dead! Someone's killed him!'

Chapter Twenty

'Hi,' I said. 'My name's Sophia Mackenzie. I'm here to see Max Clarke.'

I was standing in a quirky little reception area in a large converted semi-detached house just off Clerkenwell Green. Out of the big front windows I could see the green, a pretty church and a tea shop advertising artisan coffees.

Inside, it all was vintage colours and asymmetric bookshelves. The guy sitting at the low-slung desk before me looked as though he was an escapee from the 1950s with his striped shirt and neatly buttoned cardigan.

He blinked at me, a little nervously, as though I were a bomb that might go off. 'Max? I see ... Do you have an appointment?'

'Yes, he said to drop in ...'

There was a sudden clatter above of doors swinging back and creaking stairs.

'It's all right, Toby, I've got this.' A man had bounded down the threadbare steps and appeared on the landing. All I could make out was his smile, full of white teeth, and a mop of reddish-brown hair.

'You *must* be Sophia.'

I shrugged and let out a little laugh. 'Well guessed.'

His smile dropped a couple of notches. 'I must say, now you're here in person, how terribly sorry I am about your mother. I didn't know her that well, but she seemed a lovely, lovely woman.' He reached out, took my hand and squeezed it earnestly. It was a forward gesture but not without charm.

I tried to concentrate on it, and not the swell of feeling on hearing my mum described so.

She *had* been a lovely, lovely woman.

'Thank you,' I said.

'Look,' he said, 'I'm just about to head out for a spot of very late lunch. Can I persuade you to join me?'

I smiled. 'That would be great.'

* * *

He walked me back across the green, which was full of trendy office workers hurrying past the shops, and yummy mummies in designer sunglasses pushing their children along the narrow pavements.

Despite the glorious day, I couldn't quite stop myself from looking over my shoulder every so often, and at one point I thought Max noticed. We made small talk about my journey on the way to a large Victorian pub, and I ducked in before him.

'So, what time do you have to get back?' he asked as we approached the bar.

'I don't. Not today, at any rate.'

I deliberately made myself not think of my morning so far. My night had been sleepless and miserable, thinking about what that bastard had done to my mum, about what disaster had seemed to befall them all – someone was dead.

My call to Amity to tell them I had to stay in Suffolk to meet the doctor that morning had gone down like a lead balloon, and the memory of it made my insides clench in anxiety. I wondered if their sullenness meant they'd heard back from Scottish Heritage.

Well, if Amity were unhappy with me, I might as well seize the day and make it count. Max could tell me what had happened next in my mum's story. I'd rung Paracelsus and set up an appointment with him, then decided to check in on Monica in the café.

Rowan wasn't about as I crossed the yard. After our fight last night I didn't particularly want to speak to him, but I also didn't want our row to drag on. I needed Rowan. I needed someone I could talk to about all the bizarre revelations in the notebooks, someone who had known my mum and would be less likely to judge, and however angry I was that he hadn't believed me about the strangers following me on the train, I was just going to have to get past it.

I pushed open the café door and the scent of fresh baking – the alchemical magic of flour, butter, eggs and sugar – filled the air.

I paused on the step and breathed it in. 'Oh God, Monica, it smells fantastic in here.'

She was dressed in a neat floral apron, putting our plastic menus into the little wooden stands on our mismatched tables. She looked up, her face breaking into a grin. 'Sophia, I didn't expect you! I thought you'd be at work.'

I shrugged. 'I'm just on my way to the hospital. How are you getting on in here? Is Rowan treating you all right? Have you found everything?'

I was surprised as she came up and, without ceremony, put her arms around me, a fleeting, gentle pressure. I had a sudden flashback to my mum's notebooks, of her puzzlement at Lucy's over-affectionate embrace when she'd first arrived at Morningstar, and I nearly froze.

'Things will get better,' she murmured. Again that soft accent, perhaps Scottish in the dim and distant past. She offered me a sad smile. 'It must be so hard for you right now.'

I realized that it was nothing sinister. I was bereaved. I must have just looked like I needed a hug.

She was probably right on that score.

I sighed, surprised into candour. 'There are good days and bad days, I guess. More bad than good at the moment, but still . . .'

I couldn't finish the sentence. I only had so much bravado to go round. I was glad of my sunglasses.

'Did you have any breakfast?' she asked, stepping away towards the counter.

'Me? No, no. I'm just rushing out.'

She shook her head. 'Oh no, no, no. You can't skip breakfast. Best meal of the day. Look, I baked this just now – it's Hungarian sour cherry cake. You mix the whites and the yolks of the eggs separately then blend them together.'

She was taking up my mum's big bone-handled knife, moving to cut a slab of scarlet-studded cake that was lying on the counter.

'Oh, Monica, thank you so much, but I really can't, I've got to get to the hospital now.'

'Don't worry,' she replied, concentrating on her work. 'I won't stand over you while you eat it.' She was swiftly wrapping a very generous rectangle of the cake in one of our takeaway greaseproof paper bags, twisting the corners to seal it. 'Take a slice with you.'

The package, warm and fragrant, was being placed in my hands with a paper napkin and a wry smile.

'Enjoy.'

* * *

The hospital had been busy, everything had run late. The doctor, a tiny, exquisitely spoken woman in huge glasses, had been much more cautious than the staff nurse the night before. She shooed me into a side office, closing the door on us. There had been an 'improvement in responsiveness', but my dad, apparently, was still very, very ill.

I mustn't get my hopes up, I was told.

Of course, this immediately got my hopes up, and I felt several tons lighter as I called into his room and changed his dying flowers for a bunch of violets from Eden Gardens. I murmured an upbeat progress report into his ear, letting him know that Rowan was taking care of everything at the gardens, and when he didn't respond I tried not to let my disappointment show.

As I left I wondered if he'd known about his wife's past. The notebooks had been hidden in his shed, after all. I wouldn't wish the experience of reading those notebooks, of seeing my mum in that position, on anyone who wasn't primed for them, so I hoped with all my heart that he had already known.

Checking my phone after buckling myself into my car in the hospital car park, I noticed that someone had been trying to ring me – an unknown caller. I felt too fragile to call back and deal with any fresh drama. They hadn't left a message, at any rate.

I stared at the number – it looked like a landline but I didn't recognize the area code. I wanted to ignore it in the worst way – I was in no mood to talk to strangers.

Instead I braced myself and tapped the number, listened to it ring as a man with his arm in a sling crossed the car park in front of me.

'Hello?' The voice was female, older and strangely familiar.

'Hi there,' I said. 'This is Sophia Mackenzie. You tried to get in touch with me?' Outside, clouds passed briefly over the sun.

'Sophia! Yes, I did. It's Estella, your grandmother. I wanted to know how Jared was getting on.'

That was where I recognized her voice from. I felt a hot flush of shame. I had completely forgotten about calling her in the grind from hospital to bed to office to train station.

My life was spiralling out of control.

'Oh, yes! I'm so sorry! I should have rung, but it's been a madhouse here. I've just been in talking to the surgeon about my dad – they say he's getting better; he may wake up soon.'

Silence was the only reply.

'We just have to keep hoping, eh?' I said, trying to fill it with a nervous laugh.

'I see,' she said coolly, after what may well have been the longest pause of my life. 'Well, thank you for letting me know.'

'I'm sorry I didn't get back to you sooner,' I said, thinking perhaps I'd offended her. 'I had to go back to work, and . . .'

'That's fine, Sophia, please don't trouble yourself about it.' She didn't sound offended. If anything, she sounded *disappointed*. 'I'm sure you're extremely busy. I'll call again in a few days to see how things are going. Take care—'

'Wait,' I said. 'Sorry, there was something I wanted to ask you about. I found some notebooks of my mum's. From her teenage years . . .'

I let that hang for a second, wondering if she would volunteer anything. When she didn't I continued: 'From her time at university, and—'

'She didn't go to university,' said Estella, with a contempt that seemed so ingrained it had become impersonal, second nature.

My throat was closing, my cheeks heating up. It was as though she'd struck me. 'I'm pretty sure she did . . .' But as I said it, I felt a flash of doubt. *Had my mum been to university? After all, outside of the notebooks, she'd never mentioned it.*

There was a bark of laughter. 'She couldn't hack it, I'm afraid. Nina was . . . she had no *grit*.'

I realized, with a little flutter of confusion and anger, that being able to make this assessment pleased my grandmother. Ancient chords of envy and dominance were still being played in the background, even after my mum was dead.

You know, I thought, *with that at home, it's amazing my mum turned out as well as she did. Aaron Kessler notwithstanding.*

'I'm not sure that's fair,' I said, as politely as I could manage.

'Hmm,' said Estella, with a finality that implied I was as big a fool as my mother. And you know, maybe that's true, but I'm nothing like as easy to bully, so I forged ahead regardless.

'In the notebooks, I found references to people she knew back then. I was hoping to get in touch with them. I wondered if—'

'Oh no. We never stayed in touch with any of her friends. I doubt Nina did. I meant to ask, Sophia – Nina had a little emerald art deco ring from Thomas's mother. Did you happen to see it around the house?'

'No,' I immediately lied. I knew exactly the ring she meant. It had been returned to me in a brown paper bag from the coroner's office, together with the dishevelled clothes my mum had died in. There had been something so pathetic about her worn bra and overwashed jeans that I had wept for an hour afterwards. 'But I'll keep my eyes peeled for it.'

'If you would. Your mother's cousin Martina might like it, you know, as a keepsake.'

'I'll bear that in mind,' I said evenly. I had never seen or heard from this person in my life, and I'd be damned if I was sending her my mum's only decent piece of jewellery.

The way to remember my mum was to have been involved in her life.

'Jolly good. Well, do keep me posted on how Jared is doing. Must dash.'

I was being dismissed. 'Oh, right. Bye.'

There was an audible click as she hung up.

* * *

'I found two of the notebooks,' I said without preamble while I waited at the bar with Max Clarke. 'I don't know where the third one is.'

'Oh . . . you did?'

He had grey eyes under dark, almost bushy brows, and they watched me intently while I shifted my bag off my shoulder and opened it. 'Have you read them? Wait, let's get some drinks and sit down first.'

I ordered white wine and a fish finger sandwich on the Clerkenwell staple of 'artisan bread' before he guided me to a table in the beer garden at the back.

The sun was out, of course, but the atmosphere was dense, muggy, and a storm was coming. I vanished back behind my sunglasses, glad of the orange parasol shading the table.

'So,' he said. 'You read them.'

'Yes,' I replied. 'It was . . . it was kind of hard to do it,' I said. 'It felt like a huge violation of her privacy.' I looked at him, gauging him.

He nodded, while my fingers clenched the stem of my wine glass. Nearby, a quartet of young men in skinny jeans and elaborate facial hair were urgently discussing a planned trip to Machu Picchu for a photoshoot. Other than that, we were alone. The lunch rush was long over.

'It must have been a phenomenally difficult thing to read.' His face was kind.

A long moment went by. I couldn't speak. The memory of it was still raw; seeing her like that. She'd promised I'd be battered and bruised by the end. This part was already coming true.

'What can I do for you, Sophia?' he asked eventually.

I bit my lip and tried to compose myself. 'I need to know what's in that third notebook. I mean, I don't *want* to know, I'm pretty sure about that, but I need to. The second notebook implies that somebody . . . that there was an incident at Morningstar, and that somebody died.' I took a deep breath.

'I think it's got something to do with what happened to my mum.'

'How so?' he asked carefully.

I took a deep breath, marshalled my thoughts. 'I . . . I've never believed that my mum would kill herself. I know what the police think. But I can't' – *Just come out and say what you think* – 'I think my mum was murdered and my dad nearly murdered, and that somehow this . . . this Order of Ascendants was involved. I just . . . I don't understand why.'

'That,' he said after a long moment, 'is quite a claim.'

I offered him a helpless shrug. 'It's the only thing that makes sense to me. Firstly,' I said, 'my parents are not easy to handle, by any stretch of the imagination. My mum is needy and my dad – well, my dad isn't good with people. But neither of them has ever been suicidal. And with this book,' I clasped my hands around my head. 'I just think my mum was looking forward to life more than ever. There's . . . there's like this, I don't know, this passion for life, for justice, that comes out of the notebooks. When she's talking to me in them, she doesn't sound depressed, she sounds . . . she sounds *feisty*. Like she's ready to move on with her life. Ready to do all the things she never did.'

I folded my hands in front of me and tried to compose myself. 'I know everyone says it's my grief talking, but looking back, there was something about my final phone call with Mum. I can't help feeling that she made it under duress. There was something . . . off about it.'

He listened intently, but said nothing. I was grateful, I realized, to speak to someone who didn't try to leap in all the time, telling me what to feel or trying to give me permission to feel it.

'And the other thing is, I've realized something.' Now I'd

started talking, I couldn't stop. I felt uncorked, like shaken champagne, and everything was bubbling out. 'The police say that my parents were being continuously burgled, but that never made any sense to me either. My parents didn't own much. They'd never been targeted before. Who would burgle them? *Continuously?*

'The burglaries started about six months ago, and when you said on the phone that my mum and you had been discussing the book for that long, something twigged in my head.' I laced my anxious hands together on the wooden table again. 'Why would all this harassment begin just as she started talking to someone outside the house about her past?'

His gaze settled on me and grew thoughtful. 'You think Nina and Jared were being harassed? In the sense of a campaign?'

'Well, maybe.' I shrugged helplessly. 'I don't know. Did you have any problems? I mean, at Paracelsus? Did anyone from this order threaten you over this?'

He laughed, a short bitter sound. 'Other than the usual legal letters?' His smile faltered as I didn't join in. 'Well, I have to be honest here, Sophia. At Paracelsus we publish occult and New Age books, and we deal with difficult people sometimes. Last year we published a book on Mary Magdalene that got some fundamentalist Christians in the States very angry. But, as far as I'm aware, none of our detractors have ever done anything violent or criminal.' He shrugged. 'What makes you believe that Aaron Kessler's group was targeting your parents? Other than the burglaries? Were there other clues?'

'I don't think so,' I said, shaking my head, though I couldn't shake the thought that Rowan could be concealing more revelations from me, even now. 'But they were so alarmed that they bought a gun. Why would they do that unless they thought they were in danger?'

This seemed to make an impression on Max, whose thick brows drew together.

'I see,' he said after a long moment. 'So what can I do for you?'

Now that I was here, a reluctance stole over me. I didn't want to be battered or bruised any more.

Courage, Sophia.

I took a deep gulp of wine first.

'I have a question for you. Actually, two questions,' I went on. 'And the first one is, who died at Morningstar in 1989 and why? You've read the third notebook – what happened next?'

I sensed that this conversation made him very uncomfortable. His mouth opened and closed once, twice, and he flushed a deep pink.

'Well, you see, in terms of the third notebook, things between Nina and I had reached a difficult . . .'

Suddenly, in a lightning bolt of clarity, I understood.

'You haven't actually *read* it, have you?'

'No, I haven't,' he said with a little sigh. 'When I wrote that letter to Nina, I was expecting her to call me, to arrange a meeting where I could read it. That's what had happened with the first two notebooks as she wouldn't make copies.'

A vast disappointment welled inside me. 'You don't know what's in it?'

'Oh, no, it wasn't like *that*.' He sat upright. 'I may not have read it, but I know what happened next. You see, Nina was describing a, well, a historical event. It's just that she's the only person that was present who's ever gone public.'

A historical event? I'd seen nothing of the sort in my internet searches. 'What do you mean? Who died?'

'Peter Clay.'

Peter died?

For some reason, I had been sure it would be Tristan. I'd

spent the night imagining all the things I would do, say and throw at the despicable Peter if I ever met him. And now I learned that he'd been dead since before I was born.

I felt cheated.

'How?'

'It was a shotgun blast to the face.' Max winced. 'Quite messy.'

'I . . . I, well, what . . . *sorry*?'

Max sighed. 'Naturally, the police got involved. They ruled it an accident – drunk man trips with a loaded shotgun. There were plenty of guns in the house. But Nina told me something different. At the time, the central ritual was in full swing and everyone had taken a lot of drugs, and in the middle of this, someone shot Peter.'

'Who?'

'I don't know. Nina claims she heard the commotion and came running. She had no memory of what happened in the hours leading up to this. She was . . . out of it. They all were.'

'How was she so sure Peter's death *wasn't* an accident?'

'I don't know and she wouldn't elaborate. She did grow more guarded as things progressed.'

I tried to parse this for a long moment. To imagine my gentle, nervous, needy mother complicit in such a hideously violent crime.

Everything is lies, and nobody is who they seem.

'That's all she said?' I asked. 'That it was a murder? She didn't tell you anything else?'

He shook his head.

'So,' I said, aware that I was trembling, 'why didn't she tell the police?'

'Nina and I discussed talking to the police, but you have to remember that, even so many years later, Nina was still traumatized by her time at Morningstar and her memories of

Aaron. She just wanted to get it written down.' He met my gaze. 'Or perhaps she was protecting somebody. Some of these people she considered her friends.'

Of course – even if there was no third notebook yet, there were still the people that were there at the time, who had *known* my mum.

'This was the other thing I meant to ask,' I said. 'I want to track down the other ex-members. Do you know where I can start looking for them? In the notebooks, Mum only uses first names. I don't even know if they're real.'

'The other members that were at Morningstar with her? Yes, I know who they are.'

'You do?'

'Of course. Well, I can certainly tell you who their lawyers are. Remember, we were thinking of publishing the book, so we had to cover ourselves. Kessler, for the record, is very litigious.'

I sat astounded on the splintery pub seat as the implications of this became clear.

'I'd like that,' I said. 'The old members. I'd just . . . I'd like to talk to someone who knew my mum then. She didn't have many friends and her parents . . . you know.' I bit my lip. My phone call with Estella that morning still rankled. 'I'm not expecting much assistance from that quarter.'

'Of course I'm happy to contact them.' He drained the remains of his pint. 'But I don't think they're going to want to talk to you. They're very keen to forget they ever met Aaron Kessler.'

'Did you tell them that my mum was writing a book?'

'I didn't give specifics. I just told them that an ex-member was putting together a memoir and asked them if they'd like to read the manuscript when it was finished.' He met my gaze. 'It seems naive of me now. It probably wouldn't be that hard for them to work out that I meant Nina.'

I was thinking, thinking. 'If one of these "Ascendants" murdered Peter, they would have known they might be exposed if my mum went ahead with this.' The implications were inescapable. Not only would the murderer be afraid, the others would, too. They had all helped cover up the crime.

'Oh my God,' I said, as the full force of it hit me. 'She would have exposed them all. That was why they killed her.'

Chapter Twenty-One

I went straight to the police, asking at the front desk for Detective Inspector Rob Howarth.

'Hello, Sophia.' He was wearing a white shirt, creased by the heat and sporting slight sweat marks under the arms. He was cordial but distant, as though expecting trouble from me.

I didn't disappoint him on that score.

He took me to an interview room where I handed over the two notebooks. I told him about my conversation with Max, about the contents, about my mum's plan to publish.

As I spoke I constantly searched his damp, craggy face for some clue as to how he was receiving this new intelligence, but he gave nothing away.

'So you've no idea where the third notebook is?' he asked, not looking at me, but at the two books with their slightly faded covers. Very carefully, he pulled one over and opened it, flicking through the pages.

'No.'

'That's a shame.' He peered over my mum's handwriting. 'I'll get in touch with Kent Constabulary and ask about this accidental death.' He tapped the notebooks. 'This is an interesting new line of inquiry. Let me have a read through these, and I'll be in touch.'

* * *

When I arrived back at the hospital Rowan was in his usual chair; he offered me a wan smile when I came in and kissed my dad's forehead.

I felt a fathomless guilt. 'Look, Ro, about the other night . . .'

He shook his head. 'No, Soph, it's fine. I ought to be apologizing, not you. You've been under so much stress, and I . . . sorry. I'm just knackered.' He grinned and stood up. 'Pax.'

It was what we always used to say as children, when we made up after a quarrel – usually when my ever-present jealousy of my dad's favour made me say and do things I would later regret.

'Pax,' I agreed, and let myself sink into his arms for a second as he hugged me. 'So, how is he?'

He nodded towards my dad. 'The same. I've been telling him about planting the autumn stock.'

'Any reaction?'

'No, not today. But he might be tired out. They said the consultant came and had a look at him, so there was a lot of poking and prodding and one of those MRI things.' He hunched forward on his chair.

I gave him a measured look.

'Rowan, I had a very strange conversation today.'

'Yeah?'

'Yeah. With a man that was going to publish a book my mum had written.'

His eyes widened, the dark circles under them notwithstanding. 'Your mum wrote a *book*?'

'Yeah.' I sat down and told him everything I'd learned, ending with the revelation that my mum's book might have contained information about a murder.

Rowan just stared at me. 'Fucking hell. That's hard core, Soph.' He rubbed his chin. 'So now you really think it was one of them, this cult? That killed your mum and stabbed Jared?'

'Yeah,' I said urgently. 'I do. I think it was made out to look like a murder–suicide. But here's the thing – the third notebook, which describes the original murder, has gone missing.

Did you ever see a notebook in the house? It was probably an A5 hardback?'

He had a wary, guarded look now.

'You're quite *sure* about this?' he asked.

I ignored this question. 'Rowan, this is important—'

'I know, I know, but I never saw . . .' He seemed to be thinking. Then he trailed off.

'Rowan?'

He looked up at me. 'I didn't see a notebook. But I think I heard Nina. Typing. In the mornings. There were a few times I came through the house and she'd be in the little office downstairs, before the café opened. I never thought anything of it, I just thought she was doing the paperwork. But looking back on it, she was getting up earlier and earlier in the mornings, and the thing with Nina was, she was never an early riser.'

He glanced swiftly at me.

My mind was spinning.

I'd been so sure the third notebook was a handwritten bound book like the first two that it had never once occurred to me that it might be digital.

I had already looked at the ancient desktop computer in the office after her death, looking for some clue that would help me understand this calamity. There had been some pictures on it – nothing personal, simply photos of the gardens and grounds; the business's email correspondence, and a folder containing some old recipes and menus.

I'd clicked through everything and seen nothing out of the ordinary.

I'd have to take another look when I got in tonight.

'And what did the police say about all this?' Rowan asked.

'They think it's an "interesting new line of inquiry".'

He frowned. 'That's one way to describe it.' He shook his head. 'Bloody hell.' He looked at my dad. 'If it's true, you need to be careful. No way are you sleeping at that house any more, not till this is all sorted out.' He stood up and shook his finger at me, endearingly bossy. 'And we have to set up the CCTV cameras.'

'What CCTV cameras?'

'We bought CCTV in the end. About a month before . . . before it happened, Jared caved in and stumped up for it.'

My dad must have been desperate to consider such a thing. He *hates* CCTV.

'They're in boxes at my house. We bought four cameras and mounts and a program to view them on the PC. But we never got around to fitting them.'

I looked at my dad, lying silently on the hospital bed.

'You know what, Rowan?'

'Yeah?'

'If you could put up the CCTV, that would be great.'

* * *

'I've put the office computer in here,' said Rowan, 'it's more out of the way.'

We'd driven back to the house and collected the dusty old PC from the office. I still insisted upon going from room to room, checking that nothing was disturbed, but everything looked exactly as I'd left it.

He'd set it up in his daughter Brigit's room, on her little lilac Ikea desk. I would be sleeping in here tonight while she decamped to her brother's bed.

'Thanks,' I said, settling on her tiny, wobbly chair. My parents' PC itself, its white plastic yellowing with age, covered nearly the whole desktop, and its chunky glass monitor rested on top of it. It had been heavy – Rowan's face was still pink from carrying it up the stairs.

'I'll leave you to it,' he said. 'It's my turn to put the kids to bed.'

I nodded. 'Thanks, Ro.'

He waved and walked out, pulling the door shut behind him. 'Sleep tight.'

For something that was nearly twenty years old, the PC was still in pretty good nick, though you could have gone downstairs and made a cup of tea and a sandwich, and perhaps watched an episode of *Coronation Street*, too, in the time it took to boot up.

While I waited I took off my make-up and changed into pyjamas. Eventually, as I was smoothing my moisturiser in, the screen asked me for the password, which I knew was 'EDENGARDENS1' in all capitals.

Elite techno-hackers my parents were not.

Within moments I was in, and the screen looked exactly like it had the last time I'd logged on. The business ran on Windows XP, which I'm positive hasn't been supported by Microsoft for years. If anything happened to this thing, all our financial records would be lost.

I shook my head and muttered to myself. I would have to buy them a new laptop.

Buy *him* a new laptop, I silently corrected myself, a sharp pain knifing into my chest.

On the screen was a single folder in the corner called 'NINA', Outlook Express with its plethora of strictly business emails, and some antediluvian version of Internet Explorer.

I clicked through every single file in all the folders, even the tax documents, even the recipes, while I finally finished off what was left of the Hungarian sour cherry cake Monica had given me that morning. I read everything, right to the very end, just in case something else was hidden inside. Nothing.

On an impulse, I opened Internet Explorer, which had a very short browsing history; no more than a dozen pages. I peered at this for a while, clicking this and that, but could make nothing of it. Some supplier websites, Google and BBC Weather.

There was something so bland about this history, something so sterile and almost corporate, as though it had been constructed rather than created. No gossip, no comedy, no online shopping, no pictures of baby animals – and most certainly no social media. Nothing like mine.

It was so *lonely*, I thought. Lonely and sparse.

Troubled, I shut the computer off and went to bed.

* * *

The next day I worked from my dad's hospital room, with my phone on his bedside table.

At exactly 8 a.m. that morning I'd had an email from Benjamin:

Sophia,

Please can I have your report on the Scottish Heritage project. I have a project meeting with James in fifteen minutes and you failed to send an update yesterday.

Also, HR mentioned to me that you haven't cleared yesterday's day off through the proper channels. I invite you to look at section 5.2 of your employment terms and conditions on the intranet: www.amitynet/intra/employee-procedures for the correct process.

I hope all further extra days you take are cleared appropriately.

Benjamin Velasquez

Senior Architect

He'd cc'd James, the managing partner, in because where would the fun be in leaving him out?

I read this, my throat swelling with alarm and something a little like rage. At no point had he requested an update on Scottish Heritage – he hadn't even acknowledged my email taking the project back.

I wanted to fight back against this intransigent corporate bullying that was covering up his vicious sexual anger, but in my frayed and exhausted state, half of me wondered whether he was right. Maybe I should have written up a report for him.

I was in his power, after all. He was there, able to cover things, while I drifted in and out of work and office politics like a weak radio station. I was *vulnerable*.

I decided it was better to be safe than sorry and typed an update while I was waiting for Max to call.

When he did, it was with mixed news.

'Hi, Sophia. Sorry I'm so late getting back. It was all a bit of a faff in the end. I wanted to wait until I could tell you something concrete.'

'That's all right,' I said. 'What did you find?'

'So,' he said. 'It was four out of six in the end. We never did find Wolf – it's almost certainly not his real name, but it doesn't matter, as we couldn't track him down so he never heard about the book. Anyway, except for Tristan, the others are still alive, kicking and accounted for, which is good to know.'

'Tristan's dead, too?' I asked.

Max was silent for a moment.

'Max?' I asked, wondering if we'd been cut off.

'Yes, yes, I'm still here. He, well, he killed himself. In nineteen ninety-one.'

'Oh.' I didn't know what else to say.

I felt a wan, fleeting pity for him; golden Tristan with his trust fund. I had the distinct sense that this news would have deeply saddened my mum.

'Yes, it was very upsetting. He threw himself in front of a

train somewhere in Germany. Emily, his sister, tells me it was his third attempt. She said, "After the first two overdoses, he wanted something he couldn't be pulled back from."'

I was speechless.

'Yes,' said Max gently, 'that was my reaction at the time. I had more luck with the others. Lucy Trinder, now Lucy DuBois, is based in Paris.'

'Paris?'

'It's where Aaron Kessler first met her, funnily enough. After Morningstar, she went back there. Landed on her feet. She married this older guy – a famous photographer – had a couple of kids with him and lives in Faubourg Saint-Germain. She absolutely would not talk to me. Or you, I suspect.'

I'll bet she wouldn't, I thought viciously.

'However, Penelope and Tess are both in London. Tess Hotchkiss is a pastor now . . .'

'Tess is *what*?'

'A pastor. She counsels cult victims, believe it or not, and lives in Stockwell. Not far from where you are in Brixton, now that I think about it. She's part of some little evangelical church in Vauxhall. She wasn't that open to the idea of the book, to be honest, but somewhat less terrified and hysterical in her opposition than the others.'

'That leaves . . .'

'Penelope. And Aaron, of course. No show without Punch. We had a go at tracking down some of the servants at Morningstar – such as the cook, Michelle Lomax, and had some luck, but by the time Peter died Aaron had dismissed them and the members were doing all of the housework and maintenance.'

'And Penelope?'

'Her married name is Longman, and that's what she practises under.'

'Practises?'

'Law. She went back and finished her degree. She's a barrister now.' He paused, as though considering. 'And better yet, she's agreed to meet you.'

'She has?' I touched my dad's hand, let my fingers intertwine with his. His face was as still as always, though a little vessel beat near his hairline, a tiny sign of life. 'When?'

'How's tomorrow looking? About three?'

My mouth was dry. I had wanted to see these people, to question them, to get to the bottom of things, but now I was going to face one I felt giddy and sick with fright.

'Good. Tell her yes.'

And that's when I felt it, for the first time – my dad's rough fingers ever so gently and fleetingly squeezed my own, once, and then twice.

* * *

Penelope, not Penny, never Penny, was still recognizable from my mother's descriptions of her. That white-blonde chignon had become a tight, highlighted ash-coloured helmet. Her wispy pre-Raphaelite figure had evolved into something a little sturdier, a menopausal barrel shape her well-cut suit worked hard to hide. She had very clever-looking, cold, green eyes that her welcoming smile in no way touched.

'Sophie, isn't it?' she asked briskly, shaking my hand as I offered it.

'Sophia.'

'*Sophia*. Well, well. Have a seat. What can I do for you?'

Her chambers were in the Inner Temple, and behind her I could see the courtyard and round dome of the Temple Church, and the monument celebrating the Knights Templar rising up on its pillar; two knights sharing a single horse, rendered in bronze.

The air was scented with a fresh bouquet of flowers placed on a low table between us. Her desk was slightly to one side, a vast glass altar boasting the latest technology, crowded with folders, out of which papers threatened to burst.

But for now we were being non-official, and she took a seat on the low sofa. Her arm stretched out along its red leather back with a proprietorial air, and on her plump hand was a white-gold wedding band and matching engagement ring with a vast solitaire diamond.

I wondered if her husband knew the things I knew about her.

I settled into the chair opposite, and pondered how I was going to handle this. I could have eased into it, but something about her told me, *Cut to the chase*. Or to the quick. Either would be true.

'I'm here about Morningstar. And Aaron Kessler.'

Her stillness was my only answer. But those green eyes did not flicker. She already knew what this was about.

'As I am sure you know, my mother died recently . . .'

For a second I was distracted from my purpose, contemplating the awful finality of these words. She did, indeed, die. She was gone. And yet, in the flood of memory that washed in, she had never seemed so vital, so near me – standing in our garden, picking tiny sour apples from the tree, pacing in her room amongst her piles of papers in her bare feet, her passage stirring the dust devils in her wake.

She was gone. But she was also here. And I was here on her behalf.

'My mother recently died,' I began again, 'and I've been going through her old correspondence. I understand that you and she were in a . . . a group together.'

'A group?'

'Yes,' I said. *Yeah, you were all in a cult, remember? Having sex with rock stars on camera? Recall any of that?*

228

But I'm not here for retribution, I reminded myself. I'd come here to find out what happened to my mum. I forced myself to be calm, not to clasp my hands in my lap, not to hunch. 'A kind of . . . religious group.'

She shrugs, but the gesture is so elegant, so practised, it's like watching a performance. 'I'm so sorry, Sophia, but I've met so many people. And perhaps I was a little . . . wild in my youth, but I don't remember anyone called Nina.'

She met my eyes almost defiantly.

This I hadn't expected, this bald-faced denial, and I was completely at a loss.

'No?' I asked, trying to wrap my head around this. 'I'm surprised you agreed to see me, then.'

'Well,' she said, 'that young man from the publishing house said that your mother had passed away – there were mental problems, apparently – and you were desperate to talk to people who knew her.' She sat upright. 'He's been in contact before about this business, about some apparent . . . association between myself and Aaron Kessler.' Her voice did not change in timbre or tone, nor did her pose alter one iota, and yet I saw her absolutely harden, as though she'd turned to diamond. 'And I'll tell you exactly what I told him. I don't remember everyone I met while I was a student. I don't have to. But I very much resent these repeated assertions about me.'

I blinked at her.

'And,' she continued – there was a tiny note of triumph in her voice now – 'all of this despite the fact that nobody has ever once been able to prove any of it, nor will they ever.'

'But—'

'So, dear, I thought it best that we talk in person, so I could make myself *crystal* clear: I don't remember your mother. I don't remember Aaron Kessler. I don't know what you're talking about when you speak of this group. And, as you can tell that young man when you see him next, if I have to have this conversation again, I'm afraid I'll be forced to take legal advice.'

She offered me a tiny, almost motherly smile.

'Slander and libel isn't really my area, but happily I have very deep pockets, and many good friends that would be more than happy to act on my instructions.'

I sat in the ringing silence that followed this last pronouncement.

'I think this meeting is concluded.' She sat back on the sofa. Her gaze didn't flicker. 'I'm sure you can find your own way out.'

* * *

Max wasn't answering his phone.

I sat on the bench outside Temple Church, scowling at the pigeons pecking in the courtyard. I felt hollowed out, utterly humiliated, almost giddy with anger. That bitch. That *liar*.

And now Max wasn't picking up. He'd told me to ring him the minute I came out. I was trying not to be unreasonably furious with him, too, for exposing me to what had just happened.

This is not his fault. Or yours. Or Mum's.

I let my head rest in my hands and sighed, while passing lawyers studiously ignored me. They must see desperate people sighing every day of the week in this part of the world, I thought, and this consideration made me sit upright, not wanting to give them the satisfaction.

I was forced to admit, Penelope Longman had no more looked the sort of woman to be filmed engaging in drug-soaked rituals to access her Creative Spark than she was to sprout wings and fly.

Maybe she hadn't.

After all, it was like my mum's time at university, something there seemed to be no evidence for, something I couldn't prove.

Somewhere, church bells were ringing on Fleet Street.

For now, though, it was time to get back and check in with my dad.

Chapter Twenty-Two

'Dad?'

I stood in the doorway to his hospital room, not quite able to believe my eyes.

My father was lying upright, propped up on pillows, but despite his pallor and a kind of trembling that seemed to shake every muscle in his body, he was undeniably awake. His eyes caught sight of me and tracked me into the room, as his lips started to move inaudibly.

'Dad!' I ran up to him, hugged him in my arms, planted a kiss on his pale, waxy forehead and started to cry great whooping sobs of exhaustion and relief.

'Oh my God! Dad! When did you wake up?' I swiped at my eyes with the back of my hand. 'I can't believe it!'

'Just an hour or so ago,' Rowan's voice was behind me. 'We tried to call you. We left a message.'

My dad's voice, when it came, was impossibly tiny and low, less than a whisper; no louder, it seemed to me, than the sound of the sea in a shell. 'I heard talking.' He paused, a little wheezy, as though even this much speech was too much.

'Do you want anything?' I asked, feeling like a little girl again, babbling in my surprise, my amazement. 'Like water or more pillows or tea? I brought your slippers in, they're in the cabinet by your bed. Rowan's been looking after the gardens while you've been ill. He's been a star . . .'

I realized, with a falling sense of shock, that he might not know Mum was dead. I took his hand in mine, carefully, so I didn't dislodge the cannula bandaged to it.

I opened my mouth, closed it again. I just couldn't do this. I didn't even know where to begin.

'Your mother,' he said; and that hoarse, nearly silent sound, more like a breeze than a voice, seemed to come from the bottom of the ocean. 'I know, Sophy.'

My heart was in my mouth. It was as though he'd read my mind.

'Dad, do you remember what happened?'

He fell silent, then very slowly he raised his head again.

'Nina . . .' His eyes grew narrow, his brow furrowed. 'Your mum . . . she couldn't stick it.'

This, I had not been expecting. Not at all. Suddenly there was a hole in me, and all my feelings, all my thoughts, were draining out of me.

'Things had been . . . bad.' His voice was growing lower, slower, as if even these few words were exhausting him. 'She stopped . . .' He paused, sucked in some more air, and I was aware once again that not just his bowel but his lungs had been injured. 'She tried to . . .'

'Dad, I don't understand,' I said, but to my horror, I did. I just didn't want to believe it. 'She hanged herself? Deliberately?'

He offered me a single trembling nod. 'I tried . . .' His face was paling, whether through the memory or the effort of speaking, I could not tell.

'Dad . . .'

It was as though I couldn't breathe either. I had been so counting on another answer, that I hadn't realized how reliant I'd become on this outcome.

'I . . .' I was going to cry, I knew it. I covered my eyes with my hands, tried to pull myself together. 'I thought it was that cult.'

He blinked at me, his brows contracting together.

'What cult?' He sighed in, a hitching breath. He was exhausted. And when he said this, once again that terrible suspicion blossomed in me. The one that had bloomed within me while I had sat on that park bench in Inner Temple.

It was the one thing I couldn't admit to myself, even while it spread malignantly in my thoughts. One I had not given any voice to, but once it occurred to me, I couldn't shake.

What if none of this was real?

I mean, I knew the Order of Ascendants was *real*. Max had said as much. Aaron Kessler was *real*. The people in my mum's book were *real*.

But what if the things she said had happened weren't real? What if she'd made them all up?

How, though? And more importantly, *why*?

'It doesn't matter, Dad,' I said, and put my arms around him, kissed his warm cheek with its little sprouting of greying bristle. 'It doesn't matter. You're back with us, that's all that counts.' My tears mashed into his skin. Whether he liked drama or not, they would not stop. 'We can talk later. You need to rest.' I kissed his pale temple, where that tiny beating vein had been the only sign of life.

I waited there for a while until he drifted off again, talking only occasionally with Rowan about inconsequential things. My guts were churning, though.

Once I was sure he was asleep, I muttered to Rowan that I was going to the toilet and burst out into the hospital corridor.

'Hey,' Rowan said. 'Is everything all right?'

He'd followed me out of the room. 'Hey, Soph, it's OK. This is good news, even if what he's telling you about your mum is not what you wanted to hear. He's getting better.'

I burst into tears.

He held me, rocking me very gently, as though I was a child, while I sobbed.

He was right, of course. I was lucky. I could have lost both of them.

'Come on,' he said. 'Let's get you sorted out before you go back to your dad. He doesn't need to see you like this.' He guided me to a chair in the ward lounge, which smelled faintly of disinfectant. His hands were warm.

'You know, Sophia, I feel like . . . I dunno . . .' He looked away. 'I know you've never believed, like, that Nina would kill herself. And you were so into this alternative theory, with these notebooks and this cult, I started to believe it, too.' He sighed. 'I *wanted* to believe it.'

'What are you talking about?'

'Sophia, this shock you're in right now, I can't help feeling it's our fault.'

'What do you mean?' I had snatched up a paper towel, hospital-rough and pink, and was dabbing my eyes with it.

'Your dad and I – we should have said something to you about the burglaries the minute they started happening, but Jared and Nina didn't want to worry you or get you involved. So, like, you never understood when other people said Nina was depressed and not herself. It's all been . . . we were trying to protect you, and . . . and it's just worked out all wrong.' He offered me a bleak look. 'I'm so sorry, Soph. I really am.'

I had no idea how to respond to this. I couldn't respond, really, because I was having to start mourning my mum all over again, alongside my failure to be of any help to her. To be of any help to my father.

They couldn't even share with me that this horrendous campaign of crime had been going on.

Oh, Sophia, what is the point of you? Why are you even alive at all?

'Soph . . . are you all right? You're scaring me.'

I looked up at him, at his kind face. 'I'm fine,' I said.

'About those CCTV cameras – I've installed them, by the way. You'll see them properly tomorrow, but I still think you should stay at ours tonight.'

I nodded. He had no need to worry. I had no intention of sleeping in my parents' house that night. My mum hadn't imagined the burglaries, after all, so the CCTV would still come in handy.

'And we need to think about putting locks on the windows and fixing the pane of glass in the door,' continued Rowan. 'You know, before your dad comes home.'

I breathed out. 'Yeah. I can get started on that.'

'You know, Soph, we are going to get through this. We're going to be OK. Yeah?'

I raised my eyes to his and nodded. 'Yeah.'

'I'm going to get your dad a cup of tea, because he'll be wondering where we are. You get yourself sorted and come back in.'

'Yeah. And thanks, Rowan.'

'Oh, it's nothing . . .'

'It's not nothing.' My face was burning as I owned the truth of this. 'You've been there for them when I haven't. Thank you.'

His kiss on my cheek was warm and soft.

'I told you already. Think nothing of it. See you in a minute.'

He got up and left, while I sprawled in one of the cheap chairs, my eyes shut.

So my mum really had killed herself.

I had not, in a million years, thought my dad would confirm this when he woke up, but perhaps I should have expected it.

It's of a piece, after all.

I kept telling everyone how it couldn't possibly be true, 'because you don't understand, I *knew* her', and then it keeps being proved to me, in a thousand different ways, that I didn't know my mum at all.

I stirred in my chair.

But I didn't imagine those people on the train.

And all this started once she sent the book to Paracelsus.

I sat upright, my tears drying.

They may not have hanged my mother, but the Order of Ascendants had strung the noose.

Whatever happened, I was going to find that third notebook.

* * *

There was one last task for me that night.

'Hello?' Her voice was strained, and I had the sense she was trying to convey with her opening greeting that whoever I was, I was calling far too late in the evening.

'Oh, hello. Estella? This is Sophia Mackenzie.'

'Oh.'

Silence.

Well, nice to hear from you, too.

'It's just to say, since you wanted to know, my dad woke up today. They think he's going to be fine.'

More silence.

'They're talking about him coming home in a week,' I said, exhausted and becoming more and more thrown by her strange reaction. 'So that will be a relief.'

'Yes. I imagine it would be.'

'Yeah,' I said. 'It was touch and go for a while there.'

'Right. Well. Thank you for letting us know, Sophia. Have a pleasant evening.'

'Um, yeah. Thanks. You, too. Oh wait, I just wanted to ask—'

The click as she replaced the receiver seemed very loud.

'Oh,' I said aloud, trying to persuade myself it had been a mistake, that Estella had not hung up on me mid-speech. And when my phone rang again, I felt a shiver of relief: this was her calling back to explain we'd been cut off, and my sense of unease was all for nothing.

'Hi, Estella?'

Silence. No, not complete silence. There was some kind of ambient sound, of very light breathing – taut, controlled, as though the person on the other end of the phone was fighting some strong emotion.

I looked at the number. It wasn't Estella's, instead it read, 'NO CALLER ID'.

'Hello?'

Nothing.

'Hello, is somebody there? I can hear you.'

No reply.

The hairs on my arms and the back of my neck were gently rising.

'I'm going to hang up now,' I said, with more affronted determination than I felt.

Nothing.

And then, just as my finger moved to end the call, there was the beep, and it was over.

Chapter Twenty-Three

Rowan had been as good as his word. As we swept past Eden Gardens in my car on the way home from the hospital, I could see the rectangular box of the CCTV camera on top of the gate in the moonlight, pointing down at the main entrance.

'How many did you say there are?' I was so tired I could barely concentrate on the road; a little conversation wouldn't hurt. And there had been something about seeing it perched up there, next to the top of the gatepost – a friendly eye watching my affairs, watching my back – that comforted me.

Rowan pursed his lips. 'There are four outdoor ones. That one is aimed at the gate, the other one at the café, one at the front of the house and one at the back.' He ticked them off on his large fingers. 'And I have a confession to make.'

'Yeah?'

'Yeah,' he said, offering me a sidelong grin. 'I went mad and got two indoor ones, too. One for the café and the other one for the shed. Indoor ones are cheaper because they don't have to withstand the elements the same way, so it was only another hundred quid for both of them.'

I nodded vaguely.

'It's all done in the cloud,' he said. 'So you don't need TV screens or a video recorder. You just log in to your account and you can see it on any device, like your phone or your laptop.' He yawned hugely. ''Scuse me,' he said, blinking in tiredness.

'Anyway, they keep the footage for a month then delete it. Dead clever, really.'

'It's amazing what they can do nowadays.' I was too exhausted to speak in anything other than commonplaces and small talk. The white lines on the road were all I was capable of following. On all sides the thick, leafy underbrush and overshadowing trees surrounded us as we sped along, blocking out the moon.

'I would have got one for inside the house, too, but thought I'd better run it past you beforehand, like.' He offered me a huge, cheeky grin. 'If you were going to be streamed to my laptop in the cottage, you'd probably want fair warning before you gave us all an eyeful.'

And in my tired, almost dreamlike state, something about this hit home.

Something about cameras and being filmed.

'Sophia?'

There was something huge here, some essential point I was missing.

'Soph? Did I say the wrong thing?'

But I couldn't put my hand on it. It kept shooting away and evading the tips of my fingers.

'SOPHIA!'

His hand was on the wheel. I came back to myself – I was rolling away from the white lines, the green underbrush scraping the Ford KA, sand and gravel under my front wheel, about to hit the trees on the final bend before the cottage.

I jammed on the brakes, throwing us both forward into our seatbelts with a painful jerk.

There were at least three seconds of silence while we contemplated our brush with death.

A few feet in front of us, the trees were tall, straight and blameless.

This was all down to me.

'Oh God, Rowan, I'm so sorry.'

'It's all right,' he said, in a tightly controlled voice that very

240

much implied it wasn't. 'But if it's all the same to you, I think I'll drive.'

'There's no need. Sorry. I . . . I just thought of something, I've forgotten, it doesn't matter now, and—'

'Sophia . . .'

'No, it's OK. It's literally two minutes. I'm just so tired. I need to get to bed. I have to go back to London again tomorrow and—'

'Stop right there. You are going nowhere. This is fucking nuts, and you're going to get yourself killed.' He threw off the seatbelt with a snap and jerked open the door on his side.

'What are you . . . ?'

He crossed the front of the car, lit in hectic white by the headlights.

'Rowan?'

He pulled my door open.

'Keys.'

'Rowan, I . . . don't be like this. I'm sorry . . .'

'I know you are. I *do* know you're sorry. But you are also stubborn as fuck and completely insane.' He flung out an arm, pointing back up the road. 'Sophia, no one could *possibly* live like this, commuting hundreds of miles and working and looking after your dad. With all this drama going on something has to give – you're a fucking time bomb waiting to go off. You're going to give me the keys *now*.'

He held his hand out in front of me.

I turned off the ignition and dropped the keys into his hand.

He grunted. 'Right. Good. Out.'

Shamefacedly I shuffled out of my seat and into the passenger seat, strapping myself in.

He turned the key with a vicious twist that made my KA grind in pain.

I winced.

'Be nicer to my car, Mr Heavy Hands.'

He raised an eyebrow at me. We moved off with a little jerk of the accelerator.

I tried and tried, but could not recall what had distracted me as he drove. It was too late, and it was too gone, and in a minute or so I was fast asleep.

* * *

Somehow I had been woken and guided into the house, and then Kayleigh was there, in what my exhausted, semi-dreaming memory interpreted as a plush dove-grey dressing grown. It felt soft against my arm as she led me upstairs to the little bedroom papered in Pokémon and the characters from *Frozen*.

'Thanks, Kayleigh. G'night.'

She kissed me on the top of my head. 'Get to sleep, Sophia. You need to rest.'

I collapsed on to the tiny bed, my eyes fluttering closed. I was just switching my phone to mute, so it wouldn't wake the house in the morning with the alarm, when it went off, startling me. I rolled over on the bed and picked it up, light-headed with exhaustion. It was a central London number and I let relief flood through me. 'Max?'

'Um, no,' the voice was female, tentative, with a slight West Country accent. 'Not Max. Is this Sophia?'

I frowned at my phone. What stranger would be calling me at eleven at night? 'Yes,' I said, with a touch of anxiety. 'Who's this?'

'Ah. Well.' There was a long intake of breath, like some-one preparing themselves for a difficult or unpleasant task. 'You don't know me, but I knew your mum. My name's Tess Hotchkiss. I was in the Order of Ascendants. With Nina.' I could hear her swallow, her throat dry with nerves. 'Max

Clarke just gave me your mobile number . . . I hope you don't mind. He said you wanted to speak to me. You have questions, I suppose.'

Suddenly I was wide awake again.

'Yes,' I said. 'You see, she died . . .'

'I already know. Max said as much. I'm very, very sorry for your loss. When I knew her, Nina was a very special person. She had a gentle, luminous spirit, but underneath she was very strong. Of all the people in the order, she was my favourite.'

I blinked at this, tears rising within me to hear her so praised. I thought the same, too. 'I . . . thank you.'

'This must be hard.'

I bit my lip and tried to master myself. 'It's been very difficult, because of the way she died, and my dad . . .'

'Yes, I was surprised to hear she'd married.' I didn't have the heart to correct her. 'You know, after the order collapsed, I didn't want contact with any of them.' There was a pause. 'It was . . . a very dark period in my life.'

'I . . .' I sat upright on Brigit's little bed, trying to take this in.

I was speaking to *Tess*.

'I – well, I met Penelope Longman and she said Mum had invented the whole thing . . . and I mean, for a minute there . . .'

'I'm sure she did say that.' There was a rueful amusement in her tone. 'Ah, Penelope. She hasn't changed.'

'So it did all happen?' I asked with rising excitement. 'At Morningstar? The way my mum described it?'

'I haven't read these notebooks everyone's talking about,' said Tess, 'but, yes. The things Max told me she'd written were all broadly true.'

I felt a huge, flooding relief and gratitude towards Tess. My mum wasn't a crazy person, or a liar.

'I'm just . . . I'm so grateful you called. I – I have some

questions . . .' I had a billion questions, in fact, but now I had the chance, most of them were too insanely personal to ask – How did sharing Aaron with my mum and the others work? How did you feel about being whored out to a drug dealer? And who murdered Peter, do you think?

I had no idea where to even begin.

'I mean, I knew nothing about this,' I said. 'My *dad* knew nothing about this. In the notebooks my mum says she met Aaron and Lucy at some gathering, and then within a week she's sleeping with him and has abandoned her university course to live at Morningstar.' I could hear my voice ratcheting upwards, a slightly hysterical note to it.

'Yes,' said Tess with an unruffled calm. 'That sounds about right.'

'OK.' I rubbed my temple. 'I guess I just don't understand why. Or even *how* . . .'

'Ah. Well. The why and the how.' There was a crisp sympathy there. 'The *how* is that Lucy was dispatched to Cambridge to find potential new members. At the time I joined, we were all based in a big house in Chiddingfold, down in Surrey, which Aaron had bought with his royalties – it was nice enough, but *nothing* like Morningstar. Most Ascendants didn't live in, but shared houses and flats nearby. There were about thirty of us. Some Aaron had met in the band or at festivals, like me, and some just gravitated to him through word of mouth. It was this chaotic, hand-to-mouth existence between royalty cheques supplemented by leaning on working members for donations.' She sighed. 'But I do believe it was an authentic thing, at least then. We were a community.'

'So, what happened?'

'Tristan happened,' said Tess, with a hint of sadness. 'He was the *why*, bless his daft heart. He was in this very, very vulnerable place and he walked right into Lucy's arms, then

Aaron's. He fell and he fell hard. He gave them everything, including Morningstar.

'I think Aaron, who has a certain innate snobbery, realized that we could do with attracting more Tristans. Getting rid of the more peripheral members, the ones that didn't contribute – anything other than their love and time anyway – and replacing them, or at least exploiting them at arm's length. That was Lucy's remit. Find better people. *Richer* people.'

I snorted out a laugh. 'My mum wasn't rich.'

'No?' asked Tess mildly. 'She looked good on paper, from what I heard. They sounded her out and checked out her background after the first meeting. Her father owned a very successful double-glazing business, and Nina was an only child.'

'I . . . Sorry, they checked out my mum's background?' A chill of horror and pity went through me. 'I had no idea it was all that . . . *organized*.'

'Oh yes. They had a list of requirements. No point investing all that time and energy in her if she didn't meet the criteria.'

'The criteria?'

'Yes. She was potentially rich. She had a submissive, biddable personality – that was important after the disaster with Sarah Lowe, who'd got the police involved when she walked out, claiming she'd been held against her will.'

'Had she?' I asked, horrified.

'Oh, absolutely yes, by the end,' said Tess, as though the matter wasn't worthy of further consideration, 'and while the police wouldn't pursue the charges – they thought it was a domestic matter; it was a different age then – Aaron wasn't interested in making the same mistake again. He isn't fond of the wrong sort of attention, despite having an inexhaustible thirst for the other kind.'

I didn't know what to say to this. The cold-bloodedness of it chilled me.

My poor mum. She'd been invited to this party to meet a rock star – her life about to begin – and already she was being sized up as prey. Including background checks.

A thousand tiny details from the notebooks flooded in. Lucy twirling Mum before Wolf and Tristan, as though she was an acquisition. The way they'd assumed she'd be staying – *knew* she'd be staying.

'And, of course, Nina was beautiful, so Aaron would enjoy sleeping with her. That was important, too.' Tess sighed. 'Sorry. I appreciate this is probably hard to hear.'

It was very hard to hear.

'But I still don't understand,' I said, because I didn't. 'Even with his charm, his fame and his beautiful house, why would you? Why would any of you? There must have been something about this guy. I mean, what was he like? Aaron?'

She paused, lost in thought. In the background, I could hear the wail of a police siren coming from faraway.

'It's a surprisingly difficult question to answer,' Tess said. 'I suppose what he was . . . he was very good at creating the space that you populated with your dream of him – with what you needed from him.

'For instance, I needed him to love me, and also, because I was quite young, to parent me. To take control. My own parents were – *are* – lovely people, looking back, but they had enormous problems which I was incapable of appreciating at the time. And suddenly there was this older man, completely charming, utterly focused and willing to set boundaries for me.' She sipped something. 'It took a while for that perception to change. And of course, once you're on his bad side . . .'

She let it hang there.

'His "bad side"? What do you mean? Has he ever threatened you? Or tried to intimidate you into staying silent?'

'What, threaten *me*?' Tess laughed; a hollow, cracked sound. I found it impossible to marry up this sinister, cynical noise with the childlike, sunny Tess from the notebooks. 'Oh, no. Aaron isn't remotely interested in *me*. For the same reason he probably wouldn't be interested in your mother, ultimately – especially once her parents dropped her. For someone who banged on incessantly about the illusory nature of material possessions, he was surprisingly venal. He would consider us both failures.' She snorted. 'We couldn't even be blackmailed because we had nothing to lose.'

'*Blackmailed?* What do you mean?'

'What I say. A thousand pounds says that Aaron's still in touch with Lucy and Penelope, if only indirectly. They are high-profile people with families and business partners who know nothing about their pasts, and they're keen to keep it that way.'

'But how would he . . . ?'

'Oh, he runs a charitable fund so people can contribute to his "great work",' I could almost hear the air quotes her hands were making, 'The Society for Spiritual Enrichment. One of his little toadies was around here a few years ago, suggesting that I start chipping in if I knew what was good for me, and I sent him away with a flea in his ear. After all, what would our Magus have done? Told people I was in his spiritual sex cult?' Again that dark chuckle. 'Sophia, I tell people that *every single day*. For God's sake, it's printed in the introduction to our cult outreach services.' She paused. 'Don't get me wrong. I would never name and shame the others, but I've never hidden my personal involvement.'

'You think he blackmails the others? Really?' I tried to imagine the terrifying Penelope Longman, QC, tolerating such a thing, and failed.

'Oh yes. It's easy to overstate how much Aaron made as a

musician as there was never another successful record. If you'd had to sit through any of his dreary solo projects, you'd understand why.

'I do know, with my cult outreach hat on, that he strips the assets from the current members as well – but even so, he's a man with expensive tastes, no conscience and a long memory.' She sighed. 'Oh yes, he's blackmailing the old guard. I'm sure of it. And I don't know if you know this, but a lot of what went on was on film.'

Of course it was on film. And, as Wolf had observed to my mum at the time, that would have huge consequences.

'Yes. I read that. In fact, I was wondering about what happened to Wolf,' I said. 'Max hasn't been able to find him. Do *you* know where he is?'

She sucked her teeth contemptuously. 'No, and I've no interest in finding out. He was like Peter, another leech. He was our "cameraman". I can't even remember, to this day, how Aaron got us to agree to it.' That chuckle again, only gentler. 'But we did. We always did.'

I was astounded by her attitude. 'How can you be so calm about all this? What these people did to you . . .'

'Do I seem calm to you?' She seemed genuinely surprised. 'Hmm. I suppose I must. But if I am, it's because I've spent decades trying to make sense of my hurt and anger. I had *so* much anger, Sophia. After Morningstar I went to some very dark places.' I had a sense she was fading out, gazing backwards into some well of unpleasant memory. 'Sometimes you have to live through the darkest hour before dawn. I gained things from it, though. I found my purpose. I found God.'

'Is this your purpose, then? What you do with the cult outreach?'

'Yes.' She was animated again now, talking about her work. 'We run something called the Free Minds Shelter.'

'And you help people escape from cults?'

She sighed, as though considering. '"Cult" is such a loaded word – not every non-mainstream religious movement is a cult in the way you and I would describe it. Generally, though, when we counsel people here, we say "cult" when we mean something dangerous and "NRM" – New Religious Movement – when we don't.

'We each have specialties; particular movements that we know well and keep tabs on. Ebele is all about Christian and charismatic cults – this is a huge problem in London so she's always busy. Mine is self-counselling and lifestyle, Eastern mysticism – there are lots of cults building up around mindfulness lately. Alex deals in pressure selling and commercial outfits – get-rich-quick schemes, pyramid selling, etc. He's a lawyer so he can give advice to people.'

'*Pyramid selling?* That's classed as a cult?'

'Oh, you bet it is.' She was clearly absorbed by the subject. 'It's an epidemic.'

'I'd never thought about it that way,' I said, pondering. 'I thought a cult was . . . religious in some way.'

'Oh no, no, you don't need to be remotely spiritual to be taken in. All you need to be is manipulated into a position where you surrender your control. And if that's your definition, we all brush up against cult behaviour all the time. Have you ever had a job where the company culture was to work around the clock, even though you were never offered overtime? Had a boss that used to give presentations exhorting you to do more, constantly offering a programme of non-optional events you feel you have to attend to fit in? Ever felt guilty about leaving before eight, nine or ten o'clock at night? Or later?'

Had I ever. She was talking about Amity. 'I . . . yes. Yes, I definitely know about that.'

249

'Precisely. And if you think about abusive relationships, exactly the same is true. Have you ever had a conversation with someone you know is in a bad place in their relationship and you ask them why they don't leave, and they tell you that you don't understand, their partner is actually very thoughtful and kind sometimes? And they love them?'

I was silent, thinking.

'And yet,' she continued, warming to her theme, 'you see that the abusive person cuts their victim off from friends and family, constantly belittles them in public, and seems intent on destroying their independence. And you think, how can they stay in that relationship? And you also think, *why* do they stay in that relationship? You may even get quite angry at them and blame them, wonder if they're stupid, or maybe even mentally ill.'

'I . . .'

'You see, Sophia, it's not about logic. The *mechanism* is the thing — not faith, or politics, or love, or work, or money, or self-improvement. Those things are all incidental. Once you internalize somebody else's will as your own, the mechanism works exactly like a *trap* — easy to get in, very hard to get out.'

I sighed. I realized I was just going to have to admit it. 'I'm having trouble with this. I don't understand how someone could get mixed up in something like this, like my mum did.'

Like you did.

Again, that cracked laughter. 'It seems very odd, yeah? What people don't tell you is that when you join, it's the loveliest, fluffiest thing in the world. Everyone's *so* happy. Everyone's your *friend*. You have so much in common with them. You feel as though you've found your real family. And once it changes, well, it's too late to leave. You've bought in; lock, stock and barrel.'

I yawned, rubbing my bleary eyes with my free hand. I was

so tired, and yet I didn't want this conversation to end. It felt good to talk to someone who understood. 'All of this must have been such a burden to my mum. She never even told my dad she was in this thing.'

'Oh, Sophia, I know it's hard to understand. Really, I do. Please don't feel bad about it. But also, please don't feel that something was intrinsically wrong with Nina.'

'I guess.' I sat for a minute, deep in thought. I was beyond exhausted now. There would be a chance to talk to Tess again, I realized, and it was late. I should let her go to bed.

'I just have one more question,' I said. 'Well, the main question, really. What do you think happened to Peter Clay in the end? My mum seemed to think he was murdered.'

It was a stupid question, insensitively put. If I hadn't been so tired, I would never have asked. And, of course, it seemed impossible that this lovely woman, this pastor who was reaching out to me, would have had anything to do with that.

Didn't it?

The change in atmosphere, even through the phone, was palpable.

Tess fell silent for a long moment. 'I wouldn't know,' she said, but her voice was suddenly clipped, as though she didn't want to talk about this. 'I woke up to Lucy telling me to pack my bags the next morning.' She snorted. 'I never saw Aaron or Peter again. In person, at least.'

'Oh,' I said, 'it's very late and I'm keeping you up – is it OK if we talk again at some point? I think Rowan and Kayleigh will stage an intervention if I try to go in to work tomorrow, so I'll be available here if you are.'

'Yes, of course,' she said, and the warmth was back again in her voice. 'You'll have many more questions, I know. Call me anytime you need to talk. I mean *anytime*, Sophia. All right?'

'All right,' I said. 'Goodnight, Tess. And thanks.'

'Sleep well.' She was gone and I was alone, on Brigit's pink bed.

I had really liked Tess.

I had liked how she'd spun the straw of her exploited, miserable Morningstar experience into a new gold of helping people. I had liked how she had tossed away her girlish trappings and transformed into somebody quite kickass.

But I had also read the notebooks, in which my mum had implied it was Tess who discovered Peter's body – 'He's dead, he's dead! Someone's killed him!' – and I was convinced I had caught Tess in the middle of an outright lie.

Chapter Twenty-Four

I woke up again with full daylight streaming in through the windows, and a small person crawling over my back with deliberate movements, as though they'd dropped a tenner around here somewhere and were looking for it.

'Sophia!' said a little voice with great urgency, right next to my head.

I did not move, nor speak.

'Sophia!'

I kept my eyes tightly shut.

'SOPHIA! ARE YOU AWAKE YET?'

'Good morning, Riley,' I grunted. 'What are you doing?'

'Nothing.' This was clearly untrue, as he was clambering up to the top of the bed, his small feet and hands leaving little bruises on my back and arm as he reached the pillow. It was impossible to resent this though – Riley is just too bloody adorable.

'Why are you in Brigit's bed again?' He parked his nappy-clad backside on the pillow next to my head with a little squeak of plastic and cloth. It smelled as though it could do with a change.

'Because I climbed in the window first thing this morning and ate your sister all up.'

His vast blue eyes narrowed at me. 'You didn't eat Brigit. She's downstairs with Mummy.'

'Oh well, then I'll just have to eat you instead!'

I made a grab for one of his chubby little feet and made to put it in my mouth while he shrieked gaily – this was one of his favourite games. I blew raspberries against the pink, soft sole, which made him dissolve into fits of laughter.

'Sophia?' called Kayleigh. 'Are you all right up there? Is he bothering you?'

'Not at all!' I shouted down.

'Send him down when you like, his breakfast's here.'

'All right!' I turned to my small struggling victim, who chuckled happily. 'Go on, go down and get your breakfast, Riley. I need to get ready.'

As he toddled off, I reached over and wearily switched my phone off mute. There was a kind of slimy wetness in one corner, and I wondered whether Riley had put the tempting candy-pink cover in his mouth at one point.

There was a message from Tess: 'Call me any time you need me. I'm serious. Tx'

I also had two new voicemails – one from Max, saying he was sorry he'd been unavailable all day, but he hoped that Tess had been in touch, and some mobile number I vaguely recognized, until I realized it was the one Tess had just messaged me on.

She'd tried to call me again at 7:38 this morning.

I hit the voicemail icon.

'Sophia? It's me, Tess.' Her voice was high, nervous, nothing like I remembered her being last night. Something had rattled her. 'Sophia, I started poking around last night and I think I've found Wolf. We need to talk in person, as soon as possible. Can you call me back?'

She paused, and in the background there was the crank and roar and whoosh of London; it almost made me homesick. In her sigh, I sensed her disappointment and frustration at my not answering my phone in person.

'Be careful,' she said. 'God bless.'

I stared at the phone. *What the hell?*

The message was finished, and my phone was asking me if I wanted to call the number back – of course I did.

It rang and rang and rang. I wanted to leave a message, but there was no voicemail.

Tess had found Wolf.

She hadn't sounded particularly happy about it. She'd also told me to be careful.

I felt cold again, and frightened.

And I had that feeling again, like I'd had in the car as I'd been drifting off last night – that sense that I was missing something very obvious, very plain. I just couldn't figure out what it was.

* * *

Olympia at Amity was strangely upbeat when I called. Yes, of course she'd let everyone know that I was working from home today. How wonderful that my father was feeling better, what a huge relief! Naturally I wouldn't be in the office. They'd see me when they saw me. I must take care.

When I hung up, I felt more confused than I had in weeks. Was this it, finally, the soft-shoe shuffle as they moved to get rid of me, sugar-coated in politeness to avoid even the seeming of wrongdoing as they moved my case through the belly of HR?

Benjamin was a senior architect, after all. One of James's inner circle. I, on the other hand, was eminently dispensable.

I wandered back into the genially messy kitchen, where the kids were engaged with half-full bowls of cornflakes. Brigit grinned brightly at me, one of her front teeth missing. It had fallen out two days earlier, and I understood the Tooth Fairy had been particularly generous.

'How did it go?' asked Kayleigh. She was scrambling eggs they'd collected this morning from the hens out back, and that and the wholesome scent of toasting bread and melting butter was making my mouth water. 'Were they all right with you?'

'They were. Suspiciously so, if I'm honest.'

'How d'you mean?' Kayleigh snapped the kettle on and came over to the table, wiping her hands with a checked tea towel. Behind her, Riley was running in small circles with his arms out, still clad only in his underwear, and she reached and stilled him by gently resting her hand on his head, impeding his momentum.

I sighed and shrugged. 'Oh, I dunno. They're normally bears with sore heads when I talk to them about the situation here, and today they were super-nice.'

Kayleigh looked at Riley over the shoulder of her dressing gown. 'It can't be helped, Sophia. So much has happened. You need a break. You scared Rowan last night.'

'I know, I'm so sorry.'

'No, no, he's fine. But we're both worried about you. Promise us that today at least you'll have a proper day off.'

I opened my mouth to insist that no, I couldn't, but there was something in her pale, honest face that made me think twice. Hell, she's always so nice to me, despite the fact that I nearly killed her husband last night.

They might even be on to something. Maybe I *was* overdoing it.

'I can't promise to do no work,' I said. 'But I'll mostly be staying around here today, though I'll probably go to the hospital a bit later.'

Kayleigh winced. 'I suppose that will have to do. Thank God it's the weekend tomorrow. Have they said when Jared's coming home?'

I shook my head. 'No. Hopefully soon. And that's another thing. The house will have to be made ready – it'll need cleaning. I was wondering if you knew anyone in the village who needs the work?'

'Sure. I'll ask around. Actually, Sophia, I meant to ask, did you ever find the . . . you know, what you were looking for?' She lifted her hands and discreetly mimed pulling a trigger.

It took me a second to work out that she meant the missing shotgun.

'The what? Oh, *oh*, no. No I haven't. I found the cabinet, but it was empty.'

'Mummy,' said Brigit suddenly, 'Did you tell Sophia about Daddy's note?'

'No, I . . .'

Brigit seized her chance to be a partaker in adult affairs, a bearer of tales, a mover and shaker.

'Sophia! Daddy left a note for you on your laptop! He said it was important and we had to remember to tell you in case you didn't see it.'

'Did he? Where?'

'Brigit, let Sophia have some breakfast first . . .'

But Brigit was on a roll. She dropped her spoon into her bowl with a noisy clatter, splashing milk over her brother, and pointed to where my laptop lay on the counter near the microwave, charging.

'It's there, it's there, look!'

'I won't tell you again, eat your breakfast, missy,' said Kayleigh. She jerked a thumb at the laptop. 'This is how you access the CCTV Rowan set up for you . . .'

Of course. I was on my feet, and saw on the cover of the laptop a single yellow Post-it note in his untidy print:

https://www.goldstarsurveillance.co.uk/securecloud/3D82A84B
Username: smackenzie@theamitystudio.co.uk
Password: j3h9ddgf1

'Ah!' I said, twitching the note off the cover and carrying it to my seat. 'Brilliant!'

Then Kayleigh dropped a plate of scrambled eggs on toast in front of me, and I forgot all about the CCTV, at least for a little while.

* * *

The website had been a little confusing, but eventually I managed to log in, after which I found six squares on my personal page, each sporting a small whirling icon.

I waited for a few minutes, fresh coffee cooling at my elbow, and was about to give up when a dialogue box opened: 'If this is your first time logging in to your account, there may be a 5- to 10-minute delay establishing a connection to your feed. Please be patient!'

I sighed. I was not in a patient mood, but I doubted there was any way to communicate this to my laptop, short of smacking it with a hammer.

Kayleigh had set off with the kids at ten. They were all going swimming together at Beccles Lido, then stopping for a McDonald's, taking advantage of the summer sunshine for the day. My dad was in assessment appointments until one, when I would go over and see him.

At some point I was going to have to explain to him everything I had learned about my mum and the cult.

The thought made me feel a little nauseous.

I'd tried Tess three times and had no response. I told myself she was doubtless a very busy woman, but it didn't make me feel any better.

I couldn't stand feeling so useless, so I decided to tinker with the SH project this morning while I waited for my dad to be free. I clicked open my VPN, my link with Amity.

It looked very crowded in there.

I sat still for a long moment, hardly breathing.

All of my missing files had been returned. Clicking on their details, it was clear I hadn't simply mistaken their location – they had all been created, or rather recreated, from new sometime late yesterday evening. It was definitely my work, back from some electronic sojourn that no amount of squinting at the file details would reveal anything about.

Perhaps it had all been a simple IT glitch. Though I couldn't shake the feeling that they had been returned to me in order to head off any complaint I might make about them going missing.

Olympia had been very nice on the phone that morning.

I buried my head in my arms.

Suddenly I remembered my conversation with Tess the night before: 'All you need to be is manipulated into a position where you surrender your control.'

I could appreciate that Amity were disappointed in my continued patchy attendance and unscheduled absences, but it wasn't a situation I had chosen or could fix instantly, and we were all just going to have to live with it.

One thing was for sure – I was so fucking done with surrendering my control to them.

I opened my browser again and, as if by magic, I was watching six different still views of Eden Gardens. Nothing much was happening in any of them. I could see no people.

I clicked on CAM 1. This appeared to activate the feed for the camera – this must be the camera I'd seen last night, mounted on the top of the gate. It showed me grainy footage of tarmac, the sweep of the drive up to the gardens, a tiny fraction of the café with its grubby picnic benches under the awning. They were empty. Suddenly Rowan was there in the truck, heading towards the camera, and I could even make out his face for a few seconds in the windscreen – he looked distracted and drawn, as though something was on his mind. The back of the truck was full of broken old equipment he'd been talking about taking to the dump yesterday.

Then he drove away into the bottom of the frame and was gone.

Everything was working as it should. I should relax more, I supposed.

I clicked on CAM 2 and, true to Rowan's word, it showed the café, the building's single door in the centre of the screen. I was about to try another camera when the door opened and Monica appeared.

Perhaps she had just come out to feel the sunshine on her face, but I lingered, intrigued. Her figure was too faraway at this angle to make out her expression with the blurry quality of the video stream, but her head seemed to be moving, as though looking for someone.

I realized something – there was a secret power in this, in watching people who don't know they're being watched, and it was a thrill with a dirty, disreputable edge. I wasn't sure I liked it, or what it said about me.

I was about to click CAM 3 when I stopped.

Monica had turned and shut the café doors; she was bent over the handle, her arms moving. Near her hands, a bright pixel flashed, something metallic catching the sun, then it was gone.

She was locking the café doors. With a final gesture she turned the sign on the door over from OPEN to CLOSED.

It was only an hour until lunchtime, our busiest period.

She straightened and quickly walked away to the left of the camera's view, then vanished.

What the hell?

CAM 3 showed the interior of the café, empty and lifeless, a full pot of coffee visible on the hotplate. CAM 4 was the back of the house, with birds sporting back and forth over the hedge in dark blurs. Nothing else.

CAM 5 was the gold.

It was the front of my parents' house, and I could tell that the camera was mounted on top of my dad's garden shed, not far from where my mum had hung herself. There was the long narrow drag of vegetable patches and the tiny square of lawn, but the focus was zoomed in on the front door.

Monica entered the screen from the side, using the garden gate, through the door I knew was marked PRIVATE. Though the image was still grainy, I saw her hand go to her pocket, and realized, with a little flush of indignant disbelief, that somehow she had obtained a copy of the key.

Only my parents and I have the key to that gate.

Well, no. I'd given Rowan my mum's key while he was helping out after her death.

Why would Rowan give that key to Monica?

She crossed the lawn quickly and I waited to see what she would do – did she also have his key to the house?

She didn't approach the house, though. Instead she turned, and with a thudding heart I realized she was heading towards my dad's shed, her walk a swift, jerky gait. In the screen, she grew bigger, and her face was visible – it was nothing like the open, friendly expression I saw whenever I dropped by the café. Her mouth was a taut white line, her head constantly turning nervously, to see if she was being observed.

There was something terrifying about this, as if, even though I was two miles down the road, she was somehow walking straight up to me as I loitered above the threshold of the shed, the tree that had been my mum's gallows shading us both with its branches. My mouth was dry, my heart pounding. I didn't know this person.

When she suddenly stopped, her mouth contorted into

261

a shocked snarl and I jumped in my chair. It was as if she had seen me.

Her lips moved and she spat out something, a curse perhaps, though I couldn't hear the words as there was no sound on the camera. She stood, not moving, as though stunned. I realized, with a little burst of insight, that she'd spotted the camera. She must not have known they'd been installed.

As quickly as she had come, she turned on her heel and walked back up the garden, letting herself out through the gate. I tracked her progress back through the cameras to the café; noticing how she fumbled, dropping her keys and quickly picking them up again as she let herself back into the building, forgetting to turn the sign around again from CLOSED to OPEN, or perhaps deliberately choosing not to.

I clicked CAM 3.

I was inside the café with her now. She walked quickly round to the back of the counter and pulled on her apron, tying it tightly, her fingers snagging in the ties, and then retreated to the back of the kitchen. Then I saw her no more.

What the hell?

Within moments I was calling Rowan.

'Heya, can't answer the phone right now.' (I swore quietly to myself – I had come to know his answerphone message like the back of my hand in these last few weeks; he'd be driving) 'but leave a message and I'll get back to you. Peace.'

'Rowan, it's me. I just saw something really weird on the CCTV. Please call me the minute you get this, and don't talk to anyone else about it first. Especially not Monica, OK? Speak to you soon.'

I hung up.

It was a half-hour drive to the recycling, and even then he might have not heard his phone or muted it.

I watched the screen. Monica reappeared now, carrying one of her cakes. She cut it carefully into slices before lifting it on to the cake stand and putting the glass lid over it.

I should call the police, shouldn't I? But what would I say? Rowan might have given her the key, for all I knew.

But why would he do that?

Even then, after what I'd seen, my mind still sought some reasonable explanation. But it just wouldn't do.

Perhaps I should go over there.

Once the idea entered my head, I couldn't shake it. I had been shadowed by death and darkness for the past few weeks, and I had had enough – more than enough.

It was madness to go over there and accuse her on my own – but that wasn't my intention. I could go over there on some pretext, and sit in the café. I'd say it was a beautiful day and I just wanted to do a little work before I set off for the hospital to see my dad. I could make sure she made no other forays into places she didn't belong, at least until Rowan got there and we could, together, decide what to do. Confront her together, if necessary.

It was quarter past eleven now. The café would start to fill with visitors before too long – it would be a public place.

Safer, perhaps, than this house.

I snatched up my car keys and was out the door.

Chapter Twenty-Five

When I drove up to the gates I was already having second thoughts about my hasty plan. Monica's sprightly red Toyota Yaris was parked up against the fence at Eden Gardens, with its Baby on Board sticker and collection of cuddly toys gathered on the parcel shelf.

Perhaps I had imagined the whole thing.

She had gone into my parents' garden, with a key she had no business possessing, and approached the shed, before spotting the newly installed camera and turning back.

The most she was guilty of was trespassing, if that.

But in my heart I knew. The bald account of her actions was one thing – innocuous; dishonest but not sinister, easily explained away. That wasn't the problem. It was her face, her true face, the one I had seen when she'd spotted the camera. There had been something almost feral, unhinged, in it.

Monica was not who she seemed.

Sitting in the car, I burst into tears. I had *liked* her. My sense of betrayal billowed about me like a stormy sea. Not just betrayal, but fear.

Who was she, really? What did she want?

What did they all want?

You know what she wants. She's one of them. She's after the notebooks.

Pull yourself together, Sophia. The police have the first two notebooks now. You're going to go in there, keep an eye on her and wait for Rowan. She doesn't know you've been watching her – she probably thinks you're at work. Everything is going to be all right. And you and Rowan can confront her together, or call the police.

Come on.

* * *

'Hi, Sophia,' Monica said as I walked into the café, trying to aspire to a dishevelled nonchalance I absolutely did not feel.

You would never, in a million years, have imagined there was anything wrong. Everyone keeps telling me I'm under too much stress, after all, and maybe I was imagining things. Her pretty blonde hair was tied up on top of her head, her apron sprinkled with a pattern of tiny yellow primroses.

The only strange thing had been the sign – the one on the door, that still read CLOSED. I turned it round to OPEN as I passed it. I left the door propped wide, letting the sunlight in, though my mum had always disapproved of this, saying, 'It lets the flies in.'

'How are you feeling?' she asked.

'Better,' I said. 'Slept for the first time in ages.' I gazed around the café, at its order and cleanliness and, more saliently, its emptiness.

My heart sank.

'Dead again, I see.'

She shrugged. 'It's still only half eleven.' In terms of non-chalance, she had me absolutely beat. 'It'll pick up soon.' She turned back to the kitchen. 'Can I get you something to eat?' she called over her shoulder.

'No thanks, I had a big breakfast this morning.' I sat down at the table by the door, pulled out my laptop. 'I was just going to get a cup of coffee and do some work.'

'Oh, let me get that.'

'You don't have to.'

'No, I insist. It's why I'm here, right?' Her smile was huge, brilliant, but still . . . there was something about it. It was too wide, too high, and in its shadow I saw that feral snarl I had seen in the camera.

I realized I wasn't the only one who was rattled.

I smiled back, both of us exchanging rictus grins across the floor of this building where my mother had spent the last twenty-seven years of her life.

I was aware of the coffee being placed in front of me as I opened my laptop. 'Sure you don't want some cake to go with it?' she asked. 'I can recommend the lemon drizzle.'

'No thanks,' I said, shaking my head. 'I need to cut down. I'm gaining so much weight . . .'

'Nonsense, if anything you're wasting away. Just a little piece?'

'No,' I said, and the vehemence in my voice was like a gun going off.

She went still, her face blank, confused. I had gone too far.

'Sorry, Monica, I didn't mean to . . . you know what, cake would be lovely.' I offered a wan smile. 'The diet can start tomorrow.'

She smiled back. 'It's always a day away, right?'

As she vanished, I rubbed my face with my hands. In the background I could hear a vague buzzing – the electrical fly killer.

That noise had haunted my childhood. It had always made me anxious. I thought about them – those flies being lured in by food, then the pretty lights, then the zap of electricity. Everything about it seemed an offence against hospitality. My mum hated it.

Fucking hell, when is someone else going to come into this café? What if they don't? I tapped in my password quickly to unlock my laptop, aware of her approaching behind me with the cake. I didn't want her to see it, to learn what the word was.

My lock screen vanished, and we were both greeted with the sight of www.goldstarsurveillance.co.uk's website, complete with six views of the business and the gardens.

I'd forgotten to close it when I'd rushed out of the house.

As if to mock me, the café's tired wireless signal tore into vigorous life, with CAM 3 resolving almost immediately into a little cameo; the café, with me at the table with the laptop and her at my shoulder, gazing down at the screen, plate of cake in hand. An infinitely recursive loop of both of us watching ourselves on a computer screen.

My body froze, and I was aware of her behind me, gently, slowly, setting the cake on the table next to the coffee.

Panicking, I quickly shut the browser, but too late, far too late, and when I turned to thank her for the cake, she didn't even reply, instead drifting back towards the kitchen.

I was trembling.

I could attempt to act as though the incident with the screen meant nothing – after all, she knew that we'd installed cameras now, that was the whole point. I'd seen her react to them. I could just bluff it out.

Or, and this was the option that was winning out as I heard her moving about in the kitchen, I could pick up my bag, phone and keys and run. Run and not stop until I reached my car.

To my left was the café door, and the sunlight was a golden path across the worn flagstone floor. A mere five steps away, if that.

My car keys were on the cheap Formica table. My phone was in my handbag. I just had to curl my hand around the keys, making no noise, slide the strap of my bag up my shoulder, and vanish out of that open door.

'It was an accident.'

She was at my shoulder again. I hadn't heard her approach.

'What was?' I turned around, trying to keep my voice neutral.

And that was going to be harder to do than you might expect, because she was holding a knife.

It was the big chef's knife from the kitchen, my mum's favourite, the one she had always used to slice the vegetables for salads and soups, with the bone handle and rusting rivets that always seemed to be impossible to clean – and yet she could never bear to throw it away or replace it.

Monica's fingers were wrapped around that bone handle, and her knuckles were white.

I swallowed hard. Everything was rapidly becoming unreal, as though I was seeing the world through gauze.

She wasn't smiling any more.

'You don't understand,' she said, and the words seemed to growl out of her, through the barrier of her gritted teeth. 'You don't know how to let go. You don't know how to really exist in the world, to feel the Creative Spark. You just skate along the surface, just like the rest of the human dross. You betray your heritage.'

In the silence that followed I could hear the anodyne noises of the café at rest – the coffee pot burbling, the buzz of the fly-killing unit.

She loomed over me, trapping me in my seat against the wall and the table. She was growing increasingly agitated.

I gazed up at her.

She couldn't stand over me like this. That had to change. If she went for me now with that knife I would have no way to escape.

And that was what she was building up to. Her trembling was growing more intense, her knuckles more white.

'What was an accident?' I asked sharply.

This seemed to derail some private train of thought. She blinked, as though recalled to herself, and for a second she was hollowed out, pale, as if at some awful memory.

'You need to give them to me, Sophia. You need to give them to me, or, even though I don't want to, even though it is forbidden, I will hurt you. Do you understand?'

I offered her a quick tight nod.

'I'll give them to you, I promise,' I said. My mouth was dry, it was hard to speak. 'Don't hurt me . . . I have them right here . . .'

She must mean the Morningstar notebooks, my mum's book – what else could she mean? – but when I picked up my laptop there was a flash of something between puzzlement and rage in her face, as though she had expected something else.

'They're digitized, they're in here.'

She reached out to snatch the laptop, and the knife dropped down, just momentarily.

I smashed the sharp edge of the laptop into her face. I had aimed for her temple, but missed, glancing it, cutting her across the brow. The bright line of blood was instant, shocking in its scarlet immediacy.

I shoved her backwards, hard.

I scrambled for the door, over the table, but she did not fall over. Instantly she was after me, and I felt the whoosh of the knife at the back of my head against my hair.

I fell over the table, tumbling to the flags, barely feeling it, as she darted around it, the knife clutched wickedly ahead of her.

I rolled to my feet, my bag forgotten, the keys forgotten, and bolted for the open door, out into the blinding daylight.

She was a mere second behind me, and I knew she would

catch me. I screamed as her hand closed in my hair, jerked me back, and the knife came down, stabbing into my jacket, just missing my back.

There was a roaring, and shadow, and suddenly Rowan was there in the truck. I had a glimpse of his amazed face through the windscreen as he pulled to a stop and leapt out. The knife sank down again, snagged in my jacket, then tore downwards along my back. I wriggled out of the way, my hair tearing out in her clutching hands, but still I felt it slit my skin. Rowan was running towards me, his eyes perfectly round and his mouth wide open, bellowing my name.

The knife was suddenly under my chin.

This was it, I realized. This was where she slit my throat, and I would die.

I grabbed the blade with both hands, feeling it bite my skin, and Rowan rushed her.

She shrieked with rage and a thin stream of terror, and suddenly she let me go, the knife sliding against my palms as she took it with her.

'Soph!' Rowan was on the ground, my hands in his. 'Fucking hell! Stay here!'

I don't know where he thought I might go, but I stayed there while he called 999, and barked about a stabbing, yes, police, ambulance, yeah, whoever you can send, bring them along, and he was wrapping my hands in my slashed jacket and telling me everything was going to be fine, just scratched, I'd be fine.

'Where did she go?' I asked.

'I dunno. Forget about her . . . what the—'

'She's gone to my dad's shed. They're looking for something.' My teeth chattered. 'They're still looking for my mum's notebooks. They *must* be. She wanted t-to know where *they* were . . .'

'Calm down, calm down, Soph.' He stood up, raising his hand to shade his eyes as he looked towards the drive. 'The ambulance will be here in a minute.'

'No it won't,' I said. 'We're miles from anywhere out here.'

He pretended not to hear this.

'Help me up,' I said.

'I don't think—'

'It's all right, it's just cuts. It's the shock, more than anything. Did she get me in the back?'

He glanced around me. 'A little. Just a cat scratch.'

'Help me up.'

He was reluctant, but he helped me to my feet and held me while I tried to get my bearings. Everything seemed unreal, and I felt cold, but I explained my morning – the CCTV and its revelation, my trip to the café, Monica's strange words and violent reaction.

'Why on earth did you come here and sit in the caff with some nutter?' He shook his head. 'I wonder about you, Soph. I really do.'

'I thought we'd have customers! That it would be a public place! I'd be able to keep an eye on her and she wouldn't do anything with witnesses there. I didn't expect . . .'

The memory of opening the laptop and the surveillance cams on it burned. How stupid can one person be?

All was silent, except for birdsong and the faraway sounds of traffic, the breeze gently agitating the leaves in the trees. We contemplated it for a moment in silence.

'Where do you think she's gone?' I asked.

'No idea. Let's go back to the truck and if she shows up again, we can drive away. I'm not really up for a round two.'

I nodded. In my heart, though, I knew she had gone. She might have tried my dad's shed again, but there was nothing in there.

Rowan supported me as I stumbled back to the truck. The engine was still idling, and he handed me up into the passenger side.

'She had a key,' I said. 'A key to the garden.'

'What?' Rowan was distracted, his face tight.

'Monica had a key to our garden.'

'I didn't give her one,' he answered, alarmed and stung – something of my suspicions must have showed on my face. 'Mine's . . .' he started checking his pockets. 'It's not . . . oh, shit. Shit. I don't have mine. I think I left it on the counter in the café this morning. Shit, Soph. I'm sorry. I'm so sorry.'

'It doesn't matter,' I said, weary and nauseous. 'She didn't get whatever it was she wanted.'

'She's left her car,' said Rowan, pointing.

I blinked. Indeed she had. The sporty red Yaris sat quiescent next to the fence.

An alarming thought suddenly occurred to me.

'Rowan, what if she goes after my dad?'

He shook his head. 'Why would she?'

'Why would she go after *me*?'

'Because you'd rumbled her. And even if she did go after Jared, she won't get to the hospital before we do, not without a car or money. I'm more worried about the cottage. What if she takes it in her head that you've hidden the notebooks there and heads off that way? I'm not having Kayleigh and the kids come home to find her there – fuck knows what might happen. We need to wait here for the coppers,' he said. 'They'll know what to do about this.'

I nodded through my shocked fug.

Rowan rang the police again, asking for Rob Howarth by name, and I listened to him explain everything that had happened that morning, while I sat on the dusty vinyl seat, staring vacantly through the window, crushing some unused fast-food napkins from the truck into my bloody palms.

Tess.

The thought was as swift as a lightning stroke.

I need to tell Tess about this.

Rowan had fetched my bag from the café, and with my bloodied, numb fingers I searched for and found my iPhone, punched in Tess's number and held the phone to my ear.

I got out of the truck, not wanting to talk over Rowan's conversation. He had got hold of Kayleigh, and I could see he was getting emotional. I let my feet slide down to the tarmac, raising a placating hand towards his surprised face and furrowed brow. I wouldn't be going far.

I took a long nervous look around me. There was still no sign of Monica.

Tess's phone rang and rang and rang again. That said, something was different. There was a sort of weird echo, an ambient trilling . . .

Her phone was ringing.

Her phone was ringing *nearby.*

I let the handset fall away from my ear, listening to the birds and rustling and faraway traffic of Eden Gardens.

It was definitely a ringing phone.

With a sick knot of horror, I realized it was coming from the boot of Monica's car.

'Rowan.'

'Love, can you please just take the kids to your mum's, just while we—'

'Rowan . . .' I repeated.

'I know, and I'm sorry, but Sophia needs to go to A&E . . . no, no, she's fine, but her hands have been cut.'

'*Rowan!*'

273

'Hang on a minute, love . . . bloody hell, Soph, what *is* it?'

I didn't reply, I just let the trilling speak for itself.

His expression emptied as he realized where the sound was coming from.

'Kayleigh, I have to go. I'll call you right back.' He looked at me. 'Who are you calling?'

'Tess,' I said, unable to take my eyes off the red Yaris. 'She's a woman that left my mum's cult, years ago. She got in touch last night and told me to be careful.'

He had various tools in the back of the truck, but in the end he risked going back into the café, where he found Monica's beige jacket while I watched hawkishly from the café door. Her car keys were in the pocket.

'Come on,' I said. 'Tess could be in there, in the boot. She could be hurt.'

'She could be in there,' he replied evenly, though his face was deathly white. 'As for the rest . . .'

I knew exactly what he was thinking as we stalked up to the Yaris nervously, because I was thinking the same thing.

And when he pressed the key to unlock the boot, while I kept nervous watch and the faraway howls of police sirens grew nearer and nearer, I saw immediately, with a heart-stopping jolt of horror, that we were both right.

Chapter Twenty-Six

It was the reporters who made it all happen in the end. It was they who brought out into the open what the passing decades had failed to expose.

When the police arrived at Eden Gardens in a storm of sirens, we had been driven away and questioned separately – Rowan at the station, me in the A&E department at the hospital my dad was staying in, while my wounds were bandaged. My injuries looked much worse than they were, but my hands required an annoying level of gauze that made doing anything difficult.

I handed over the login details to the cameras without demur. During the questioning, the detectives, a man and a woman, had been interested in what I had to say about Morningstar, and I had waxed lyrical, frequently gesturing at DI Rob Howarth, who had stood silently in the background, describing my mum's notebooks, which I had already handed over.

'Did the other notebook ever turn up, Sophia?' he'd asked patiently.

I shook my head. 'No.'

I made sure to tell them about Tess's final phone call, and the warning about Wolf.

Once they were done with me, I'd called Max right away and told him everything. A Morningstar true believer had inveigled her way on to the staff, had murdered Tess Hotchkiss and attempted to murder me.

'You're serious?'

No, I thought with a flicker of pure frustration, *I'm telling you all this for a dare.*

I swallowed and tried to pull myself together. It wasn't his fault the whole story sounded so far-fetched.

I was outside the Royal Suffolk's A&E department, trying to hold my phone in my bandaged hands. 'Yes, I'm serious.'

'Are you all right?'

'I'm fine. They've bandaged me up and—'

'*Bandaged* you? You were injured?' He sounded horrified.

'I . . . a little. Look, it's really nothing. A few defensive injuries; what are they between friends? And Rowan is fine.'

'And they've caught this woman?'

'No. That's just it. They don't know where she is. But she doesn't have her car.' I wiped at my brow with the back of one bound hand. 'It's . . . Tess was in it.'

I thought back to what had awaited us in the boot as Rowan had opened it. Tess curled up on her back, her salt and pepper hair slicked and spiked dark red, her face misshapen with the ferocity of the blows, almost as though she was melting like candlewax; one snow-white hand, with a plain gold band on the ring finger, resting over her breast.

Rowan had turned away and vomited near the front of the car.

I hadn't moved. I stood there, the lid of the boot like an awning, and made myself stare down at her.

The second of the Morningstar Ascendants to end up dead in a month.

'Tess Hotchkiss is *dead*?'

'Yes.' I held my breath, wondering how to say this. 'You know, you might want to start thinking about your personal safety, too. This woman is still out there, and I think you, and probably everyone else at Paracelsus, might be vulnerable right now.' I winced, sweat running into my wounds. 'These people aren't taking prisoners any more.'

That did it for Max. He wanted me to come to London. He would put me up in a hotel, so we could talk about what to do next in terms of Nina's book, but there was absolutely no way I was leaving. My life was here at the moment and I was going nowhere.

I told him I'd be in touch soon.

Despite his protestations, I hung up and went back into the hospital.

* * *

By the time I sat down with my dad as he gingerly tackled the small, bland dinner in his hospital room that evening, Rowan, Tess and I were the headline story on the news – one person dead, another injured at a garden centre in Pulverton. Karen Ince, who sometimes called herself Monica Hardy or Antonia Lister, was armed and potentially dangerous, we were told, and should not be approached.

They even had a clip to accompany the news segment, and it wrung my heart to watch it. It was Monica, in the café, at about ten o'clock that morning, unaware of the internal camera, washing Tess's blood off her hands. The reason she'd been tying on a new apron when I saw her was that she'd stuffed the bloody one she'd worn earlier in the café rubbish.

As I watched her ball the material up and crush it down into the pedal bin on national television, I felt caught in a vast, obscene disconnect. I had been the crazy daughter in denial about my suicidal, mentally ill mother, blaming some cult, constantly asking for more time off work, nosing like a conspiracy theorist around the offices of the great and the good – a lone, isolated Sophia in my own paranoid, furious world. Now, in the blink of an eye, my personal tragedy was being consumed by millions as they sat down to their egg and chips, waiting for *Strictly* or *The Great British Bake Off* to start.

'Both Theresa Hotchkiss and Karen Ince were former members of a group now called the Society for Spiritual Enrichment, an organization alleged to be a "dangerous cult", led by a former musician called Aaron Kessler and based in his mansion in Kent . . .'

The eyes of the various newsreaders glittered over the television – *Cults! Rock stars! Murders! We've struck gold tonight, people!*

You'd have thought it would make me feel more believed, more grounded, but weirdly, it was the exact opposite. I felt more exposed and lonely than ever, even more of an outsider, and the only good that could come out of it was if this woman was captured quickly, before she could hurt anybody else.

Terrible as Tess's murder was – I saw her blood-spattered face every time I shut my eyes – it wasn't even the most troubling thing on my mind at that moment.

The thing that disturbed me most was this: how had the media found out about Morningstar? I certainly hadn't mentioned it to any of the reporters who'd constantly been trying to contact me all day. I had stuck with the police's recommended statement, as had Tess's colleagues at the cult outreach project. When I'd spoken to Ebele, Tess's co-worker at the church, I'd had the uncomfortable feeling that she thought *I* was the leak.

Somebody was talking about Morningstar and my mum.

My dad watched the TV digest of these events silently, picking through his beef pot pie.

In my pocket, my phone buzzed. It had started to ring steadily throughout the afternoon, so I switched it to vibrate. Then Do Not Disturb.

If I'd stood up now and left the ward, I wouldn't have made it as far as the corridor without being tackled by a reporter. It was only the constable lounging on one of the chairs outside that kept them out of Dad's room.

I wondered if they were hacking my voicemails yet. How long before they got in touch with Amity? Before they started rooting through my love life?

'This is a mess, right enough, Sophy.'

My dad gazed up at the wall-mounted television, chewing slowly.

'Yeah,' I said wearily.

He looked about to say more, but then gave up, simply sighing and shaking his head.

'Look, Dad, Kayleigh's found someone to clean the house when they discharge you, but I really think—'

'I know what you think,' he said. 'But believe you me, everything will be better once I get home. That woman will never come back there now.' He snorted. 'She's already done all the damage she can.'

'I wish I had your faith.'

He shrugged gingerly.

'What do you think she wanted?' I asked.

'You know what she wanted,' said my dad. 'She was one of that cult. The ones you told me about. She wanted to intimidate your mum.' He licked his lips and gestured at the television. 'It was probably her that kept breaking into the house. Her or another one of them.'

'Dad, Mum was already gone when I hired Monica.'

'All right. Not just her. All of them.' He wiped a little drool away from the corner of his mouth, his brow wrinkling in impatience. 'They want to stop this book of your mother's, whatever that is.' He scowled.

I didn't answer. I was thinking of how miserable, desperate and despairing my mum must have been to contemplate such a horrible death, to attack my dad.

'I know you don't like to hear this, but your mum was . . . Christ, she was . . .'

I waited in silence. I understood his anger, I just didn't want to engage with it. Perhaps I was a little angry, as well, or it just hurt too much. Silence was all I had.

He threw down the fork irritably. 'Oh, forget it.' He leaned back. 'I just need to get home.'

'There's no rush. Anyway, you're staying in this hospital until Tuesday, whether you like it or not.'

He seemed about to say more, but something about my face must have given him pause. Instead he moved on to his little pot of fruit jelly, and the news moved on to tomorrow's weather – hot again, with the possibility of summer storms over the weekend.

* * *

'Good morning, Sophia.'

It was DI Rob Howarth, tapping tentatively on Dad's hospital room door.

I stirred in the chair, rubbing my eyes, all my bones aching. I had spent the night in my dad's room, in the chair next to the bed, and the nurses had brought me a blanket and pillow.

'I'm sorry, I didn't mean to wake you.' Howarth appeared genuinely apologetic.

I was starting to like him a lot more lately, now that he seemed to be taking me seriously.

'It's all right,' I whispered, and yawned hugely.

I looked over at my dad. He was fast asleep, but already I could see a big improvement, at least relatively speaking. His cheeks were pink, the remains of his springy hair somehow more vital.

I reached over and kissed his bald brow.

I got to my bare feet, still dressed in yesterday's clothes, my cut hands bound in clean white bandages.

'Let's go out into the corridor,' I said softly, forcing my feet into my sandals. 'I don't want to worry him.'

Howarth nodded. 'Yes. I have some things to tell you.'

* * *

In the corridor, we passed the constable who had kept watch overnight. He offered us both a pleasant nod.

'Shall we get a coffee?'

I agreed, yawning again. 'Have you caught her?'

'Sadly no, but we don't think she's in the area. We spotted her on CCTV last night at a motorway services on the M6. She must have hitch-hiked.'

'Perhaps,' I said. 'Or she has an accomplice? Maybe this Wolf gave her a lift, who knows? Tess did warn me that he was around. Or maybe Penelope or Lucy have spirited her away somewhere to save their reputations. Maybe they're all in this together.'

He shrugged. 'She was alone on the camera. Anyway, she has family in Scotland. We think she might be going there.'

All around us, the hospital was starting to come alive, morning staff emerging from offices after handover, bed washes about to begin. They'll wash my dad first, if memory serves, after the meds, so it was just as well we were heading down to the coffee shop.

My dad didn't like being helpless. And he certainly didn't like me seeing him that way.

In the coffee shop, we found seats at a small table between a gasping woman in a dressing gown with a tube attached to her nose and a young couple, the woman hugely pregnant, constantly stroking her extended belly through a thin checked nightdress.

'When did Tess die?' I asked when Rob Howarth returned with a white coffee and an almond croissant for me, a cup of tea for himself.

'Yesterday morning, we think — a few hours before you found her, though the post-mortem won't be until later today.' He tore open a little packet of sugar and poured it into the tea. 'We think Tess Hotchkiss came out here, looking for you. She caught the Lowestoft train first thing, then a taxi to Eden Gardens. She went into the café, asking for directions to the house, and we think "Monica", or this person who calls herself Monica, recognized her as a person opposed to their religious group. She killed her with the same knife she attacked you with. It's captured on your CCTV.' His eyes met mine over the lip of his cup. 'You could go back to that morning and view it. I wouldn't recommend it, though.'

'Don't worry,' I said, shuddering. 'I've got no plans to.'

'Tess Hotchkiss was stabbed so hard in the head that the knife pierced the skull in places.' He sipped his tea, his expression thoughtful. 'It was an extraordinary attack. You're extremely lucky to be alive, Sophia. So much so, we're wondering if she intended to kill you at all.'

'I don't feel lucky.' I didn't know what else to reply. 'Did the people at Tess's church say why she came all the way out here to see me?'

'No.' He put the cup down. 'Presumably, from what you've told us, it was in connection with this "Wolf" character.'

'Will you question Aaron Kessler?' I asked.

There was a long pause.

'What?' I asked in the face of his silence. 'Did I say something wrong? I mean, he's the one thing all these people have in common.' Suddenly I was filled with a burning rage.

'So, Sophia . . .' He was crimsoning a little, his mouth compressing, as though he were getting ready to tell me to calm down.

'No,' I snapped. 'Don't you dare "So, Sophia" me. I don't understand what the problem is. I've been saying all this from day one – it's *very* simple. We went through all of it again yesterday, after this crazy woman nearly slit my throat—'

'Sophia—'

'My mum was in a cult years ago and writes a book about it, right?' I furiously counted these events off on my bandaged fingers. 'A book that will ruin reputations left, right and centre. A publisher approaches the people involved and says, "Hey, this is happening, what do you think?" And almost immediately my parents are put through a six-month campaign of intimidation and criminal damage.

'This so stresses out my mum that she hangs herself and attacks my dad when he tries to stop her. Right? And then, no sooner is she dead, than strange people start following me. One of Aaron Kessler's little worshippers even gets a bloody job working for me in my café, all the better to keep searching the house. And then, when someone who's spoken out about the cult in the past pitches up, she *stabs her in the head* and hides her in the boot of her bloody car!

'These people – Penelope, Lucy and Aaron Fucking Kessler – all of them, all want to stop this book being published because of something my mum says in it. Every single thing that's happened supports this view, and people are now *dead* because of this! So don't "So, Sophia" me, *Rob*. Will you question Aaron Kessler?'

The entire coffee shop had turned to stone. The pregnant woman, obviously in some distress, was still breathing shallowly and rubbing her belly, but her partner was staring at me. The other customers were staring at me. Even the girl working the counter, with her green apron and name badge reading 'Hi I'm Valentina!' was staring at me from over the top of the cake stands.

I crossed my arms mulishly and ignored them all, focusing on Rob.

Of all the people present, DI Rob Howarth seemed the one least taken aback by my outburst.

'Sophia, I understand that you're very upset.' His tone was calm, almost apologetic.

'You think?' I snarled.

'You may not believe me, and that's your prerogative, but here's my problem. All these things that you've described, when you say them like that, they do indeed sound like a story. A logical flow of events, if you will.' He set his tea down on the table. 'But in this cult of yours, anyone can take a load of details, throw them together and make a narrative out of them. Anyone can have a story; it doesn't make it true.' He shrugged. 'I need more than a narrative. I need physical evidence.'

'How much more evidence could you possibly need?' I snapped.

'These connections, Sophia – they're nearly thirty years old! There's no evidence that Lucy DuBois or Penelope Longman have any connection to Aaron Kessler that isn't purely historical. No evidence that the woman you called "Monica" ever burgled your parents' home. She only started working at the garden centre a week ago.'

I groaned aloud. He just didn't get it. 'Look—'

'By your own admission,' he said, not rising to me, 'you've never seen the people you allege followed you on the train again. We'll naturally keep investigating, but there's no proof that this was anything more than the work of a single random mentally ill person. Someone who became inflamed when she heard her religious group was under attack in the press because of a book that was going to be published, and who acted alone, breaking into the property, insinuating herself on to your staff, and ultimately killing Pastor Hotchkiss.'

'Acted alone?' I let out a harsh bark of laughter. 'Really? So I imagined the couple on the train, then?'

There was a long pause.

'In answer to your original question, yes, we did question Aaron Kessler. I spoke to him yesterday. He's co-operating fully with the investigation. He gave us this woman's name – her real name – her address, and a lead on the sister in Scotland.'

'But Tess . . .'

'Why would he want Pastor Hotchkiss dead? As he pointed out, she's been "maligning his religion" for the past twenty-seven years. Why would he suddenly want her killed? Why would anyone? There's no logical reason for it.'

I wanted to grab him and shake him. 'Because of the book Mum was writing! The stuff in the notebooks!'

'But you've never found the third notebook, which is supposed to contain all these revelations,' he said, still infuriatingly calm and sympathetic. 'Have you?'

'No,' I said. 'But . . .'

'Has Max Clarke ever explicitly told you what these revelations are?' He glanced at his watch.

When he said 'Max Clarke' I caught a note of disapproval, which was just subtly different enough from the stoic delicacy with which he treated me to notice.

'As far as I know, he just told them that an ex-member was writing a memoir of her time with them in the Eighties. They worked out themselves that he meant my mum.' His expression didn't change, which nettled me. 'Which I still think is enough to be going on with.'

'Perhaps. But I've been reviewing the files on Peter Clay's shooting, and while it's not the most thorough investigation, I can't see anything unusual about it. As for the rest, you could argue that Mrs Longman and Mrs DuBois showed questionable judgment at times, but while their behaviour might be personally embarrassing to them now, other than the drug use, it was never illegal.'

'What's your point?'

'Think about it, Sophia. Why would anyone want Tess Hotchkiss killed? Who gets anything out of it – except for one unstable woman who saw her appear at your house and recognized her as an enemy to a cult she's involved in?'

I sat there, my mouth opening and closing, until finally I managed to say: 'If nobody wanted her dead, then why is she dead? Why is this happening?'

'Mr Kessler thinks—'

'Mr Kessler,' I snapped. 'He's *Mr Kessler* now. Oh that's just great!'

'Sophia, I know this is hard, but you need to hear this. Mr Kessler was approached about this book months ago and told his . . . followers, or whatever they are, not to speak to anyone in the press about the revelations in it. This woman, who had always been "fragile", left the estate shortly afterwards. They reported her missing to the police in Kent months ago.' He shrugged. 'You may not like him, but the fact is, this man and his followers have done everything right.'

He sipped his tea, for all the world looking perfectly comfortable.

'I don't understand why everybody is so relaxed.'

'We're not relaxed, Sophia. But even though we haven't absolutely identified who we think was breaking into your parents' business, and why they were behaving in this way, we have different lines of inquiry now.' He tilted his head to the side.

I only sighed.

His hand reached out and gently touched mine. 'This has been a horrific tragedy,' he said. 'Karen Ince is a dangerous person and we won't be happy until we've caught her. But at least we have a handle on where she's likely to be.'

'Do you have a handle on whether she's got my mum's shotgun?' I asked bitterly.

'No,' he said. 'For the record, we don't think she does. There could be a perfectly innocent explanation for the missing gun.'

I just looked at him. 'Like what?'

'Your father tells us that your mum was in the process of selling it.'

'He did? When? Who to?'

'He told us yesterday. He says that after they bought it, having the gun in the house just made your mother more anxious. We can't find the paperwork, but the buyer may not have submitted theirs yet.'

Really?

I was torn between relief and suspicion that it wouldn't turn out to be that easy. I would have liked to have known who the buyer was. There had been nothing about it in the Eden Gardens emails.

'We're watching Karen Ince's sister's house. A whole team of armed response officers will be waiting for her.' He offered me a tiny smile. 'We think this is the end, Sophia.'

I bit my lip. 'Yeah?'

'Yes. You can go home now.'

* * *

My dad was awake when I got back to the room, and to my surprise he was sitting upright in the chair I'd spent the night in.

'Dad!' I said. 'Are you sure you should be doing that?'

'Doing what?' he asked. His voice sounded fainter, but much more like himself. 'A fella can't sit in bed all day.' He licked his dry lips. 'And there's so much to do. Rowan's a good lad, but I know the place will be a bloody mess.'

I sat down on the bed. 'I think he's been doing fine.'

'How would you know?' asked my dad with a slightly testy air. 'You've never been interested in the business.'

'You've never been interested in what I think about the business, so I stopped bringing it up.'

He leaned back in the chair. 'Touché.'

Silence fell. The elephant in the room was enormous now, crowding us out.

'Dad?'

'What?'

'About Mum.'

He was silent for so long that I didn't think he was going to reply. When I glanced sideways at him, I realized with horror and grief that his eyes were wet.

My dad never cried. Never ever.

'Dad?'

'I'm fine. What about your mum?' He turned and met my gaze, and his expression was almost challenging.

'Did you really not know that she was . . . well, in this cult before you met her?'

'Of course not,' he said. He seemed almost offended that I would ask something so stupid.

He looked away then, and I knew that if I looked into his face, I would see tears again.

Out of respect for him, I pretended not to notice.

'So,' I said, swallowing. 'She really killed herself?' I tried to master myself. 'Are you sure it wasn't . . . I didn't believe . . .'

He just nodded at me, his eyes cold and terrible. 'Of course I'm sure.'

I shouldn't be questioning him on this now, I realized. Or perhaps ever.

'And she finished that book of hers,' I said.

'Yes.' His voice was faint and he rubbed the bandages on his swollen belly, making me think of the pregnant woman downstairs. 'She did an' all. That was a surprise.' He snarled then. 'I can't believe she did this to me. I . . .'

The tears leaked down his face, as his jaw clenched and teeth gritted, as if he could force them back in.

'Dad,' I said softly, horrified. I reached out.

'Don't,' he snapped. 'Just *don't*.'

I didn't say any more.

Chapter Twenty-Seven

It took the weekend to clean the house from top to bottom in time for my dad's return. The three village girls Kayleigh sourced to help out – Lena, Jenny and Agneta – were cheerful and thorough, and it felt good to have human life in the house again, even if only for a few hours. They kept finding things – bits of jewellery and scraps of broken objects under tables and beds – which they presented for my inspection, like cats who have caught birds and mice. They found no shotgun or notebook, but then you can't have everything.

The downstairs bathroom was converted for my dad's use through the expedient of a tin bath we'd found upstairs and a low stool – he'd be sleeping in the dining room, which was being co-opted for his bedroom. I expected a fair amount of resistance to this, but he'd had surgery only fifteen days earlier, and it was ridiculous to expect him to go up and down stairs, and hike out to his little shed in the garden.

I had a feeling I would have to be firm on this point.

I was overseeing the reconstruction of his bed in the room downstairs on Sunday afternoon when my mobile rang.

I didn't recognize the number – probably another journalist. I had set up the phone so numbers I didn't recognize went straight to voicemail; I would call them back should they merit it. It was therefore no surprise when a second or two later the phone chimed to let me know there was a message.

Being in no hurry to listen to the cozening familiarity of yet more reporters, laced with the occasional threat – 'If you don't talk to someone soon to get your story across, Sophia, you may find it leads to unpleasant consequences down the road' said one particularly unctuous git – it was at least another forty-five minutes before I lifted it out of my pocket and raised it to my ear.

There was a long pause, as if someone were collecting their thoughts.

'Sophia, this is Emily Corben, the facilitator here at Morningstar. I'm calling on behalf of Aaron Kessler. He wants to meet you in person.'

Her voice was perfectly even and controlled. It would have been difficult to pick her out from an electronic, computerized voice in a line-up, except that somewhere in the background a door creaked open at her end and her voice grew slightly fainter, as though she'd turned to glance over her shoulder at somebody.

I wondered if Aaron Kessler was in the room while this message was being delivered.

'Mr Kessler doesn't care to travel much and you'll have to come to the house, so we'll arrange a car for you. Let me know when and where you would like to be collected. You may bring anyone you like with you, if you wish, but you must come. Thank you.'

* * *

A minute later, I called Max.

'What do I do?'

There was a businesslike yet breathtaking presumptuousness at work here – up to and including getting someone else to make the call, as presumably the Magus himself was too busy sleeping in till noon.

Everything about it assumed I would be going. It put me in mind of my mum's notebooks and the letters she'd received. She'd flirted with not going, and yet gone.

I, at least, was not so biddable.

'What do you mean, "what do you do"?' asked Max. 'You're going to *go*, aren't you?'

It took me a second or two to wrap my head around the fact that this was his response, and when I did . . .

'What? Are you *mad*? Who's to say I'd ever get out of the building alive?'

In the kitchen Agneta and Jenny, who were scrubbing the scaled sink and had been giggling together, went quiet.

'How do I know that that crazy bitch Monica, or Karen or whatever her name is, isn't hiding there?'

'Sophia—'

'No. No, thanks.'

Max sighed. 'Sophia, listen to me. Aaron Kessler is far too self-interested to harm you. This is a charm offensive. The book's going to happen, and he knows it, so this is him mitigating the fact . . .'

I blinked. Did I miss a meeting somewhere?

'What do you mean, "the book's going to happen"? The final notebook is still lost. We've only got the first two . . .'

There was a pause.

'Now, Sophia, there's no need to give up. We do have the first two notebooks and, you know, we might be able to get some . . . auxiliary writers in to finish the book. I mean, the timing now is just so perfect.'

'"Auxiliary writers"?' I blinked again, surprised not just at the suggestion but its tone. 'The book's the story of my mother's time at Morningstar, so unless one of the other Ascendants, or whatever they were called, wants to finish it, which I can't see, what could auxiliary writers do?' The more I thought about it, the more it rankled. 'And what is an "auxiliary writer" when it's at home anyway?'

'Well, rather than it being an autobiography as such, under the circumstances we could publish an exposé on Aaron

Kessler and the cult. We could put you in touch with someone, a journalist that we trust, who could—'

A journalist?

'I can't even think about that right now, Max, I really can't.
There is too much going on here.'

'Naturally not,' he agreed quickly. 'But please, just think
about it. You wouldn't have to go to Morningstar alone. I
would be happy to come with you.'

'I . . .'

'Look, just think about it. Aren't you even a little bit
curious?'

* * *

I was still thinking about this conversation as I lay in my
bed back at Eden Gardens on Sunday night.

Most of all, I had to be honest with myself, I was frightened
of agitating the group any more, with my dad wounded
and he and I alone in the house. Every time I shut my eyes, I
could see the blind, unswerving glare of the woman on the
train, the same glare Monica had when she stood over me
with a knife in the café.

The police may have promised us regular patrols and panic
buttons while Monica was still at large, but I wasn't a fool.
That wouldn't be an indefinite arrangement. My dad and I
would still have to live in the world that came after.

I lay on my back, staring at the ceiling, the moon casting
the silhouettes of tree branches on to it in a kind of shadow-
play. There were no sounds in the hot, still night, only the
occasional rustle and flap of wings, or the faraway drone of a
lone car on the main road.

Was this going to be my life now, lying awake every night,
listening out for broken twigs and squeaking hinges, freezing
whenever the security light flicked on or the phone rang?

If only I'd been able to find the final notebook. This constant anxiety might at least have had a point.

Typing, typing, Rowan had said. *In the morning.*

The clunky old computer was back in the office now, and I stomped downstairs and switched it on, waiting impatiently until it booted up. Again, the mail, the folder called 'NINA', with four more folders inside it – 'BUSINESS', 'RECIPES', 'TAX' and 'HOUSE'. I'd been through every last one with a fine-toothed comb, but I went through them again anyway, trying not to dwell too hard on the contents – pictures of her standing outside the café; her hair in a blue scarf printed with swallows that I'd given her for Christmas, and her anxious, diffident smile.

I wiped at my eyes with the sleeve of my pyjamas. I should give this up and go to bed.

All right, I decided, I would try one last thing.

Into the PC's search box I typed 'morningstar' and hit enter.

The icon whirled for a few seconds and the computer made a ratcheting, ticking sound. I rubbed my eyes and yawned.

When I opened them I saw exactly one result:

C:\Documents and Settings\Nina\NINA\Recipes\
MORNINGSTAR3.DOC

It had last been modified five days before my mum's death. But why hadn't I . . . Ah. *Ah.*

I clicked 'NINA', then 'RECIPES', then right-clicked to expose the 'Show Hidden Files' option.

And there it was: MORNINGSTAR3.DOC.

The missing third notebook. What else could it be, with a name like that?

I was light-headed as I opened it, waited for the ancient

version of Word to kick in, and my heart started to pound at the back of my throat. *Oh God*, I thought, *this is it. What is in here?*

Then: 'Enter password to open file MORNINGSTAR3.DOC'

'Oh, you have to be kidding,' I hissed. 'Mum, what are you doing to me?'

Chapter Twenty-Eight

It was almost dawn before I gave up on unlocking the password for MORNINGSTAR3.DOC.

Of course I tried 'EDENGARDENS1'. I tried 'MORN-INGSTAR1' and 'A4RONK3SSLER' and every iteration and fragment of mine, hers, the Ascendant's and my dad's mutual lexicon that I could think of, in small letters and caps and in numbers. I tried dates and pet names and addresses. Book and movie titles.

Nothing worked. Whatever the password was, it was not obvious.

I'd need expert help, I realized as I squinted at the screen, to unlock it without damaging it. Perhaps the police, or even Max – though the more I thought about it, the more reluctant I was to share this find with him.

Instead I emailed the document to myself and stored the copy in my iPhone.

I sighed and let myself relax a little, my tiredness tinged with elation.

I found you, I thought to myself, cradling my phone to my breast. *I found you.*

Back in bed, though my eyes were huge and heavy, they would not close, and my room was growing lighter every minute with the rising sun.

I wondered about Aaron, the dark god of my mum's notebooks, and the deadly charisma that had snared these people to their deaths.

And, if I were being completely truthful, didn't I also want to try myself against it? To feel those arrows shot against me and resist them?

To see what the big deal was?

It was madness, though. Worse, it was arrogance.

I lay for hours, thinking, and in the end I knew what my answer would be.

I was going to go to Morningstar. I was going to get in that car (with Max as chaperone – he had seemed absolutely desperate for the dubious honour), and go to that house, that darkness that had haunted my mother's dreams, and confront the spider at the centre of the web.

I was going to look that bastard in the eye and let him know exactly what I thought of him.

If nothing else, I owed it to my mum. And to Tess.

With that decided, it was as if a great weight dropped from my very soul. Within minutes, I fell fast asleep.

* * *

After I'd sent copies of the file to Rob Howarth and my friend Orla, who managed her company's IT department ('It might be tomorrow till I find someone, is that OK, Soph?'), I called Max and told him of my decision.

'Will you come with me?' I asked him.

'Of course, of course!' he said. I could almost hear him beaming down the phone. 'I'd be happy to.'

'Thanks. I can't help thinking it's better to do it sooner rather than later—' I began.

'I think that, too,' he agreed, cutting across me. 'Any time works for me, Sophia. Just text me the time and I shall be at your disposal.'

'Great,' I said, a little taken aback and, to be honest, a little disquieted by his enthusiasm. 'I'll let you know.'

* * *

Next, after a cup of coffee and a slice of toast, I rang Emily Corben. I felt I needed fortifying first.

I was at the cottage – I'd dropped by to return Kayleigh's Dyson to her – and called the number from the sofa while Riley climbed over me once more, demanding to know who I was talking to.

'Hush now,' I told him, raising the phone to my ear.

It seemed to ring for a very long time.

'Hello?'

'Oh, hi, is this . . . Emily?'

'Who's calling?' Again, that controlled, almost robotic voice.

'This is Sophia Mackenzie. I got your message.'

Silence.

'I'm willing to talk to Mr Kessler,' I said, the words feeling strange as I said them.

'Good. Is tomorrow convenient?'

I blinked. Tomorrow my dad was coming home. I stroked Riley's head as he fell on to the sofa next to me. 'I . . . well, yes. I guess. It would have to be the morning. I need to be back here in the afternoon.'

'The car can meet you at ten tomorrow morning.'

'Oh. *Oh*. Well, to be honest, I would prefer to drive Max and myself down, so if you give me the address . . .'

'That won't be possible.'

Again, she sounded like a computer-generated voice.

'Ah,' I said, thrown. 'It's just that I have some errands to run first.'

'The driver can take you anywhere you want to go.'

'Who are you talking to?' demanded Riley loudly as he attempted to crawl into my lap.

'Nobody, Riley, just some people. Sorry about that,' I said into the phone. 'I . . .'

'Do you have *children*?'

The question was like a gunshot. It was the first time she'd sounded ruffled. Well, *ruffled* was the wrong word. *Intense*, might be better. *Concerned*, possibly.

But why?

'Who, me? No. Not at all. This is just my friend's son.'

'I'm afraid we'll have to insist on the car,' she said. 'Mr Kessler and the community like our privacy here. We don't allow outside vehicles on to the grounds.'

'Oh, I . . .'

'If you'd like to make your own way down to Kent, I suggest our car collects you from Lullingstone Roman Villa. Mr Kessler looks forward to seeing you then. Goodbye.'

There was nothing but the purr of the dialling tone.

* * *

The next day, I drove into Dartford, where I'd agreed to pick Max up outside the railway station, rather than fighting upstream like a salmon through the London rush hour. From there we would go on to Lullingstone to meet Aaron Kessler's driver.

I'd torn down the M25 that morning, all the while trying to come up with possible passwords for Mum's Morningstar3 document. It was doing nothing to raise my mood. Rowan was going to collect my dad from hospital in the afternoon, once he'd been signed off on the doctor's rounds, and part of me was hoping the doctor would have second thoughts. Dad was safer where he was.

As far as I knew, Karen Ince was still on the run, though she'd apparently been sighted near Lockerbie. The CCTV cameras were now turned towards our house, and we'd been told to call at even the slightest sign of trouble.

I wished I could say it was enough to make me feel safe.

* * *

Max was standing outside the doors of the new railway station in Dartford when I pulled up, talking urgently into his phone. There was an odd moment when he saw me. His eyes widened, and his hand clenched around the device, as though I'd surprised him in a guilty act, and within seconds he finished the call.

Though he managed a smile when he got in the car, I was still unsettled, but I couldn't put my finger on why.

'Carry on with your call, if you like,' I said evenly, as we pulled back out on to the high street. It was busy and the traffic was fractious, like my nerves. The sky was grey, that metallic gunmetal colour that precedes a summer storm.

'No, not at all, it's just office stuff. How are you?' he asked, dropping his backpack into the footwell between his feet.

'I've been better.'

'Yes, yes, of course,' he said, noting my bandaged hands as they gripped the wheel. The dressings had scaled down to a few thin wraps of gauze now. 'Wow. It must have been terrifying. Any news on the woman who did it?'

He seemed bursting with excitement, and it was rubbing me up the wrong way. I didn't see what there was to be happy about.

I shook my head. 'She's still on the run, apparently. Spotted near Lockerbie. They think she's trying to get to her sister's place near Glencoe.'

'That must have been really scary,' he said passionately.

'Yes. I thought I was going to die.'

I could hear my own voice and realized that it sounded flat, unfriendly. Markedly so.

A conviction was growing inside me, had been growing inside me since the weekend, as more details had come out about Morningstar, about my mum's suicide and about the book. Details such as how many Ascendants had been there in 1989; pictures of a handsome young blonde man with a tentative smile – Tristan – and talk of his gruesome foreign suicide; pictures of Tess, an attractive, stout, middle-aged woman with salt and pepper hair, smiling at the camera. All these things that should not necessarily be linked automatically in the mind, as Rob Howarth might say, and yet somehow they were.

I was turning off, heading back towards the M25. We were about twenty minutes away from the meeting point.

As if sensing my withdrawal, Max turned to smile at me. 'You don't need to be nervous. Aaron Kessler will be at his most charming. He always is when he wants something.'

I nodded, distantly. Behind us, the struts of the Queen Elizabeth Bridge rose like a mirage in the distance, sunlight touching its tracings, just for an instant, before the grey shadow of the clouds moved over it.

It smelled like rain and tarmac through the tiny open gap in the driver's side window, and the scent lent me perspective in my sleepless, overwrought state.

'What do you think will happen if we never find the third notebook?' I asked.

I hadn't told Max about the discovery I'd made on my mum's old PC last night, and every instinct I'd had during this journey so far screamed that this was the right decision, at least for now. At least until I'd read it.

'What?' he asked. He seemed distracted – his phone was continually vibrating, and he was diverting calls. Perhaps he was very busy, but I don't remember him being in such demand when we'd had lunch the week before.

'What happens if we never find the notebook?' I repeated. 'If it's gone for ever?'

'Well, as I said, the material we have is still interesting. We can still use it – in one form or another. It's the perfect time for an exposé on Aaron Kessler and his group, with all of the publicity this case has raised.'

'Perhaps.' I pulled out on to the motorway. I felt sick to my stomach. 'Perhaps.'

We drove in silence to Lullingstone and turned into the car park Emily Corben had suggested. Trees overhung it and the air when I got out was heavy and humid. I'd worn the lightest work suit I had and already beads of sweat were gathering at the nape of my neck and slithering down my cleavage. I was glad I'd worn no make-up.

Max leapt out of the car, and once again I wondered at his enthusiasm as I followed him out, locking the car behind me, my bag over my shoulder. The car park was practically empty, and I could see nothing that looked like a chauffeur-driven luxury car, unless Kessler had been forced to downgrade to a VW Polo with a dented wing.

'So how do you think this will go?' I asked, tucking my arms around me despite the hot weather.

'I don't know. We can press him about Peter Clay – he doesn't know we don't have the third notebook yet.'

'I suppose.'

'All the media and publicity will have rattled him. If we can get an exclusive now . . .'

I gave him a sideways glance while my hand drifted protectively down towards my phone.

'What do you mean? What exclusive?' I asked sharply.

At that moment the car arrived, and there could be no mistaking which car it was, even though this wasn't the Bentley of the notebooks but a gleaming silver-grey Mercedes Benz, driven by a man in a charcoal uniform with a peaked cap.

I looked at Max, with his hipster hair, pointed shoes and hungry eyes as the car rolled towards us.

His excitement was palpable. His eyes shone with it.

And suddenly I knew that what I'd been thinking all the way here was true.

'You set this up,' I breathed. 'You set all of this up.'

His smile didn't move, but his eyes were blinking just a little bit more than before.

'What do you mean?'

'You told those reporters about Morningstar, about my mum being in that cult, about how it related to Tess and the others!' I said. 'That's where they got it all from.' I fought to control my growing rage, my sense of betrayal, which, once let off the leash, was threatening to consume me. 'I didn't understand where they'd unearthed all the information from so quickly, how they'd worked it all out, how they'd joined up the dots.' I felt incandescent with fury. 'They got it from *you*.'

'Sophia, that's very—'

'*True*,' I snapped. 'It's very true, isn't it, Max? You wanted to whip up excitement for the book. And to do it you put me and my sick dad in the most appalling position – those reporters were hunting us at the hospital like *animals*. My God, did you set up this meeting with Aaron Kessler, too? Was this *your* idea? Did you give him a prompt, tell him to get in touch with me?'

'Now, Sophia, calm down. This is such a golden opportunity for us, for all of us – your dad included. We're doing this for Nina, after all—'

'Don't you *dare* tell me to calm down! Don't you dare say my mother's name! When were you going to let me in on all this? You unscrupulous bastard!'

'Listen,' he said, and his voice sounded an octave higher and a little desperate. 'It's not like that.'

But it was like that. It really was. It was the only explanation.

I knew what I was going to do next, but the only way to move through the madness of the decision was not reflect upon it.

He was absolutely depending on getting into this meeting with Aaron Kessler, on obtaining this 'exclusive'.

I forced myself to look calmer, and instead just shook my head at him sadly, as if in defeat. I opened the door and quickly slid into the backseat of Kessler's car.

Meanwhile Max had to go round the back to get in the other door, which gave me all the time in the world to just lean over and lock it.

'Drive,' I said to the chauffeur, as Max tried the door a few times, having not quite understood yet. 'You're just here for me, right?'

The driver looked over his shoulder at me as Max knocked on the window, still thinking this was an oversight. The driver was young, his head shaved under the cap, and florid tattoos crept up his neck from his chest.

He nodded.

'Then drive. Not him. Just me.'

Max was pounding on the door now, saying, 'Sophia? Sophia!' and his voice was muffled by the tinted glass, though not enough to disguise his panic.

'*Drive*,' I said again. 'Take me to Morningstar.'

Chapter Twenty-Nine

The sulky sky did not change on my journey to meet Aaron Kessler – dark grey clouds billowed over the horizon, but some sunlight fingered in through the gaps, making fields of rape and corn glow a dull gold, as though a thin band of summer was trapped between heaven and earth.

I held my phone, pretending to be busy answering texts and carefully looking connected to the outside world – like somebody that would be missed if something happened to me.

Mostly, however, I was trying to guess that password still.
creativespark1?
No. Dammit.

Now that my fury and indignation were receding, I started to wonder if I'd overreacted. Max was a treacherous shit, true, but in retrospect I'd still rather have had him sat there beside me.

My fear was ratcheting up in slow degrees. I no longer wanted to meet Aaron Kessler – I wanted to go home and lie under the covers of my bed, or perhaps quietly prepare something to put in the oven for my dad that night.

Stop it, Sophia. Don't be a coward. Face this man. You owe it to your mum. You owe it to Tess.

My phone chimed. I'd received an email.

Sophia,

We have to talk about Scottish Heritage. I will see you tomorrow at noon.

James

I sighed. Amity. They were the last thing on my mind right now. I was sick of being worried and defensive with them, constantly on the back foot. They either liked the Scottish Heritage design or they didn't. They either let me cope with these extraordinary events or they didn't. But I wouldn't be handing any more of my power over to them. Not to them, and certainly not to Benjamin.

Let them fire me if they wanted to. It was just a bloody job, at the end of the day.

I glanced up at the driver.

'Excuse me, how much longer will it be?'

He pretended not to hear me.

'Excuse me,' I said more loudly. 'How much—'

'Forty minutes,' he replied. But his head twitched, as though he was nervous, and amongst the tattoos creeping above his collar, I spotted it – a cross within a circle.

'You're one of them.'

He didn't answer.

'You're one of the order – an Ascendant. I recognize the tattoo.'

His attention remained focused on the view out of the windscreen.

'How long have you been at Morningstar?' I asked.

Still no reply.

'They told you not to talk to me, right?'

After a few seconds more of silence I sighed and turned back to my phone, feigning an indifference I didn't feel. I wondered if he could see my fingers shake as they touched the screen.

Ascend4nt . . . No. You tried that last night.

'Suit yourself,' I muttered at him.

* * *

After half an hour of winding through the Weald on narrow green roads, the arrival itself was a surprise – suddenly we turned into a wooden and iron gate set into a high wall, and the driver leaned out of the window and tapped a code into an electronic box mounted on a pole.

I stirred in the back seat, swallowed hard and put the phone away.

We were rumbling along a drive, the one described in the notebooks. The well-kept gravel swept away towards the house, which was lined with neatly pruned hedges and solar-powered lighting.

The house was exactly the same, and yet also completely different from how I had imagined it. It was a kind of fortified Tudor manor, surrounded by a moat and dotted with leaded windows. I understood how it must have seemed like a castle to my mum, but in actual fact it wasn't very large, and the drawbridge looked like a Victorian reconstruction – it was a folly, more than anything, the germ of an ancient building painted and propped into something it wasn't.

What did strike me immediately was the complex at the back of the property. Clean new accommodation blocks had been built, about three storeys high, none of which would have existed when my mum had last visited. There were four of them, surrounding a low, flat-roofed building which was either a cafeteria or meeting place.

Business must be booming.

I was driven past apple trees and beehives, a neatly trimmed labyrinth of hedging which must be the Yew Maze I had read about, and three very glossy, well-maintained Range Rovers with 'The Society for Spiritual Enrichment' and the cross–circle logo painted on the side.

It was the spookiest thing, to see this place that had struck my mum as a kind of paradise, and to find it pretty and prosperous, but still very corporate. Soulless, in fact.

I felt strangely cheated on her behalf.

A woman was waiting at the door – she was in her thirties, perhaps, and good-looking, in a smart grey suit; her hair that exquisite variegated blonde that denotes a good colourist. She regarded me unsmilingly as the car pulled up, and it was obvious, from the way she was dressed to the way she watched me, that she was someone who could mimic being a normal person, but who had little or no truck with the real world.

In the upper windows, I glimpsed movement. A face had appeared, then another, but they vanished quickly once they saw me look up.

I realized that I hadn't been afraid – not really afraid – until this moment.

The door was opened for me, and I emerged into the pre-storm stillness. It was as though, our suits notwithstanding, I was visiting an isolated tribe member from the Amazon, who might react in unpredictable ways at any moment, in line with diktats and agendas I could only guess at.

Her amulet swung from her neck on a thin gold chain. If she saw my eyes drop to it, she gave no sign.

'Sophia Mackenzie? I am Emily. Please follow me.'

She didn't offer to shake my hand and didn't inquire about my journey. Instead, she turned on her heel and I trailed in her wake, clutching my handbag under my arm, across the little drawbridge and through the big door.

Several things were becoming very clear.

In my line of work, I know a building like this needs a good deal of expensive upkeep. Even a small fortified manor with generous but not extensive grounds like this one would cost between fifty and seventy thousand pounds a year to maintain. The blocks built at the back with their cladding and landscaping looked a cool million pounds taken as a job lot.

Aaron Kessler obviously wasn't having problems sourcing that kind of money. Even without his followers, finances like that would make him a difficult, intractable enemy.

My guide was silent. She seemed almost to glide ahead of me.

Passing by a large mural, I realized it was the order's symbol, wrought in iron and gilt, with a colourful silk backdrop. In front of it was an altar with fresh flowers. The whole thing was brightly polished and vibrant.

As she passed it, Emily made a little gesture of obeisance.

I was struck by the complete contrast between appearances and belief, and full of questions. What was it exactly that they worshipped here? How did a little gang of believers clustering around a spoiled and petulant man-child become this . . . this . . . whatever the hell this was?

I realized I was being led up to the long gallery, and that at the end of it was Aaron's study, where my mother had been sent to open the safe and ended up nearly freezing to death in the barn.

I clutched my bag more tightly.

There was no sign of any other people, but I knew they were there. What might have been voices stilled as our footsteps passed by closed doors, beams creaked above. From somewhere below, I could hear a faint banging of pots.

And then the door was suddenly in front of me and Emily was knocking on it, with the kind of head-bent deference you might expect of someone rousing the Pope.

'Yeah?' came a low male voice. 'What is it?'

'Sophia is come.'

What a strange word choice.

Silence. Then: 'Send her in.'

She opened the door, and since it was what I'd come for, though my knees shook, in I went.

* * *

The room was smaller than I'd thought it would be. It put me in mind, with its finicky untidiness, of my dad's shed – except that my dad's shed didn't have a fur rug and an open fireplace, which was dark and empty now, since it was summer.

A clock on the mantelpiece tocked sonorously.

Aaron Kessler himself occupied an ornate wooden desk chair. The rugs were thick and springy, the furniture spotlessly dusted, though crowded with small pictures, ornaments and *objets d'art*; fresh flowers bloomed from a vase on the mantelpiece. My mum had mentioned gold discs and photos of the band, back in her day, but there was no sign of these now. His identity as Aaron Kessler of the Boarhounds had been shed, like a snake's skin.

Now he was his own creation.

And unlike the house, he was almost exactly as I had imagined him. Long dark hair framed his face, and it still had its lustrous colour. I wondered if he dyed it. His eyes were brown – that jet-black colour that looks pupil-less in certain lights.

There appeared to be no chair in the room other than the one he occupied. I realized that people who came in here were expected to stand while they talked to him.

'Are you going to ask me to sit down?' I asked.

He regarded me intensely for a long moment, then moved to his feet, silently offering me his chair with a languid wave.

With surprising agility, considering his age, he launched himself upwards, taking a seat on the desk facing the chair.

'Thank you.' I settled into the chair, uncomfortable with the way it remembered the warmth of his body.

I was being wrong-footed. He was being neither portentous

and mystical, which I would have found absurd, nor cheerful and friendly, which would have appeared insincere, nor even aloof, which would have been alienating.

But you were told this. He's always who you need him to be.

He was dressed in a white shirt, thankfully buttoned up today, and a pair of dark grey trousers – not for him Emily's business suit. He wore no amulet, nor jewellery of any kind.

'So, at last it's Sophia.' He half-smiled to himself and cocked his head to one side. 'You've made me wait.'

'I'm right on time.'

He laughed. 'Yeah, perhaps you are.' His eyes narrowed. 'Why have you come?'

'You invited me.'

'Yes, I know I did. My real question was, why did you accept?'

'I'm here because of my mother. I don't know if you remember her—'

'Of course I remember Nina.' He folded his arms at me. Through the shirt, his muscles were still surprisingly defined. He was very good-looking, and it was distracting me.

'Right. Good. Because I think there were probably a few girls coming through here, and you can't remember them all.' I folded my arms right back at him. Was that the right thing to do? Was I mirroring him? I unfolded them.

'Would you like something to drink?'

'Considering that I've read my mother's notebooks, I think I can safely answer "no".'

His laughter was as unforced and sunny as if I'd made a little joke about the weather, rather than about drugs and his ghastly ritual. He had white teeth. Like the car, he at least was well maintained.

'That was a long time ago. And you can't be that afraid of me, Sophia, or you wouldn't have come here alone. Having spoken to Max Clarke, I know that it was you that blew him out on this trip, and not the other way around.'

I didn't know what to say to that, so instead I just shrugged. 'This is family business.'

'It most certainly is.'

He had instantly become serious, and those dark eyes fell on me. 'You have questions for me.' He held his hands wide, as though about to start conducting an orchestra. 'And you've come a long way. Ask.'

'Did you kill my mum?'

'I was told that Nina killed herself.'

'She was driven to it – the burglaries, the harassment. My dad says she couldn't stick it any more. Was that down to you? I'll ask again. Did you kill my mum?'

He cocked his head at me again with a little shake, as if I had disappointed him.

'No. But you know that already.'

'Why would I know that?'

'Because you know everything, Sophia, if you'd only look inside. You are the World Soul. You are the avatar of divine wisdom.'

A beat.

'I'm really not,' I said. 'And I'm afraid I'm going to have to insist that we keep this conversation confined to the real world. I don't share your beliefs.'

'You have no idea what they are, so how would you know?'

'Mr Kessler . . .'

That laughter again, dark and rich. '"Mr Kessler"! So formal. You've already let me call you Sophia.'

I had the strangest feeling then – as though this predator was grading me for my predation skills, and finding them wanting, and that this was personally disappointing in some way.

I just stared at him. *Don't back down.*

'All right, if you like.' He smiled and shook his head, as though indulging a child. 'Let's do this the boring, inefficient way, then. You know I didn't kill Nina because I didn't have opportunity, means, or motive.' He smiled again. 'Did I leave anything out?'

'I think you had all three.'

'How do you mean?'

'You sent people to harass my mother. Once Paracelsus told you she wanted to publish her notebooks, you tracked her down, and your Ascendants made my parents' life a misery until she—'

'You've no idea why you're here, have you?' He offered me a half-smile, and there was a wisp of pity in it. 'Why I invited you to come? It makes me wonder if you've even read all those notebooks of Nina's.'

This observation was so prescient, I started.

'Now, why would you come all this way without knowing why? Hmm. Now I feel *bad*. Like I have you at a disadvantage.'

'I would have thought that would please you,' I said evenly.

'Not at all!' He swung his heels against the desk. 'I can see that you think I'm your enemy; that I was Nina's enemy, but I only want the best for you, Sophia. I wanted only the best for Nina, but in the end, she was like they all were . . .' His gaze flicked away to the ceiling, then back to me. 'They had too much negative energy.'

His self-absorption was breathtaking.

'What about Tess?' I asked. 'Is that why she's dead? She wasn't *positive* enough?'

He threw up his hands, as though rejecting this utterly. 'That was an accident. Karen had been sick on and off for years. What were we supposed to do? Throw her out? The regimen here now is so much more demanding than in your

313

mother's time – we dropped the drugs and decadent living years ago.' He sighed. 'It was a tragedy, and a lesson to us all.'

'A lesson to Tess, certainly.' I held up my bandaged hands. 'And to me.'

'There was never any need for Tess to die. It did not serve anyone's purpose. We'd fenced together on and off for years when she swapped the Creative Spark for her Lord and Saviour, Jesus Christ,' he said this last in a mock-American accent. 'All her death achieved was to bring unwelcome media attention here.' He snorted. 'It was something she never managed in life.'

He narrowed his eyes at me again. 'And as for you, Karen would never have harmed a hair on your head. She knew who you were.' He waved a hand, as though taking in the whole building. 'They all know who *you* are.'

Me?

'And who am I, exactly?' I asked.

'I told you, Sophia. You're the World Soul. You're divine wisdom, crushed into a mortal dream state, a sort of Sleeping Beauty. In the end your prince will come to kiss you, you will wake and the world as we know it will end.'

His expression didn't change throughout this speech.

'Really?' I sighed. 'I asked for that, didn't I? You do seem to know a lot about me.'

'Of course I do.' He raised his eyebrow, cocked his head at me. 'I created you.'

'Sorry?'

He pursed his lips, as though thinking. 'Well, Nina helped.'

I took his meaning instantly, though I tried not to. I opened my mouth and closed it again.

'W-what are you trying to imply?' I said, my throat bone dry.

'Don't be stupid, Sophia. It's not a good look on you. I'm asserting, not implying. They're different. You're mine. We all performed the ritual to call down the Creative Spark and it worked. Nina drank the Sacred Draught. I went into her and she bore fruit. You are it.'

Profound silence followed this statement, broken only by the slow tock-tock of the mantelpiece clock.

This was why I'd been invited here, I realized. This was what he had expected me to confront him with when I arrived.

It was how he suspected I hadn't read all the notebooks.

Good God, what else was in there?

'You're not my father. I have a father. Jared Boothroyd.' My voice was tiny to my own ears, like a little girl's.

'Jared?' His eyes widened and his mouth screwed up, as though he tasted something bitter. '*Jared*, is it? What, you think *that* guy is your father? Not even *he* believes it, I guarantee it. Why should you?'

And as he said it, I knew it was true. It made perfect sense.

Why had it never occurred to me, even while I was reading about my mum and her intense sexual attachment – no, *obsession* – with Aaron in the months leading up to my conception?

But to own this possibility was to lose both of my parents all over again. Certainly to lose my dad again, or at least my biological connection to him, after only just getting him back.

And despite these insidious doubts, right now my dad was the person I most wanted to see in the world.

'I want to go home!' I was going to start weeping soon, and I'd be damned if I'd let him see it.

'I don't think you should. We should talk, Sophia. This changes things—'

'I want to go home!' I shouted. 'I want to go home RIGHT NOW!'

'Sophia,' he said, with the commanding tones of someone who was rarely contradicted. 'You have to calm down. We have to talk, seriously, about the future.' He stood up and walked towards me.

A horror came over me then, that he might touch me.

I would not stay here a moment longer.

I bolted out of the chair and dived past him to the door. It took a second to work the medieval latch with its scraping metal device, and he was nearly at my shoulder before it flew open and I was in the long gallery, running for the stairs.

'STOP HER!' he bellowed, emerging into the long gallery behind me. The house seemed to come alive. Doors opened, and below there seemed to be hundreds of them some-how, congregating in the hallways, whispering to one another through the cracks in barely open doors, though there could have been no more than twenty people in the house.

As I tore down the stairs, the blonde woman, Emily, stood, her arms outstretched as though to catch me. I swerved around her as she swore, pelted for the front door and shoved it open.

I ran across the drawbridge, the wooden timbers bouncing beneath my pounding feet, and threw myself in the car, slamming the door after me.

'Drive!' I shouted at the driver, but he didn't.

I was not his master.

Aaron was, and he crossed the drawbridge a minute later, taking care not to run. At the vast oak door, a plethora of pale faces peeked out at me. They were old, young – there were even some children.

One, with a pixyish haircut and sharp chin, I thought I recognized.

Aaron leaned over me, speaking to me through the window.

'Sophia, you need to calm down and come back inside.'

'No! Absolutely not! You let me out of here NOW.'

'There's so much to tell you, so much you don't understand.'

'If you don't let me out of here!' I screamed in my hysteria. 'I'll call the police, do you hear me?' I waved my phone at him.

I had had enough revelations for one day. I needed to go home, lick my wounds and think.

The threat of the law was at last enough for him, though.

'When you calm down and are capable of rationality,' he said, 'we'll talk again. You need to process this. I get it.' He stood back and smiled. 'We'll speak again soon enough.'

He smacked on the roof, and the driver pulled away while I wept.

I had no idea where he was going to take me. Through my tears I could see that we were following the same route back to Lullingstone that we had taken.

A few times I caught his eyes in the rear-view mirror, studying me. Just his eyes, though his jaw was obviously tense, the muscles in his shaven neck working.

He pulled into the car park, next to my KA. I wondered, distantly, how out of all these cars he knew which one was mine.

He got out to open the door and held it.

'Will you be all right?' he asked. 'Should I get someone? Do you want to go back?'

It was the first time I had seen him properly. He looked very young, and alarmed, as though even this little bit of interaction with me was forbidden.

'You don't have to worry about me,' I mumbled. 'I'm fine.'

'I do have to worry,' he said.

I felt a twinge of gratitude then, that at least someone around here was a compassionate human being.

Then he said, 'You're the Sacred Lady. The World Soul.'

I got out of the car without another word or a backward glance.

Chapter Thirty

'How did it go?' asked Rowan.

I was back in my car.

I'd been sitting there for two hours, perhaps a little less. The Mercedes had rolled away, leaving me alone and desolate. Everything seemed slightly unreal.

There was no sign of Max. I wondered, distantly, how he'd got back to London. More than anything, I was horribly relieved he hadn't been there with me.

What are you talking about? Max knows Aaron Kessler is your father.

The thought came to me instantly. He'd known, of course he'd known. The way he'd said, during that first phone call, when I'd told him my mother was dead, 'This is *Sophia* I'm talking to?'

He knew. My mum must have told him.

'Y'know, Rowan, I . . . I don't really . . .'

'Soph?'

'I . . .'

And then I burst into tears again.

'Soph? Sophia! Did they hurt you?'

'Not physically.'

'I'm coming to get you.'

'No,' I said, pulling myself together. 'Absolutely not. I wasn't hurt, I'm fine. It was just . . . well, I found out some things. Does Dad know where I went today?'

'No, I don't think so.'

'Good. Rowan, you have to promise me never to tell him.'

'Why not?'

'It's just . . . they said things about Mum. Things he doesn't need to know, all right?'

He was quiet. 'All right. Listen, about your dad.'

'Is there something the matter?'

There was a long pause. 'He's not himself. I'm worried about him.' He breathed out. 'He's saying some very strange things. He's very upset, you know, about your mum.'

'I know, Ro, I know.' I stared out of the window, at the trees. The storm hadn't broken yet, but it would soon, and the air was hot and still. 'I know. He's really angry at her.'

And if he ever learned what I'd just learned . . . Oh my God, how could he know Aaron was my father? He hadn't even known my mum was in the order!

He must never, *ever* find out.

'I'm on my way back. I'll see you then.'

'OK, Soph. Drive safely.'

He was gone.

I lingered for a long moment, gazing at my phone. The third notebook was once again under my fingers, that blank request for a password. I must have typed in dozens and dozens of them since finding the document last night. My cut palms hurt with the effort.

Aaron had called me the World Soul.

You know, now I thought about it, so had the driver.

On a whim I tapped in 'worldsoul'.

Then 'WorldSoul'.

Then 'TheWorldSoul'.

And at that, it sprang open.

The Third Notebook

Chapter Thirty-One

I don't remember much about that morning after the ritual, Sophia, except that I felt unbearably nauseous and bruised all over, and there was a bitter, chemical taste in my mouth. They'd come to me as I lay on the grass near the Yew Maze, the sun rising over its untidy tops. I had a sense of Lucy and Tristan, jackets thrown over their robes and their feet thrust into wellington boots, urging me to 'get up, get up, you have to get up now', and exhausted as I was, in the end I responded to the naked fear in their voices and let them guide me back to the house.

The feeling had come back to my feet, and my toes sang with pain. I was shivering, but mostly I wanted to sleep.

'Where's Aaron?' I asked. The dawn was rosy pink, the sky tinted like blood in bathwater.

'Upstairs,' said Tristan, trying to sound upbeat, but there was a cracked note in his voice.

'I had a bad dream. Tess was screaming about someone being killed. Did something bad happen?'

'It's all right, Nina, don't be scared – it's going to be fine,' said Tristan. 'But we do need to go back to the house now.' He was walking quickly, they both were, and it was hurting my feet. I wanted them to slow down. I reached out to grab Tristan's coat, roughly thrown over his robe, and as my hand closed around the cloth I could see it was covered in something, dark red scales of dried blood that fell off my skin as it moved.

I gasped then and stood stock-still.

Lucy gently but firmly pushed me forward.

'You need to have a bath. We all need to clean up, Nina.' She pushed me forward. 'Before the police arrive.'

* * *

There was the shower, and I realized with a little shock that Lucy was in the shower with me, still wearing her bra and knickers, which was strange, but no stranger than anything else that had happened in the last few hours. Our robes lay in a discarded pile on the bathroom floor, before Tristan gathered them up in his arms and bore them away.

Lucy's hands on my head were hard and rough as she washed my hair and scrubbed my fingernails. 'Stand up, Nina,' she commanded, when I decided I was tired and would like a little sit-down before the shower went any further.

Whatever was in the Sacred Draught was intense, and it was coming in and out like waves at sea. Sometimes I was awake, realizing I was covered in blood and that I could remember nothing of the ritual. Then, within a few minutes, I was melting under the buffeting water, and it seemed to me that Lucy was singing as her hands moved through my hair and that we were mermaids now. I kept asking her what the song was.

'For fuck's sake, Nina, for the thousandth time, I'm not *singing*. Stop being silly and try to concentrate. We're in trouble.'

I must have been driving her mad. I'd had a larger dose. Its bitter, sickly taste was the very last thing I consciously remembered. We'd been standing in the dining room with the others, and Aaron had offered me the cup half full of purplish liquid, wine adulterated with God knows what, and I had drained it all on his orders, after the others had taken only a few swallows.

Lucy, of course, was sober now.

'Is Aaron OK?' I asked. I'm ashamed to admit that this was all I cared about.

'Aaron's fine, sweetheart.'

'What about the others?'

'Everything's fine,' she said, but her voice was tight. 'We're going to sort it out.'

Then she was roughly towelling me, attacking my hair with a comb and hairdryer, and I was aware of Tristan rubbing hard at the bath with cloths and something that smelled like bleach.

This struck me as rather fastidious. I'd never seen Tristan clean anything in his life.

'Is there nothing we can give her, you know, to bring her down? Should we give her some black coffee, or something?' he asked.

'No. She needs to sleep it off.'

I was led up the stairs, which seemed to go on for ever. The fire in the long gallery was cold ash. We passed the open door to the dining room.

All traces of the ritual were gone, the candles vanished. The space looked oddly vacant, even with the instruments stacked in their usual places.

Then I noticed, almost in passing, what it was. The recording equipment had disappeared.

'Where's Aaron?' I asked again, drowsily. Suddenly I'd never been so tired.

'Upstairs. But he's asleep. Everyone's asleep. Come on.'

'You said the police are coming.'

'Yes. There was an accident,' said Lucy. 'But it's going to be fine. We're going to take care of everything. We just have to stick together, all right?'

This filled me with such nameless dread I could do nothing but nod. I had a quick flashback of tugging at Tristan's coat and seeing blood on my hands.

Had I dreamed that? The blood? I couldn't trust my senses or memories.

'I want to sleep, too.'

'Yes,' said Lucy. 'And you will, sweetheart.'

'Did something happen to Aaron?' I asked again, voicing my darkest fear. 'You'd tell me, wouldn't you?'

'Of course, sweetheart.' Lucy's eyes were tearing up. 'Aaron's fine. But Peter . . . Peter had an accident.'

I did not need to ask any more. I already knew, in my heart of hearts, what the rest would be.

I glanced down at my scrubbed hand, now pink, the secret gaps beneath my fingernails sore and sensitive.

Nothing would ever be the same.

* * *

'So, Miss Mackenzie, you know that we just need to take a statement.' A pause. 'Are you all right with that?'

I was in the morning room with a big man in a grey coat who sported a dark blue tie, with what looked like a darts' league insignia on it. He had a tiny moustache, almost but not quite like Hitler's, pouchy eyes and curly hair, his pink scalp gleaming through in places.

His name, he had told me, was Detective Inspector Derek Holmes and he was writing things down on a big pad.

Next to him was a smaller, thinner man in another cheap suit. He'd been introduced, but I didn't remember his name. He didn't speak, he just stared.

It filled me with horror.

I had never really spoken to the police before, other than to ask directions. Now I was about to lie to them.

Penelope's disdain for me had utterly vanished as she'd talked me through the story she'd devised and the role I was to play; her lips had been as white as her skin.

We had to get this right, she'd said. Every detail had to match up. We were all in this together now. Do you understand, Nina?

Well, I assumed we were in it together. I still hadn't seen Aaron – not since the ritual. He hadn't been present for Penelope's briefing.

326

I nodded stiffly at Detective Inspector Derek Holmes and sniffed. My hands were in my lap, one of them crushing a paper tissue already damp with tears.

They'd both appeared just as Peter's body had been carried out of the house by the ambulancemen. Good cop, bad cop.

'What were you doing last night?' asked the detective.

'Nothing much,' I said in a faint, sad voice, just as Penelope had coached me. 'We had dinner and some drinks afterwards.'

'So, as much as you can remember, Nina – can I call you Nina? – what do you remember happening?'

'We cooked a meal.' I scrunched the tissue to my face. It came away wet. These tears were a source of amazement to me – was I crying out of fear? For Peter?

For myself?

'And who was present at this meal?'

'Aaron, Penelope, Lucy, Tristan, Peter, Wolf and me.' I thought hard for a minute. 'And Tess.'

'So Peter was at the table? When did he arrive?'

'About half four, five o'clock I think. I don't remember exactly. We had started cooking.'

'Then what happened?'

'We all sat down to dinner. Aaron gave a toast, I think.' I spontaneously added this little fictional detail. There hadn't been a meal, of course. But as Penelope had pointed out, there was no way we could tell the police what we'd really been up to. We had to appear to be normal, unremarkable people, and as far as the police were concerned, normal, unremarkable people cooked meals and gave toasts. They didn't don robes and engage in secret rituals. Aaron had made his wishes very clear to Lucy and Penelope, I was told. We had to persuade the police that what had happened to Peter was a terrible accident, and as normal, unremarkable people, we were naturally distraught about it.

'And then?' he asked.

'We all went upstairs.'

'Upstairs. Where to?'

'The dining room – but we don't use it for that. The instruments are set up in there. Aaron and the lads played them.'

'And you had more to drink?' He licked his lips.

'Yeah.'

'And what time did you go up there, do you think?'

'I . . . I don't know. About quarter past eight, maybe?'

'And you all went up together and carried on drinking.'

'Yeah, we were all there.' I let out a little sob. 'Having a good time.'

None of this had happened, of course, but you would be hard pressed, based on the evidence, to work this out. Penelope's cleverness had been extraordinary this morning. She had filled and drained glasses with spirits and wine, asked us to press our lips to them, and then placed them around the dining room, to create the illusion of an abandoned party. Perhaps she knew to do these things from the sketchy legal training she'd been pursuing before she threw it all in to follow Aaron. Or, I thought with a hint of distaste, perhaps it was just her terrifying native cunning shining through.

I sobbed again, not so much grief-stricken as overwhelmed and terrified at my daring.

'Take it easy, love. Did you have anything other than drink at this party?'

'Like what?' I asked, though I knew exactly what he meant.

'Any drugs?'

This was the first time the other man had spoken. He had a deep voice that somehow didn't seem to go with the rest of him. I blinked at him in alarm.

'No,' I said quickly. 'No, I didn't . . .' I tailed off.

'How much had you had to drink, then?' asked Derek Holmes.

'I'm not sure. Three, maybe four glasses of wine? And some brandy?'

'About what time did you go to bed?'

'Early. I felt a little sick. About half ten, twenty to eleven. I honestly can't remember. It was early. For us. The others stayed up.'

'And . . .'

'And I fell straight to sleep,' I said. The tissue was little more than wet shreds in my palm.

'You didn't hear anything after that?'

'I'm sorry,' I lied. 'I never heard a thing until the shot. I was in bed. I ran down the stairs . . . I shouted for the others, but nobody answered. They'd gone out. There's no phone here so I didn't know who to call. There was blood everywhere in the hall. All over my feet. And his *head* . . .'

I burst into tears again, and I could almost feel the unspoken communication over my head between the two men.

What it meant and how this had gone, I had no idea, but when the detective carefully helped me to my feet, his hand lingering just a little too long on my back, I had a feeling I knew.

* * *

This is the story we had come up with between us:

The others told the police that I had felt sick and gone to bed early, and that they had all put on thick coats and boots, taken two torches and gone out to watch the stars together. It had been a beautiful clear night, with a full moon.

After a little while Peter had complained of being cold – he'd brought only a thin jacket. He'd seen a deer in the trees near the grounds and he kept saying he'd like to shoot it. Peter was very fond of shooting, if not very good at it. Aaron had several licensed guns. Aaron had a lot of expensive toys lying around the house.

Everyone told Peter not to be silly, he was too drunk to handle a gun, and what would they all do with a dead deer at this time of night anyway? He seemed to accept this, but still complained of being cold.

They had given him one of the torches and he had gone back to the house. They thought he'd gone to get a coat.

When they'd heard the shot, they'd just assumed he'd seen the deer and taken a pot shot at it nearer the house.

But it turns out, he'd been carrying the gun back outside and his stumbling foot must have caught on one of Morningstar's uneven flagstones. His finger had been on the trigger and, unfortunately, the gun had come up and shot him. No one discovered him until I heard the shot, came down in my nightgown and found him lying there with half his face blown away, my bare feet puddled in his blood, my hands raddled with it as I'd tried, in my dazed, shocked state, to shake him awake.

My screaming had drawn the others back to the house.

A tragic, tragic accident.

It was as good a story as any. For all I knew it might have been true.

I'd hated and feared Peter. If I'd heard, for instance, that he'd been killed in a car crash during one of his many murky trips to London, my reaction would probably have been delirious relief. But here, like this, his death filled me with cold horror and a numbing dread.

I remembered next to nothing of that night – just bits and pieces. I remembered that there had been cold flagstones, and that I had laid down on them, naked, and that the crown of flowers on my hair had fallen away, but that was all of the ritual I could recall. The next fragment of memory had been on the stairs, when someone was shouting at me – male voices, very angry, warped and distorted, like a tape that was slowed down, but the note of rage and sheer panic had been unmistakeable.

Then that rolling boom, like thunder.

I had been terrified, and that's when I'd run out and into the grounds.

That was all I could remember.

The others kept telling me it was an accident, a terrible accident. That Peter had been off his face; he'd freaked out, picked up the gun – we'd done nothing wrong, after all. It wasn't as if we were lying to cover up a crime. It was just an accident.

We were simply protecting ourselves from a materialistic, judgmental outside world that wouldn't understand us.

Most importantly, we were protecting Aaron, protecting his good name, protecting his nascent solo career, which would be launching any day now that the ritual had been completed.

It had been an *accident*.

But me?

I wasn't so sure.

* * *

Throughout this long day, I didn't see Aaron once; at least, not until the end of it.

I was passing by the windows in the long gallery when I glimpsed him stood on the drawbridge with the two policemen, shaking hands with them one by one. They were leaving.

My heart began to pound and my mouth was dry. I needed to see him. I needed his embrace, for him to tell me that it was all right, that I had performed as required, both in the story for the police and in the ritual, which now seemed a mere dream.

As I waited restlessly for the police to go, I brushed my wild miasma of hair, which had dried into strange twists and crimps, changed into tighter jeans and applied a little slick of lipstick to offset my white face, which was still wan after last night's adventures.

Whatever Aaron and the police were talking about, it seemed to go on for a long time.

But eventually they turned on their heels and left, their cheap shoes thudding against the drawbridge planks. I smoothed down my clothes and headed off down the stairs to find Aaron.

331

I emerged on to the landing just in time to see him climb the stairs and enter the long gallery opposite.

'Aaron!' I shouted out.

The most peculiar thing happened. It was as if I was invisible, or a ghost. He did not turn round or acknowledge me in any way. His angular face was as impassive as a marble angel's. He must be lost in his own thoughts, I reasoned to myself, but there was something in the determined set of his shoulders that coldly told me yes, he was aware of me.

He just didn't want to acknowledge me.

I leaned across the wooden balustrade, gripping the ancient handrail. 'Aaron!'

He opened the door to the master bedroom and went in.

I stood for a few moments, breathless, wondering what this could mean. A cold shiver was moving up my spine, my throat was tightening.

I crossed the landing, skirting the handrail, the wooden floor creaking beneath my pounding feet as I raced down the long gallery, ignoring Wolf as he sat huddled in front of the fire, his face ashen.

'Nina,' he called after me.

I ignored him. I was outside Aaron's door, but now I was here, I had no idea what to do.

I knocked, tentatively.

There was no reply.

'Aaron?'

I tried the door.

It was *locked*.

I attempted to turn the handle a few times just to be sure. I had never known Aaron's door to be locked. Usually, just the force of his personality was sufficient to repel the uninvited.

'Aaron! Aaron! Let me in!'

I was aware that someone was at my shoulders, grabbing at me with hard hands, and they smelled of cigarette smoke and weed. I was wrapped against his chest as he pulled me backwards.

'C'mon, Lucy, help me out!'

Both Wolf and Lucy were pulling me away from the door into the long gallery, and I didn't understand what was going on, I tried to resist.

'Let go of me! Let go! Aaron? AARON!'

They dragged me away, and in my weakened state, though I fought and wriggled, I was as helpless as a kitten.

I was borne back into the long gallery and forced down into one of the chairs in front of the fire.

'He doesn't want to see you,' said Lucy. 'He doesn't want to see anyone.' She folded her arms at me, not quite meeting my gaze.

I blinked at her, tears running down my face. What Lucy was saying didn't make any sense. How were we supposed to know what to do now? Why was Aaron angry at me?

'Why not?' My teeth were bared at her, and I contemptuously shook off Wolf's lingering hand. 'What's going on?'

Penelope had appeared in the doorway, as though drawn by the furore.

'Now, now, Nina. It's been a long day for everybody. Perhaps he'll feel differently in the morning,' she said smoothly.

I burst into heartbroken sobbing, and I was conscious of Wolf's arms settling around me, him murmuring into my hair to 'let it out, let it all out'. I hated it, and the smell of him, and I was about to shake him off when I realized how selfish I was being. Of course Aaron was distraught over the loss of Peter, and nobody had thought to comfort him. Aaron, who gave so generously to us all, when we gave him nothing back.

And now I was adding to his troubles.

'He must be grieving,' I said, wiping at my eyes. 'He must miss Peter.'

Penelope and Lucy shared a look.

'It's been a very long day,' repeated Penelope with a finality that brooked no riposte. Her usually perfect hair was messy, straying out of its braided crown. 'Let's get something to eat and have an early night.'

* * *

When I woke the next morning it was still dawn. I lay there, disoriented, conscious only that I wasn't alone – there was movement in my room, rustling, the sound of drawers being stealthily opened.

'She's awake.'

I rubbed my crusted eyes and blinked. In the chilly semi-darkness Penelope and Lucy seemed everywhere.

It took me a couple of seconds to realize they were packing my few possessions into a pale blue knapsack.

'What . . . what are you doing?' I sat up in the bed, suddenly wholly conscious.

'Nina,' said Penelope firmly, as though addressing a recalcitrant child, 'Aaron's been thinking. With what happened to Peter, it's best that we all think about what direction the order is headed in and take some time and space for ourselves. The driver's here, and he'll take you to wherever you need to go.'

'What? I don't have anywhere to go!'

'It won't be for long. Just while we sort this thing with Peter out,' offered Lucy with a weak smile.

Penelope's expression didn't change – or perhaps it did, and that shadow of triumph was back, its lines accentuated by the way the pre-dawn light silhouetted the pair of them.

Good cop, bad cop.

Instantly I understood everything.

'You're throwing me out?' My stomach bottomed out. I felt like I was falling. Penelope's next words sounded as though they were coming from a very faint radio station playing faraway.

'Nina, there is absolutely no point in making a fuss. Aaron has made his mind up.' She brushed back her icy hair from her face, and from this gesture, with its languidness, its showy affect, I guessed how much she was enjoying this. 'You need to leave with the others. Right now.'

'I want to talk to Aaron first!' I snapped, my jaw trembling.

'Aaron isn't here, sweetheart,' said Lucy. 'He went out this morning. He needs his space too.' Her eyes looked huge in the gloom. She was already in full make-up.

'But . . . but where will I go?' I asked, bewildered. 'I have nowhere left to go.'

'Why don't you just go back to college?' drawled Penelope, as though the subject bored her.

I scrambled away from them over the bed, stunned. 'I can't, they'll have expelled me by now – Aaron said . . .'

'Then go back to your parents, but you can't stay here. We're shutting the house up. We're all leaving.'

'I can't go back to my parents!' I looked wildly between them both, as though they had lost their minds. 'You know I can't!'

'The world doesn't owe you a bed for the night,' snapped Penelope, all control vanishing, her green eyes narrow with malice. 'Get in that car with the others, or we'll call the police and they can throw you out into the street like the little tramp you are.'

* * *

Tristan and Wolf were already in the car as I was led, sobbing, to it, as though it were my gallows. Tristan was pale and shaking, every blue vein in his face visible, but Wolf had a kind of morbid cheerfulness that seemed to want to burst out of him, a mood he also seemed to be working hard to restrain.

'You all right, love?' he asked as I climbed into the car. He moved next to me and put his arm around me. The smell of stale fags was overpowering, but this kindly human contact comforted me nevertheless. 'Cheer up, darling. It's for the best.'

This was too stupid to even reply to. The only reason I'd let the others pull me out here was because I was afraid of upsetting Aaron even more. I had persuaded myself, I think, that this wasn't real – this was a test, and at the last moment he would appear, call me back in, and I would throw myself at his feet and wrap my arms around his knees. Together we would weather out this horrifying storm of death and fear.

I kept waiting for this deliverance.

It kept not appearing.

Our driver had reappeared, though. We no longer merited a uniform, it seemed, and he was in old-man slacks and a pale blue shirt. He still neither looked at nor spoke to us.

Even in the depths of my misery, I wondered how he had been contacted, considering there were supposed to be no phones in the house.

But these thoughts were interrupted by a sudden terrible, hideous wailing.

It was Tess.

'NO! NO! NO! AARON! AARON! HELP!'

Penelope and Lucy were wrestling Tess out of the door, and she was still in her clothes from the night before. Her face was bright red and streaked with tears, her mouth a scarlet wet maw as she sagged in their arms and let out a high keening, which might have been words, or might simply have been random syllables, a lost language of grief.

Penelope was furious, and the more Tess resisted, the more savage she became, kicking out the skinny bare leg Tess put down to brace herself against her forward momentum, grabbing Tess by the hair as her head sank into her chest. Lucy just pushed, her face slightly turned away, as though despairing of trying to comfort Tess and just desperate to get her in the car.

This spectacle filled me with a pure throbbing sense of terror and loss. I was experiencing exactly what Tess was, only Tess was physically expressing it.

This was it. It was *over*.

I would never see Aaron again.

Wolf was unbuckling himself from the seatbelt with hard jittery movements, his face set like iron. The car door was flung open, the cold air hitting me as he jumped out.

'Get your fucking hands off her!' He shoved Penelope back with ruthless contempt. 'She's just a kid!'

He took Tess in his arms, Lucy releasing her. 'Come here, love. Come here. It's all right. It's OK.'

Tess still wailed, striking out weakly at him. 'I don't want to *go*! I want to stay here . . .'

'No, you don't. No you don't.'

'I do! I want to stay!' Tess's face crumpled and her resistance collapsed. Her hands fell straight to her sides. 'I want to stay with Aaron.'

'That's not going to be possible, baby. And he's too much of a despicable coward to tell you that to your face.'

'No, no, don't say that . . .' Her eyes were huge, as though she was hearing unbearable blasphemies, her hands knitting in her thick honey-coloured hair.

'All right. Have it your way.' He petted her head, as though she was a panicky young animal, smoothing her hands where they were gnarled against her scalp, and shhing her as she rocked on her feet, racked with sobs. 'Come on. Come on now. Come with us.'

Tristan had got out of the car now and took Tess's little suitcase from Lucy, as it was clear the driver wasn't going to do this.

Tristan popped the boot and dropped it in, hiding them all from my view for a second. All I could hear was Tess, weeping, and the faraway calls of pheasants somewhere in the grounds.

'Where you off to now, love?'

It took me a long moment to work out where the voice was coming from, and then I realized it was the driver. There was the flash of his attention in the rear-view mirror.

'D'you have parents? Do you want to go there?'

His face turned over his shoulder – he had pockmarked skin and a large, bulbous nose lined in tiny purple blood vessels, but in his little grey eyes and locked jaw I saw two competing impulses existing in tandem – a reticent, stoic pity balanced against a desire to have absolutely nothing to do with me or any of us. We were trouble.

I shook my head.

'I can't go to my parents'.'

'You sure?' He turned his pockmarked face back to the front. 'I think you should.' His voice was even. 'They'll be worried.'

'I doubt it,' I muttered bitterly.

I had the sense he wanted to say more, but instead he just sighed, a tiny sound of breath. 'Then where?'

'Cambridge. Mill Road.'

'You got family there?'

'Friends,' I said. 'But I think you should take Tess back to where she needs to go first.'

His only reply was a single nod.

* * *

Our driver honoured my request and took Tess home first. She wept all the way to Reading, with such abandonment that I was sure she would make herself sick. I had the peculiar feeling of almost envying her the paroxysm of her utter despair.

I myself could feel nothing – it was as though the world was made of cotton wool. Or rather, it had ended, and I was living through the split second between the detonator sparking and the explosion, and this moment was going to last for the rest of my life.

Wolf was talking to Tristan.

338

'Are you joking? He couldn't go abroad if he wanted to. He just said that to get us out of the house. Peter Clay was shot dead in his fucking hallway. There'll be an inquest.' Wolf scowled, resting his head on the rain-pattered window and letting out a sigh. 'He'll probably love the publicity, the prick.'

'You think he'll stay at Morningstar?' Tristan rubbed his pink eyes. 'With the girls?'

Wolf's laughter was shocking, raucous. 'Well, I think half of that's right.' He leaned forward and tapped on the driver's seat. 'Mate, can I smoke in here?'

'Do what you like,' came the gravelly response. 'It ain't my car.'

Tess continued to sob quietly, huddled against the window. Her top and jeans were soaked with it. I had the sudden morbid fear that Tess might cry herself to death; actually die of a broken heart.

I lied to the police.

It came to me like a sudden thunderclap, as the fuse burned down and the explosion finally came.

I lied to the police.

It had seemed bearable, in the floating world of Morningstar where we all had each other, but now, now that everything was ripped apart, the appalling magnitude of my sin towered above me, towered above all of us.

In my head I heard it again, that storm of furious, yelling male voices from the night of the ritual, cut off by that rolling boom.

I lied to the police, and I think I lied about a murder.

Chapter Thirty-Two

Wolf stayed in the car with me. Tess was gone and Tristan had been let out in Oxford, and parted from us with a sheepish little wave.

He's going straight back to Morningstar to beg to be taken back, I thought with the insight or paranoia of a jealous lover, and suddenly a voracious desire grew within me to go with him, to try again. Perhaps Aaron had changed his mind in the intervening hours, realized that he'd been too hasty.

How could Aaron manage without us? He'd be so alone.

'So what number do these friends of yours live at, love?' asked our driver suddenly.

'I don't know,' I said. 'I think it began with a one, though.'

He sighed, but I didn't care. I was exhausted now – bone-deep tired – and if I had to knock on every door on the street to find Rosie, that's what I'd do.

After all, I had no other plans.

And maybe, after a day or two, I could start to think again about Aaron – find some way to make clear to him that no matter how upset he was about Peter he didn't have to send me away. I was there for him, for ever and always.

I loved him.

I would find my way back to him. Somehow.

* * *

Rosie lived in number 137, and when she threw open the door and saw me standing dishevelled and wan on her doorstep (I must have knocked on twenty doors before finding the right one) she squealed and embraced me tightly.

'We've all been so worried about you!' she said, squeezing my arms. 'And who's this?'

Wolf stood behind me, smoking a tiny roll-up and holding his rucksack and the large black case he'd brought from Morningstar.

I'd asked him in the car: 'Is that Aaron's video camera?'

'What do you think?' The others were gone, and he seemed to have relaxed into a complacent cheerfulness.

'You stole that.'

'Not at all.' His eyes glittered in malicious amusement. 'I took it in lieu of my wages.'

I could think of nothing to reply.

'He's a friend of mine,' I told Rosie. 'From . . . the house.'

When I'd asked Wolf in the car where he would go, he had simply shrugged. Somehow, and with me not quite understanding the mechanics of it, he had followed me out of the car, so that now I'd be asking Rosie to put him up, too.

I could not bear to object. With Wolf gone, even though he had been a peripheral and cynical member, my last link to Aaron and Morningstar would be gone, too.

Rosie nodded. 'Welcome,' she said, opening wide the door and letting us both in. 'Come on in.'

* * *

Rosie's comfortable little flat was perched jauntily atop a betting shop and next door to a curry house. Delicious smells frequently wafted in through the open window on to the street, though I was too heartsick to eat.

My first surprise was waiting at the kitchen table.

'Hello, gorgeous!' It was Piers, ebullient as always, sitting in a Sisters of Mercy T-shirt with a can of bitter in his hand, a pile of books and notes in front of him. His hair had been cut short, shaved in fact.

He leapt up and seized me, swinging me around the room, and in the centre of my misery I felt a little flare of joy at seeing him.

'Piers! What are you doing here?'

'I *live* here. Me and Rosamund – we're an item now.' He moved next to Rosie and put his arm shyly around her. 'I only moved in at the weekend. Strange days, eh?' His gaze lighted on Wolf. 'Hiya, mate, I'm Piers.'

'Wolf,' replied the same coolly, though he took Piers's proffered hand and shook it.

'So what happened?' asked Piers as we sat down at the table and Rosie put the kettle on, Piers taking his books and dumping them to the side.

'Is this a visit?' asked Rosie, and there was something almost nervous about the question. 'Or have you . . .'

'We left,' said Wolf. 'Some daft twat was messing about with a gun while he was pissed and shot his own head off, and after that our buzz was kind of harshed.' He shrugged. 'It was getting old anyway.'

The other two were silent. I felt I ought to add something, to clarify, as this explanation seemed to have stunned our hosts.

I opened my mouth. 'I—'

'So we caught a lift down as far as Cambridge,' said Wolf, as though I hadn't spoken. 'D'you two fancy a spliff?'

* * *

Wolf and I slept in the tiny crowded living room, in the midst of Rosie and Piers's shared jumble of books. I took the couch and lay there, staring at the glow-in-the-dark plastic solar system that had been glued to the ceiling.

Nearby, Wolf snored gently on the floor, supported by a couple of sofa cushions. It had been a difficult evening. Piers had clearly found Wolf intimidating, but had tried to warm to him. Somehow, though, Wolf had sensed Piers's unease, and wanted to capitalize on it, talking to him with a kind of patronizing familiarity, only asking if he could smoke or use the loo while he was in the process of getting up or doing these things.

Rosie he barely acknowledged, treating her like one of the Morningstar girls, someone that brought glasses and food and provided colour while the men talked.

Rosie had grown chilly, and seemed unlikely to thaw towards him.

My thoughts were lost in a maze, like the yew maze at Morningstar. Sometimes Aaron was before me, and his eyes were vast and tragic. I had betrayed him. We had failed. We had been too full of negative energy and brought death into the house.

But sometimes my memories of Morningstar scalded me into shame, as though I was being doused from a boiling kettle – *he used you, he used you like a thing, and when the going got tough, he threw you away like a rag!*

At other times I thought of Detective Inspector Derek Holmes in his darts' league tie and Hitler moustache, and my heart nearly stopped beating in fright.

* * *

For the first few days, I lived in terror of a knock at Rosie and Piers's door, of the police wanting to take me in for questioning. After all, what would happen if they wanted statements about Peter's death and they couldn't find us? Wouldn't we look guilty? Perhaps we should go back to Morningstar, point this out to Penelope or Lucy, who could perhaps reason with Aaron.

I mentioned this to Wolf one morning, after Rosie and Piers had gone out.

He shook his head at me. 'I took care of it. I went to the police station yesterday. I'm not stupid.'

'I just thought that if we told Penelope or Lucy . . .'

'What? What could they do?'

My mouth was dry and I swallowed. 'They could talk to Aaron.'

His brows beetled together and then a light seemed to come on. 'Oh, you think those two are still there. At Morningstar.'

'What do you mean?'

343

He let out a bitter little laugh. 'You think he chucked the rest of us out and let them stay? Really?'

'I don't understand . . .'

'Nina, the minute he got them to do his dirty work for him, he'd have showed them both the door.' Wolf was sitting at the kitchen table with a mug of instant coffee. His constant chain-smoking was starting to get on Rosie's nerves, I could tell, and there was obvious tension between him and Piers. It was hard to discuss it with them, though, as I never seemed to be alone with Rosie. Wolf was always there.

And now the story of our time at Morningstar had become Wolf's narrative of it – the careless account of Peter's accidental death, the tawdry failure of the whole experiment, everyone's gullibility and stupidity.

Everyone's except Wolf's.

'You think he threw them out as well?' I asked. I found this nearly impossible to imagine.

A bark of harsh laughter. 'Petal, I know he did.' He lifted his mug and slurped. 'He wouldn't have thought twice about it. He just needed them to get you lot out first. Divide and conquer.'

'How do you know that?'

Wolf grinned. 'You should have heard him talk, the minute you girls and Tristan weren't in the room.' His voice dropped a register as he mimicked Aaron's hoarse murmur. 'I think it's not working because the other guys are wrong, man. They're all so weak and negative, man, I need to get rid of them all and start again, but you'd stay on, right, Wolf? I'd still need a cameraman.' He rolled his eyes contemptuously. 'Man.'

I simply stared.

'I don't . . .'

'Why are you surprised? He was a selfish, narcissistic *dick*.'

'Well,' I said, feeling a sudden rush of protective rage, 'if he was that terrible, why did you stay with him for so long?'

344

And then a peculiar thing happened. Something bleak and un-guarded flitted across his face. 'I had my reasons.'

Silence fell, and he was looking at me, his usual aura of defensive cynicism gone, and I realized that I absolutely could not listen to what was going to come next. I needed him. I couldn't do this post-Morningstar world alone, and I could not afford to be boxed into a corner with him that would require a single unambiguous answer.

'I'm going out,' I said. 'I need a walk. I need to think.'

'I'll come with you—'

'No, I'm going on my own. I need to be on my own.' There was a rising hitch of hysteria in my voice. 'I'm never on my own!'

'You're fucking off back to Morningstar, aren't you?' he sneered. At that moment he'd never looked more like his namesake, as if the very hackles on the back of his neck were standing up. I thought he might snarl.

I thought he might bite.

'No.' I snatched my coat with quick, trembling fingers. 'I'll be back at lunchtime. I just need to get out.'

* * *

'You've got a problem there.' Rosie rested her hand on her chin, let her pale eyes settle on me.

'What do you mean?'

I hadn't gone back to the flat at lunchtime. I'd spent three hours in the canteen in the Institute of Astronomy, drinking endless cups of tea with Rosie, as earnest young men and women in jumpers and jeans with their arms full of notes and books had come and gone.

At first I'd felt horribly guilty. I was taking up Rosie's hospitality and privacy at home, and now I was hunting her down at the institute.

But I had to talk to somebody.

I'd composed the apology I was going to give Rosie for

disturbing her studies, for taking up her flat, for never replying to her letter while at Morningstar, when she saw me, checked that I was alone, and then jumped up and hugged me, as though she'd been here waiting for me all along.

'Let's get a cuppa,' she'd said.

I'd talked for hours, my voice hoarse and buzzy, my eyes pink with tears. I'd talked about Aaron, about Morningstar, about how much I missed him and it, about how I knew I was a fool but I could see no other life.

Rosie had merely nodded and listened, for once without judging.

'You've got a problem in Wolf.'

I shrugged. 'I don't know.' But I did.

'You do.' Rosie offered me a look over the top of her glasses. Her hair, now dyed black, was pulled back tightly on top of her head and tied with a scrap of lace. Her denim jacket bore the badges of bands I'd never heard of – who were Fields of the Nephilim? 'He thinks you're together, it's just that *you* don't know it yet. This is why he's so weird and undermining with Piers, cos he thinks Piers is after you.' Rosie rolled her eyes and took a sip of her tea. 'Have you thought about what you're going to do next?'

'I can't see past this inquest.'

'That could be months away. And here's the thing, Nina – if the police thought you were involved somehow, you'd have heard from them by now.'

'I don't . . .'

'It was really sad what happened to this Peter, but if you're not involved, then what is there to worry about?'

'Oh, I don't . . .'

'See, Piers and I were talking to your tutor. At St Edith's.'

I froze. 'You talked to Dr Eddingley about me?'

Rosie sighed. 'I know it sounds interfering. But I feel terrible about what happened. I knew Aaron Kessler was bad news when we met him, but I didn't want to seem like the uncool girl, the one

346

who made a scene, and Piers was enchanted with him, and well, I could have handled it all a lot better.' She sniffed, with a little toss of her head. 'Basically, I thought about myself first. So.'

'Rosie, you're not to blame for my mistakes.' I was humbled. 'None of this is your fault.'

She shrugged this away. 'Well, anyway, we spoke to your tutor.'

I simply stared.

'And he reckoned that you'd only missed a term, so if you made a submission and explained that you were having, shall we say, emotional problems, they might let you restart the year in October. You haven't officially been sent down yet.'

I didn't know what to say. I'd despaired of ever returning to university after the casual way in which I'd left it. I wasn't prepared for the sudden breathless squeezing of hope within my breast.

'Rosie, that's so lovely of you to think of me, but even if they took me back, how would I live till then?'

'You could get a job. They're always looking around here. The tourist season will start in a couple of months anyway. You could wait on tables, or pull pints, or sell punt tours in the streets. You could even sign on.'

I considered this for a long moment. 'But how would that pay for my rent, my grants? I can't ask my parents for anything. I think Daddy might wring my neck if he ever saw me again.'

'Firstly, I don't think that's true, and secondly, *you* will always be welcome to stay at the flat, and for as long as you need to.'

Rosie looked away. There was a long second of silence. There had been no doubting that very definite, singular *you*.

'And Wolf?'

Rosie raised her shoulders in a shrug. 'I hate to turn anybody out, but you said it yourself. He's like this bitter, angry, chain-smoking shadow. He constantly follows you around, *speaks* for you, tries to control where you go and what you do. He's got money for tobacco, but he's never offered us a penny towards his keep—'

'I haven't offered you anything,' I said, mortified.

'That's different, Nina. You're our friend – what we have is yours. But we don't know anything about this guy, except that he was involved with Aaron Kessler somehow. And to be blunt about it, neither do you.'

I fidgeted at this. Yes, Wolf was annoying to Rosie and Piers, I could see that. But he was the only other person I had access to that understood the Morningstar experience.

To let that go would be like letting Aaron go.

I said as much.

Rosie looked quickly over each shoulder, as if to make sure she wasn't being overheard, then she leaned forward and whispered, stabbing the table with her finger, 'Nina, you were a harem girl for that man. You were a slave – someone to be used and lent out when necessary. They locked you in a barn overnight where you nearly froze to death for *disobedience*.

'They have got so thoroughly and completely into your head that instead of wanting to call the police, you wait by the phone every day hoping you'll get called back there. They're a mind-control cult, Nina.'

'But . . . you don't understand . . .'

'No, I don't understand. I wasn't there. But I think you have been through a terrible experience and you are vulnerable; so, so vulnerable.'

She grabbed my wrist gently. 'And listen. This is what this Wolf character sees in you. This is why he doesn't like us, because we want you to get better, to be free and happy and in charge of yourself again. He wants you to stay this way because then he has a chance of keeping you.'

She let me go.

'Just make sure you don't sleep with him.' She reached over and grabbed my cup. 'With a fella like that, you'll never be rid.' She shook it. 'Another one for the road, missus?'

Chapter Thirty-Three

Tearing up the motorway, the third notebook and contents fresh in my mind, I was nearly killed three times on the journey home from Morningstar. I pulled out in front of lorries and changed lanes on the motorway without looking, angry cars honking at me.

It was very hard to concentrate on anything that wasn't happening inside my own head.

I'd only had time to read the first dozen or so pages, but I was already running very late – I had to go home and get my dad settled.

I would read the rest tonight, once he was in bed and I was back in my little room upstairs, where there was no danger of him finding this document and asking me questions about it.

I shook my head, trying to dispel the thousand crowding thoughts surrounding me and focus on the road.

Aaron Kessler couldn't be my father. That was obscene, ridiculous – Jesus, I'd been actually kind of attracted to him. The memory made me shiver, as though filthy things had fallen down the front of my dress and I needed a long shower and a scrubbing brush to be rid of them.

But another part of me knew there was nothing ridiculous about it. My conception was suspiciously close to the time my mum left the order. My dad must have come later and taken me on as well, without knowing the full story, and together they had resolved never to mention the matter of my parentage to me.

You can see why they might have thought that was for the best.

Or maybe, I thought, with a growing sick feeling, she had passed me off to my dad as his. My mum hated confrontation and was a hardened procrastinator. Knowing her, it was entirely possible she had just neglected to mention Aaron and his role in my conception for over a quarter of a century.

I didn't know how I felt about all this. I was furious that she hadn't told me, yet knowing didn't make me any happier either.

I wasn't going to worry about it now, though. I was going to Eden Gardens to see Dad and make him the cauliflower curry I had planned. We would have a quiet night in together. I wouldn't mention visiting the man who might have fathered me, instead I'd take on my mother's job of making him cups of tea and listening to him grumble about immigrants and the government.

We would get through this.

Dammit, I thought, with an angry shake of my head. I'd forgotten to ask that bastard Aaron about Peter Clay, or Wolf.

Tomorrow. Tomorrow I would think about all this.

Tomorrow was another day.

* * *

I pulled up at the gates of Eden Gardens, heartsick and exhausted, only to find them closed and padlocked.

A homemade sign on a square piece of plywood read CLOSeD UNTiL FURTHeR NOTiCe. I recognized my dad's peculiar typography. Normally my mum wrote the signs.

It was only four o'clock in the afternoon.

I got out and unlocked the gates, wondering what all of this meant, and deciding nothing good.

* * *

'Dad?'

The shed was as I remembered it. I hadn't been inside it since I'd found the notebooks in there.

He was sitting in his chair, at his desk, breathing hard, as though he'd been exerting himself.

'Dad! Are you all right?'

He didn't acknowledge me, but he didn't object when I came in and picked up the filthy coffee cup that had been left by the police.

'I was shouting for you all over the house and you didn't answer. You worried me,' I said, coming up to him and kissing him. He was very tense, his skin cool, and I sensed he would have liked to pull away. He was probably cross I hadn't picked him up from the hospital.

At that moment I didn't care how crotchety he was. I was just so glad to be here with him, faraway from Aaron Kessler and his horrifying assertions. 'So Rowan dropped you back, did he?'

'Yes,' he said, as though everything was ordinary, and we hadn't been through this all-involving experience of near-death, grief and terror together. But his voice was rough and faint.

'I'm sorry I couldn't be here, but I had to meet someone about Mum.' I stood, stretching my back after my long drive, and then I noticed something strange.

The stepladder was out, and the sight of it gave me a jolt. I looked up – above my head a little panel in the wood was open – it had been designed, clearly, to look like natural planks, and through the gap I could see the corner of a black plastic suitcase.

'What's that? I didn't know there was a false ceiling there.'

He grunted.

'How clever is that? You always were good with wood.' I frowned at the case. 'What's that up there?'

'Insurance.'

'Insurance against what?'

He grunted again.

'You know, Dad,' I said, 'I could go off on this big rant about how you've been very sick and shouldn't be climbing stepladders and engaging with clandestine joinery, but I'd be wasting my time, wouldn't I?'

He didn't answer for a few moments. I sensed that he'd exhausted himself, and was furious at how long it was taking him to recover.

He was going to be a terrible patient, as always. That much was plain.

I looked at him, with his shaking hand and pale face, and felt a sudden surge of affection for him. Whatever Aaron had said, it was this man here who had been the stable presence in my life, the one who fixed things, provided and made things safe.

And now I was going to do the same for him.

'I was thinking of making curry for dinner. I've got some wine in, and that beer you like. Will that do?'

He nodded.

'D'you want a cup of tea?'

He nodded again. 'Before you go, I need you to fetch that down,' he said. 'It's too heavy for me.' He coughed. 'I'm too weak.'

'That case?' I peered up at the disarticulated wood, and then eyed the stepladder with distaste. 'All right.'

Steeling myself, I mounted the stepladder, sticking my head through the hole. The dust had been disturbed – other things had been up here recently; he must have taken them down.

Why was he doing this now?

'I saw that sign on the door,' I called down. 'Don't you think "until further notice" is a bit much? People might think we're shutting permanently. It'll scare custom away.'

'They can think what they like,' he said unhelpfully, his voice was little more than a whisper.

This is a problem, I thought with dull dread. My dad wasn't sociable. My mum had handled the whole 'dealing with people' side of things here, and it wasn't clear how he'd manage without her.

We needed to replace Monica straight away.

The case was heavy – there was something substantial in it that gave off a plasticky rattle when I moved it.

'Bloody hell, Dad, have you got a body in here?'

His answer was a kind of wheezy snort that might have been laughter. 'Almost, but not quite. Set it on the desk.'

I bore it down the stepladder carefully and put it on his desk. It wasn't that big, but it was full of some kind of equipment, something roughly the size of a sewing machine.

The case was moulded black plastic, and specially made to contain whatever was inside, shadowing its weird bumps and being slightly asymmetrical. It was covered in dust and crusted insect droppings, and I slapped my dirty hands against my trousers in disgust after gently lowering it on to the desk.

I stood back. 'What is it?'

'Never you mind. Were you going to make some tea?'

'Suit yourself.' I wasn't in the mood to quarrel with him, especially not tonight. 'I'll be back in a minute.'

* * *

I set the dirty cup in the sink and filled the kettle, looking around at the freshly cleaned kitchen. I would cook, that's what I'd do. It would calm me. And all of these huge things, these revelations, could wait until tomorrow. They would change nothing tonight.

I went over to the cupboard by the old Aga, looking for my dad's favourite mug, which wasn't on the draining board.

Lying on the counter was an opened letter with some kind of dark threatening letterhead. Official letters had become a constant thing since my mum's death, and I had learned to pay them no mind. They would all be got to in good time. But it was strange that this one was lying opened in here. Perhaps it was from the hospital.

I read it, then read it again, three times in all, while my blood froze.

Re: Notice to Vacate
Dear Mr Boothroyd,

This letter is to notify you that you are hereby given thirty days to remove yourself and your belongings from the property formerly known as The Old Mill, Pulverton, Suffolk.

The owners are within their rights to demand you leave immediately. In consideration of your recent ill health, however, a total of thirty days from the date of this letter will be granted to you to find alternative accommodation.

Please leave the property in good condition, having had it thoroughly cleaned, and deposit the keys at Newmarket Estates, Undley Road, Beccles.

Note that if you do not comply with these terms we will be forced to commence eviction proceedings through the courts.

Thank you for your swift attention in this matter,

Yours sincerely,
Daniel Babcock

This missive has been sent by a firm called Daniel Babcock and Associates, on behalf of Thomas and Estella Mackenzie.
Estella.
That was why she'd wanted me to tell her how Dad was doing. It was so she could start the process of chucking him out

on the streets. At the funeral, I remembered she'd said she wanted to 'talk about the house'.

I was breathless, stunned at their ruthlessness. It had never once occurred to me that my parents didn't own this house outright.

'What the hell is wrong with these people?' I muttered to myself as the kettle boiled.

I made him some tea, just how he liked it, strong and with two sugars, and I put one of the little Bakewell tarts he enjoyed on a plate.

I need to stay calm, confident and strong. Dad needed care, not anxiety.

The garden was cooling down, the sun getting lower as I went out, carrying my little burdens to the shed. High summer had passed and soon Eden Gardens would grow red and gold, the air earthy and damp with falling leaves.

Except we won't be here to see it.

And what are we going to tell Rowan?

The thought made me dizzy and sick. Rowan depended on Eden Gardens to feed his wife and children.

As I stepped past the squashes we grew near the fence, I heard a creaking noise behind me, as though the garden gate had swung open, just a fraction.

I froze.

'Hello?'

There was no answer.

I turned, my heels sinking into the mulch, but nobody seemed to be there.

I was about to go up and check the lock – in my disordered, distraught state I might have forgotten to shut it behind me, and that was it, swinging in the breeze . . .

'Sophia!' called out my dad from the shed. 'Sophia, come here, quickly!'

His voice was urgent, alarmed.

I looked towards the garden gate, and then carefully carried the tea and cake over to the shed, looking back over my shoulder constantly.

'Dad, I think there's someone . . .'

It took me a minute or two to make sense of what I was looking at.

'Dad,' I said, in the quietest, most even voice I could manage, 'what are you doing?'

He was standing up and facing me, the black case open on the desk. Within it I could see something bulky, with a lens and a handle – some kind of camera. Stuffed in with it were dozens of old video cassettes, plainly labelled with dates and the occasional name: '29/10/88 – SARAH', '3/2/85 23:47', 'Tristan – 4/6/87'.

But this wasn't what was holding my attention.

Instead it was the shotgun he was pointing at my face.

'Dad?'

'I'm not your dad, as you well know. You were at Morningstar today, right? Didn't you meet your real daddy there?'

Rowan, I thought. Rowan had seemed cagey on the phone when I'd told him not to tell my dad. He'd probably already told him, and didn't want to say.

'Dad,' I said, fighting to stay calm. 'Stop this immediately. Put the gun down. You're upset. I know you're upset—'

'Upset?' His eyes were bright and wet with tears. 'You have no idea, Sophia. No idea what that means. You know, when Nina's monstrous Mummy and Daddy let us stay here, after her grandfather died and they didn't want to pay fucking tax on the sale, the place was a shambles. It stank of corpses. Literally *stank* of death, because the old fella had died here and they never visited, heartless twats that they were; he was half rotted away by the time he was found.'

He took a step nearer, the barrel of the gun shaking. It would have been easy to knock it out of his hands, but I was too far away.

'No water, no heat, no electricity, your mum practically about to drop with you.'

I was transfixed, speared by his rage and despair.

'I built this place out of fucking nothing, all for her, even though she'd never give me a straight answer. "I don't know if Sophia is yours." "I don't know if I still love Aaron." She just kept me hanging on and hanging on and *hanging on . . .*'

'Dad—'

'Stop calling me that!' he screamed, his anguish apparent, and as much as I was terrified, his pain was awful to behold, an unassuageable agony. 'You even *look* like him! Is it *you* that's going to inherit this place, is that the plan? Once your grandad and granny throw me to the wolves?'

Wolves.

I stared at the tapes, the camera, him, in disbelief and dawning realization.

My dad is not my dad.

Suddenly everything snapped into place. *Of course. He's Wolf.* This was what Tess had been on her way to tell me when she'd died. This explained her urgency – she'd had to do it while Dad was still in hospital and unlikely to see her. And she would have wanted to do it face to face, while I was sitting down, presumably.

'D—' I took a step backward, my heart pounding. It was as though I was falling, and my legs were trembling, about to give way. 'Please don't do this. We can talk about—'

'You can blame Nina for this, Sophy,' he snarled. 'She's leaving me, she says, she's had enough, she'll risk it all, them finding out about Peter, everything. She'll go to you, she says . . .' He swiped at his wet face with the back of his hand. 'The

357

heartless, stone-cold bitch! I would have given my *life* for that woman!' His eyes were huge. 'Did you plan it together?'

She's had enough, she'll risk it all, them finding out about Peter – he'd known about the book Mum intended . . .

It could only mean one thing. One horrible, inescapable thing; the only thing that fitted the facts.

'Dad,' I still couldn't wrap my head around it. 'You killed *Mum*?'

Even in his extremity, the deed seemed too huge to acknowledge. It was as though I hadn't spoken. 'We'll all go together, like we were meant to, like we should have, if you'd come home that night . . .'

'Dad, you don't want to do this.'

'No,' he said, and a strange calm seemed to come over him. 'I don't, but that won't stop me.'

His expression grew flat, emotionless, and I knew, in that second, that he was going to kill me, and that no words or pleas would spare me.

'I'm not building all of this out of nothing, building you and her out of nothing, just to lose it all.' Tears were falling down his face, but it was as though he was no longer connected to them, to any human emotion I could recognize.

'Goodbye, Sophia.' He raised the gun and steadied it. 'We'll both be with your mum soon.'

I threw the hot cup of tea in his face.

He let out a yowl of rage, and I turned on my heel and ran, scrambling like a mad thing towards the garden gate, my feet tripping over the lines of squash and courgettes, getting entangled in the netting over the brassicas. I fell forward on to my belly, my cheek grazing the damp soil, and inhaled its earthy scent.

He was coming after me as I tried to flounder to my feet. 'Hold still . . .'

I flopped over on to my back, my foot hopelessly caught.

Oh, please let it be quick . . .

He stopped just before my feet, the gun aimed at my chest. He was breathing hard, very hard, though whether this was with rage, despair, or post-surgery exertion, I couldn't tell.

I opened my mouth to plead for my life, though my voice was dry as dust.

'It's an irony you'll never be able to appreciate,' he said. 'But this was how I got your mother. I shot that dirty fucker Peter Clay right in front of her, to keep him off her, and she was too out of it even to remember afterwards.' He was gasping, finding the strength to raise the gun. 'A shotgun,' said my dad, breath sawing in and out of his lungs. 'That's funny. It's how it began, and how it's going to end.'

'Dad, please, no, please don't . . . please, I'm begging you, please don't do this . . .'

And then someone stepped out from the hedges lining the fence. He was a shadow behind my dad, with long dark hair, high cheekbones and intense black eyes.

Aaron Kessler.

I couldn't move. For a nightmare moment, I thought I was dreaming him.

He was carrying something, long and thin, and I realized it was a tyre iron.

'Hello, Wolf,' Aaron said.

And then he brought it down hard on top of my dad's head. The gun fell away.

My dad – Jared – was still for an instant, trembling, before sinking to his knees in the soft mulch of Eden Gardens, then toppling forward, like a felled tree.

* * *

'Why did you come?'

The police were clearing everything away. They'd asked

their questions and let me go, and my dad, heavily concussed, had departed in the ambulance.

Part of me felt I should have gone with him, but everyone – the police, the ambulance crew and Rob Howarth – thought this was a very bad idea. Maybe it was.

After all, it takes a little while for the heart to know what the mind understands – he'd killed my mother.

He was not my friend.

Aaron had refused to answer any police questions, very politely but firmly stating that he never spoke to law enforcement without his lawyer present, as a matter of course. Various threats about arrest were made, and dismissed with his contemptuous silence.

I didn't think he was going to answer me either, at first, as we leaned against the garden fence. I could see SOC officers moving around inside my dad's shed.

Aaron sighed. 'I never realized, until you said his name today, that the man living here with Nina was Wolf.' He leaned back on his hands and raised his eyes to the stars. 'I don't watch much news. It's not good for your mind, you know – your spiritual development – and anyway, I have people for that.'

If he noticed my curious look, he gave no sign.

'Jared Boothroyd. Been a long time since I heard that name.' He closed his eyes. 'A long time.'

I waited, shaking. Aaron was like something I had dreamed, of a piece with the rest of my evening.

He slouched against the wood. 'Once I realized it was him, it all made sense. Nina was never interested in Wolf in that way at Morningstar, but he was obsessed with her.' He smiled, as though at a happy memory. 'Nina was a beautiful woman – so fragile, so innocent, and yet strangely strong. She could get you that way.' Aaron stretched out his legs and struck a fist against the place where his heart would be. 'It makes sense that he followed her. But me, I always wanted to catch up with Wolf one day, because he stole something very valuable to me.'

'The Morningstar tapes,' I said, hearing the quiver in my voice. 'You came for them. Alone. Because the others all believe you had them all along. That's how you lean on them for money. If it came out that they'd been hiding in a garden shed somewhere in Suffolk for the past twenty-odd years—'

'I don't know anything about that,' he dismissed this with a wave of his hand. 'But once I knew it was Wolf out here, I had to confront him. I thought it was time somebody did. Anyway, what makes you think I'm alone?'

I was such a fool. Of course he wasn't alone. His driver would be nearby, and anyone else he'd wanted to rustle up.

I gazed at the trees around me.

I shrugged. 'Well, thanks for saving my life.'

'You don't have to thank me for that. Gratitude exists only where there are alternative courses of action, Sophia. You're worth much more than the tapes.' He rose to his feet. 'We should watch them. You'd find them ritually instructive. Your conception is on one of them.'

'I'll pass, thanks.'

There was a long, cool pause. Then he said, 'I'm going to call my lawyer.'

I felt oddly calm, considering all that had happened. You'd think I would be devastated. But I wasn't, not really. I felt vindicated, as though a secret subconscious belief I'd harboured had been proved right.

My mother hadn't killed herself. My mother had fought to live, fought to tell her story of escape and rebellion and love that had ended in slavery, fought to escape this mad Eden with its controlling Adam, who had loved her too much and not at all.

She had not been saved, ultimately, but now, at least, she would have her justice.

Chapter Thirty-Four

It had been nearly three weeks since we'd been thrown out of Morningstar.

I took some of Rosie's advice at least, and after the first week I wrote to the college. A fortnight later they wrote back. I opened the letter with shaking hands, standing at the kitchen counter in the little flat, while Wolf watched daytime TV and smoked.

The college would entertain my appeal. I must write, formally, setting forth my case, by March 21st.

I read it again, the paper trembling in my hands.

I already had the feeling it was too late.

'Summat the matter?' barked Wolf.

It was as though he had a sixth sense when something moved me – he could feel it from across town. I would be lying if I said it wasn't impressive.

'No, no, not at all.'

* * *

I couldn't sleep that night. I lay on my back, staring up at the ceiling with its green glowing solar system, unable to stop the tears.

Morningstar, for good or evil, was lost to me. I was adrift in a cosmic darkness, with only luminescent plastic planets to guide me.

I tried to suppress a tiny sob.

On the floor, in his pool of blankets, Wolf stirred.

'Are you all right?'

In the dim light, his eyes reflected tiny glints.

'I'm fine,' I said, but my voice broke, my tears locked in it.

Before I knew it, he was next to me, warm like an animal, and his arms were snaking around me.

'Nina . . . Nina, it's gonna be all right.'

I shouldn't be encouraging this, I knew, but in my loneliness and misery, any contact was a comfort. I let myself cling to him for a moment.

His lips brushed my cheek, my throat, his perpetual stubble scratching across my skin.

'No . . .'

I tried to move away and push him off, but his grip tightened. 'Shh, shh, easy now . . .'

'Wolf, stop it, I don't want—'

His mouth was on mine, stopping up my words, and his hands were roving over me, pushing up my T-shirt, kneading my breasts. There was the coolness of his tongue on my nipple and then the warmth as his mouth closed over it, sucked and laved me, and though I pushed, as hard as I dared, I could not detach him.

And I wasn't sure I wanted to detach him. I was so wretched, so alone, so frightened, that the animal flare of sex, any sex, offered up a sliver of distraction, of oblivion.

I didn't resist any more as he roughly pulled off my knickers and buried himself deep inside me. In his thrusting greed and enthusiasm he was a stranger to me as he moved hard against and within me, the moon dousing him in pale light, his shoulders white, his lips wet and dark. The others must be able to hear us in their room; and I thought that perhaps he wanted them to, or simply didn't care.

Eventually my orgasm came like an afterthought, and he let go then with a shudder and a long loud groan before sinking into me. Then all was quiet apart from our breathing and the random shouts of a few drunk students ambling back to their digs in the street below.

'Wow,' said Wolf. 'I have wanted to do that to you since the minute I laid eyes on you.'

I didn't have any answer to that.

He kissed me then, arranging us both stagily for sleep, my head against his bare chest. Part of me suspected that this was so Piers and Rosie might find us that way in the morning.

Rosie, who'd said, 'Just make sure you don't sleep with him. With a fella like that, you'll never be rid.'

'Are you all right?' he asked.

I wasn't. Now it was over I was more despondent than ever, more lonely. I'd just made everything worse. I was going to cry again, out of my old grief with this new ingredient of shame.

'Hey, hey, what's the tears for?'

'You didn't use a condom,' I said, for lack of any other way of verbalizing my despair.

'You didn't argue at the time.' He grinned, and when I didn't answer he kissed me. 'Don't worry, babes. You can get that morning-after pill. It'll be fine.'

I still didn't reply. Clearly there was no point.

And it didn't really matter that he hadn't worn a condom, because I was quite sure, from the absence of my normally clockwork-exact period, that I was already pregnant.

* * *

'Bloody hell,' had been Daddy's words upon first seeing me when I arrived home with Wolf.

Mummy was speechless. It was the first time I think I'd ever seen her cry.

I was six months gone with you, already feeling huge and ponderous, some vast, sway-bellied grazing mammal.

Within me you were kicking urgently, as if somehow you were able to see my mock-Georgian family home with its oversized conservatory, chintz sofas and horrified parents, and had decided you had better places to be.

At my side, Wolf had made an effort. He'd shaved, so his chin and cheeks were pink and razor-burned, and he'd changed into relatively clean clothes that we'd purchased from a charity shop in Oxford.

We'd been on the road for months. I'd called Rosie twice with the end of my few coins and tried to explain what had happened.

'Nina, LEAVE HIM!' Her confusion and her growing disgust with me were almost palpable.

But I couldn't leave him, and I dared not tell her why.

It wasn't as if I hadn't tried.

We'd been in a café in Cambridge when I attempted to explain that we were not only through, we had never begun.

Piers and Rosie had evicted him the evening before, in a storm of shouting and smashed furniture. He had urged me to meet him the next day to talk it through, and as this had been the price of him leaving without further violence, I'd agreed without hesitation.

'Here you go.' He placed the cup in front of me. 'Drink up. That's the end of our cash.'

Next to us, a tired-looking family of Mum, Dad and two small children were pressing cake into their mouths.

'We can get a ride from the coach station here to Manchester,' he was saying. 'After that, we're sweet.'

'I'm not going anywhere with you,' I said, and my nerves were singing, my voice tight. 'I just agreed to see you because you deserve to be told face to face. We're not together and we're not going to be. I'm going back to Rosie's after this.' I laced my fingers together on my lap. 'On my own.'

His face transformed instantly into a searing, murderous rage. I think, if we'd been alone, he would have hit me.

'Don't you fucking dare,' he hissed. 'Just don't.'

'Wolf, I don't know how else to tell you—'

He reached forward, grabbed the lapel of my jacket and hauled me closer. It's easy to forget what men could get away with back then. People would think we were 'having a domestic'. If he wasn't physically punching me, it was unlikely anyone would intervene. His face was inches from my own.

'What gives you the fucking right,' he snarled into my ear, 'to get me in this much fucking trouble and then dump me?'

'I don't . . . I didn't . . .' I yelped, terrified at the change in him.

'Listen, you silly cunt, you *shot* a man,' he whispered. 'I've been trying to fucking *protect* you here. If you leave me swinging, I'll do the same to you.'

I was stunned into silence. 'Wha— what are you talking about?'

'Peter Clay. It was *you*,' he whispered coldly in my ear. 'You were off your face when you wandered downstairs. Uncle Petey saw his opportunity with you off your tits and grabbed you. Some stupid tosser had left the gun cabinet unlocked, and *boom*. You shot him.'

'I . . .'

'You'd be in a fucking cell right now if it weren't for me,' he muttered, his spittle flecking my cheek, his breath blazing against my skin. 'Don't even *think* about leaving me in the lurch.'

He thrust me back into my seat.

I blinked, a bone-deep dread and terror settling over me.

'Excuse me, love,' said the man at the next table, still chewing his food. 'Is everything all right here?' His wife scowled at Wolf.

Sophia, I had no memory of the night of the ritual, except that there had been a noise, a noise like rolling thunder, and a storm of raised male voices, and then my hands had tasted of iron and salt.

There was one other thing, and I realized it in a flash of insight. I had *hated* Peter Clay. Not only on his own account, the dirty, lecherous, would-be rapist, but also because I didn't yet have the emotional machinery to hate Aaron the way he deserved. Nothing Peter did or said to me happened without Aaron's implicit permission, but to admit this to myself would be to admit that Aaron was the bully and fraud Wolf claimed he was.

If Peter had tried to force himself on me while I was in that subconscious state, without inhibitions, then yes, I could imagine me

367

shooting him dead. The gun cabinets were often left unlocked, and I knew where they were.

I started to shake.

Across the table Wolf glared at me, his arms crossed, as though daring me.

'Yes,' I replied to the man, my voice barely a whisper. 'Everything's fine.'

'Just a difference of opinion, mate,' said Wolf, not bothering to look at the man. He grinned at me then, and there was a hint of triumph in his face.

* * *

We dossed with various shady characters he knew for the next few months – squats in Preston, Manchester, briefly Leeds. I was growing and splitting my clothes – you were increasingly apparent and eager to make your entry into the world. I couldn't understand your rush. The world didn't seem a place I would be in a hurry to meet, at least not then.

I realized that I would have to go back to my parents and ask them for help. There was no way I could have a baby here, living like this in filthy, freezing rooms, where Wolf smoked what joints he could muster and we eked out our dole giros with what he could steal and sell. The inquest kept being delayed and delayed. Wolf kept track of these things. I didn't have the heart, nor the courage.

Sometimes I wondered if prison might be better than this, and then, beneath my heart, you would stir, as though urging me to think again.

Eventually we hitched a lift back down south. I'd considered calling my parents, warning them, but ultimately my courage deserted me.

And now, here we were.

'How long . . .' sputtered Daddy, gazing at my swollen belly.

'The baby's due in September.' I placed my hands over you, to protect you. My mother's face contracted into a scowl as she saw my filthy, torn nails, my dry, dirty hair.

'Yep,' said Wolf, smiling at them both. 'It's a little girl, they tell us. Amazing what they can do in hospital nowadays.' He slurped tea from Mummy's bone china. 'We couldn't be happier.'

* * *

We lasted roughly eighteen hours there, even with Wolf on his best behaviour – he was Jared now, his given name.

By breakfast, arrangements had been made that he and I would move into the Old Mill, my grandfather's house in Suffolk, which had been standing empty for the best part of a year after he died. We could live in it 'for a little while'. Daddy would send us a stipend until Jared got a job. This money would go to Jared, as clearly I couldn't be trusted with it, Mummy observed, unable to look at my swelling belly.

Daddy would drive us there now.

I couldn't escape the feeling that they were desperate for the neighbours not to catch sight of us. They needn't have worried. After being back for less than a day, I had no desire ever to return. Even Wolf was a better bet.

Once the inquest was over, I thought, as Daddy handed us the keys and left, not even consenting to enter the house – instead leaving us on the step, his disgust with me a palpable, living thing – everything would be different. I would rally my strength, consider how I might escape this relationship I didn't want and couldn't feel.

But then, on an icy night on the first of October, in an overheated hospital bed, while I screamed and screamed and screamed, you happened.

And you swept all before you.

Until you left me, I never looked back.

Chapter Thirty-Five

It's a beautiful day on top of Mount Vesuvius.

Perhaps the day is a little too beautiful – the hour-long climb to the top at its nearly forty-five-degree angle has exhausted us, and we're drinking lukewarm Orangina under the awning at the edge of the crater, surrounded on all sides by enthusiastic teenagers taking selfies against the vertical shaft of Vesuvius's business end. Above, the sky is a perfect cerulean blue.

My companion's name is Marco, and he's an interior designer; he's self-employed, but he occasionally contracts for Amity. He's Italian – Veronese – but lives in London now. He is tall and gangling and usually his hands are expressive and mobile, though today they hang limp. He is as crushed by the heat as I am. In the distance, the Bay of Naples is a smear of blue and gold in the heat haze.

I told him I had always wanted to see a volcano, so here we are.

'Is it worth it?' he asks me, his hand on the small of my back.

'Yes,' I said. 'But there's no lava. I thought there would be lava.'

He laughs out loud. 'No, no lava. But see this?' He points to the dusty centre of the crater, with one or two small scrub brushes growing on it, as though daring the mountain's ire. 'This is the most dangerous volcano in the world, *mia Sophia*, and it's overdue for a big eruption. If this goes off, all those people down there' – he waved his hand towards the Bay of

Naples, with its carpeting of houses, cafés and gardens – 'they are gone. Everything they have is gone. Just because a thing is quiet and there is nothing to see, does not mean all is well. Things seethe beneath the surface. Pressure builds up. Then *boom*.'

We started dating eighteen months ago, shortly after my Scottish Heritage project was picked up. Scottish Heritage loved the design, but more crucially, James did: 'Benjamin asked my opinion on this. He had problems with it. But that's a true Amity design.' He had addressed me in his office, while I clung to the seat of my chair with my hands, like a little girl, expecting to be fired. 'That's Frank Lloyd Wright reimagined. It's world-class work.' He snorted. 'Sometimes Benjamin can be a little *unfocused*.'

I hadn't known what to say, but that was fine, because James is usually happy to do all the talking.

With James's patronage, a number of things changed for me, and almost immediately.

At any rate, it explained why Olympia had suddenly started being nice to me. And as James was the one who properly introduced me to Marco at the Amity summer party, I am having a hard time staying mad at him, sociopath though he is.

He was Cleo's crush, but by then, Cleo was gone.

When I told James about my deleted files, he launched a full investigation, and the audit trail had led to her, of all people. They even caught her on CCTV. When confronted, she told them Benjamin had put her up to it. Why she'd gone along with it wasn't clear, but thinking back to the morning the files went missing, I remembered her dishevelled appearance and guessed she'd been sleeping with him. Perhaps that had been the first time, or perhaps it was an on-and-off thing. Ultimately, it didn't matter.

Out of the mess of revelation, office backstabbing and betrayal this exposed, the only thing that really floored me was *Benjamin and Cleo? No way is he her type.*

Because, of course, I think as I take the bottle from Marco and sip, I have had a crash course in revelation and betrayal. I have lost and found a mother, and I have lost and found a father.

A father of a kind, at least.

The thing that makes me saddest about all this is that my mum wasted all those years. Left emotionally insecure by her selfish, self-absorbed parents, she had been easy prey for Aaron, and then, when he threw her out, rejected and damaged, she was easy prey for Wolf. It took her over a quarter-century to find the courage to move on and try again.

And once more her incipient boldness was crushed out of her before it could begin.

As the revelations have come out of my dad's – Jared's – trial, I still can't wrap my head around the fact that it wasn't the book that killed my mum after all.

It was that she was leaving him.

Strange as it is, I pity him, too. Though I haven't forgiven him, or seen him since his trial. That's not likely to change.

The thing I remember most clearly is the tape.

I don't know how they got it – Aaron must have handed it over to the police, doubtless for his own purposes. It was seven minutes of badly lit, blurry footage of one of the ritual's aftermath, with growly, incomprehensible sound.

It opened on a woman, more like a girl, lying in abandon on the parquet flooring. She was clad in a single long silky garment, her dark blonde hair spread around her, her eyes closed. Empty glasses and crushed flowers lay nearby.

It could only have been Tess.

Other than her, the room appeared empty, but there were

sounds, something like footsteps, fidgeting, the sound of a lighter being ignited and the sucking in of smoke.

This must be Wolf – Jared, my dad. I realized that he was behind the camera, sober – perhaps the only person in the house still in possession of his faculties as he was not part of the ritual.

Minutes passed in this manner, the girl not moving, the camera not moving, and the sound of someone picking through the tapes, vaguely whistling.

Then there was a terrible female roaring from some other room, the splintered, ancient sound still capturing with crystal clarity her terror, rage and sense of affront.

I realized with a start that the voice was my mum's.

'GET AWAY FROM ME! GET AWAY FROM ME! DON'T FUCKING TOUCH ME!'

Now, on the camera, I could see him as he emerged from behind it, and I recognized him immediately, though he had more hair then, his bald spot no bigger than a fifty-pence coin at this point. His fast, sturdy gait was as familiar to me as my own face, as he appeared in shot, stepping over Tess, vanishing out of the door and running towards the sound of my mum's voice.

The camera never showed his face. But I can imagine his expression.

There was more shouting – the terrible sound warping and shredding it into incomprehensibility. In the foreground, all remained still, the camera pointed forwards and Tess lying there, like a dead woman.

Then there were shouting voices, a resounding boom: the muzzle flash flickering against the wall in the hallway, as though lightning had struck indoors.

At that, Tess jerked awake.

* * *

They caught Karen Ince living rough somewhere in Glasgow in the end. I'd been girding my loins for that – yet another trial – but it never happened as she was judged unfit to plead. I couldn't have been more relieved. If she was genuinely ill, I pitied her, too.

I never found out who the couple following me on the train were, and Aaron professes to know nothing about it. Me, I have my doubts. I remember that sharp little face, gazing down from one of the windows at Morningstar. Perhaps he sent them, just to keep an eye on me; perhaps they were pilgrims on their own account. I'll never know.

I think sometimes of those endless phone calls my mum used to make, urging me to come home. Why had it never occurred to me that she was crying out for help, and that the solution was not that I retreated back into Eden Gardens, but that she leave it and Jared and join me in the world?

It was a conclusion she came to herself in the end. It was what the book was meant to do.

It was this conclusion that killed her.

As for Jared – it feels strange to stop calling him Dad. I do think he loved me, especially when I was younger. I remember him making me wooden toys, and showing and explaining the plants to me in the garden, tending to me as he did them. It was as I grew older, I think, that he started to pull away from me. Perhaps he saw Aaron in my face.

He was happy enough, though. He had what he wanted – he had Nina, and his own business, and for someone who came from nothing, he must have felt like a king in his own little domain.

Except that it wasn't his domain, he'd merely borrowed these privileges, in the same way he borrowed the privileges of Morningstar, with its constant supply of drugs and girls. He was for ever helping himself to other people's things, and then getting furious when the original owners wanted them back.

Things like Aaron's camera, or Eden Gardens, or my mother's autonomy.

I haven't decided what to do with the notebooks yet. I haven't shown them to anyone except Rosie and Piers. I tracked them both down soon after Jared was arrested, and was astonished at how quickly I warmed to them both. I see them on average once a fortnight now, for dinner in their shabby-chic semi in Stoke Newington or to look after their cats while they travel.

They are a font of information – perhaps the only one I have – on what my mum was like before this tragedy overtook her.

I will never have any love for Penelope, whom I have spoken to again recently, but I was moved, despite myself, by Lucy, who flew over from Paris to meet me in the end. She looked haunted, and drank a great deal in the restaurant where we had dinner.

I found out that Aaron had bitten her very hard in the last few years – he'd received a massive bill for back taxes on Morningstar, despite his prospering 'seminar' business, and all the old members, including herself and Penelope, had been made to bear the strain.

Lucy was a mess – a well-coiffed, designer-clad mess, with enormous childlike eyes in her taut, Botoxed face, and I was acutely aware that she was only talking to me now because she had to. She wept over dessert, and I was mortified even as I pitied her cosmic self-absorption. After her initial hastily delivered platitudes on my mum's death (she failed to mention Jared) she didn't refer to anybody's tragedy besides her own for the rest of the evening.

I had power over these people now, each of whom had had a hand in ruining my mother's life.

What to do with them all?

I am conscious that Tess could have exposed them

whenever she'd wanted, but out of mercy chose not to. Maybe I should be guided by her and her hard-won equilibrium.

They're their secrets to keep, after all.

* * *

That evening, after dawdling through the ruins of Pompeii with Marco, sharing a hand-held parasol as we amble through the columns and snatches of fresco, we catch a bus back to Rome. It's forty degrees in the Bay of Naples, which is by the sea, so Rome itself is a staggering bastion of heat and humidity.

We go back to our hotel, dug into the ruins of Trajan's market, and share a cool whirlpool bath and some bottles of Peroni. We are both too exhausted for sex, instead tenderly washing the sharp, gritty volcanic dust from each other's bodies and hair while the air conditioner burrs quietly in the background.

I love this hotel, with its Imperial cellars and Renaissance terrace, where we sit and eat breakfast. I love that it has its feet in the ancient world, its head in the clouds.

Already it's inspiring my next project, a small luxury hotel that Marco will be interior designing. We joke amongst ourselves that one day, if we save hard and are very lucky, we might be able to afford to stay in it for a night after it's built.

While Marco goes downstairs to check a few things with reception – we are going to dine out under the stars overlooking the Roman Forum, eating good pasta and, if I have any say in the matter, drinking lots of good wine – I sit naked at the dressing table and open my laptop.

There's an email from Rowan. Rowan lost his job when Eden Gardens closed, and it was one of the darkest times in our friendship. He was devastated and frightened, with two young children to support and, had I but known it, another on the way. He'd had no idea that my parents had no legal rights to the house or gardens.

I didn't expect my grandparents to relent – not after what Jared did to their daughter – but I'd hoped they'd sell the gardens to Rowan and me as a partnership. However, the instant they learned that Rowan had an emotional identification with the place and with Jared, and had worked there all his adult life, we suddenly found there were mysterious 'new offers' all over the show, keen to drive up the price.

Their greed and mean-spiritedness were a revelation at the time, though in retrospect, I'm not sure why. They wanted nothing of Jared's to survive, including his business, no matter who they took out on the way.

In the depths of my bemused grief, I had a brainwave.

I took Rowan out, got him drunk and pitched the idea to him. I owned the supplies, the machinery, the kit – my grandparents owned only the land, after all; the business was a different thing entirely.

We could start over.

It wouldn't be easy. We'd need to borrow money, get a mortgage for a new site and have agreements drawn up. Rowan was a labourer – he didn't even own the cottage he lived in. If we were to raise capital, it would have to be done by me.

But he and Kayleigh would be partners, not employees, and we had a customer base we could take with us. I would be the silent partner, leaving the running of the business up to them until they could afford to buy me out. I knew they were a safe pair of hands.

It had been touch and go. We found a site, then it fell through, then another, which also fell through. Then we found the perfect place, a little garden centre off the main road to Southwold.

After that everything was go, go, go. And it hasn't stopped since.

I'm sufficiently mean-spirited myself to drive by the old

house occasionally and inspect the rusting gates, the ever-changing litany of estate agents' signs, while the grounds grow wild within. Despite, or possibly because of, their greedy attempts to fleece Rowan and me, my grandparents have never found a buyer.

I have no interest in buying it or living there myself now that the business is secure elsewhere. In the end, it's a place I escaped from and my mum didn't.

I no longer have anything to do with the house or its owners.

* * *

The second email of note was from Aaron Kessler.

I sat there, considering it for a long moment, wondering if I was going to delete it unread.

In the end, I opened another bottle of beer and clicked on it.

Sophia,

I hope this finds you well.

I know you said you didn't want to hear from me again, and I guess I'm OK with that if that's what you really want.

I guess, I thought to myself, *that you're* not *OK with it, since I'm hearing from you.*

I raise the bottle to my lips.

But anyway.

It was pretty crazy by the end, I know, but I still feel we have a lot we can teach one another. We're blood and that's a very deep and sacred thing.

I was thinking about this last night and I remembered that I never told you how I met Wolf, so maybe you'd like to know.

We were in Thailand, and it was September, monsoon season, and you couldn't go anywhere or do anything because it was so hot and humid you thought you'd die, so you just had to stay in air-conditioned bars and drink and watch the girls go by. It was something else.

I had gone out there to find myself, back in the days when you could tell people that and they wouldn't laugh in your face. The Boarhounds were just breaking out, so nobody knew who I was. I was just exploring, trying to be free.

That's where I met Wolf. He told me he was a landscape gardener, but he'd been fired from his job over some misunderstanding about petty cash. So he's out here, working bars, taking pictures. He might publish them in a book. They're good pictures, he's got a visual eye.

So I said, come with me, and take pictures of my journey before that happens, and that's what we did.

It was great at first, it was full of love and adventure and amazing spiritual insights. On the last night I was lying out on the beach at Tapao under the stars and I had a vision that I had to go home, I had to stop fucking around and start my mission. I told Wolf this, and we were on the next plane.

When we came home I thought it would be the same, but it wasn't. It erodes you when you aren't doing things for yourself, when you're being kept. All things must strive or die. I know you feel this, from meeting you, from what people tell me about you, you're a striver. I like to think you get that from me.

Anyway, Wolf's going to be in prison for a long, long time. Even though he stole from me, part of me will always love him, remembering those times we were happy and free in Thailand. I hope part of you will feel the same one day. It's not good to hold on to old resentments, Sophia. They're what kill us in the end. Take it from me.

Transcend this, if you can. I know it's a big ask, but try.

It's not what I expected, but he's actually said something almost sensible.

I don't know how I feel about Jared, but hating him won't bring my mother back.

He's asked, a couple of times, through his lawyer, to write to me. I have always refused.

But maybe my biological father is right. Maybe I should allow it. Maybe.

I do think he loved your mother – there was a lot to love about Nina, though I guess you already know that – but even at Morningstar he wanted to possess her exclusively, to own her, and that's not the way.

If we never speak again, promise me one thing – you'll never allow yourself to be owned.

Maybe, one day, you'll be ready to take your place amongst us. Maybe not. But I hope so. It will always be here for you. The Ascendants are told to remember you in their prayers and offerings every day.

You'll never be forgotten.

I had become litany. Who would have thought?

That said, there is something in being forgotten that I would quickly learn to appreciate. I remember those people on the train; Monica's mad stare; her shaking, white-knuckled grip on my mum's knife.

And suddenly I feel cold here in Rome, for the first time since I arrived.

So that's all I've got for now, apart from one more thing. I just wanted to say that you're a magical creation, unique in all the universe. You are the order's greatest single success.

Never change.

Better go,

A.

I sat there for a long time, thinking. That's how Marco found me.

He gestured at my nakedness and bent down to kiss my shoulder. 'You're wearing this to the restaurant? It looks very good, but I'm not sure it fits the dress code.'

'Sorry, Marco. Sorry. I got distracted. There was an email from Aaron Kessler.'

'How does he know your email address?'

'How does he know anything?' I rubbed my eyes. 'He has people to find out these things.'

'What's he saying?'

'He says that I am a "magical creation, unique in all the universe".'

'I see,' he raised an eyebrow at me. 'That is quite a boast. And what do you think about that?'

I sighed and smiled at him.

'I think you could say that about anybody.'

Chapter Thirty-Six

'What the fuck is this?' Jared asks Nina.

It's been building in him all day.

It is a beautiful, blessed July evening, and Eden Gardens smells of blossom and rings with the ratcheting calls of magpies. He's been out planting and his clothes are still dirty.

She is working at the kitchen table, putting together a late supper for them to have at the bottom of the garden, under the fairy lights. She slices the small, sweet tomatoes they grow here, before dousing them in balsamic vinegar and herbs.

She glances up, knife in hand, and with a sick, sinking feeling she sees that he is holding her notebooks. He must have found her hiding place at the back of the wardrobe, which implies he's been searching the house.

His face is hectic with red and white patches, as though he has been dealt a mortal blow.

'Did you write this?'

The question is absurd. Who else could have written it?

It occurs to her then that maybe this is a good thing. She is going to have to tell him sometime. This doesn't change her plans, the ones she made after she realized that Sophia was gone and never coming back.

It merely accelerates them.

'You shouldn't be looking at them.' She straightens and faces him. 'They're private.'

He backhands her across the face, and she is thrown down on to the floor in the kitchen, catching her head on the edge of the sink unit.

He has started to hit her more and more often now. Once Sophia left, it's as though some secret obstacle of shame has vanished.

Her birdlike hands flutter to her dark scalp. Blood flows freely, wetting the webs between her fingers in scarlet.

'I have fucking worked and slaved for you. For twenty-seven years, I've been the breadwinner, I've been putting fucking clothes on your back and paying for you – and paying for Aaron Kessler's little bastard . . .'

This she cannot stand. She will not tolerate him speaking about Sophia that way.

'Jared, you've always known the score there. I don't know which one of you is her father . . .' She tries to rise to her feet, but she is dizzy and feels sick.

But what she doesn't feel is afraid, as foolish as this is. They are on this course together now, she and he, and it must be pursued to the end.

'Come off it, Nina, she even *looks* like him. She has for years. Aaron, who threw you all out once he was bored with you. I, meanwhile, have been busting my arse for you, and' – his face contorts – 'and you're still obsessed with that fucker!' He shakes the notebooks at her. 'Even now!'

'I'm not obsessed with him. I've just never worked through it before.' She is tired of sitting on the floor, of cowering, so she lifts herself up. 'I want people to know what happened to me. I'm sick of hiding from it.'

'Were you ever going to discuss this with me, since I'm in it?' He throws his hands wide.

'Eventually.' She rubs her bruised cheek.

'What the fuck does that mean?'

'I'm leaving you,' she says. She lifts her hand away and inspects the blood.

'You're what?' He lets out a snort of bitter laughter, but

there's an alarmed question in his voice. 'And where would you go?'

'I'm not sure yet.'

'Oh you always say this when you get a mood on—'

'No,' she says, and she feels very calm. 'I almost never say it. I just think it. But now I'm saying it.'

'You wouldn't last two days without me,' he sneers.

'I think I would.' Her hand closes on the kitchen roll and she pulls a piece off. She looks around. 'I've had enough. I want a fresh start. I've been living here, hiding here, for twenty-five years and it's *suffocating* me. I want to go back to college. I want to go back to the world.'

The silence broadens between them. He realizes she is serious.

'How long has this been brewing?' he asks, crossing his mud-stained arms.

She dabs the towel to her scalp. 'Since Sophia left.'

'Sophia,' he hisses. Sophia, Aaron's bastard, the root of all evil. For a moment, his jealousy is like a chemical burn. 'Of course. Because fuck knows *I'm* not enough for you.'

Nina thinks, contemplates, and while she doesn't realize that these are the words that will kill her, she knows that once said they can never be taken back.

'You found me in a very vulnerable place, and despite everything I said to you, you spun that into a relationship. You've had over a quarter of a century out of me, and that's more than enough.' She adjusts her dishevelled yellow blouse. 'My life went on hold when I arrived at Morningstar. This is where it starts again.' She crushes the towel to her head to stop the bleeding. 'I'm sorry if I hurt you—'

'HURT me?' he bellows, and Nina is amazed that they can't hear it up at Rowan's cottage. 'Hurt me, you treacherous cunt?' He snatches up the notebooks, shaking them in her face. 'The way you fucking *talk* about me in here! Like I was shit on your shoe! Is this why we're having the break-ins? Is it your Lord and Master Aaron and his little army of dipshits expressing their disapproval of your fucking literary ambitions?'

She starts guiltily, and her face says it all.

'You want to be careful, Nina,' he says, playing his trump card, the one that has always sufficed before now. 'If you want to get chatty, I can get chatty too. I'll bet there's still someone out there who would like to hear what really happened to Uncle Petey.'

Nina has been expecting this.

'They'd have to prove it, though, wouldn't they?' she says. 'And I think that would be difficult to do now.'

'Yeah? But would you risk it?' He leers at her.

'Yes,' says Nina, and for the first time in twenty-five years she realizes this is true. 'Yes, I would.'

***

Jared storms out and into the garden. Its peace, its order, the glowing fairy lights all mock him.

He has done everything he can for her, and it means nothing. He's built this place out of nothing. He's built *her* out of nothing, the cold-hearted, ungrateful, worthless bitch.

He fucking *killed* a man for her, after all.

He shot that Peter Clay right in the face. He'd found the dirty bastard pawing at her as she stood there screaming in her drug-drenched fugue, and he'd seen red . . . He'd been lucky to get away with that.

He wants to kill her, to grab that thin, fragile bird's neck and squeeze until her eyes pop out, until she feels just the tiniest part of the pain and anxiety he is now in. He's been wanting this, on and off, for years, but lately he thinks about it all the time, has thought about how he would accomplish the deed. Considering it is satisfying but terrifying.

It is not, however, more terrifying than the loss of her.

Aaron Kessler, to whom Nina was an insect, is worth more than him to her, he realizes. Sophia, who spends her life avoiding her mother's phone calls, and who's abandoned them both to live a highfalutin London life of men and drink – her fucking father's daughter, all right – is worth more to her than him.

So, it was like that, was it?

He wants to kill her. Yearns for it. No, he wants more. He wants to *hurt* her while he's doing it.

And once the doors are open and he fully owns it, then nothing else will do.

He takes the notebooks into his shed, shoving them on top of the pelmet. Nina never comes in here if she can help it. He can move them into the hiding space he's built for the camera later.

For now, though, he has more urgent plans.

* * *

'Call Sophia,' he says.

He's come back into the kitchen. It's two hours later and he's calm again.

She watches him carefully, as though aware this is a trap. In the last few moments she felt a change in the atmosphere, something sinister, something she doesn't recognize.

'She won't come. She never comes. It's Friday, she's probably out.'

'Call her anyway. Tell her it's important, don't tell her what it is. I'm going to fix these fairy lights; they keep flashing.'

He turns on his heel and walks back out into the garden.

She calls Sophia and is confronted by her furious resistance.

386

And just for once Nina wants to say what all these phone calls hint at, to just speak out loud: 'I'm calling because I love you, and I miss you even when we're in the same room together. You are all of love I know in the world, and tonight, that's important.'

But she doesn't. She doesn't want to frighten or upset Sophia. Tomorrow, they'll talk. There's always tomorrow.

Part of her suspects that Sophia will approve of the new arrangements Nina has in mind. Sophia has never been close to Jared, subconsciously deterred by his glowering self-absorption. It doesn't matter either way. The changes will happen regardless.

Nina replaces the receiver and carries a cup of tea down to the table at the bottom of the garden.

He is on the stepladder, fiddling with the wires.

'Is she coming?' he asks.

'No. She's out at a nightclub. She's over the limit, she says.'

'Hmm. Sounds like her.'

Everything could almost be normal. But even though she's always said she is not remotely psychic, she has put the kitchen scissors in the back pocket of her jeans, under her blouse.

He will not be hitting her again.

This is so true, if she but knew it.

'This is no good,' he says. 'It's knotted; my fingers are too big. I'll hold it straight while you undo it. Don't want a fire.'

A fire sounds unlikely to her, but she isn't interested in quarrelling with him any more. Now the cat is out of the bag, things will start to happen. She needs to find a place to live. She needs work. She has no doubt that there will be plenty of quarrelling to do then.

She places the tea on the table and joins him on the stepladder, him coming down a step or two so she can go up.

She can't see any knots in the wires.

'What do you want me to do?' she asks.

'Hold still,' he says, and his tone is blasé, almost too blasé, and she knows what he is about to do even in the split second before the loop goes over her head.

Her fingers flail behind her for the tree, searching for purchase. He is gone, and she knows instantly that he means to kick the stepladder away.

Her terror is boundless, as is her disbelief. Why is he doing this? He, too, will be destroyed.

'Enjoy this, Nina, you ungrateful bitch. You ruined my life. Sophia and I will be following you soon enough.'

Something galvanizes Nina, then, and she remembers the scissors just as the noose draws tight. The strung lights prevent the noose from completely closing, but she still can't get her head out, and at the moment it doesn't matter. All that matters is that she stops him hurting her baby girl.

As she reaches up to cut the wire, he sees the scissors and snatches for her hand, but she's too quick for him.

The scissors sink deep into his belly, once, twice, and it is this second blow that unbalances him. He falls away, and the stepladder with him, the scissors embedded in his flesh.

Nina scrabbles for the tree, for the branch above, as her eyes grow bloody and turgid and her breath is cut off by her own weight. Her twitching feet grow still.

All of the lights are growing dim.

The last thing she thinks is, *Sophia*.

Acknowledgements

I'd like to thank the indefatigable team at Michael Joseph for all of their efforts – in particular my editor, Maxine Hitchcock, as well as Clare Bowron, Eve Hall and Emad Akhtar, all of whom offered invaluable suggestions on the text. Thanks are also due to Sarah Harwood, Beth Cockeram, Nick Lowndes and Shauna Bartlett. The more I work with you all, the more I am blown away by your dedication and creativity. You are all awesome and it's been a privilege.

Once again, all praises are due to my unflappable agent, Judith Murray, and everyone at Greene and Heaton, who I am grateful for every single day. Thanks a million.

I'd like to thank Treadwells Bookshop in London, who were a fund of research material, books and excellent advice on paganism and occultism – anything I got wrong is entirely down to me. Everyone I dealt with in the pagan and magical communities was never less than brilliant, clever and kind. I am a guest that came knocking and now may never leave. Thank you.

My research on cults took various twists and turns, too many to recount here, but should anyone be looking for a place to start, I can recommend *Combating Cult Mind Control* by Steve Hassan, 1988, published by Freedom of Mind Press, and reissued several times since.

I'd also like to thank the following: Chuck Dreyer, Gordon Fraser, Melanie Garrett, Lucia Graves, Dave Gullen, Sumit Paul-Choudhury, Michael Row, Gaie Sebold and Ally Shaw, all of whom were with me when I first came up with the idea in a farmhouse out in South Wales. Thanks to KD Grace for being there for me (we will get back to Avebury some day!), Cambridge Writers for giving me excellent critique on the first few chapters, and Louise Dean and the rest of the Kritikme Krew for some splendid advice and good laughs.

I'd also like to thank my family – Mum, Dad, John, Atsuko, Joe, Darla, Aiden, Arcadia, Finn, Rain, Remy, Oliver, Jacqueline and Lance – for being themselves.

And finally I'm going to take this opportunity to welcome Asta and Hallam to the world. Have fun, you two. Go nuts.

Don't miss Helen's next
unforgettable thriller

FIND ME

Coming 2019

Available to pre-order now